RED
RAG
BLUES

RED
RAG
BLUES

DEREK ROBINSON

CONSTABLE • LONDON

For Sheila

Constable & Robinson Ltd
3 The Lanchesters
162 Fulham Palace Road
London W6 9ER
www.constablerobinson.com

First published in the UK by Constable,
an imprint of Constable & Robinson Ltd, 2006

A copy of the British Library Cataloguing in
Publication Data is available from the British Library.

ISBN-13: 978-1-84529-299-7
ISBN-10: 1-84529-299-5

Printed and bound in the EU

NOT IN
THOSE SHOES

1

In 1953, the average New York hoodlum took no interest in current affairs. Sammy Fantoni was different. He read the *New York Herald Tribune* from end to end, every day. 'Improve your mind,' his uncle, who was also his employer, told him. 'Feed your brain. Learn about the country you love. What you don't understand, ask me.'

Sammy was surprised by how much he understood. Of course he took a professional interest in violent death, and 1953 had its fair share of bad blood between the other New York families: Gambino, Colombo, Bonanno, Genovese, Profaci. The *Trib* did an excellent job of reporting Mob killings. And one day he saw a piece in the national news about lynching. 'Nobody in the US got lynched last year,' Sammy said. 'First time that's happened since they kept records. What's up?'

'One is tempted to blame the sudden rise of television,' his uncle said. 'Arkansas has ceased to make its own entertainment.'

Sammy gave it five seconds' thought and moved on. 'How about the Yankees? If they win the Series again, that'll be the fifth straight year. Some sports writers say it's gettin' boring.'

'Americans have no concept of eternity,' his uncle said. 'That's why they invented baseball.'

Sammy didn't understand that either. Probably a joke. The hell with it. Plenty other stuff in the *Trib*, good reassuring stuff.

1

Eisenhower got sworn in as president, in 'fifty-three, and the *Trib* told Sammy that Ike said the US Seventh Fleet would no longer prevent Nationalist China from attacking Communist China. Sammy looked at the map. The Nationalists had Formosa. The Reds had all the rest. So it was like giving Puerto Rico permission to invade America. Sammy relaxed. He was thirty, he'd done his stint in the military, he didn't want to go back into uniform. He'd voted for Ike to *end* the Korean War, not to start a new one. He liked Ike, an American through and through, a guy who wouldn't take any subversive crap from anyone, like belonging to the Communist Party of America, which just got thirteen punks tossed in jail. He read about Loyalty Review Boards and the hard work they did, all across the country, making pinko people disprove that they were disloyal, or else they lost their jobs. Damn right! Why wait for tomorrow's traitors to betray America when you could flush out the bastards today? You know it makes sense. The *Trib* said the dollar was strong, 'fifty-three was looking good, the country was on the up.

Only thing Sammy disagreed with the *Trib* about was when it reported a smart-ass called Charles E. Wilson of Detroit, who said what was good for General Motors was good for America. Well, it sure as hell wasn't good enough for *this* American. Sammy took his brown Pontiac convertible to a man who customized cars. 'Beats me why I bought this heap,' he said. 'No class. No tailfins. No *difference*.' And the guy agreed.

Now, on a sunny summer's morning, he was driving west across Manhattan in his blood-red Pontiac, the top down, 200 pounds of added chrome shouting class at the world, and sitting beside him was Julie Conroy, a piece of female beauty that turned his voice husky every time they met. He had picked her up at her apartment. She wore a tailored two-piece of cream linen that made the mailman drop a couple of letters. No hat. Black hair curled like a dark sea in a light breeze, a phrase he remembered from a movie review in the *Trib*. 'You look like a million dollars,' he'd said.

'I feel like a buck and a quarter. Not enough sleep.'

He had held the car door for her and said, 'You ever get your hands on a million, buy A.T.&T.' See, he read the business pages too.

Now he turned north on Riverside Drive. 'Okay if we take the bridge?' he asked. 'Small piece a business I gotta do in Jersey.'

Traffic was light. Trees were in full leaf and the sunlight made them bright as new paint. Clouds were up high, quietly going about their business, which didn't include blocking out the sun. She rested her head and closed her eyes. That felt good. This trip was probably a big mistake, so enjoy what you can.

Sammy stopped at the George Washington. She opened her eyes. He paid the toll and got a receipt. 'Tax-deductible,' he told her.

'Huh.' She thought about that as they crossed the bridge, about making a tax return when your business was crime. Too complicated. She gave up. The bridge flexed and trembled. The Hudson was far below. She closed her eyes and imagined they were flying.

Hackensack looked like a nice place. Plenty of big old clapboard houses in wide streets. Sammy found the one he wanted. He parked and got out. 'Five minutes,' he said. Julie watched him open the trunk. He was dressed for Wall Street except that the pants, lapels and tie were too narrow. He walked to the house, swinging a baseball bat. Now that was too corny to be true. All the same, it put a chill in the sunshine.

He was back in four minutes, tossed the bat in the trunk, got in the car, drove away, first using his indicators and checking his mirrors, considerate of his valuable passenger.

'You gonna tell me?' she said. 'Or should I assume the worst?'

'I did my sister a favour. Her boy Jimmy ain't gettin' good enough grades at school. She's upset. I discussed it with his headmaster.'

'Using a baseball bat?'

'Never touched the guy. He agreed, Jimmy's been gettin' a raw deal. It's the school's fault.'

'Or maybe the kid should work harder.'

Sammy left Hackensack behind, and put on speed. 'Nah,' he said. 'My way's better.'

She wondered how much of it was true. None, maybe. Or maybe the truth was even worse.

She'd met Sammy at a party in the Village. He'd looked and sounded like someone from *Guys and Dolls*. They'd talked a little, danced a little, he'd been very attentive, and as he drove her home – for which she was grateful, the rain was bouncing knee-high off the pavement – he'd made a remark that he obviously thought was respectful. Complimentary, even. 'Any time some guy annoys you and you want him whacked, or maybe semi-whacked,' he'd said, 'you call me.' He was serious.

At the time, it had seemed almost touching, in a quaint, New Jersey way. Now, she wasn't so sure.

2

The *San Felipe* was a medium-small passenger liner, not nearly big enough to qualify for one of the huge berths on the west side of Manhattan, where fire boats pumped great fountains and whooped triumphantly to welcome the likes of the *Queen Mary*. Instead the *San Felipe* docked on the Jersey shore, at Hoboken. No bands played at Hoboken, no flash bulbs popped.

Luis Cabrillo was in the saloon when the ship tied up. He was playing backgammon with a fellow passenger, Dr John Barnes. Cabrillo had joined the *San Felipe* in Caracas, Venezuela. Barnes and his wife came aboard at Havana. They had been in Cuba for the annual convention of the American Psychiatric Association. The *San Felipe* was not a fast ship, and the two men had played a lot of backgammon. They finished this game, and Cabrillo lost on the last throw. 'Another?' he said. They re-set the board.

Barnes was in his sixties, built like a foreman carpenter, wore a corduroy suit. Cabrillo was half his age, and by contrast he looked slim, almost sleek. He wore a double-breasted blazer from a good tailor, charcoal-grey flannel trousers, suede shoes. His face was as smooth as an olive. Mostly it was as expressionless as an olive too.

They played fast, slapping the pieces, flicking them into corners. Luis paused, as still as a statue, then doubled the stakes. 'Well, sure, I need a new car,' Barnes said, and accepted. Luis threw the dice. 'Not a pretty sight,' Barnes said, and promptly redoubled. Luis accepted. Later, he re-redoubled. Barnes accepted again and said, 'If this goes wrong I may have to sell the old car.' But nothing went wrong for him.

'Thank you,' Luis said. 'Jolly good sport. How much do I owe you?'

Barnes opened a notebook. 'Seven hundred and three dollars. Please forget it. I've already forgotten it.' Luis was writing. 'It's of no importance,' Barnes said. 'I've been flat broke, often. It's a temporary inconvenience, nothing more.'

'You're very kind. This is a charge on my bank in Caracas.'

Barnes took the cheque. It was signed *Count de Zamora y Ciudad-Rodrigo*. 'I hope you won't be offended.' He struck a match and set fire to a corner. 'Here in the US it's a criminal offence to bounce a cheque.' They watched it burn in an ashtray. 'Tell me one thing, and then we'll go our separate ways and I'll sleep easy tonight. What plans have you got? In America?'

'I plan to join the Secret Service.'

'Uh-huh.' Barnes stirred the grey flakes with a pencil. 'I expect their number's in the phone book.'

Mrs Barnes came in. 'Our bags are ashore, John.'

'Okay. Mr Cabrillo tells me he plans to join the US Secret Service. What d'you think of that?'

'Not in those shoes,' she said firmly.

'Why not?' Luis asked. 'Most comfortable shoes I've ever had.'

'Fine in Venezuela. Okay on this ship. But take it from an American, you won't get anywhere here in suede.'

'What happened to the land of the free?'

'It's available in every style and colour,' Barnes said, 'except suede.'

★

The arrival hall on Hoboken dockside was unlovely when it was new, and that was long ago. Black ironwork was gaunt and skylights were grimy. Immigration officials sat at a row of metal desks. One of them studied Luis Cabrillo's passport. 'Is that a British name?' he asked.

'From the Norman French. An ancestor was the bastard son of William the Conqueror. The family . . .' Luis stopped. The man was flicking through the pages of a thick ledger. He failed to find a Cabrillo. The book flopped shut. 'What's the purpose of your visit to the United States?'

'I wish to play backgammon.'

The man waved away a fly that was trying to sneak through immigration. 'You mean tourism?'

'Do I? Jolly good. We'll make it tourism, then.'

The man thought about that. He handed Luis a printed sheet of paper. 'Read this. Tell me if you answer yes to any question.' He sat as motionless as a sack of coal.

Luis read, and smiled. 'Surely only a lunatic would answer yes.'

'Sign at the bottom.'

'With pleasure.' Luis had a flamboyant signature. 'Now, if I try to overthrow the government by force, you can charge me with perjury, and serve me right.'

The immigration official's expression had never changed. 'I don't like you, Mr Cabrillo,' he said. 'If it was up to me, I'd refuse you entry to this country. You're a smart-ass. That's un-American. I hope you get your smart-ass well and truly kicked. Now beat it.' He stamped the passport.

Nearly all the baggage had been claimed. Luis quickly found his suitcases and a porter. 'Got anything to declare?' a

6

customs officer asked. 'Nothing,' Luis said. 'Thank Christ for that,' the man said. 'Now I can go eat.' He chalked the bags, and Luis walked out of the echoing gloom and into the sunlight. He paused to look around, and a bum with a tin cup immediately stepped forward and said, 'Spare a dime, buddy?' Luis searched all his pockets, and found a coin. 'This is all I have.' He dropped it in the cup.

'Jeez,' the bum said. 'I think you need it more than I do.' He fished it out, gave it back, and shuffled away. Luis looked at the porter. 'This is America,' the porter said. 'Even the bums got standards.'

A blood-red Pontiac pulled up to the kerb. 'What kept you?' Julie Conroy said. 'We've been here for hours.'

'I wonder if you could take care of the porter,' Luis said. 'My small change seems to be unacceptable.'

'Sammy, pay the porter,' she said.

'Sure, sure.' The bags went into the trunk. The porter was amazed to get five dollars. By now Luis was sitting in the car.

Sammy got in, checked his mirrors and used his indicators, and eased into the traffic. 'What d'you think of America, Mr Cabrillo?' he asked.

'I think somebody could make a fortune filling in the potholes,' Luis said.

'Land of opportunity,' Sammy said. 'Everyone says so.'

★

The *San Felipe* was not an important ship, and Hoboken didn't rate highly, so the FBI sent a new agent, Fisk, fresh from the Bureau's academy, to check the passenger manifest. He found little of interest, just a French film director with a Russian name, and a wheelchair case who had been acquitted on fraud charges involving a Canadian copper mine with no copper in it. That was long ago. But Fisk was young and keen. He chose a good viewpoint and used binoculars to watch the other arrivals go through customs and immigration. Luis Cabrillo's body-English interested Fisk. Most arrivals were in a hurry to get their passports stamped and go. Cabrillo talked and talked. Gestured. Wore his blazer like a cape, loose over the shoulders. Fruity shoes, too.

When Cabrillo was at last admitted, Fisk went over to the immigration officer. The man showed him the name. 'Smart-ass,' he said. 'Comes into this country like he's going to the Roxy. Like it's a costume party. I hate a smart-ass.'

Fisk drove back to the FBI office on East 58th Street and reported to his supervisor, Prendergast.

'French film director,' Prendergast said. 'No. It's always raining in black-and-white on some pathetic chain-smoker. And forget the wheelchair. Two strokes and a kidney stone as big as the Ritz. That leaves this Cabrillo. No doubt about who met him?'

'I was only twenty feet away. Sammy Fantoni, with girl-friend. I checked the plates on his Pontiac.'

'No uncle?'

Fisk shrugged. 'Wouldn't know him if I saw him. Isn't he a recluse?'

'Sort of. Since his wife died, he don't get around much any more . . . All right. Open a file on Cabrillo. Anything else?'

Fisk hesitated. 'What's the Bureau's stance on Cuba? Dr John Barnes, American citizen, just back from visiting there. He's a psychiatrist.'

'Mr Hoover approves of Cuba. It's stable, pro-American, good cigars. But psychiatrists, Mr Hoover disapproves of. They're unstable, secretive, possibly anarchic, probably un-American. Don't open a file on Barnes. I'm sure we have one.'

Sammy took the Holland tunnel into Manhattan, then Third Avenue uptown. Luis was in the back seat. He said little. Too much to see. At one point Sammy broke the silence. 'My uncle's dentist used to live down that street,' he said. They looked. It was just a street. 'He moved to Denver,' Sammy said. 'Nobody ever figured out why.' He swung into 84th Street.

He carried the bags into the apartment. It seemed crowded

when three people were standing in it, trying not to look at each other. 'I forgot to introduce you,' she said. 'Luis, this is Sammy Fantoni.' They shook hands. 'I don't have a car,' she explained. 'Sammy offered.'

'Awfully decent of you,' Luis said.

'My day off,' Sammy said.

'Yes? What business are you in?'

'Sammy's in recreational equipment,' she said. 'I could use a beer. There's a deli on the corner.'

'I'll go,' Luis offered. 'That is, if they'll let me charge it to your account.'

'My account. Now there's two words I never thought to hear together . . . Sammy, you go. Get us some sandwiches too. Swiss cheese and ham on wholemeal for me. Luis wants a BLT on white toast. No pickle.' Sammy saluted and went out.

'I've never even heard of a BLT,' Luis said.

'Trust me. I know your taste. You've put on a pound or two. Suits you. You were kind of gaunt in those days.'

'It was that frightful wartime food the English gave us. Fish pie. Toad-in-the-hole. Porridge. Spam. You're looking awfully well yourself. That's a jolly pretty outfit.'

'Used to be my interview suit.'

There was a pause while they took a long look at each other and assessed the differences that eight years had made. 'Spiffing,' he said. 'Utterly delightful. Now why don't you show me the rest of the apartment?'

'This is it, pal. Bathroom's through that door. One walk-in closet. Bed. Convertible couch.'

'Dear me.' He strode slowly from end to end, counting the paces. 'In Caracas, my bathroom alone was bigger than this.'

'So why leave?'

'All my money was spent.'

'*All*? Not even you could do that. Don't lie to me. Not now.'

'I must admit, there were other reasons. But crucially it was a question of cash.' He bounced gently on the couch, testing the springs. 'And in my hour of need, you were the only person I could think to turn to.'

9

'Well, think again. I'm broke. Worse than broke. I'm unemployable.' He raised an eyebrow. 'You don't want to know,' she said.

'Oh.' He stretched out on the couch. His feet overlapped the end. 'Not what I expected. A desperate situation, isn't it?'

'Cut the bullshit, Luis. Being broke in New York is no joke.'

'Madrid was nothing to laugh about. At least here we're not surrounded by Fascists and Nazis.'

'You reckon?' she said. 'Stick around.'

★

Madrid was where they first met, in the summer of 1941. Hitler had conquered most of Europe and now he was carving large chunks out of Russia. Britain, he said, would have to wait her turn. The future looked very German. All the more reason to enjoy the present.

They had a few good weeks together, and then suddenly Luis left, went to England, on business. Well, he was Spanish, and Spain was neutral; but Julie felt sure his business was spying for Germany. She travelled to Portugal, hoping to catch a plane to the US, and hey! there was Luis, living in Lisbon. She'd been half right. He'd been recruited by the Madrid office of the *Abwehr*, which was German military intelligence, and code-named 'Eldorado'. But while the *Abwehr* believed him to be spying in England, he had gone no further than Lisbon. All the top-secret information he sent to Madrid came from his imagination. Luis sat in his room in Lisbon, asked himself what the Germans would like to know, and turned his answers into utterly convincing intelligence reports. He knew they convinced the *Abwehr* because the *Abwehr* kept paying him. They paid him a lot.

Julie cancelled her flight home. She moved into his apartment and became his business manager. They made a hell of a good team. His output was phenomenal – far more than one spy in England could have produced. But Luis had invented a

10

network of sub-agents, fearless and prolific and reporting to him; and naturally Madrid *Abwehr* paid him for their efforts. The Eldorado Network was a spymaster's dream. Then the British found out.

Their Secret Service, MI6, persuaded Luis to become a genuine double agent. He and Julie went to England and worked for the Allies until the end of the war. He was part of the Double-Cross System, which 'turned' enemy agents and created a steady flow of false information, lightly speckled with fragments of truth. The Allies' best deception plans were reinforced by Luis's lies. MI6 still called him Eldorado, although Madrid had changed his code-name to 'Arabel'. Whatever the label, the product never failed to please. Luis sent the *Abwehr* radio bulletins by the hundred, written reports by the thousand, all priceless intelligence, which was rapidly transmitted to the High Command in Berlin. To the very end, the Germans trusted him. They never stopped paying.

There was a price for illusion. Julie paid it. The strain of living with a professional liar was great. Sometimes Luis behaved as if his phantom sub-agents were real. When the *Abweh*r wasn't sufficiently grateful for their reports, he became moody, sour, resentful. When the *Abwehr* sent warm congratulations, Luis became smug. He was more comfortable in his fake world than in the real world.

He and Julie were still in love, but it was a prickly, arm's-length kind of love. And when the war ended, and suddenly nobody needed double agents any more, his brilliant bullshit had no market value. Thanks to the *Abwehr*, he had a fortune tucked away. On a grey and gloomy day, he and Julie took a long, sad look at each other and agreed they were incompatible. He caught a plane to South America. Big mistake. She still had a husband somewhere, left over from pre-war, a footloose newspaperman called Harry whom she hadn't seen in four years. She went looking for him. Not a happy idea, either.

★

11

'Look, this is important, so don't give me any of your bullshit,' Julie said. 'Have you any funds? Investments? Property?'

'When did I ever give you any bullshit?' Luis asked.

'Eight years ago. You gave everyone bullshit, remember? You were in the bullshit business. You couldn't tell the truth if it took its clothes off and sang *Rule Britannia*.'

'Dear me,' he said. 'You Americans can be awfully Prussian. Sometimes I wonder whether you might have been happier fighting on the German side.'

'You wonder. All you ever did was wonder. That's how you ended up working for both sides at once.'

'Well, if I did, then so did you.'

Sammy Fantoni had gone, and they were strolling in the park next to Gracie Mansion, the mayor's official residence. Dogs chased squirrels, contrary to city bylaws, and challenged His Honor to come out and stop them. The East River surged past, keeping Queens and Brooklyn at a decent distance from Manhattan. An old man was feeding gulls, tossing up bits of bread as the birds swooped and flailed and grabbed. 'Look. He thinks they are his friends,' Luis said. 'He is a fool.'

'Have you got any money?' she asked. 'Anywhere?'

'None. No dollars here, no cruzeiros in Venezuela, no Swiss francs in Zurich. I'm totally broke.'

'Then you're a bigger fool than he is. At least he can afford bread. Why the hell did you come here? New York is absolutely the worst place to be broke in.'

'Is it? I can think of worse places. Siberia is uncomfortable, and large parts of China are not at all attractive.' Julie groaned. He said: 'When you want to make money, go where people *have* money. Right? New York is rich. Besides . . . I wanted to see you again.'

'After eight years?' They sat on a park bench. 'We agreed, back in 'forty-five, remember? End of story.'

She was hunched and tense. He was relaxed, sprawling, his arms hooked over the back of the bench. She kicked his ankle. 'Hey!' he said. 'That wasn't a very kind thing to do.'

'Did I get your attention? Listen. This is not a kind city. New Yorkers murder each other for no reason at all, it happens every day. *You*, you're not even American, you're an alien. What makes you think anyone here is going to be nice to you?'

'Why are you so angry? And don't hit me.' He raised an arm in defence. That annoyed her; she got up and walked away. 'We only just sat down,' he called. 'It's all rush, rush. I'm an old man, I can't stand this pace.' But he followed her.

'You're thirty-four,' she said. 'And you're an idiot. You had at least a hundred thousand pounds when the war ended. A quarter of a million dollars, give or take a buck. That's more than most Americans make in a lifetime. How could you possibly spend it all? Where did it go?'

'Oh . . . here and there. This and that. I had some bad luck at the track.' She looked at him as if he had said: *there was a hole in my pocket.* 'All right,' he countered, 'how come you're broke?'

'I got fired.'

'There you are, then. You've been working, and look where it got you. I haven't been working, but at least I enjoyed myself.'

'Let's get out of here.'

They passed the old man, no longer throwing bread in the air. He was mopping a sleeve with his handkerchief. 'Little bastard shat on me,' he said. Luis smiled, courteously. 'That's New York for you,' he said.

They were on 84th Street again before Julie spoke. 'How did you know where I live?'

'Simple. MI6 has a man in Caracas, awfully nice chap, we played tennis. Anything I can do to help, he told me, just ask. So I did. He got in touch with Kim Philby, and Kim did the rest.' Luis leapfrogged a fire hydrant. 'You liked old Kim, didn't you? Best brain in MI6, and manners to match.'

'You're telling me the British Secret Service knows where I live.'

'Evidently so.'

They stopped at York Avenue. The traffic thumped past,

an unhurried tidal wave. Luis was puzzled by Julie's attitude, her seriousness, the flickers of annoyance that flared into anger. At Hoboken he'd expected a kiss, even if it was just a brush of the lips on his cheek. But no kiss. No handshake. They hadn't touched in any way. She kept coming back to money. During the war, money had never excited her. *He* had been the one always concerned about getting paid. Now their roles were switched. He could sense the tension in her body. The lights said WALK. They walked.

'Would it be insensitive of me to ask about your husband?' he asked.

'Dead. Car crash in Belgium. Four years ago.'

'Oh dear. I never met him, of course, but — '

'Don't let it bother you. Belgium, for God's sake. What a dumb place to die.'

That seemed to dispose of Harry. Luis allowed a decent interval to pass, and asked: 'Where does Sammy Fantoni figure in your life? He seemed very attentive, and . . .'

'We met at a party. He's a hood. He thinks he's in love with me.'

'A hood? A gangster? Such a cordial chap.'

'Yeah. If I asked him to, he'd cordially break your arms. As a demonstration of affection.'

For once, Luis was silenced. They went back to the apartment.

THE VOLCANO DROPPED OFF

1

Luis had picked the best day to arrive. Once a week, Julie and three others ate supper at the cheapest pasta joint in Manhattan. It was called Vesuvius and it was far to the east of Greenwich Village, even beyond the Bowery, out where the rent was very low. The owner cooked the food, served it, washed the plates. Enrico was very old, face like a pickled walnut, had fought the Austrians when Italy was on the Allied side in the First World War, later got slung in jail by Mussolini for his politics. Came to America, got his citizenship, did time for smuggling booze out of Canada during Prohibition, learned to cook in Sing-Sing. 'No family,' Julie told Luis. 'Enrico takes in waifs and strays like me and the rest of the supper club. All you can eat for a dollar, sometimes wine too. Enrico won't take more than a dollar a head. Politics.'

'What politics?'

'Ours and his. Act polite, don't talk smart, and he'll feed you too.'

A taxi came to pick them up. She introduced the driver as Herb Kizsco. Fiftyish, bald as an ostrich egg except for a thick grey ruff, long face that would have suited an El Greco cardinal. 'Herb knows more about Shakespeare than even Ann Hathaway did,' she said. 'Unless, that is, he was really Francis Bacon, in which case I guess she married the wrong guy. Is that right?'

'No,' Herb said.

'Good. Shortest lecture you ever gave. Let's go.'

He drove over to Park Avenue and turned south. The meter was not on. 'I like Park,' he said. 'I like cruising past these doormen, all blowing whistles and waving, busting a gut to get a cab for their rich tenants. Let 'em take the Subway, I say.'

'Subway stinks,' Julie said.

'It wouldn't stink for long if they had to ride it. The mayor himself would be down there, spraying Chanel No. 5.'

'I hate Chanel.'

'Comes the bloody revolution, you'll get Chanel whether you like it or not.'

'Is there to be a revolution?' Luis asked.

'It was a joke,' she said. 'I like Herb's jokes. I always have.'

They turned west on 42nd Street. Beyond the cinemas and the soft-porn peepshows, the buildings became hulking, grimy, industrial. Herb stopped outside the steel-shuttered offices of a corsetry distributor and honked his horn. After a minute, a woman came out of a side door. She was a short and chunky redhead, hair in a scarf like Rosie the Riveter; keen, alert face, or maybe she was just hungry. No make-up; denim skirt and jacket; old sneakers. Age thirty-plus.

'Bonnie Scott, meet Luis Cabrillo,' Julie said. They shook hands. 'Bonnie was the best fiction editor this side of Chicago.'

'I met Graham Greene once,' Luis said. 'Awfully nice chap.'

'Huh.' Bonnie was impressed, but not much. 'What did you talk about?'

'The war, and the dreadful damage it did to literature. Graham thought that Hemingway's metaphors, in particular, had suffered horribly.'

'I'm so hungry, my stomach thinks my throat's been cut,' Bonnie said. 'Is that metaphor bad enough for you? Let's go.'

Herb drove downtown on 9th Avenue, took 14th Street east all the way across town to Avenue C, and found a block of tenements that looked just like the next block and just like the last ten. Fire escapes zig-zagged down every building. One house had been gutted by fire; smears of smoke blackened the tops of windows. Kids on roller-skates were playing street hockey. They parted reluctantly. Their voices were unbroken

16

but the curses were adult enough. 'Are we still in Manhattan?' Luis asked.

'I sometimes wonder that myself,' Herb said. 'In the greater sense, does Manhattan exist, or are we all just looking for it?'

'There's Max,' Julie said. 'He's looking for us.'

Max was six-two, late thirties, dressed mainly in army surplus clothing. 'You're late, and I'm starving,' he said as he got in. His voice was as rich as rum.

'If you're in such a hurry, get out and take a taxi,' Herb said, driving on.

'Not wise. They shoot taxi-drivers on sight in Avenue C.'

'Actors ought to be shot on sight,' Bonnie said, casually.

'Her ex is an actor,' Julie told Luis.

'Allegedly,' Bonnie said.

'In that case he should only be allegedly shot,' Max said.

Herb had to slow and swerve to avoid some garbage cans. 'This is a truly terrible part of New York,' he said.

'Max Webber, meet Luis Cabrillo,' Julie said. 'He got his fruit boots in Venezuela.'

'I got the clap in Guatemala,' Max said. 'It happens.'

They crossed into First Avenue, drove a few blocks, turned left into 5th Street. By now Luis had no idea which was east or west. The shape of the conversation baffled him too. It was rapid, clipped, throwaway. Nothing anyone said seemed to lead anywhere. Caracas had not been like this. He kept quiet and looked out the window. The view was grim and repetitive.

'At last!' Julie said. 'Shangri-la.'

Enrico's restaurant was small. The name *Vesuvius* was spelled out in thick plywood letters. Most of them had lost their paint. There had once been a neon-lit eruption, but the volcano had dropped off and now only the dead lava-flow clung to the building.

Max led the way in. Their arrival was like a happy invasion, everyone smiling in anticipation of greeting Enrico and his steaming pasta. The old man wasn't there. The place was empty. No customers. No message, no notice, no explanation. 'Huh!' Bonnie said. Herb dragged a bentwood chair from a table and sat astride it. 'Too damn quiet,' he said.

17

'There's Apache up in them hills.' A priest came out of the kitchen. 'Don't tell us he's dead,' Herb said.

'Enrico? No, no, he's alive. But he's in prison, poor fellow.' A hint of Dublin in the voice, a rusty streak in the grey hair, a calmness that suggested the priest knew of many worse predicaments than being in jail. 'I visited him this morning. Complains about the food, but then so he should, it's abominable, if they had any brains they'd put him in charge of the kitchen, but when did you ever see a jail with any brains?'

'What did he do?' Julie asked. 'Why is he inside?'

'Well now, that's a bit of a mystery. All we know for sure is some people from the Immigration Department came and took him away.'

'Enrico's a citizen. He showed me the papers.'

The priest nodded. 'They'll have to let him go. The thing is, he's been questioned rather a lot by a couple of men in similar suits who are nothing to do with Immigration. They want to know all about his customers. The ridiculous part is they already knew everything. Whenever Enrico forgot someone's name, they reminded him. So what do you make of that?'

'They've been watching the place,' Bonnie said. She walked to the window. 'There's probably a telescopic lens pointing at me right now.' She waved. 'Shove it, buster!'

'No need to shout,' Herb said wearily. 'Just talk to the bugs.'

Gloomy silence. Luis leaned against a wall. He had no idea why they were so angry, so grim; but he knew it was caused by more than the absence of pasta. He was hungry. If they couldn't eat here, he hoped they would rapidly move on.

'I guess Enrico looked after a lot of guys like us,' Max said.

'You four were kind of special,' the priest said. 'He asked me to be here tonight, so I could explain the situation to you. Said to wish you good luck, and stay strong.' He rattled a bunch of keys. 'I have parishioners to visit.'

They went out and sat in Herb's taxi and watched the priest lock up and walk away. He had thick rubber soles and a long stride. A priest on the Lower East Side did a lot of walking.

★

18

They had to eat. No money for restaurants, coffee shops, cafeterias, bars.

'If we can't eat out,' Bonnie said, 'we'll have to eat in.'

'Don't look at me,' Julie said. 'Four people going into my apartment means an orgy. I'll be out on my ass in the morning.'

'We'll be quiet as mice,' Max said.

'Give me a break. You know what landlords are like in this city. Single woman tenant equals whore. I can't risk it.'

'I'm out,' Herb Kizsco said. 'I'm living in the Bronx now.'

'I can't cook,' Bonnie said. 'Con Ed just cut off my gas.'

'I know a guy would reconnect you,' Julie said. Bonnie was interested. 'He charges ten bucks,' Julie said. Bonnie lost interest.

'That just leaves you, Max,' Herb said.

'I have plates. Unfortunately . . .'

'Nothing to put on 'em,' Julie said.

'Well, let's go *some*where,' Herb said. He started the engine. 'It's bad enough being hungry without looking at the crappiest street in the cruddiest part of Manhattan.' He drove on. After a couple of blocks, he said: 'I'd hock the gold in my teeth if I had any gold in my teeth.'

'Would some gold help?' Luìs asked.

Nobody laughed. If it was a joke, it bombed. 'Gold would undoubtedly help,' Herb said. 'An ingot, for instance, would be useful.'

'I have this.' He showed them a fountain pen. It was dull yellow.

'Gold-plated?'

'Heavens above, no. Solid gold.'

'I know a pawnbroker, stays open till midnight,' Bonnie said. 'Bleecker Street and Sixth.'

She got twenty dollars for the pen. They bought all the fixings for spaghetti Bolognese, plus French bread, a pint of olives, a pound of Parmesan, much fruit and a gallon of Californian red. She gave Luis the change. 'We need coffee,' Max said. Luis bought coffee. He turned to Julie and murmured, 'Do I tip the man?'

'Only if he sells you his sister. Come on, let's go.'

Max's apartment was at the top of the building. He used four keys to open four locks. The door was sheet steel. 'Wait a second,' he said. 'Give the roaches a chance to hide. They own the damn building, after all.' He marched in, loudly. 'I'm home, darlings. Had a good day at the beauty parlour?' Small vermin hustled and scuttled and found sanctuary in dark corners.

With the first glass of wine and the prospect of hot food, everyone cheered up. They drank Luis's health, asked him what he thought of New York. He said he was impressed by the height of the skyscrapers and the depth of the potholes. Herb congratulated him on a perceptive image. 'Symbolizes the irony of capitalism,' he said.

Max asked: 'Everyone want garlic in their sauce?'

'Not me,' Bonnie said.

'Tough shit. Majority rule. That's democracy for you. Ironic, ain't it?' Max was chopping onions. 'What are politics like in Venezuela, Luis? Any revolutions while you were there?'

'Oh . . . I believe there was a small one. I was fishing that weekend up in the mountains, with the British ambassador's wife. Charming woman. Quite devastating with a nine-foot split-cane rod. She could drop a fly on a sixpence.'

'That's like a dime,' Julie said.

'We had a revolution in this country, once,' Bonnie said. 'Wasn't popular. Didn't last.'

'Personally, I never saw anything wrong with King George the Third,' Herb said.

'Me neither,' Julie said. 'A warm family man and a real affectionate tyrant.'

'What this country needs is the Affectionate Tyranny Party,' Herb said. 'Any bastard doesn't vote for us will get lovingly assassinated.'

Now Luis knew it was all just a joke; but nobody laughed. Nobody even smiled. New Yorkers puzzled him.

Max made a lot of spaghetti and it tasted good. Luis thought the wine was young and coarse, but it was certainly the right drink for their food, this company, these surroundings. He had watched the pasta sauce being fortified with

20

garlic, oregano, paprika, ground black pepper, cumin, basil, old black coffee. Max had tasted it and then stirred in some chilli powder, tasted again, added more chilli. This was not subtle food. This was not a sophisticated gathering. The men had not shaved. The women were without make-up. The apartment was bare of paint or wallpaper. They sat on upturned milk crates and ate off a door that rested on two trestles which were stencilled NYPD – DO NOT PASS.

From time to time, Herb went to the window and looked down to make sure his taxi had not been stolen.

After dinner they talked about Enrico's arrest, and about work, or the hope of work. Herb was sick of driving a taxi but he couldn't quit until he found a job that brought in regular money. 'I coach some kids at Warners. They're scared they might get tossed out unless they open a book once a term,' he said. 'Makes a few bucks. Peanuts, but it's cash in hand.'

'Watch your back,' Bonnie warned. 'One of those kids might be a snitch for the IRS.'

'I hear there's money writing stuff for students,' Julie said. 'Essays, theses, term papers.'

'I'd sooner shine shoes,' Bonnie said.

'Didn't you have something going with one of the studios?' Max asked. 'Some screenplay thing?'

'This schmuck at Warner Brothers wants to make a biopic of General Patton. I gave him a screenplay, he gave me zero. Said it's not suitable. Screwed again.'

'No contract?' Julie asked.

'If I'd asked for a contract I wouldn't have got the work. The schmuck knows I'm in a fix.'

'Time I got back to the hack,' Herb said. Dinner was over. He drove them to the Subway. Luis bought tokens. Mr Fort Knox.

★

Julie and Luis rode the Third Avenue El to 86th Street. She took him to Mooney's Bar, found a booth, ordered beers. 'So now you know,' she said. 'The blacklist is alive and flourishing, and it'll get you too if you don't watch out.'

'Blacklist? What blacklist?'

She eased her shoes off and flexed her feet. 'No jokes, Luis. You never could tell a good joke, and the blacklist is about as funny as a boil on the backside.'

'Are we talking about American politics?'

'No, we're talking about American hysteria. Of course it's politics. McCarthyism. HUAC. The witch hunt for Communists, real or imaginary. Nixon's holy crusade. Hollywood pooping its pants whenever someone names names. *That* blacklist. Don't tell me nobody in Venezuela heard of it. The shit's been flying for years.'

'I had my bellyful of politics in the war, writing all those reports for the *Abwehr*. When I arrived in Caracas in 1945 I vowed never to read a newspaper again, and I never have.'

'*Time* magazine? *Newsweek*? *Readers'* goddamn *Digest*?'

'No.'

'They don't have TV in Venezuela?'

'I never looked at it.'

She sucked the suds off her beer and watched him, warily, as if this might be some elaborate hoax. 'What have you been doing for eight years?'

'Enjoying myself. Keeping fit. I swam in my pool every day, played tennis, golf, a little polo. Kept a Bugatti, competed occasionally. There was always horse-racing and high-stakes bridge. Trout fishing in the mountains. But mainly I read. Foyle's of London sent me a crate of new novels every month. Pure delight. Some American authors. Very talented.'

'The great American talent is publishing stuff that doesn't get you labelled pinko and slung in the pokey.' She finished her beer and stood up. 'Got to work.'

'Where?'

'Here. Waitress. I do the graveyard shift, midnight till four. The tips aren't bad, and I get a free hamburger for breakfast.' She gave him her spare keys. 'Don't play the radio, and stay out of my bed. See you at dawn.' She came back to ask: 'Was that solid gold fountain pen really yours?'

22

'A golf trophy. Runner-up in the Venezuelan Amateur Open, 1951.'

'*Olé* in spades,' she said, and went away again.

2

Next day she slept until noon, took a shower, and dressed in one of Harry's old shirts. Luis had been out and bought a loaf and a small jar of Maxwell House, which left him with less than a dollar. They ate a late breakfast of dry toast and black coffee. 'Last night you spoke of HUAC,' he said. 'What is HUAC?'

'No.' She looked at him as if he had spilt ketchup down his shirt. 'No.' She took her cup and padded, barefoot, to the window. 'I have to live with that horseshit but I don't have to talk about it.'

'Terrific legs,' he said. 'The ass was superb, I remember. May I see the ass?'

'Go to hell, Luis. Go back to Venezuela, you don't belong here.'

'I can't go back. That shirt is the most provocative thing you have ever worn.'

'Christ . . . I'd go straight to Venezuela if I could. If I had any money.'

He went over and stood behind her and wrapped his arms around her waist. She put her cup on the windowsill. She held his wrists, lightly. Whether she was resisting the embrace or endorsing it, neither of them knew. 'We were always happy in bed,' he said. 'Isn't that right?'

'Yes, sort of. And if we go to bed now, I'll be stuck with you. Sex is fun but it isn't simple and right now my life is too complicated already.' She spoke flatly and without emotion. Luis could think of no reply. They stood for a long minute, looking out the window. Eventually the doorbell rang.

It was Bonnie Scott. She had four tins of smoked oysters, part of a food hamper sent by her rich aunt in Philadelphia who had heard that she was unemployed and not eating properly. 'This is my aunt's idea of K-rations for Manhatta-nites,' Bonnie said. 'There was a jar of caviare too, not the best Beluga, she apologized for that. I traded it.' She waved a bottle of French white wine. 'You guys ready for lunch?'

'Permanently,' Julie said.

They ate, and talked about Enrico's arrest, the notorious squalor of the Tombs, his chances of getting bail. Luis wanted to know more. 'What is HUAC?' he asked.

'Shit,' Julie said. 'There he goes again. He's been locked in the toilet since 1945, reading Proust. He knows nothing. Walk him round the block, Bonnie, tell the poor bastard the facts of life. I have to wash my undies.'

'Are those the only shoes you have?' Bonnie asked him.

'The best suede. Very comfortable.'

'Sure. Don't blame me if you get kidnapped by the New York City Ballet.'

They strolled down First Avenue.

'HUAC,' she said. 'You've honestly never heard of HUAC?'

'There was no reason. I didn't intend to leave Caracas, so why should I follow American politics when I could spend my time reading the best American novelists?' Luis was beginning to resent their poor opinion of his Venezuelan lifestyle. 'Truman Capote, Herman Wouk, Norman Mailer, Bellow, Salinger. Where would you go to find the truth? The *Daily News*, or John Steinbeck?'

She grunted. 'I certainly wouldn't quote *The Grapes of Wrath* to HUAC, which incidentally stands for the House Un-American Activities Committee, a bunch of bad-breath bigots who could prove the Pope's a card-carrying tool of the Kremlin if they tapped his phone, and God knows they're probably doing that already.'

'Un-American,' Luis said. 'Like doing something that's not cricket.'

'Spare me your English jokes, old sport. I've been grilled by HUAC and it was no comedy.' Luis looked interested, so she told him.

First, she was served a subpoena to appear before the

24

committee. Failure to appear was contempt; she could be jailed for that. So she wore a sober blue dress and went. She knew what they were going to question her about.

Back in 1947, working for a small New York publisher called Goblin Press, she'd edited two short satirical novels. They were about life on a US Navy ship during the war in the Pacific. The ship manufactured condoms in a great variety of sizes, textures and colours. The author was a happy, funny, middle-aged man who looked a bit like Spencer Tracy, only taller. He enjoyed being taken to lunch, and he was content to let Bonnie edit his manuscripts. His name was Gibbon Connor Rail, Gib for short, and he would talk about anything except his experiences in the navy. He declined to supply a photograph for the book jacket. 'Show the ship's cat,' he said. 'More brains.' She found a picture of a sardonic cat. The books sold well enough to cover their costs. Goblin Press was satisfied.

Three years later, Bonnie saw Gibbon Connor Rail's picture in *The New York Times*. He was Mikhail Bolgarik, an attaché at the Soviet embassy, declared *persona non grata* by the State Department and now on his way back to Moscow. 'Pity,' her boss said. 'I'd hoped he might have a big book in him. A desk job at the Kremlin will destroy his talent. Incidentally, I was never totally convinced by his name.'

'Gibbon Connor Rail,' Bonnie said. 'What's wrong with it?'

'Gib Rail is Big Liar, backwards.'

She was startled, and defensive. 'You forgot the Connor,' she said.

'Think about it. Conner. One who cons.'

'My God . . . If this gets out, Goblin is going to look pretty stupid.'

'Yes. Fortunately, both titles are out of print. With luck, no one but us will know.'

Soon, Bonnie and her boss moved on. She joined a bigger publishing house, worked hard, got known as a skilled editor with an eye for new talent. He made a career move: he became a theatrical agent. In 1952, he appeared before HUAC as a friendly witness. They asked him questions and he told them what they wanted to hear.

Chairman: Have you come across any blatant Communists in the course of your professional career?

Witness: In my experience, good actors are seldom blatant, and Communist actors even less so.

Chairman: I see. How many Communist actors have you known?

Witness: Let me answer that in this way. I know of certain people in show business who would not raise a finger to help this Committee fight the Communist conspiracy for world domination: Paul Robeson, Sam Wanamaker, Zero Mostel, Humphrey Bogart, Jules Dassin, Larry Adler . . .

He was on safe ground here. All these people had already been denounced by HUAC.

Chairman: Any others?

Witness: There are certainly many actors whom I personally would never cast in a truly patriotic American play or movie . . .

And he read out a list of seventy-three names, some famous, some retired, some just starting their careers, and none represented by the witness's agency.

The committee was impressed. The chairman remarked that the list included writers. Did the witness know of any specific Communist attempt to infiltrate the US with dangerous written material?

Witness: In 1947 a Russian KGB officer, working undercover in New York and using an alias, succeeded in getting two books published here, satirizing the US Navy. I never met the man, but I understand the editor, Miss Bonnie Scott, knew him well and worked closely with him.

That was more than enough. HUAC subpoenaed Bonnie. She confirmed everything. Counsel for the Committee suggested that the two books were subversive of the American armed forces. Bonnie said that the American armed forces seemed to have survived the attack in good shape. 'No thanks to you,' the chairman said. Her publishers sacked her before the day was out.

'For what?' Luis asked.

'Guilt, of course. Guilt by association. Guilt by implication. Guilt by gobbledegook. Who gives a shit for what? Nobody takes a chance with HUAC. Hell, they might subpoena the company *chairman*, for Christ's sake, demand to know why he hired a known Communist sympathizer and saboteur of the American Way of Life! He might go before the Committee and get his answers scrambled, next thing you know, the shareholders are screaming blue murder! Jesus Christ Almighty, get that goddamn woman out of here, before she contaminates us all!'

They turned the corner of 81st Street into York Avenue and headed back to the apartment.

'So what do you do for a living now?' he asked.

'No publisher will touch me. Once in a while, a friend pays me to read a manuscript, give an opinion, just as long as my name isn't on the report. People are scared.'

He stopped, and looked around. This was a quiet, unexciting part of town, a bit shabby but comfortable in the warm afternoon. Couple of bars, deli on the corner, a dry cleaner and laundry, a fruit and vegetable store spilling on to the sidewalk with a kid using a watering-can to keep the stuff cool and fresh. Nearby, two old guys were sitting at a card table, playing chequers.

'What are people afraid of?' Luis asked her. 'Nothing is going to happen to America. This is the safest country in the world.'

'Sure. But the Commies'll getcha if you don't watch out.' When Luis laughed in disbelief, she nodded towards the two old guys. 'Ask them what they think of Communism . . . Nah, that's too easy. Make it Socialism.'

Luis strolled over to them. 'Excuse me,' he said. 'I don't mean to interrupt your game.' They wore woollen undershirts, yellow with age, and they squinted through storebought spectacles.

'That's all right, sonny,' one said. He made his move.

'It's just that I'm running for office and I wondered if I could count on your vote. I represent the Socialist Party.'

'Get a cop,' the old guy told his friend.

'Please, that's not necessary,' Luis said. As the man got up, Luis made a gesture of restraint. It was only a gesture.

'You touch him,' the old guy said, 'I'll turn your brains into Cream of Wheat.' Somehow a blackjack had appeared in his hand. Luis backed off. Bonnie came to save him. 'Forget it,' she told them. 'He's three bricks shy of a load. Some days he thinks he's Napoleon.'

'Well, I ain't too fond of the French neither,' the old guy said fiercely. 'They're all Commie bums.'

'Sure they are.' Bonnie hustled him away.

Julie was sitting on the stoop, waiting for them. Bonnie told her about the two old guys, the blackjack, the threat to call a cop. 'Now you know,' Julie told him. 'Lucky you didn't get a poke in the chops. Last week I saw a kid get thrown off a bus just for carrying a copy of *Das Kapital*.'

'Doesn't anyone protect freedom of speech?' he asked. 'Surely the authorities . . .'

'Hey! Stay away from the authorities. Keep your mouth shut. Otherwise you might end up in the cell next to Enrico.'

'Or worse,' Bonnie said.

Luis had a gold ring. They hocked it and ate supper at a German beer-cellar on 86th Street: franks and sauerkraut plus beer, and apple pie for three. Now he had two dollars. He left one as a tip. 'You're insane,' Julie said. She picked it up and gave it to him. 'I have been a waiter,' he said. 'This is no time to cheat the workers of their due.' He put the dollar back. 'Leave it there, or I shall stand on a chair and sing the *Internationale*.'

'How does that go, again?' Bonnie asked.

'The workers' flag is deepest red, the something something blood they shed,' Luis said. 'After that it gets rather left wing.'

Bonnie went home to the garment district. Julie went to Mooney's, to work the graveyard shift. Luis went to bed. The fold-out couch was not comfortable. Something would have to be done about that.

28

BECAUSE THAT'S WHERE THE MONEY IS

1

Luis was often surprised and pleased by the skill of his subconscious. He took a problem to bed and woke up, effortlessly, with a solution.

Julie was asleep. He kept the curtains closed, shaved and showered as quietly as possible, made a cup of black coffee, put on a clean shirt and a quiet tie in the colours of an ancient British regiment, and chose his light grey summerweight suit. According to the New York phone book, the offices of the FBI were on East 58th Street.

It was a pleasant morning, promising a day suitable for drinking white wine in the park; he looked forward to that. Presumably Julie had a nice frock she could wear. If not, there were frock shops. He passed a couple of them as he walked to the Subway. It was a busy neighbourhood: stores, restaurants, cinemas. Luis approved. He liked tradesmen to be on hand when needed.

The Subway train smelt of rancid hair-oil and its passengers hadn't smiled since Prohibition ended, but it rushed Luis downtown at raucous speed. He got off at 58th Street. By the time he reached street level he had turned so many corners that he was confused: which way was east? Where was north? It took five minutes of going the wrong way before he found the FBI building.

The exterior was blank and easily washable; it might have been designed by a blind architect. The interior took no chances either. A man in a suit sat at a desk with a plaque reading *Information*. Behind him were an American flag and two portrait photographs, one of President Eisenhower, the other of Bureau Director J. Edgar Hoover. They were facing each other. The Director looked like an ageing pug, and the President looked as if he was wondering whether to take him for a walk or let him suffer a little longer.

'Sir?' the suit said.

Luis touched the plaque. 'I have information.'

'Yes?'

'Albert T. Falcondale, charged in Los Angeles with embezzlement, jumped bail. I know where he is.'

The suit took a thick ring-bound manual from a drawer, consulted the index, put it back. 'Not a federal offence,' he said. 'Try California. They might be interested.'

Luis was taken aback and tried not to show it. The fellow was treating him with steely politeness. Yet Al Falcondale had got away with a million dollars, Luis knew it, he had partnered Al in the Caracas Golf Club foursomes. His stomach growled, a comment on the FBI's indifference. 'There are other criminals,' he said.

The suit produced a yellow legal pad and a pencil and slid them across the desk.

Luis wrote a large dollar sign and slid the pad back.

'The Bureau does not pay informants.'

'You expect something for nothing?'

The suit tore the page from the pad and screwed it up. He did this without malice. The cost wasn't coming out of his pay cheque.

'There is another way,' Luis said. He had banked on getting 1,000 dollars from the FBI. His information was genuine: Caracas had a small but rich population of Yankee crooks, many of them regular golfers. 'I enrol in the FBI as a special agent. I have experience. During the recent unpleasantness in Europe I was an Allied agent at the highest level.'

'Every FBI agent must be an American citizen, and have a law degree or be qualified in accountancy.'

'I'm wasting my time here.' Luis's stomach agreed, and so did the suit: he made the smallest of nods. Luis left.

He walked to Fifth Avenue and immediately suffered an attack of envy. Everything and everybody was so rich, and it was all being done so easily, so confidently, as if Fifth Avenue had a *right* to be rich. The Plaza hotel, the Pierre, great cathedrals of success. Saks, Peck & Peck, Tiffany's, Cartier's, Bergdorf Goodman, Harry Winstone, places where if you had to ask the price, you shouldn't bother people by coming in at all. The casual swagger of the customers told him that money was not one of their worries.

He got as far as St Patrick's cathedral and sat on the steps. *Déjà vu* was nibbling at his concentration. He had been in this situation in 1941, penniless in the wealthy heart of Madrid, desperate to get a job as a spy. But on that day in 1941 he had eaten breakfast. That was the difference. Now, when he counted his change, his fingers were trembling. A bus went by. It carried an advertisement for a steak house. Saliva surged around his tongue.

A man with a pushcart was selling pretzels. Luis bought one. It felt like Bakelite and tasted like cardboard, but it fooled his stomach into thinking real food was on the way.

Money, he thought. *Made by selling things. You sell your time, your talent, your property. Or, in the case of that bum at Hoboken, your self-respect. You simply blackmail someone into paying up*. A faint idea stirred in a distant corner of his mind. He pursued it, caught it, and shook it to life. 'Bloody hell,' he said aloud. 'Has it come to this? Surely you can think of something better?' No reply.

In a drugstore he found a phone and a phone book and the listing for the British Consulate.

It was several blocks away, which gave him time to work on his opening lines. *Déjà vu* helped. He remembered how he got into the German embassy in 1941. 'Keep it simple,' he murmured. 'Very short, very simple.'

The woman running the reception desk was English. 'Have you an appointment?' she asked, pleasantly.

'Intelligence,' Luis said. 'Military intelligence.' He went

and sat in a chair and picked up *The Times*. He turned the pages slowly and quietly while he tried to hear what she had to say, but she was expert at shielding her voice on the phone.

Visitors arrived, respectable people with honest appointments. Others left, their business done. Luis read a report about Korea. Not a happy place. There had been a war; he recalled looking at battle scenes on a newsreel while he waited to see *High Noon* in a Caracas cinema. War had ended now, it seemed. Neither side won or lost. Nothing new there. Damn good movie, though. Grace Kelly's smile would melt the elastic in an archbishop's underpants. Luis turned the page and found the county cricket scores. A stocky young man appeared beside him. He had curly sandy hair and a fighter-pilot's moustache.

'Frobisher,' he said. 'I don't believe we've met, have we?'

'Oxfordshire are doing jolly well, aren't they?' Luis said. Frobisher cocked his head as if he were slightly deaf. 'County cricket,' Luis explained.

'To the best of my knowledge, Oxfordshire don't play in the county championship.'

'Of course they don't. Just checking.' Luis folded the newspaper. 'Thomas Ford the Third. Responsible for security at all Ford plants. That includes England.'

They went to Frobisher's office. Luis was invited to sit. Frobisher perched on a corner of his desk and took note of Luis's suede shoes, which were beginning to look a bit weary. 'We have to be awfully careful,' he said. 'Now, if I ring your Detroit office, they'll vouch for you, won't they? What's the number?' His hand rested on the phone. Luis chewed gently on his upper lip. 'I expect it's on your business card,' Frobisher said. Luis stopped chewing, and looked at a mounted photograph of Spitfires on patrol. 'So you're not Thomas Ford the Third,' Frobisher said.

'No. Still, it was a start. Would I be sitting here if I'd told that charming lady the truth? She would have given me several forms to complete in triplicate and then made an appointment for next Tuesday with the Second Secretary for Commercial Intelligence. That's no good to anyone. I want to see your top man in military or political intelligence.'

'I shall need a name.'

'Tell him I'm Eldorado. If that means nothing, tell him to ask Kim Philby.' Luis glanced at his watch. 'It's tea-time in London. Kim will be tinkling his teacups.'

Ten minutes later, Frobisher ushered him into a large corner office and withdrew. A man in a tweed suit was frowning hard at a piece of paper. 'I'm Harding,' he said. 'Philby's given me three questions to ask. If you get any of them wrong I'm to assume you're bogus, which is a painful condition in my department, often leading to death or disablement.'

'Dear Kim,' Luis said. 'Ever the charmer.'

'One: who was Nutmeg?'

'Ex-Indian Army officer. Worked for the Ministry of Food in Cambridge.' Easy. Nutmeg had been the code-name of an Eldorado sub-agent.

Harding grunted. 'And Wallpaper?'

'Faggot lecturer, University of Birmingham.' Another sub-agent. 'Next.'

'Who killed Haystack?'

'I did. Too damn lazy.' All mythical sub-agents. Piece of cake, Luis thought.

'All the loonies pass through here,' Harding said. 'Last week it was Mahatma Gandhi in a tartan loincloth, yards and yards of it, she must have weighed sixteen stone. I told her the orange lipstick was a mistake, and she became violent. That was when I began to suspect she was not who she claimed to be.'

'What did she want?'

'Money. What do you want?'

Luis walked to the window and pretended to enjoy the view. He hadn't expected Harding to be so blunt. Instinct warned him away from a blunt reply. 'I wish to give London an opportunity to become a partner in a business venture,' he said. 'My wartime memoirs are almost ready for publication. They should sell very well. But the manuscript is a mess, all in longhand. I need to get it professionally typed.'

'Bring it here. We'll do it for you.'

'I wouldn't dream of imposing. A thousand dollars should be adequate to cover the cost.'

'Blackmail,' Harding said. 'Well, it's not up to me.'

Luis waited in the next room. Harding's secretary brought him coffee. He loaded it with sugar; his system had long since lost faith in the pretzel. There was nothing to read. He thought about Julie and all the things they could do with a thousand dollars. He should have asked for two thousand. Or five thousand. Great Britain owed it to him. In the war, Eldorado had been worth two armoured divisions, a battleship and six squadrons of Lancaster bombers. Someone in MI6 had told him so when he got his MBE.

The door opened. Harding beckoned. 'London says I can give you one hundred dollars,' he said. 'And that's all.'

Luis went in. He didn't know whether to feel dismay or delight. An hour ago he would have run through mud to catch a hundred-dollar bill. Now he had talked himself into being worth five grand. 'I feel like Mahatma Gandhi,' he said. 'I feel like a fight.'

'Not with me. There are six ways to break a man's arm without using weapons and I invented three of them. I taught unarmed combat to Commandos all through the war. Scots were the worst. Pain threshold so high it went off the clock. God help the Glasgow police if any of my pupils survived.'

'How many arms did you break?'

Harding looked away. His mouth curled; he almost smiled. 'Official secret. More than a few, let's say. Blood all over the floor, sometimes. If you bleed on my carpet I'm stuck with the stain. Consulate's on a very tight budget.' He unlocked a desk drawer and took out money. 'First, I need to know where we can contact you.'

Luis briefly thought of giving a false address: the Athletic Club, or the Pierre Hotel. But what if London tried to buy his memoirs? Philby might find the other nine hundred dollars. Perhaps even more. He wrote Julie's address on the blotter.

Harding gave him four twenties, a ten and two fives. 'Britain has a desperate foreign-exchange crisis,' he said. 'Nobody's allowed to take more than twenty-five pounds a year out of the country. What you've got is the funds for an average British family's foreign holiday.'

'Can't stand around chatting,' Luis said. 'Lunch calls. A dozen *escargots*, a *coquille St Jacques*, a nice *blanquette de veau*, and a little *tarte au citron* to finish.'

'May it rot your guts like battery acid,' Harding said pleasantly. 'My secretary will show you out.'

When Luis had gone, Frobisher came in. 'All on tape, sir,' he said. 'Rather a smooth customer, I thought.'

'Slippery. According to Philby, the man is a naturally gifted liar. Can't tell the truth to save his life.'

'So he's lying about his memoirs?'

'Probably. But London thinks it's worth a hundred dollars to find out. Officially, Philby's retired, so he's got time to worry about posterity's opinion. He wants to know what Eldorado's written. So do we. Here's the address.'

Frobisher copied it from the blotter. 'I never realized you were expert in unarmed combat, sir,' he said. 'Is it hard to learn?'

'No idea. All codswallop. Can't break wind, let alone break arms. And Gandhi in a kilt and lipstick – all tosh. Fooled him, though. Nobody more gullible than a liar.'

'How very true.' As Frobisher smiled at Harding, he thought: *Which makes you gullible too*. But he said nothing more.

2

A plate of veal and peppers cost seventy-five cents. Peach pie and ice cream was thirty cents. Coffee, a dime.

Luis had followed some men who looked like truck drivers into a diner off Seventh Avenue. Truck drivers knew the best places to eat; well-known fact, and it turned out to be true. When he was full of good American grub, New York ceased to be a battlefield and became a parade ground where talent and opportunity marched side by side. Success was simply a matter of picking your partner.

He had invested a nickel in the *Herald Tribune* and now he

checked out the employment pages. Clearly, the economy was buoyant. Thousands of jobs. Accountancy, law firms, banks, hospitals, real estate, airlines, construction, all were clamouring for help, expert help, qualified help, experienced help. That wasn't Luis. He read Art Buchwald's column, didn't understand the jokes, left a fat tip and went out into the streets again. He felt less buoyant than the economy and he didn't know where he was going.

Somewhere in the low Fifties, between Madison and Park, he saw a sign that said JOBS and headed for it, mainly because his feet were hot and he wanted to sit down. By the door a brass plate, tanned olive by carbon monoxide, identified the Aace Employment Bureau. He climbed three flights of stairs, the last uncarpeted. The door was open. A man in his twenties sat in an old-fashioned barber's chair with his feet on a desk. He wore khaki pants, tennis shoes and a faded blue windbreaker with the sleeves rolled to the elbow. He was reading a book called *Pro Secrets of the Hollywood Songwriters*. He put it face-down on the desk. 'One good number on the Hit Parade,' he said. 'That's all it takes, and then you retire on the royalties . . . I'm Mike Morgan. You're looking for a job.'

'Correct. Luis Cabrillo.'

'What sort of job?'

'You seem pretty comfortable. I'll take yours.'

'Cost you ten grand. That includes seven years remaining on the lease. And the name, Aace Employment. My old man's idea. First listing in the Yellow Pages. Please . . .' He waved Luis to a chair.

'Despite which', Luis said, 'business would seem to be less than hectic.'

'Who needs hectic? I get the first week's pay as commission. Two clients a day keeps me afloat.' Morgan took a small steel gyro, a toy, and made it spin on the desk. The thing hummed as it wandered. 'Dad left the business to me. He died while I was in Korea, defending freedom, justice and democracy. We looked all over, but we never found any freedom, justice or democracy to defend. Ain't that funny?'

'Strange indeed.'

Morgan shifted a coffee mug before the gyro could bump into it. 'If you had ten grand you wouldn't be here. So . . . got any marketable skills?'

Luis thought of saying: *I can lie convincingly.* But he shook his head.

'Go wash windows, then. Schlepp garbage cans. Be a messenger. Sell newspapers. There's a hundred ways to make a buck out there.'

'Messenger? Like a courier?'

'No. Like a guy who delivers documents, stuff can't wait for the mail. Everyone uses messengers. Ad agencies, lawyers, banks, brokers, even me sometimes. I can fix you up with a job. You want to be a messenger?'

They watched the gyro. It was running down, developing a wobble. It flirted with the edge of the desk, came back for a second look, toppled and tumbled to the floor.

'Wise choice,' Morgan said. 'Messengers get paid peanuts.'

'Thank you for your time,' Luis said. Morgan picked up his book.

3

Luis stood on a corner and looked at Madison Avenue. If this was the Mecca of American advertising, it went about its work very discreetly. All he could see was banks. Big solid banks. First National City. Marine Merchant. Chemical Bank. He craned his neck and searched for more. Manufacturers Hanover. Dime Immigrant. Was that a bank? It had a Wells Fargo truck outside.

All these banks, all that money.

Luis, daydreaming, remembered Willie Sutton's reason for robbing banks. 'That's where the money is,' Willie had said. Here, now, in this one sunny stretch of Madison Avenue, there must be fifty million dollars doing nothing in those banks. Just lying in bundles of notes, getting older, going nowhere, buying nothing. Luis had another thought. Those notes kept shrinking in value. Inflation nibbled like mice. Even at only one per cent per annum, fifty million dollars was worth half a million less than a year ago. Yet nobody caused an uproar about that. Nobody sent the FBI to Washington DC to arrest the Willie Suttons in government who had quietly siphoned off the loot. Nobody complained, so presumably nobody suffered. Bank robbery, like everything else in life, was relative. Do it with a gun and you go to jail. Do it with statistics and they let you teach at Harvard Business School. Amazing.

Luis went for a stroll. He had the whole afternoon to kill.

Without really looking, he saw a couple of messenger agencies, so Morgan was right. Then, somewhere near Lexington Avenue, on 49th Street, he passed a tired-looking building that advertised offices to rent by the week, day or hour. He wondered what type of business would rent its premises by the hour. Several possibilities suggested themselves. One generated half an idea. He walked around the block and developed the idea further. Then he went into the building and rented a small room on the second floor for two hours. It cost him ten dollars.

Next he went to Bloomingdale's and bought a pair of light leather gloves. He wore them when he visited a stationery store and bought ten large, strong envelopes, a block of writing paper and a ballpen. He borrowed a Manhattan phone book and looked up ten banks with branches no more than a few blocks from his office. He wrote ten messages in block capitals, put one message in each envelope, sealed them, and addressed the envelopes to the banks. As an afterthought he wrote "Any Teller" on the envelopes.

He went to a messenger agency he'd noticed on Lexington Avenue. 'I need ten messengers,' he said. 'They must deliver these ten envelopes at exactly two forty-five p.m. and take what they're given and bring it to me immediately at this address. Is that possible?'

'Strictly routine,' the man said. 'Deliver, pick up, deliver. Where's the problem? Forty-five bucks.'

Luis recoiled. 'Isn't that a bit steep?'

'You want it good or you want it cheap? My guys do good work. Cheap, you can get elsewhere.'

Luis paid.

★

Messengers were a mixed bunch. Some had just left school with no qualifications except the ability to make a delivery and, if necessary wait, for a reply. Others were elderly men with sore feet who needed the pay to boost their Social Security benefit. A few were recent immigrants with little English. All had one thing in common: boredom. Walk around Manhattan all day, carrying stuff you don't know what it is, soon you switch off the brain. What's to get excited about? Ain't gettin' paid to think. Paid to walk.

Billy Ogilvy was seventeen, six foot two, waiting for the army to claim him. Interested only in sex, at which so far he had had limited success. If he saw a good-looking girl his pupils would dilate spontaneously. Otherwise he had no reason to put his face to work. His features were heavy. They fell into a natural scowl and he left them where they felt comfortable.

He went into a branch of First National City Bank at two forty-five p.m., as ordered. He joined the shortest queue. It took him four minutes to reach the teller. He gave her the big envelope. First half of his job done. She was young and pretty and his eyes widened to get a better view. He rested his elbows on the counter.

She slit the envelope, took out the paper, read the message: *I have a gun. Put all your money in envelope and seal it. Do it now. No alarm! Gun is loaded.*

Instinctively, she glanced at Billy Ogilvy. He looked her in the eyes. He was frighteningly calm; he might have been waiting for a bus.

The bank had a simple policy for this situation: give the robber your money and let him go. On average, a hold-up cost less than a thousand dollars. For that, it wasn't worth risking anybody's life, especially a customer who might get

39

caught in the crossfire. She took all the paper money in her tray, stuffed it in the envelope, sealed it with sticky tape, gave it back, and held up her hands, palms outward: empty. Billy turned and left. It was the first time she had been robbed and she suddenly found herself frightened, breathless, trembling. It took her an absurdly long moment to find the silent-alarm button. By then Billy was gone, lost in the crowd.

As instructed, he delivered the envelope to Luis in his rented office on 49th Street, got his signature (G. Washington) on the job sheet, and went away. Two more messengers delivered bulky envelopes to Luis in the next ten minutes. Maybe more were on their way. Or maybe trouble was coming. Enough was enough. Luis quit.

He walked out of the building, carrying all three envelopes in a Bloomingdale's bag. The day had changed: now colours were brighter, sounds were sharper. As he reached the corner and looked for a taxi, a police siren screamed and wailed. Another siren did battle with it. A taxi saw Luis and swung to the kerb. He got in. Two police cars bullied through the traffic and stopped halfway down the block. Their sirens faded into a long, low sob and died. Cops ran into the office building. 'Goodness!' Luis said. 'What's all that about?'

'Late for their coffee break, I guess,' the driver said. He was black. He wore a knitted woollen cap and he chewed a toothpick.

'Uptown,' Luis said. He didn't laugh. He didn't smile. He was beginning to feel like a New Yorker.

★

For the NYPD it was rapidly turning into a busy afternoon in Manhattan. Two shootings, one fatal, in Spanish Harlem. East River Drive closed near Bellevue by a multiple pile-up. Anonymous bomb threat to City Hall. Knife fight in Chinatown: three victims. Truckload of furs hijacked near Penn Station. Shots fired at 125th Street and Columbus; passing fire truck hit. Plus minor crimes and misdemeanours all over the city, such as the lady on West 12th Street who threw her husband out the window without opening it first. He landed on a passing musician. Sheer bad luck. She was a big woman, and unrepentant. She flattened three patrolmen before she was cuffed and led out. By then a crowd had gathered. Kids on the roof tossed garbage cans at the patrol cars, missed, killed a dog. Officer fired warning shots. Small riot. It was that sort of a day.

The officers who responded to alarms at ten midtown banks flooded the area. At five banks the robbers had got away. The rest were old, slow and bewildered; they willingly gave up their envelopes and their instructions. Police found an empty office, rented in the name James Madison. 'He was a regular guy,' the office manager told them. 'Dressed nice. Paid cash.'

'You didn't suspect anything?' a detective said. 'You never heard of James Madison before?'

'Sure. I go to the fights. That's the guy built Madison Square Garden, right? Could have been a relative. How should I know? Ain't clairvoyant.'

The last two messengers turned up, bearing envelopes, which they refused to release unless somebody signed their work sheets. 'You're looking for a James Madison, right?' the detective asked them.

'Hell, no,' one said. 'Thomas Jefferson.'

'James Monroe,' the other messenger said.

'Let me out of here,' the detective said. He drove to the messenger agency and questioned the boss. 'Ten messengers, to go to ten banks. Didn't that strike you as unusual?'

'No. Why should it? Kind of job we handle all the time.'

'And the ten deliveries from the banks to a rented office?'

'So what? Most the offices in Manhattan are rented. *This* office you're standing in, it's rented. The guy was polite, he paid cash. See?' He had found the paperwork. 'William McKinley. All kosher. Strictly routine.'

'Yeah. President McKinley was assassinated in Buffalo in 1898.'

'Before my time. Maybe this is a relative . . . Hey, look at this.' He had the messengers' job sheets. 'McKinley signed

41

different names. G. Washington . . . A. Lincoln . . . U.S. Grant.'

'Cute,' the detective said. 'Cute as crabs.'

One thing, there was no lack of witnesses. No lack of descriptions, either. Depending on who you believed, the suspect was a clean-shaven twenty-five with grey eyes and no scars, or a forty-year-old with a Clark Gable moustache, brown eyes and a birthmark like a strawberry on his neck. The birthmark was Billy Ogilvy's contribution. 'Which side?' the cop asked. 'Right,' Billy said, and touched the left side of his neck. The cop reversed his pencil and rubbed out birthmark. Billy saw that, and was hurt. 'You'll never catch the guy,' he said. 'I met him. He's a mastercrook.'

Ten banks, no leads: it was a headache. Bank robbery was a federal offence. The NYPD gladly turned it over to the FBI. The banks had lost five thousand bucks and change. Let Hoover's agents bust their nuts over it.

★

Luis kept five hundred dollars and put the rest in a safe deposit box which he rented at a branch of Chase Manhattan on 72nd Street. Then he took a cab to 84th and First. No cops in sight. Julie was sitting on the stoop, reading the *Trib*. 'Someone left it at Mooney's,' she said. 'I can't afford newspapers. That bastard McCarthy's muckraking again. See? Says he's found more Reds in the State Department.'

'I thought we might go to Central Park and drink some chilled white wine. Have you got a nice frock to wear?'

She squinted up at him: he was standing with his back to the sun; his face was a dark blank. 'You sound like Daddy Warbucks,' she said. 'I'm not Li'l Orphan Annie.'

He laughed. 'I haven't the faintest notion what that means.'

'Means you're out of your depth. Something else you don't know.'

They went inside. He showered, and changed all his clothes. 'Jolly warm, New York,' he said. 'Is there a laundry handy, by any chance?'

She was watching him dress. 'On every block. They like to be paid. And I'm behind with the rent. So what makes you so chipper?'

'Chipper . . .' he murmured. 'I knew a chap in Madrid who was chipper. Freddy Ryan. Remember Freddy? Trained with me to spy for the *Abwehr*, until they shot him. Poor old Freddy. Didn't look chipper when he was dead. Looked as if he'd been kicked in the goolies.'

'This is America. If you mean nuts, say nuts. Let's go.' She was wearing jeans and a t-shirt.

'Like that? It's a waste of your legs. Haven't you got a pretty frock?'

'Wrong gal. Shirley Temple I'm not.'

'America has ruined you.' But even that didn't make her smile.

4

Fisk had a guilty secret. He liked crime. For him, a day without crime was flat, dull, worthless. That was why he had joined the FBI. He had a law degree from Yale, his family were Presbyterians, and he couldn't do wrong any more than he could play the bass saxophone, so crooks fascinated him. He and they were alike yet unalike; a puzzle and a challenge. He felt much the same way about women. In a flash of inspiration he suggested to the manager of the messenger agency that the person who hired ten guys to rob ten banks might have been a woman.

The manager was amused. 'You saying I don't know Arthur from Martha?'

Fisk's supervisor, Prendergast, looked on. When the FBI had taken the ten-bank steal from the NYPD, Fisk had been eager to be involved. 'Bring your notebook,' Prendergast said. 'You can take statements.' They had questioned many people and they were getting nowhere. Now the kid had an original idea. 'What's on your mind?'

'The nature of the crime. It's evasive, there's no risk of violence to the criminal. That's how a woman would rob a bank: get someone else to do it.'

'Listen, sonny,' the manager said loudly, 'if it's built like a man, talks like a man, and grows hair on its knuckles it ain't a woman.' He was annoyed at having to tell his story all over again.

'I arrested a female, couple of years ago,' Prendergast said. 'Walked like Betty Grable, talked like Joan Crawford, when we searched her she was hung like Roy Rogers and his horse Trigger, both.'

'That's different,' the manager said. 'This still wasn't no woman.' He pictured Luis. 'Most I can say is maybe the guy was a fruit, on account of he was wearing fruit boots.' They were interested. 'You know,' he said, 'them soft suede things look like the fairies made 'em.'

It was a lucky break. Well, law officers have plenty of bad luck; they also have good luck once in a while. Fisk phoned Immigration at Hoboken, got the contact address which Luis had given: an apartment on East 84th Street. 'I want a black bag job on that apartment as soon as possible,' Prendergast said. If the money was there, the case was closed. That kind of search wasn't legal, but this was the Bureau. Who gave a shit about the law?

★

They took a taxi to Central Park South, to a hotel she knew. The foyer was a cool and lofty place with an ambitious fountain. Bronze statues of naked youths danced in a circle through the spray. Their streaming, glistening skin made them look as if they were on the spree. 'I come here a lot,' she said. 'Just to look around. It's free. I want to be like them. Run in the rain.'

'Something I'd buy a ticket to see,' he said, and regretted it. Too flip. Her silence made it worse. 'Sorry,' he said. She walked away. For the first time since he arrived, he thought perhaps she disliked him. That raised a flutter of panic.

Without Julie he would be alone in New York, alone everywhere, in fact. Spending money had kept him busy in Venezuela; but it hadn't created a different person.

They went into the restaurant. He ordered a bottle of Blanc de Blanc, a plate of *hors d'oeuvre,* some breadsticks. Spending money helped the little panic to fade.

'Herb Kizsco came by the apartment,' she said. Luis had to work his memory: Kizsco, academic, head like a melon, got fired, drove a taxi. 'He heard Enrico was let out of jail. Seems the church hired an attorney to put the squeeze on Immigration.'

'That's good.'

'Yeah. Except, those nice folks from Internal Revenue were waiting. They want to audit his tax returns for the last seven years.' She ate an olive.

'If Enrico charged a dollar a meal, he couldn't have made any profit.'

'Forget profit. They'll find mistakes, irregularities. Anything they want to look for, they'll find, they always do. They'll put him out of business. He might as well quit.'

'That's persecution. Surely the government — '

'The government's running scared, just like the rest of us. The whole country's scared shitless.'

Luis looked around. The place was calm, quiet, prosperous, unhurried. This wasn't York Avenue, where people lived on the sidewalk in their undershirts. This America was as solid as Fort Knox. He wanted to know why Julie had been fired, but instinct said this was not a good time to ask. So he smiled instead. Back in the old days, his smile had worked like sunlight on flowers. Not now, though.

'I hope you can pay for the booze,' she said. He nodded, and kept the smile burning. 'This morning you were flat broke,' she said. 'Now suddenly it's taxis and frocks and imported wine.'

'Busy day. My associates negotiated profitable deals with several banks.' He forked an anchovy.

She thought about that. He gave her more wine. 'Luis, I know you better than anyone in the world. I know your beautiful body, every square inch of it.' Hope lurched in his loins. 'I know your shabby soul,' she said, 'and I know your cock-eyed mind. Whenever you sound pleased with yourself, you're lying.'

'I have five thousand dollars and change.'

'Good. Tomorrow you can get an apartment of your own.'

For a few seconds they looked each other in the eye. Both were afraid. Julie was afraid that she would fall back in love with a man who could only be trouble. Luis was afraid he would lose the only woman he could be honest with. Also dishonest with.

The moment passed. They talked about harmless things: Manhattan, what to see, what to avoid.

Time to leave. He signalled for the bill. The waiter looked young enough to be his son. 'Suppose I told you I was a Russian spy,' Luis said to him, casually, as he sorted out money. 'What would you do?'

'I'd expect a good tip, sir.'

'Yes? Why?'

'It's a bull market, sir. From what I hear.' He was quick and cheerful. Luis laughed, and added more to the tip.

When they were outside, she said: 'Smart kid. Just don't judge everyone by him. Can we afford the movies? Then dinner?' He smiled, and waved down a taxi. 'Don't do that Russian spy crap again,' she said. 'It gives me cramps.'

5

The first man into the apartment wore Con Ed coveralls. He carried a Con Ed toolbox and, if pressed, he could show ID from Con Ed. He got in by using picklocks that were not Con Ed issue. He was a retired cop who did illegal entries for the FBI. He preferred the Con Ed identity because it let him search anywhere for gas leaks or faulty electric cables, including under the floorboards. Nine times out of ten, your amateur robber hid his stuff under the floor. Tenth time, he buried it in the backyard. People did what they saw in the movies. No imagination.

But he found no scarred wood, or scratched nails, or disturbed dust: the floorboards hadn't been moved since Pearl Harbour. He went down the hall and peeked at the backyard. Kids on a tree swing. Guy poking burgers on a barbecue. Forget it.

He went back to the apartment. Somebody knocked on the door, so he opened it. Repairman from New York Telephone. 'Name of Conroy?' the man said. 'Fault on the phone?'

'Join the party. Hey . . . You're with the Bureau, right?'

They studied each other.

'Used to be,' the repairman said. 'I remember you now. NYPD? Yeah. Small world. I retired, but the pension sucks, so I work freelance. Break-ins, bugs, taps. Same old stuff. British Intelligence hired me. They want to know, did this guy write his life story yet. You?'

'Lookin' for bank robbery evidence. Hell, it's all paper. Work shared is work halved, right?'

Together they searched the apartment, inch by dusty inch, and found nothing. They were drinking Julie's coffee when the landlord came in, followed by the two old guys Luis had offended on York Avenue. They were all drunk. The landlord was one boilermaker short of being fighting drunk.

'The fuck you two pricks doin' in my buildin'?' he shouted.

'Fixin' the leak in your worn-out gas stove,' the Con Ed man said.

The landlord sniffed the air, hard. 'You smell anythin'?' he demanded. The two old guys sniffed. 'Ain't no gas smell in here,' they said. 'No, sir.' One of them clacked his teeth, which the excitement had loosened.

'No pleasin' some people,' the Con Ed man said to the phone repairman. They were unworried. They had the force of injustice on their side.

'Get your ass outa my buildin', boy,' the landlord said. 'Ain't no gas smell here! Shoot your mouth at me, I'll stick this fist in it.'

47

'Reason there ain't no gas smell, pop, is because I just fixed the damn leak.'

'This *my* buildin'! Anythin' leaks, I get told first!' He was so furious that he was spitting a fine spray. 'How the fuck you get in here?'

'Door was open. Look, since you're bein' so damn reasonable, tell you what I'm gonna do. This your buildin', you're entitled to one hundred per cent of it, and that includes the lousy leak in your stinkin' stove, so I'm gonna take this big heavy wrench an' give a good hard smack, right where I fixed it. See? Where the gas smell came from. Your smell, right? You want it back? You can have it back.'

'Sure he wants it back,' the repairman said. 'Belongs to him.'

'Call a cop,' the landlord told the two old guys. One of them picked up the phone. 'Dead,' he said.

'I'm fixin' that,' the repairman said. 'Takes a while. Want to wait?' The landlord grabbed the phone and flung it at him and missed. 'That's not your property!' the repairman warned. 'Belongs to the phone company!'

The row was still raging when Julie and Luis walked in. 'There's the sonabitch!' the two old guys cried. 'That's the lousy Commie bastard!'

'You're outta here,' the landlord told her. 'Bad enough you're a whore, but look at you, whorin' with *this* stinkin' Commie! Out!'

'The man's right,' one of the two old guys said. 'Ain't American,' the other said. The Con Ed man and the NY Telephone man slipped away.

'Pack your stuff,' Julie told Luis. She dragged a suitcase from under her bed. Ten minutes later they were on the corner of First, looking for a taxi.

'Why would the phone company send a guy to fix the phone?' she said. 'It wasn't bust. It got cut off a month ago, when I couldn't pay the bill. And I never asked Con Ed to fix anything.'

A taxi slid alongside. 'What's a good hotel?' Luis asked.

'They're not interested in me,' she said. 'They know everything about me. So it has to be you.'

SWEET
CHEAT

1

They stayed at the Drake. Separate beds.

Next morning, while he was in the bath, she took his suede shoes and $20 from his wallet, went out and bought a pair of black loafers, same size and width. She came back without the suedes. 'I'm not going around this city with a guy looks like he plays with the pixies,' she told him. 'I've got my reputation to consider.'

'May God forgive you. I never shall.' But the loafers were comfortable. Later that day he bought another pair, in brown.

By then, they had sublet a small penthouse apartment on Central Park West. 'It's cheap because it's short,' the agent said. 'The tenants are in Europe for three months. They return, you're out. Have a nice summer.'

'Ample time to achieve our goal,' Luis said. 'We are rabid Marxist-Leninists. In three months, all this will be Bolshevik.' He waved a hand at Central Park. Julie shook her head.

'That's nice,' the agent said. 'The doorman's name is Mike. Tip him five bucks a week. Don't water the cactus. Anything else I can tell you?'

'For an underground movement, we're awfully high up,' Luis said.

'It's just an act,' Julie said wearily. 'He's just an actor.'

'Sure.' The agent gave her the keys. 'I nearly voted Democrat myself, once.' At the door, he paused. 'Nearly forgot. The hot water is very, very hot.'

49

Luis was playing with the TV. 'It's such a hulking great thing, yet it creates such a terribly small picture,' he said. 'Can't see any future in it. Not much present, either.'

She switched the set off. 'Look: put your tiny brain in gear. You want to get us dumped on the street again? Jokes about Bolsheviks in Central Park don't play in this city. You listening?' She shoved him until he stumbled. 'What d'you think the agent meant when he said the water's very, very hot? Wake up, Luis, for Christ's sake.'

'Um,' he said. 'Perhaps even double-um.' He went away and took a shower; came out wrapped in towels. 'Absolutely right,' he told her. 'Very hot indeed.'

★

There was a phone, and it worked. She asked Bonnie Scott to come over for lunch. Bonnie arrived hungry.

'Do me a favour and tell him again,' Julie said to her. 'HUAC, McCarthy, the blacklist, the witch hunt. He won't listen to me. What the hell do I know? I'm unemployable.' She went off to the kitchen.

'Oh, Christ,' Bonnie said. 'Give me a drink.'

Luis found half a bottle of Scotch. 'No ice, I'm afraid. We forgot to plug in the fridge.'

'That's classed as an Un-American Activity. Next thing, you'll tell me you listen to *The Flight of the Bumblebee*.'

'Shouldn't I?'

'Rimsky-Korsakov, old sport. Russian.'

'He's dead.'

'Dead means nothing. Nobody mentions Rimsky-Korsakov on Voice of America, unless they want to get canned.'

'Is that the same as fired?' Luis stretched out on a settee. 'I've been fired, several times. I don't think Voice of America circulated in Venezuela.'

'It's a radio station. In Europe. Beamed at the Iron Curtain. Paid for with US tax dollars.'

'Ah, I see. Propaganda.'

'No. Well, yes, some of it. The point is McCarthy and his

sidekicks have got every government employee wetting himself in case someone tells McCarthy the guy prefers Prokofiev to Cole Porter, or he saw *The Battleship Potemkin* when he was in college in 1934, or he reads *War and Peace* in bed.' Bonnie ran out of breath.

'Tolstoy is vastly over-rated,' Luis said. 'I would seriously question the judgement of anyone who wastes much time on *War and Peace*.'

'The hell with Tolstoy. This isn't about Tolstoy.'

'*Potemkin* is different. I enjoyed the film enormously. The sequence of the baby-carriage bouncing down the steps is high comedy. Just thinking of it makes me hoot.'

'Enjoy your thoughts, friend. I know guys who've been kicked out of their jobs for less. And believe me, nobody's brave enough to screen *Potemkin* anywhere in the US.'

'All governments are neurotic,' Luis said. He raised a foot to admire his new loafers. 'I knew a British civil servant whose career was blighted when his wife said cricket was silly. Which it is. Of course, baseball is even sillier.'

'Ever seen a game?

'Heavens, no.'

'Then you got no right to condemn it.'

'Goodness! What an intolerant nation you are.' He smirked at Julie, who had come out of the kitchen to get a Scotch. 'I think I'm doing rather well,' he said.

'You quit thinking in 'forty-six,' she said, and went away.

'Forget baseball,' Bonnie said. 'Take government of the people, by the people, for the people. Lincoln said it must never pass away. Well, buster, it's gone, and Voice of America's just one line on the tombstone.'

'For doing what, exactly?'

'Who cares? Poor bastards aren't accused of anything, so how can they defend themselves? What McCarthy says, goes. At Voice of America, half the staff went.'

Luis eased his shoulders. 'I never listen to radio,' he said. 'All gabble, gabble, gabble,'

'That's just an example. A symptom of the disease. Any level of government, McCarthy or HUAC just gives them a

51

nasty look, and *kazaam*! Everyone's running in circles to prove he's loyal.'

'Yeah.' Julie was leaning on the kitchen door, listening. 'And the best way to do that is fire the next guy. *He's* the traitor. Now you've done your duty. Country's safe. So are you.'

Luis shrugged. 'Maybe the next guy *was* a traitor.'

'Who says?' Bonnie demanded.

'Yeah,' Julie said. 'What if a guy went to a couple of Party meetings? Never joined, just listened. What if he had a dog called Molotov?' She went away again.

'I would ban all dog-owners on sight,' Luis said. 'The world would be a better place without dogs.'

'You'd probably ban radio, too,' Bonnie said.

'Splendid idea. And shoot broadcasters on sight.'

'Forget it, Bonnie,' Julie called from the kitchen. 'Just let it go.'

'Anyway,' Luis said. 'I have no sympathy for government employees. What makes them think they deserve a job for life? Nobody else has one.'

'Not the point!' Bonnie was prowling the room. 'There are men, and women too, who do their job well, get caught up in this witch hunt, disgraced, sacked, maybe they know what they're accused of, maybe they don't . . .'

'Ah! Now I understand.' Luis clicked his fingers. 'Life isn't fair. Get the phone book, I'll find a dozen lawyers only too happy to take this dreadful Senator McCarthy to court.'

'You don't understand,' Bonnie said.

Julie reappeared. 'He's got his head up his ass.' She went away.

'I'm the one with solutions,' Luis said. 'You're in love with problems.'

'Listen: McCarthy never fires anyone. How can you sue him? What he does, he puts the fear of God into some dusty corner of government. Soybean subsidies. McCarthy makes a speech: he's found twenty-three card-carrying Communists in the federal government's Division of Soybean Subsidies! Instant panic. The Kremlin's got a plot to fuck up American farmers! Run for your lives!'

'Where's the proof?' Luis asked.

'Here's the clever bit,' Julie said. She was carrying a tray of soup and sandwiches.

'The Agriculture Department doesn't wait for proof,' Bonnie said. 'They up and fire two dozen people.'

'Security risks,' Julie explained.

'Which just goes to show that McCarthy must have been right all along,' Bonnie said. 'Each time he does that, he gets more power. He points, and everyone poops their pants.'

'He's unstoppable,' Julie said. 'Like bubonic plague. Eat, eat.'

They moved to the table. Spoons got handed around. Bowls of soup. Salt was passed. 'So now you know,' Bonnie said. 'That smell you noticed when you got off the boat was fear.'

'Kindly explain one thing,' Luis said. 'Why is the government interfering in the soybean market?'

'I quit,' Bonnie said.

'The government doesn't give a subsidy to new novels, does it?'

'I double-quit.'

'And good fiction is far more important than soybeans.'

'Drink your soup,' Julie told him, 'before the strychnine gets cold.'

2

A mile to the south and three hundred yards to the east, Special Agent Prendergast was reviewing the Ten Banks Con with Agent Fisk. It didn't take long. They had a heap of witness statements which more or less agreed about what happened, and totally disagreed about what the guy looked like. No fingerprints. No physical evidence except the demand notes. And now the suspect Cabrillo had vanished.

'Too bad our Con Ed man didn't tail him,' Prendergast said.

'We didn't hire him for surveillance, sir,' Fisk said. 'We hired him to burgle the apartment, period.'

'The Bureau doesn't burgle,' Prendergast said sharply.

'When we send a man in, it's a black bag job. It gives us deniability. The Bureau has no record of last night.'

'Of course.' Fisk checked his fly. It had become an automatic reaction when he made a procedural blunder. All fully zipped. 'I still think it was Cabrillo,' he said. 'We locate him, he vanishes. Too big a coincidence.'

'Maybe. Did he know we located him? If he didn't know, why would he stick around? This is New York. People move. What do we know about the Conroy woman?'

'She's broke, sir. Owed rent. Maybe that was his motive for hitting the banks.'

'So now he's rich. Why doesn't he just pay the rent?' Fisk had no answer. 'The man we want is a thinker,' Prendergast said. 'Most criminals like to act but hate to think, because thinking is such an effort. He's the opposite. Couldn't rob a gas station if you gave him Genghis Khan for back-up. All his activity is between the ears. That's where we'll catch him. He thinks he knows everything. Well, nobody knows everything.'

3

Harding had been with MI5 or MI6 since the beginning of the Hitler war, and he had no illusions about the kind of men who were attracted to work in intelligence. Some were crooks. The winds of war scattered money and they wanted it. Some were dreamers, romantics who believed secrecy had a magic quality. Some were crusaders, determined to save their country by subterfuge. These types were dangerous men who killed their friends and chalked it up to bad luck, and went on and did it again. Fortunately they were few, and usually, in time, they managed to kill themselves.

Most of the other people in intelligence were as sober and hardworking as accountants but secrecy breeds arrogance as night grows mushrooms, and every intelligence organization has its share of shits. Harding had known the good and the bad. The best of the good, in his opinion – the cleverest, most balanced, certainly most successful and yet still the most approachable – was Kim Philby. Shame about the early retirement: a great waste, Harding thought. Still, friends were friends. He made it his business to know Kim's home number.

Early in the afternoon, he called Philby and reported that a search had turned up no sign of Eldorado's manuscript autobiography. 'Of course it may be in a suitcase in a locker in Penn Station.'

'Or it may be on a publisher's desk,' Philby said.

'Yes.'

Pause.

'Even from three thousand miles, I can hear you wondering,' Philby said. They both laughed. 'Why should it matter? War's long since over. We won. Who cares what a superannuated double agent has to say?'

'But you care, sir.'

'Luis Cabrillo has more enemies than he knows, some of them quite frightful types. It would be unwise to excite them. Luis worked day and night for the Allies. Hate to see him killed.'

'All three of us agree on that, sir.'

It won a chuckle from Philby, which made Harding's day.

4

Luis annoyed Bonnie Scott.

She'd given up talking about the blacklist and the witch hunt to anyone who wasn't in the firing line. People didn't want to know. Some were crusading anti-Communist bigots. Some were tired survivors of the Depression years who would agree with anything rather than risk losing their jobs. Most were ordinary Americans with a gut feeling that McCarthy must have stumbled across some vast Commie conspiracy, otherwise why all this panic every time he turned over another rock? So what if he didn't have class? Who would you sooner have as sheriff: John Wayne or Fred Astaire? Well, then.

But Luis Cabrillo was a clean sheet. He arrived in New

York knowing nothing about McCarthyism, and when he was told, he refused to take it seriously. His dismissive shrug infuriated Bonnie. She phoned Max at his fortified apartment on Avenue C. Max had a suggestion. 'Billy Jago,' he said. 'Let's go now.'

'Will he be in?'

'Is Bismarck a herring? See you at the ferry.'

Bonnie, Julie and Luis went by Subway. They took the express and got off at South Ferry. 'Told you it was fast,' Julie said to him.

'Not fast enough. A chap can take only so much advice about rectal itch.'

Max was waiting for them. He looked pleased. An old friend had promised him work, recording radio commercials for Standard Oil of Indiana. He couldn't do it as Max Webber, so he was calling himself David Meyer. 'Guy I knew in the army,' he said. 'Got hit by artillery, ours, theirs, who cares? We shovelled Italian dirt into a mattress cover and buried it and called it Meyer. So now I use his name. Touching, ain't it?'

They were getting on the boat.

'You've got a very recognizable voice, Max,' Bonnie said.

'Nobody's going to recognize me in Indiana. Hog-callin', that's their idea of vocal talent. And I get paid cash.'

Luis wasn't interested in Indiana. 'Where are we going, and why?' he asked.

'Staten Island,' Max said. 'To see Billy Jago.'

'Who is?'

'Best writer-director I ever worked with.'

'Thank you. I think I see a rough sailor. I shall go and invite him to have energetic sex in the scuppers. I'm sure he'll know what they are.' He walked away.

'Why are we wasting our time with this clown?' Max asked.

'We have nothing better to do,' Julie said, 'and he's going to buy us all dinner.'

'The man is a prince.'

Luis rejoined them half an hour later, as the ferry was docking. 'I've been talking to the captain,' he said. 'Staten Island is a dump. They grow potatoes and eat their young.'

56

'We should take some beer,' Max said. 'To wash down the young.'

Luis bought two six-packs of Miller. They got a taxi and headed for the other side of the island. 'Bloomfield?' the driver said. 'That's marsh out there. Mafia bury their mistakes in Bloomfield.'

'I'll show you the turn-off,' Max said.

'This entire island's a turn-off,' Julie said. 'No offence meant.'

'You should come in winter,' the driver said. 'Gets real depressin'. On a good day, folks have to stand in line to shoot theirselves.'

'Good heavens,' Luis said.

'See that?' The taxi slowed and shuddered over a stretch of corrugated road. 'Lousy Commies built this road on the cheap.'

'What do people do on a bad day?' Luis asked.

'A bad day? Folks go down their nucular bunker, practise getting A-bombed by Stalin.'

'Stalin's dead,' Bonnie said.

'Yeah, sure, that's what he wants you to think.'

Staten Island was dull. After Manhattan, everything seemed low and scattered. The weather was discouraging: a beige overcast hid the sun. Luis noticed that a lot of telephone poles were not quite upright. Even the seagulls were sluggish.

'Make a right here,' Max said. The taxi jolted down a one-track lane that had grass growing in the middle. After half a mile, the jolts were harder and the grass was higher. 'Hope you can swim,' the driver said. 'We're gonna run out of island.'

'There it is,' Max said.

Billy Jago lived in a bungalow. Wind and rain had stripped the paint; now the place was bleached wood. The porch was trying to collapse. Some window-panes were bust; curtains had been stuffed into the holes. A thin path went through weeds and brambles to the front door. When the wind blew, the path was lost.

Max asked the driver to come back in an hour. Luis paid him. There was no place to turn. He reversed down the lane, cursing steadily.

'This is what blacklisting does to people,' Max told Luis.

57

'Billy refused to testify when HUAC subpoenaed him. They got him for contempt of Congress. He did six months in a federal penitentiary. Came out, none of the studios would touch him. He's been living here for a year and a half. If he was a horse, someone would've shot him. As it is . . . see for yourself.'

Max went first through the weeds and marsh grass. He rapped on the door and it swung open a couple of inches, so he pushed it and went in. 'Hey, Billy!' he called. No answer. 'Watch your step,' he muttered. 'This ain't exactly prime real estate.' Some floorboards were split, some had snapped and left holes. Mildew was growing up the walls.

Billy was in the kitchen, at the back of the bungalow. He didn't hear them come in. He was standing by a window, watching something through binoculars, totally absorbed.

'Brought you some beer,' Max announced. Billy lowered the binoculars very slowly and turned like an old man, shifting his feet before he swung his body. It was a big body, which surprised Luis. He had expected Billy to be a skinny hermit, but the man was taller than Max. He seemed broader, too, although his shoulders slumped with the effort of carrying anything as heavy as binoculars. His face was the giveaway. It was gaunt. Deep vertical lines dragged the flesh together like accordion folds. The beard was thin and patchy and hid nothing. Jago had lost the beef that went with his height. His clothes were baggy.

'Brought you some beer,' Max said again. 'You remember Bonnie? Julie? This is Luis. Just arrived from Venezuela, we're teaching him American history, reckoned he ought to see some famous monuments, Grant's Tomb, Chrysler Building, Billy Jago's hideaway.'

Luis dumped the beer and shook hands. The bony fingers would not let go. Billy peered down. 'Luis,' he said. 'As in the heavyweight champ.' His voice was light and husky from lack of use. At last he let go.

'Good to meet you,' Luis lied. Billy's breath stank like a broken sewer. Luis backed off, pretending to take note of the kitchen. It was a dump. His hand was sticky where Billy had held it. He took out his handkerchief, wiped his nose and his fingers at the same time. They smelled faintly of shit.

'Didn't you write a movie script about boxing?' Julie asked Billy.

'Yeah. Wrote it for Brando. We were in discussion when I . . . uh . . . lost my way.' Behind the beard a smile flickered and died. 'It's lying around here somewhere.' He waved the binoculars.

'What were you looking at, out there?' Max asked.

'Airplanes. Newark airport's a mile or so thataway. I watch the big birds come and go.' He ducked his head and raised his arms, and swayed to left and right, banking, climbing. 'They sail on the air. Steel eagles. Show never stops. Free admission.'

'I hope you're taking care of yourself,' Julie said. She picked a couple of empty cans out of the sink. They were beginning to rust. She looked for a garbage bin. It was overflowing. She put the cans back in the sink. 'You eating enough?'

'Women,' Billy said. 'First thing they do is try to improve you.' His voice was being worn down; it wasn't much more than a whisper. Luis had been opening beers. Billy accepted one, used both hands to hold the bottle at arm's length like a new-born child. 'Ah yes,' he said. 'It has its father's face. I'd know it anywhere.'

With the beer to oil his throat, his voice strengthened. He showed them around the bungalow. One room was much like another: peeling wallpaper, broken ceilings, the spicy, musty smell of damp, cardboard boxes split and spilling clothes, books, scripts, reels of film, curling photographs, chipped plates, a football gone flat, a typewriter with no ribbon.

'Sorry about the mess.' Billy said. 'We've got the Republicans in.'

They ended up in the kitchen again. Billy had found a leaking cushion and sat on the garbage bin. His visitors sat on the floor. Outside, the haze was developing into a thin fog. 'This is fun,' Billy said.

'Luis doesn't believe in the blacklist,' Julie said. 'We brought him along to improve his education.'

Luis smiled amiably. By sitting near the back door, which was permanently ajar, he avoided the worst of the smell: the sickly, cloying smell of a place too much lived in and never cleaned.

'Blacklist,' Billy said. 'Oh, I don't know about that.'

'Just tell him about HUAC,' Bonnie said.

'Not much to tell.' He got up, rearranged his cushion, sat down. 'All over very quickly.'

'You got shafted, Billy. How was prison?'

He scratched his neck and examined his fingernails. 'Not like it is in the movies.' They laughed, and startled him.

'I saw one of your movies the other day,' Max said. 'At the Biograph. *Low Society*.'

'Ah . . .' Billy's eyes went into soft focus.

'You directed *Low Society*?' Luis said. 'I saw it in Caracas. Very interesting film.'

'You wanted James Stewart for it, didn't you?' Max said. 'You'd have got a nomination, with Stewart. Maybe an Oscar.'

'The studio had whatshisname on contract,' Billy said. 'They made me take whatshisname.' His body was slack. Beer was dribbling down his leg.

'Well, it was still a hell of a movie,' Julie said. 'I cried for a week.'

'The scene where the blind man walks over the cliff,' Luis said. 'Superb. Comedy at it purest.'

'That scene wasn't funny,' Julie said.

'Well, they laughed in Caracas,' Luis said. Max scowled. Luis cocked his head. 'I thought you people were hot for the truth,' he said.

'Oh, God save us from the truth,' Bonnie said. She got up and took the bottle from Billy's fingers before he soaked his pants, and put it within reach. 'There's no truth, only shades of lying. You made a very good movie about that, Billy.'

'*Sweet Cheat*,' Billy said. 'Based on my novel. I can't write. Best part was the title.' He peered here and there, searching, not finding; took a deep breath; got up and shuffled out of the kitchen.

'Can't you see he's sick?' Max said to Luis. 'You don't need to be so damned blunt.'

'What illness does he suffer from? We could get treatment.'

'He's blacklisted,' Bonnie said. 'It's incurable.'

Billy came back with a copy of *Sweet Cheat*. 'Good reviews,' he said. 'Didn't sell.' He gave it to Luis. 'Keep it.' He perched on the garbage bin again.

'You should write some scripts, Billy,' Max said. 'You know people in England, France, they would . . .'

But Billy was shaking his head. 'I'm just an old fart,' he mumbled.

'Forty-two. In your prime.'

'Tell you something.' He found his beer and took a long suck. 'That Committee was right to throw me in jail. Not fit to make movies. Not fit to sharpen a pencil.'

'HUAC's full of shit,' Julie growled. He didn't hear her.

'A man is judged by his peers. That's right? My peers said . . . this man . . . not fit.' He was crying. 'Sterling Hayden, damn good actor, he named me to the Committee. So did Lee J. Cobb. And Elia Kazan. What a director. Next to Kazan . . . I couldn't direct traffic. And Budd Schulberg. Now *he* can write. Schulberg named me. Oh Christ . . .' Snot was dribbling out of his nose and he didn't know it. 'Those are the good guys. They *know* where I belong. In jail, that's where.'

Max cleaned up Billy's face and they took him to what passed as his bedroom. 'Can we get you anything?' Bonnie asked. He lay on his stained bedding and looked frightened. 'We'll come again,' she said. He didn't like the sound of that.

They walked out by the single-track lane and met the taxi, backing towards them. 'Thank God,' the driver said.

★

Everyone was quiet until they were on the ferry again.

'Billy Jago gave me my first big break,' Max said. 'Second lead in *The Devil You Know*. And he fought for me. Studio wanted to replace me, but Billy wouldn't budge, and he won. Billy liked a fight.'

'You wouldn't guess it now,' Bonnie said. The boat vibrated as it departed from Staten Island. Luis went and sat in a corner and read *Sweet Cheat*. After ten minutes Julie came and nudged him and pointed at the Statue of Liberty.

'Awfully small,' he said.

61

'And getting smaller every day.'

He thought about that, briefly, and went back to his book.

5

Question the witnesses. Re-question the witnesses. Probe. Compare. Search. The FBI worked in much the same way as any police force. Lacking a crucial clue, or a friendly informer, what other way is there?

Fisk went back to the messengers. Sometimes a guy goes home, tells his family about the excitement, it brightens up their empty lives, all of a sudden he remembers something he didn't tell the cops. Tattoo, missing finger, steel teeth, left-handed, smelled of fish, anything.

For Fisk the messengers remembered nothing new. Neither did their boss. It was possible, Fisk told them, that the man they were looking for was British. They didn't think so. Hispanic, maybe. You know, the olive skin and all? Fisk asked what they thought a Britisher sounded like. Cary Grant, they said. David Niven, with that cute little moustache. Errol Flynn, too: there was another.

Flynn's Australian, the boss said.

This was hotly disputed. Flynn killed all those Japs in Burma: I seen the movie, and Burma ain't nowhere near Australia.

Fisk stopped the argument. 'Are you saying the man we're looking for had a moustache?' Some said no, some said yes, some said depends what you mean by moustache, I mean take Clark Gable . . .

Fisk walked a couple of blocks, questioned the manager of the rented offices. 'British? How should I know?' the man said. 'I'm from Omaha. Are they the same as Irish? Brooklyn is lousy with Irish. This guy wasn't Irish.'

Fisk had a tuna sandwich and a glass of milk. He took the Subway to Queens and visited the ex-cop who had done the black bag job. 'Guy I saw was cleanshaven. As to racial origin . . . Could've have been Caucasian with a good tan,

62

maybe Hispanic, no tan at all. Not Arab, Jewish, or Negro. Help you any?'

'I'm trying to get a handle on this man,' Fisk said. 'All I know is he left Venezuela. What's he doing in New York, apart from crime?' That was where Fisk learned about the telephone company's repairman's failure to find the life story which British Intelligence wanted to read. 'You didn't report that,' Fisk said.

'You didn't ask for life stories. Gimme an extra fifty bucks, I'll tell you all the other stuff I didn't find. No striped giraffes in that apartment. No lawnmowers. No naked blondes. Unfortunately.'

'I apologize,' Fisk said. 'My remark was obtuse.' The ex-cop winced. 'Is there anything else you can tell me? Any small detail, any tiny facet?'

'No,' the ex-cop said. *Obtuse*, for Christ's sake. Fucking FBI. They all had college degrees and they couldn't find their dick with a roadmap. Fuck 'em. 'Not one tiny facet.'

It took Fisk the rest of the day to track down the landlord of the 84th Street apartment. The man had been to the ball game. Now he was in his favourite bar on York Avenue, telling the two old guys how the Dodgers blew it in the ninth. Fisk identified himself as a Special Agent. 'Hell, we knew that,' one of the old guys said. 'The haircut, the suit, the tie.'

'Is it true J. Edgar Hoover's a queen?' the other old guy asked.

'I need information about the couple you evicted last night,' Fisk said. 'Miss Conroy and — '

'Them Reds? Soon's I saw them Commie bastards in my building, plannin' their stinkin' sabotage, I applied my demo-cratic American boot to their Red asses . . .' He kept Fisk's shorthand busy for quite a while.

'Any idea where I might find either of them?'

'She had a dumb job in a bar. Which bar? Beats me.'

'Hoover never married, did he?' the second old guy said. 'Pudgy little fellah. Looks like James Cagney without the balls.'

'You want my opinion,' the landlord said, 'Hoover should investigate the Dodgers. That pitching in the ninth was criminal. They been infiltrated, you want my opinion.'

Fisk began checking bars.

6

Thirty minutes before midnight, Julie took the crosstown bus, to work the graveyard shift at Mooney's. Luis went with her. He'd failed to persuade her that he had ample money for both of them. 'You dropped in on me,' she said. 'You could drop out, just as easily.' He wanted them to take a taxi; she said if he didn't like the bus he should stay at home and read his book. It was raining. A taxi would have been good. The truth was she hated him for having been so snotty on Staten Island. So indifferent to suffering. So hard.

He bought two umbrellas on 72nd Street. 'That was lucky,' he said.

'This is New York,' she told him. 'Soon as it rains, some guy sells umbrellas.' They walked in silence up First Avenue to 86th.

The bar was hot and loud. Paddy Mooney saw her come in and beckoned. She followed him into the back office. 'I know you had your troubles,' Mooney said. He was a stocky redhead with teeth like a barricade. 'God knows I saw enough trouble in Ireland, enough to make me want to help.'

'I'm fired,' she said. 'That it?'

'Fellah from the FBI was here lookin' for you. I said the name meant nothin', but you know what them bastards are like. Ferrets ain't in it, so they're not.'

'I've done nothing wrong.'

'Ah, shit. That won't help you, nor me either.'

He gave her a week's wages and they shook hands. She walked out of the bar and into the rain. Luis followed. 'You did that,' she said. 'First you lost me my apartment, now my job's gone. What next?'

Luis flagged down a taxi. 'I suppose a roll in the hay is out of the question?' She hit him with the umbrella, hard. It broke. Of course it broke. It had been that sort of day.

7

Kim Philby ordered pigeon pie with new potatoes and French beans. His guest, Peter Cottington-Beaufort, chose roast shoulder of lamb with potatoes and broad beans. Both of them drank bottled Bass. One of the things they liked about the Oxford and Cambridge Club was its proper, traditional English food. No greasy foreign surprises. And the tables were widely spaced. No eavesdropping. Still, they spoke quietly.

'I do envy you your suits,' Kim said. 'My chap's hopeless.' Peter smiled. He had a long, thin face that went with his tall, slim body and his long, melodic name. His smile curled like a bit of ribbon: up at one end, down at the other. 'Your tailor's not your problem, old chap. He does his best with what you give him. The trouble is, you give him too much.'

'Well, I'm a bloated capitalist, I'm supposed to be fat.'

'I'm told you've cut down on claret,' Peter said. 'That's good. Drink was one reason you got pulled out of Washington in 'fifty-one, wasn't it? A bitter blow. I say: this lamb. Delicious.'

Kim frowned at his plate. 'Every time I order pigeon pie I forget what damned hard work it is.' He abandoned the pigeon and settled for the pastry crust. 'If you think I drank a lot, Peter, you should have seen what the CIA could put away. Martinis the size of flowerpots.'

'Extraordinary people.'

'CIA reckoned you were a pansy if you never got shit-faced, in their charming expression.'

Peter looked at his solid, unexciting face. No magnetic appeal there; but if you wanted quiet, unflappable, unvarying, utter competence, there was nobody to beat Philby. 'I have some mildly encouraging news. The dust has settled in America. J. Edgar Hoover still loathes you but he has called off the hunt. I believe you have something for me.'

'There's a loose cannon rolling around New York. Luis Cabrillo. Took part in our Double-Cross show during the war. It seems he strolled into the consulate and tried to sweet-talk 1,000 dollars out of our man. Cock-and-bull story about funding his autobiography. Said I would vouch for him.'

Peter thought about it as he ate his last two French beans. 'Let us consider the options,' he said. 'It could be bluff. No book exists. *Or* he's written the Double-Cross story, despite having signed the Official Secrets Act.'

'American publishers don't give a toss about the Act.'

'True. *Or* he's truffled up some juicy new secrets which he thinks British Intelligence might pay *not* to have published.'

'Then why isn't he in London?' Kim propped his head in his hands. He scarcely noticed when the plates were removed.

'One further possibility,' Peter said. 'He's found some damaging stuff about you personally. Blackmail.'

'Double buggeration in spades,' Kim said gloomily.

'Another scandal is unthinkable. I caught a lot of flak when Burgess and MacLean did a bunk, scuttling away on a cross-Channel ferry in the dead of night. They weren't very welcome in Moscow, I can tell you.'

'If they hadn't done a bunk they'd be in the Tower by now. Or under it.'

'Well, we've got to keep you out of there, at all costs.'

'That sounds like bad news for Mr Cabrillo,' Kim said.

'It's the only option, and in many ways the tidiest. Yummy. Here comes pudding.'

'Satisfy my curiosity, Peter. How did you arrive at a name like Cottington-Beaufort?'

'The hyphen is mine. Some obscure department in the Kremlin invented the rest.'

'Slightly outrageous, isn't it? Almost too English.'

'Well, you know KGB. The man at the desk always know better than the man in the field. I believe they found the names on an AA road map. Is that cream I see? Wonderful.'

AN OSCAR
FOR IRONY

1

They slept in separate beds, in separate rooms, in separate frames of mind.

Luis was happier now than he had been since the war ended. He was rediscovering the many pleasures of treating the whole world as a badly written farce which deserved to be rehashed for his private benefit. One of the benefits was money. He'd swindled the *Abwehr*. Milked them vigorously. He'd do it again to someone else. Just a question of finding another rainbow with a pot of arrogance at the end. Arrogance always paid well.

Julie puzzled him, but that was nothing new. All through the war, their love affair had been a roller-coaster ride. The longer it lasted, the faster and fiercer the ups and downs became. It trundled to a halt in 1945. The war stopped and so did they; in a curious moment of flatness and anticlimax they decided to love each other from afar. Peace made him nervous. He had seen himself married, pruning roses, selecting schools, organizing holidays. It was a ghastly outlook. He fled to Venezuela, spent money as if he could buy his future, and never once woke up without thinking of her.

Julie felt differently.

For eight years Luis had been a ghost hovering in a corner of her mind. When her life was busy, the ghost faded until there were whole months when she could barely remember his face. Then she would glimpse the reflection of a man in the window of a crowded, jolting Subway train, and Luis would spring back to life. He wasn't as splendid as he thought, but he was fun in the sack and his idea of good citizenship was to make the world dance to his tune. She missed that. Then the train stopped. The stranger turned. He was nobody. She got off the Subway and New York reclaimed her.

She revelled in the place. New York was full of fizz. It had every kind of food at all hours, every kind of manners provided they were bad, and the sort of humour that drew blood and didn't wait for a laugh. Manhattan was awash with young men out of uniform, glad to have survived, ready to celebrate. Boyfriends came and went like the weather. She was clever, got jobs, made money. Fell in love a couple of times. Being in love was like plunging down a ski slope, almost out of control. Jokes were funnier, the air tasted fresher, nothing was impossible. Soon she fell out of love. 'Who are you kidding?' she asked herself.

The years hustled by. Being a New Yorker suited her; she had enough friends, enough money, no problems. The bigots in America didn't bother her. It was a big country, there was room for a few loudmouths. Give them time and space and they'd fall on their faces. And then one day she ran slam-bang into McCarthyism, and she was the one who fell on her face.

It was a shock. Suddenly she was out of work. Suddenly the America she'd depended upon no longer existed. Friends faded away. Nobody said anything, and that was the trouble: her phone didn't ring, she wasn't asked to parties, movies, days at the beach. She was on the blacklist. She was dangerous.

No job, little money, few friends. And now Luis had blundered back. She needed a pal, someone with sympathy and compassion and tact, and fate had sent her Luis. He hadn't changed. He never faced reality. He altered it, faked it, dodged it. He was a joker. On the other hand, one small push would have been enough for her to tumble into bed with him. She knew it, and her guard went up like steel shutters in the path of a riot.

2

Max Webber wore aviator glasses for the audition. They were so black they made him look blind. He'd borrowed a leather flying jacket and a pair of cavalry breeches. He made a strong impression when he arrived at the hall, a disused gym in Brooklyn. The audition was for a modern-dress version of *Henry the Fifth* that would tour schools and colleges in New England, and he was to read for the part of the king. 'I'm David Meyer,' he told an assistant. 'Yup,' she said, and ticked his name.

When he was called, he took a chair with him on to the makeshift stage. He sat calmly until the last whisper, the last cough, the last fidget and shuffle had faded to an expectant hush. Then he let another ten seconds pass. Ten seconds is a long time when everyone is watching a man who is watching them.

Finally Max stood and spoke. He began the king's speech to his troops before the battle of Agincourt. He had the voice of a king and the bearing of a warrior, but within a couple of lines, everyone knew that this Henry was drunk. Not stupid-drunk; every word was clear, every phrase made sense. It was the clarity of the guy in the bar who should have gone home an hour ago, the guy who is impressed by his own eloquence. The longer he spoke, the drunker he got. At one point Max seized the chair one-handed and used it like a sword to emphasize his words, thrusting and slashing and fending off the enemy with a parry so fierce that he lost his grip and the chair sailed away to a splintering crash. He gave it a look of royal contempt; clearly he blamed the chair. By now everyone was laughing. This was no longer an audition; this was a performance. It won him a roar of applause.

'Can't use your interpretation,' the producer told him, 'and you know I've got to hear the other guys, but believe me, you've got the part. Stick around.'

Max drank coffee, read a day-old *Times*, talked with an old pug who had wandered in from the street, thinking the gym was back in business. 'I'm lookin' for easy work,' the pug said. 'Actin' . . . After the fight game, it don't look too heavy.'

'Piece of cake,' Max said. 'Nobody hardly ever hits you real hard.'

The producer came back, and took him aside. 'You're Max Webber. I can't use you.' He was half-accusing, half-apologizing. 'Somebody just recognized you.'

'I'll wear a beard,' Max said. 'You want, I'll *grow* a beard.'

'And it's my ass when you get exposed.'

'Who's to expose? Your show ain't Broadway. It's touring New England schools, for God's sake! Nobody's heard of me in Frozen Hollow, Maine. Christ, nobody there's heard of Shakespeare.'

'They've heard of Joe McCarthy,' the producer said. He dropped his voice to a whisper. 'Personally, I wish someone would shoot the sonofabitch. Until then . . . I had to bust a gut to get funds from educational trusts. They find out I've hired someone who's listed, they'll cut me off at the knees. Can't take the risk, Max. It's not fair on the others.'

The ex-pug saw him leave and said, 'Looks like you stopped one below the belt, pal.'

'Belts are bein' worn real low this season,' Max said. 'I got mine down around the ankles.'

3

Julie showered and dressed, and left Luis still reading *Sweet Cheat*. She ate breakfast at a coffee shop. She walked across the park and shopped at Saks Fifth Avenue for underwear. That took most of her pay from Mooney's. She changed in Saks' ladies' room and dumped her old, frayed, greying underwear in a trash can. Now she felt better. Cleaner, stronger, smarter. She could be hit by a taxi and die with pride.

The day was bright, with enough breeze to cut the sunshine. Manhattan glittered. It was full of people in a hurry to do business. She had no business and she was in no hurry, but to loiter on Fifth was to be jostled. Get on or get off: that was the motto.

She got off – off the avenue, off the island, nearly off the city. She took the Subway north, the IRT line right up through the Bronx until the tracks ended at Pelham Bay. The ride took an hour and cost a nickel. Worth it. She walked into Pelham Bay Park, where a lot of nothing was happening in all directions. Good. Now she could really relax, stop worrying. About what? About Luis. Here she was, as far from Central Park West as you could get for a nickel, and he was still as close as ever. There was no escape. She'd known it as soon as she saw him standing on the sidewalk in Hoboken. She was still in love with him, and he was still in love with her. It was a dismal prospect. It foretold a double dose of stress and folly; and the knowledge that these would be laced with moments of astonishing happiness was no consolation. 'Why can't the stupid bastard love somebody else?' she cried aloud. 'And why can't I love some other stupid bastard?' She knew the answer; she'd found it years ago, inside a Chinese fortune cookie: *The heart has its reasons which the reason does not know.* Smarter than your average fortune cookie. 'So explain!' she commanded her heart, but her heart pleaded the Fifth Amendment.

She wandered across the park and found a boatyard quietly baking, littered with hulls that would never float again and broken motors rusted solid. She walked down the slipway and checked the bay for Russian submarines. Nothing. Wrong time of day. They were all on the seabed, lunching on black bread and Borscht. Everyone knew that. She went back up and got a whiff of fried onions.

Floyd's Bar was held together with old Schaefer beer signs. The floor was last washed by the great tidal wave of nineteen aught five. Floyd was frying onions in Castrol Extra Plus. Nothing was too good for his clientele.

They were two white-haired men in painter's dungarees that should have been framed and hung in the Museum of Modern Art. Floyd was thirty-plus, built like a welterweight. The right half of his face had three days' growth. The left half would never need shaving again. A sweeping burn had turned the skin to something like pale pink plastic. The left eye was sealed shut.

71

Julie asked for a beer and listened to them arguing amiably about last year's Miss America competition, and whether the results were fixed by the Mafia or the Catholic Church. Floyd gave the men hot dogs slathered with onion. They paid and went out.

'We should of asked you,' Floyd said. 'You bein' a gorgeous dame of the opposite sex. You got an opinion?'

'Yeah, sure,' she said. 'You ever hear of a priest say anything nasty about Frank Costello, or Carlo Gambino, or Lucky Luciano, or Carlos Marcello, or anyone with an O at the end of his name and blood on his hands?'

'Jeez,' he said. 'I never thought of it that way.'

'I'm not saying all priests are bad. But you've got to be a very, very stupid Mafiosi to get excommunicated. Fix me a burger, would you? Well-done. No onions.'

While he busied himself, they talked about relative levels of corruption in the city. 'The health inspectors could close me down in ten minutes,' Floyd said. 'I make sure the right guy gets a dimple Haig once in a while. Must be dimple. The man has his standards.'

'Scotch? That's un-American,' she said. 'What's the guy got against bourbon?'

Floyd grunted, and turned the burger.

'Ask me, he's a Commie,' she said. 'He's out to cripple Jim Beam and Jack Daniels and those other good ol' boys.' Still no response. 'Looks like a case for Senator McCarthy. Send for Tail-gunner Joe.'

Floyd hit the burger so hard with his clenched fist it turned star-shaped and bits spattered all over the grill. 'That sonabitch comes through my door I'll blow his head off!' He reached down and slammed a shotgun on the bar. His one surviving eye glared.

'Ah . . .' Julie was startled. She'd strayed into a minefield. She moved cautiously. 'I guess you had a raw deal, too,' she said.

'Okinawa. Last island hop before Japan. I was a Marine. Just a grunt, just a number on a pair of dog tags. Weather stunk, jungle stunk, and the Japs . . . would . . . not . . . die.'

She almost said *I read about it* and then had the smarts to shut up.

'Squadron of Marine bombers was based on that island. Some those pilots had to be blind or dumb or drunk. Marines bombed marines. Fly-boys don't care who they dump on. Japs, grunts, all the same to them. Marine bomb hit a flamethrower and I caught a splash in the face. What the army calls friendly fire.' He patted the shotgun. 'This punk McCarthy tells everyone he was a Marine flier. He's full of shit. I'm ready to blow him apart, him and every other lying, cheating, treacherous Communist faggot stinking up this country.'

Julie blinked. What had he said? He'd said what he said. 'You sure you got that right?' she asked.

Now he was very angry. 'You ever seen Okinawa?' he demanded. She shook her head. 'You got no right to put me straight,' he said.

Julie gave up the discussion. 'My burger's burning,' she said.

Floyd swept the charred meat on to the floor with the back of his hand. 'Bar's shut,' he growled.

★

Luis took them all out to dinner. Enrico's restaurant was padlocked; the old man had gone to stay with his daughter in Schenectady. Bonnie recommended a steak house on Houston Street. They went late, so as to let Herb Kizsco finish his shift. It was midnight before they ate. The steaks arrived still sizzling. The sound was music before they invented music.

Nobody said much until the waiter cleared the plates and the frivolity of ordering dessert was done.

'Well,' Max said, 'it's tomorrow now, so I can tell you. I got subpoenaed. This afternoon I take the stand before the House Un-American Activities Committee, in Washington.'

'Oh, *shit*,' Julie said.

'Slice it where you like, that's what it'll be,' Max agreed.

'Why didn't you tell us?' Bonnie said. 'When did it happen?'

'Couple of weeks ago. Didn't want to tell anyone. Fact is, I'm sorry I've told you now. Spoils a good steak.'

'I thought everyone here had been subpoenaed already,' Luis said.

'Hell, no. Only me,' Bonnie said. 'Max and Herb got named, and Julie got screwed in some private witch hunt. Nobody gets subpoenaed unless HUAC reckons there's pay-dirt to be found.'

'So if you haven't been subpoenaed,' Luis told her, 'there's no official reason why you should be on the blacklist.'

'The blacklist isn't official, you klutz. You can't go and look it up in the public library, for God's sake. The blacklist is unofficial.' She was angry because of Max having to go to Washington.

'It's unofficial but everyone knows,' Julie said.

'That's not quite true,' Herb said. 'There's also the Attorney General's List of subversive organizations. If you can't prove you haven't been linked with any of them, you can't have a job where federal funds are involved. That's how I got kicked out of the university. I signed too many petitions when I was young and idealistic. Or, as the FBI would say, subversive. So *that* List is published. Anyone can use it to accuse somebody else of negative loyalty.'

Luis was amused. '*Negative* loyalty? How do you prove *positive* loyalty?'

'Get yourself killed fighting the Reds in Korea,' Max said. 'That's a good start.'

'What are you going to say to them?' Herb asked. 'You got a strategy ready?' This led to a rambling discussion of the Committee's techniques. Ideally HUAC wanted a witness to admit he'd been a member of the Communist Party. But it also welcomed confessions like attending a Party meeting. Subscribing to a left-wing magazine was good. Writing for it was excellent. Stated admiration for the Soviet people was really juicy, never mind that the battle of Stalingrad was raging at the time. It could make you a security risk. Security

74

against what? That wasn't HUAC's territory. HUAC's task was to identify the guilty before they could do any damage. Not easy. The guilty were a slippery bunch. 'Actor called Lionel Stander,' Max told Luis. 'Hell of a talent. Got subpoenaed. Committee asked him if he'd name un-American subversive types, and he said he certainly would. But the way he said it, everyone there knew he meant the members of HUAC. Now that took guts.'

'More guts than Gary Cooper had,' Herb said. 'He crumpled like a wet paper bag when they questioned him.' Sterling Hayden couldn't wait to sell out his pals. Ronald Reagan gave HUAC all the help they asked, and more. Walt Disney too. Scared stiff the Reds might sneak their propaganda into Tom and Jerry. The bigger the name, the louder they sang. They had too much to lose.

'I've got nothing to lose,' Max said. 'If Paul Robeson can live on the blacklist, I'm in damn good company. Right?'

They had been over this ground a dozen times before. Now it was being covered for Luis's benefit. He listened closely.

'You might end up in even better company,' Julie said. 'Ring Lardner Jr went to jail. Dashiell Hammett's still inside.'

'Writers,' Herb said. 'They're vulnerable, they *write* things. The Committee doesn't jail actors.'

'They might start with Max,' Bonnie said. 'HUAC's kind of desperate for publicity.'

'I'll give the goddam Committee some headlines,' Max said. 'I'm going to tell 'em they're worse than the KGB and the Gestapo rolled together.'

'You're not going to plead the Fifth?' Herb asked, sharply.

'Why should I? I got nothing to hide.'

'Max, pleading the Fifth is your only constitutional defence. Fifth Amendment,' Herb told Luis. 'Right to silence so that you don't incriminate yourself. Without it, they can demand answers. You refuse to answer, that's contempt of Congress.'

'Fuck 'em,' Max said. 'If everyone they subpoenaed said *go fuck yourself*, this shitty Committee would've folded years ago. There's been too much talking and not enough fighting.

I'm for freedom and justice, and I'll do what it takes to get it. Tomorrow, you check the headlines. A new war of independence is about to break out.'

'Well,' Julie said, 'it'll make one hell of a biopic some day.'

'Billy Jago could direct,' Bonnie suggested. 'Maybe they'll give him an Oscar for irony.'

'Billy Jago won't work again,' Luis said confidently. 'He'll be dead in two years.'

'*What*?' Max said. Everyone stopped eating except Luis. He was enjoying his apple pie *à la mode*. 'What did you just say?'

Luis waved his spoon while he chewed his pie. He kept them waiting. 'I've met Billy's sort before,' he said. 'One good kick in the crotch, and he never gets up.'

'Horseshit! The witch hunt gutted him,' Max said. 'The guy got screwed.'

'Don't we all? I got screwed several times. I didn't quit.'

'He's a damn good film maker. He'll be back.'

Luis's spoon swung, negatively. 'I have read his so-called novel, *Sweet Cheat*. It's a concealed confession. From the start, Jago makes his hero intolerable. Decent, unselfish, brave. Kind in thought, word and deed. Jago is itching to kill him.'

'And he dies in the end,' Bonnie said. 'I've read it too.'

'Of course he dies!' Luis was enjoying this even more than his apple pie. 'The hero is the author! But Jago's problem is he's not strong enough to dream of surviving! His awful hero is condemned on page one, but he takes an inexcusably long time to depart. As we saw, poor Billy is living up to his script.'

'That's a cruel thing to say,' Julie told him.

'Well, we all saw him. We all smelled him. The man is in a deliberate state of advanced decay.' Luis was looking at her, so he failed to see Max throw a punch that thumped him just in front of the ear. Luis and his chair crashed backwards and went through a decorative screen and down two steps and into another table where four Texas oilmen were eating seafood salad and drinking imported lager. They were hungry and thirsty and they seized Luis and flung him back. Max tried to punch him again but Herb overturned the table and Max lost his balance and went down with the debris. Then waiters arrived in a rush and the fight was over. 'Put it on my bill,' Luis said. 'Just put it all on my bill.' He kept saying it until the manager heard him.

4

'So we've got nothing,' Prendergast said.

'We've got his name and description, sir,' Fisk said.

'Cabrillo? Probably an alias. Description? We've got too many descriptions, from too many idiots.'

'I saw him in Hoboken.'

'Did you?' Prendergast got out of his chair, dropped to the floor, did ten rapid press-ups, and stood again. 'Make the heart pump,' he said. 'Get extra oxygen in your brain. *Think*, Fisk. You didn't see someone robbing banks. You saw a man in Hoboken with the name Cabrillo in his passport, which may or may not have been counterfeit. There are twenty-seven Cabrillos in the Manhattan phone book, never mind Brooklyn or the Bronx. Have you checked them?' Fisk was silent. 'Don't bother,' Prendergast said. 'They're all in Spanish Harlem, they won't tell you anything. So we have nothing.'

'We have Mrs Conroy, sir. We know she's his partner.'

'And we have her file. Which you've checked?'

'Yes.'

'And questioned her Known Associates?'

'None of them are at the addresses in the file.'

'Well, that's New York for you. Peripatetic.' He cocked an eye at Fisk.

'I know what that means, sir. There is one other link. The British Consulate.'

'Yes. We already have a transcript of the alleged Cabrillo's conversation with Mr Harding, of MI6.'

'A transcript,' Fisk said. 'That means — '

'Yes, we do. Routine. But all the transcript told us was that

77

Cabrillo's a former intelligence agent. Proves nothing. Toss five bricks in the Harvard Club and you'll hit three ex-agents, and they're all writing their memoirs.'

'Slim pickings, then.' Fisk didn't mention the fruit boots. He had lost faith in the fruit boots.

'We've got something. We've got patience. This type is a show-off. He's having fun and making money. He'll do it again. Can't stop himself.'

'Maybe he left. Maybe he's living in Lancaster, Pennsylvania.'

'Not a chance. He *likes* New York. It's got what he wants.'

'Banks?' Fisk said.

'No, not banks,' Prendergast said wearily. 'Excitement. Nobody likes banks, you cretin. The banking system is like the sewage system, only less exciting.'

'Nobody steals turds,' Fisk said, daringly.

'Is that what your investigation has turned up? Three days' work, and you've discovered that nobody steals turds?' Prendergast pointed at the door. It was a cheap shot, but then one of the perks of power in the Bureau was making cheap shots.

I KID
YOU NOT

1

Luis woke up with a plum-coloured bruise above his cheek-bone. He found Julie in the kitchen, watching the coffee percolator go bloop-bloop. She didn't look up. She might have been trying to read a message in Morse.

'Expensive evening,' he said.

'You caused it. Max stands by his friends.' She poured coffee and padded away.

'I thought those oil-chaps from Texas were awfully decent about it, in the end,' he called. No reply. Oh well.

He shaved and showered and went out to buy the papers. His bruise throbbed in time with his pulse. He saw a big drugstore and went in and asked for an eyepatch.

'Why?' the man asked. 'That eye looks okay. Ain't black, ain't bloodshot. Ice pack for that bruise is what you need. Buck-an'-a-half for the bag, get your ice at the deli.'

'Just sell me an eyepatch,' Luis said.

The man rummaged in boxes. 'If you want stuff you don't need, I got a special on hernia belts,' he said. 'Also elastic knee bandages, ideal for the hamstring you ain't suffering from.' He put an eyepatch on the counter. 'I got incontinence pads, extra large.' He was losing interest. Luis tried on the eye-patch. 'Errol Flynn,' the man said. 'Captain Blood. Lousy movie.'

'How much?'

'Hell, it's old stock. A quarter.' Luis produced a twenty-dollar bill. 'Get outta here, for Chrissake,' the man said in disgust. He walked away.

Luis sidled out. In Caracas they would have got him a chair, examined his injury, produced a range of eyepatches, offered him coffee. In London they would have apologized and wondered if by any chance he might have something a little smaller. New York turned a simple purchase into a title fight, but he was in and out fast and he got what he wanted. New Yorkers were big on giving you what you wanted. Luis found that encouraging.

The eyepatch was a success. People glanced at him, especially women. The sun was well up, the air was hot, so he took off his blazer and wore it loosely over his shoulders: the intelligent woman's Errol Flynn. He looked at himself in a plate-glass window and blinked and changed focus when he realized that someone inside was looking out at him. Clean-cut youngish woman, page-boy haircut, powder-blue smock. It was a hairdressing salon. A window display said *Blondes Have More Fun*. He went in. 'My life has been rather dull lately,' he said. 'Can you help me have more fun?'

'This is no barbershop,' she said, amiably. 'And you're no lady.'

'Hair is hair.' They were having an amiability contest.

'You don't seriously want to be blond.' Her voice had a cool confidence that made his bruise throb. 'Take that chair.' There were a couple of customers in the place, too absorbed in their own treatment to notice Luis. He sat. She put a blond wig on his head. 'See?' she said. 'Federal disaster area.'

'Somewhat yellow.'

'Makes you look like a faggot.'

'Could I be a redhead, d'you think?'

She found a hot ginger wig and fitted it. 'Now you look like a three-alarm fire. You trying to attract attention?'

'Actually, I'm on the run from the FBI.' He spoke softly.

'Yeah? For what?'

'Bank robbery.'

She discarded the ginger wig and brushed his hair smooth. 'My next appointment isn't for twenty minutes. Buy me a cup of coffee.'

They sat in the sun and drank take-out coffee from a corner deli. She said her name was Stephanie Biaggi but everyone called her Stevie because she was slim-hipped and her face was boyish. She was twenty-five and she lived in the Village with her husband Vinnie, the All-American creep. 'He crept for America in the last Olympics,' she said. 'That's the kind of creep Vinnie is.'

Luis was scarcely listening. He was in love with this brisk, vivid, delightful woman. Was it possible to be in love with two people at once? She had more to say about Vinnie, his low ambitions, his bad breath. 'How frightful,' he said. Stunning ears. Enchanting mouth.

'You're no bank robber,' she said. 'I had a boyfriend who was a psychologist, I can pick out types.'

'You picked out Vinnie.' Luis said it to make her lip curl. He loved that lip curl.

'Did it on the rebound,' Stevie said. 'All my marriages were on the rebound. It began when my fiancé, no warning, ran off with his math teacher. So I hitched up with Danny, age forty, looked sixty, had eighty-year-old kidneys. First I knew of that was on the death certificate.'

'Nasty shock.' Luis patted her thigh. Two hardhats in a passing truck shouted. He smiled proudly.

'Then I met Pierre. He was nineteen going on twelve. Face like an angel. Brains like a butterfly. Jumped off the Brooklyn Bridge for a bet.'

'Oh dear.' He took her hand. She linked fingers with him. 'And this led to Vinnie?'

'One thing that creep can do is drink. He drinks and he pukes. Two things. Drink and puke. Takes a swing at me now and then.' Luis gazed at her choirboy face, appalled at the thought of someone hitting it. 'Never connects,' she said. 'Drink and puke, that's Vinnie's limit.'

'Not a love-match, then. Why don't you divorce him?'

'Both Catholic. The families would die of shame.' She leaned against him, her head on his shoulder. Old, long-forgotten fertility rites began celebrating in his loins. 'You Catholic?' she asked.

'Was once.'

'I knew it. Soon as I saw you, I knew you're the one I've been saving myself for, and you're the one can save me.'

'That's very flattering.'

'Nothing to it. Shoot the creep in the head and dump him. Do it tonight. I can borrow a shooter. There's a really wet bog in Connecticut I know, we'll dump him there, he'll never come up. Tonight?' She squeezed his arm.

'Oh dear. Not possible, I'm afraid.' The fertility rites had shut down. He was at a loss for words; so he said something, anything to get control of events. 'I'm sure Vinnie isn't worthy of you, but . . . but why me?'

'Kill him and dump him, and you can make love to me all night. You'll like that a lot. See, I'm a virgin.'

Luis gently eased her away from him. 'Three marriages?' he said.

'Losers. I keep picking losers.'

Luis thought about it. Danny, killed by his kidneys. Pierre didn't have the brains to stir his coffee. And now Vinnie the lush. It was just conceivably possible that Stevie was the only three-time-married virgin in New York City. The sun shone, as if this were a regular day in Manhattan. Maybe she was joking. He looked at her face. Such loveliness. 'Poke the shooter in his ear,' she said. 'There's a hole in his skull, see, one shot puts his brains through the blender.'

'Look at the time! Your next appointment . . .'

She kissed him on the lips. 'You're the one,' she said. 'Come see me again.' She walked away.

Luis felt rattled. He found a large coffee shop and ordered a big breakfast. A stack of pancakes with Canadian bacon and scrambled eggs calmed his nerves. He came out and noticed a used-car lot where a building had been torn down. He took a taxi to his bank, opened his safety deposit box, and half an hour later he was driving a cream-and-brown convertible down Broadway. At Times Square he picked up Seventh Avenue and kept going downtown. He'd seen a big ad in the *Trib* for Barney's Men's Store. He bought three summerweight suits, a dozen short-sleeved shirts, other stuff. They tailored the pants while he waited. Then he drove home.

The car had a radio. Sinatra sang *High Hopes* and Luis joined in. When it ended he cried, 'That's a hell of a voice!' Sinatra's was pretty good, too.

2

'The FBI's got its knickers in a twist about Cabrillo,' Harding growled. He gave Frobisher some typewritten pages. 'See if you can make sense of it.'

They were on the viewing platform at the top of the Empire State Building. Harding put a dime in a telescope and watched some tugs nudging a liner into its berth. Like watching piglets find the teat, he thought. Curiously pleasurable.

'Well now,' Frobisher said. 'This is our transcript of an FBI discussion of their transcript of our conversations with Cabrillo. Isn't this unnecessarily complicated? If they want to know, why don't they just ask?'

The dime ran out. 'Perhaps they think we're protecting him. We did give him 100 dollars.'

'He seemed pleased to get it, too, which is odd, because they seem to think he's a successful bank-robber. How long has the FBI been snooping on us?'

'Always. A convenient arrangement. They bug our offices. We bug theirs. Now we have a little itch, but they're the ones who scratch. It helps to know that.' They strolled around the platform. 'I like it up here. Even Hoover can't bug it. And all this . . .' Harding gestured at the Bronx, Queens and Brooklyn. 'Let's take the wider view. What do we really know about the man to whom I gave a hundred dollars?'

Frobisher watched a Constellation turning on to its final approach to LaGuardia. 'Precious little, sir. Called himself Cabrillo, knew something about Cabrillo's work for Double Cross, but so did a lot of people in that department.'

'So maybe he's not Cabrillo at all. Maybe he used Cabrillo's identity to get money from us.'

'Money well spent,' Frobisher said. 'I mean, he could be bogus and still have some genuine secrets up his sleeve.'

'Or he could be a Soviet agent trying to infiltrate us.'

'Or he might be crackers.'

Harding shrugged. 'Either way, he'll probably be back. Good! Let him stick his neck out. I'll cut his phoney head off.'

As they went down in the express elevator, Frobisher reread the transcript of the FBI discussion. 'Two split infinitives,' he said.

'Go back to the office,' Harding told him. 'Make your feelings known. Somebody's bound to be listening.'

★

Luis hurried into the penthouse, tossing boxes from Barney's on to a sofa, and announced: 'This you must see, kiddo. I kid you not.' *God help us*, Julie thought, *he thinks he's learning the language*. But she followed him to the window. His enthusiasm filled the air like hay fever. 'The creamy convertible,' he said. 'I just bought it. Spiffing, ain't it?'

'Studebaker,' she said. 'Both ends look the same. Can't tell whether it's coming or going. Yeah, that's your kind of car.'

'Let's go somewhere! Get the wind in your hair!'

He was like a small boy on his first roller skates. Experience told her to mistrust his enthusiasms. She looked at the car again. He'd parked it by a fire plug. Also she was hungry. 'I know a good place for lunch,' she said. Experience groaned quietly and said she'd regret this, and she told experience to go piss in its hat. Luis was crazy, had always been crazy; but she was getting tired of being sane for both of them. They went down and drove away just as a cop was approaching the fire plug. 'Make a right on Broadway,' she said. 'Drive north for about fifteen miles. It's called Route 9. You can remember that. It's your mental age.'

She angled her seat back and let Luis do the work. Manhattan slipped by, the Bronx, Westchester. Sun and wind made her sleepy. The Hudson glinted on their left, the city was long gone, nothing but greenery, you probably couldn't get a *Trib* or a gin-and-tonic or a competent, reliable, reasonably priced hitman anywhere here. Signs appeared. 'Tarrytown,' she said. 'We're there.'

They lunched at a big old clapboard inn that looked as if it had been built lopsided. 'I'll have pigs in blankets,' she decided. Luis rolled his eyes. 'Baked oysters wrapped in bacon,' she said.

'Then the pig is on the outside. It can't be inside *and* outside. Where's the logic?'

'We're saving it for dessert. He'll have the same,' she told the waiter. 'Snow peas and baby carrots, and the driest white wine you've got.' Luis watched with pride. 'I love you when you're being brisk,' he said.

'Well, life is short. I'm hungry, you're hungry, let's get the kitchen working.'

'There you go again,' he said happily. 'New York is so refreshing.'

'Yeah? Try refreshing your memory. A few days ago you didn't have a dime. Now you can rent a penthouse and buy a car. What happened?'

'I negotiated a series of bank loans.'

'On what? Banks want collateral. You were flat broke in three continents.'

'We reached an agreement. The point about money is it's fundamentally worthless, don't you agree? Money in the bank goes nowhere, does nothing, it's a fiction until you give it its freedom, turn it loose, let it do some good . . .'

She let him burble on. He wasn't going to tell her the truth. You couldn't trust Luis even when he told the truth and backed it up with a ten-year guarantee from the US Supreme Court, because he probably forged that too.

After the pigs in blankets they had black cherries jubilee. The waiter prepared it in a chafing dish at their table. He worked quietly, almost solemnly, so that when he flared the brandy the blaze was pure theatre.

'That's dandy,' Julie whispered. The rush of the flames

85

covered her words. Luis leaned towards her. 'Sorry?' he said. *Dandy* was a dumb word, dredged up from her Nebraska childhood, so she let it go and kissed him instead. Harder than she meant. Their lips disengaged slowly.

'Best idea you've had all day.'

'Blame it on the wine,' she said. But it wasn't the wine. It was the damburst of pleasure: a summertime jaunt, a good lunch, a good-looking man who made her feel special and right now she didn't care whether he was lying or not. Also he had money. After months of scraping a living, she'd almost forgotten what a pleasure money was.

Ice cream was served with the drunken cherries. Then brandy with coffee.

'Odd thing happened to me this morning,' Luis said. 'I met a terribly pretty little ladies' hairdresser. Looked like Audrey Hepburn crossed with Jean Simmons. Name of Stevie. We had a chat, she invited me to murder her husband, chap called Vinnie. A brute and a beast, she said. Tonight was good for her, if I was free. Does that sort of thing happen often in New York?'

'She wasn't joking?'

'Well, she offered her body as reward for my services.'

'What did you tell her?'

'I was non-committal. Also scared.'

'Good. This is New York. People get rubbed out for a lot less than a roll in the hay.'

They drove back to the city. The afternoon was slack and hazy, and the air in Manhattan smelt as if it was beginning to lose the will to live.

THE WORST IDEA
SO FAR

1

Max Webber ate lunch at the Shoreham Hotel in Washington. He ate well: beef Stroganoff, sautéed mushrooms, scalloped potatoes, a half-bottle of claret. It all went on the Committee's tab. So did the hotel room and the airline ticket. His attendance mattered. Nobody said why.

Instead of having dessert he smoked a cigar with his coffee, a fine, big cigar. Why not? He was important. Allegedly.

That morning, he'd got on the plane at LaGuardia feeling slow and flat and generally outnumbered by the world. His life was going badly. He shouldn't have gone to the audition in Brooklyn. Shouldn't have announced he'd been subpoenaed: that just raised the pressure on himself. Shouldn't have thumped Cabrillo. The bum deserved it, but what if the cops had come and slung them both in jail? His stomach growled. Should have had breakfast. Someone heavy dropped into the next seat and nudged his arm. It was his agent. Harry Pinckney.

'Max! Thought I knew that noble profile. How the hell are you? We are well met. Here, look at this.' He took a bound script from his briefcase and dropped it in Max's lap.

'How the hell d'you think I am?' Max said. His agent knew all about the subpoena.

'Uh-huh.' Harry was fooling with his seat belt, tightening, slackening. He had been an actor once, before a car smash left him with a couple of scars that limited his roles to Prussian guards officers. 'I'm not just Mr Ten Per Cent, you know,' he said. 'I came along to give you moral support.'

Max felt ashamed of his churlishness, but he wasn't about to concede anything: not today. 'Moral support. Sounds like a bishop's jockstrap.' He opened the script. 'What's this crap?'

'Cold War drama. Interesting character called Gunning Broom. See what you think.'

'I know what I think. I think I'm blacklisted.'

'Just read. Where's the harm?'

By the time they landed at Washington Max had read it twice. A hundred pages. Some complex action in America and Russia. Probably run two hours. Working title: *Logjam*. Simple story-line: Gunning Broom is a young US academic who stumbles on a Soviet spy ring in America, can't prove it, infiltrates to seek evidence, gets sucked in too far until he himself looks like a traitor, finds himself on the run with wife and teenage daughter.

Conflicting loyalties, tough decisions, frequent surprises, black humour. Some strong bad guys, which made Gunning Broom even stronger.

'Well, crap it ain't,' Max said.

'Keep it. You like Gunning? Might have been written for you.'

'Nothing's written for me, Harry. You know that.' But his agent just shrugged.

They shared a taxi from the airport to the hotel. Harry kept the taxi. He had other people to see.

Max was still keeping the fire going in his big, important cigar when Harry came into the restaurant. 'Can we use your room?' he asked. 'Jack Delmonico's in the lobby. Very keen to meet you. Remember Jack?'

Max remembered. Years back, Delmonico had directed a movie Max was in called *Kentucky Blues*. Afterwards Jack went on to bigger things. His handmade Italian shoes proved it. They took the elevator, and made small talk about Washington's steamy summer. Max's room was blessedly cool. He dumped his cigar before it bored the hell out of him.

'Warners have signed me to direct *Logjam*,' Jack said. 'You've read the script?'

'Intelligent, pacey,' Max said. 'Pretty good.'

'Well, it cost us enough. Not that money always buys quality.'

'The studio thinks *Logjam* spells Oscar,' Harry said.

'Those bums never could read,' Max said. They laughed, although the line didn't deserve it, so he smiled. Why not?

'Sometimes their bullshit is good, honest manure,' Jack said. 'Warners' budget for *Logjam* would buy a small South American republic. And we're casting now.'

'Yeah? You can have me for nothing. Except of course you can't.'

Delmonico strolled to the window. His seersucker suit was so fine that sunlight shone through it. 'We've talked to Bob Mitchum, Jimmy Cagney, they're interested. Cooper, too.'

'Gary's not just a cowboy,' Harry said. He was resting on a sofa, feet up. 'Look at *Fountainhead*. He was an architect in that.'

'Sure. Bogart read *Logjam,* said he'd play the elevator operator, anything. I told him it's a matter of balance.'

'What's your ideal team?' Harry asked.

'Lauren Bacall. Jimmy Stewart. This new kid James Dean for contrast. On the Russian side, Burton and Ustinov, they're fluent in broken English, which is essential, and I'm looking at Jean Simmons to play the mute girl agent.'

'Jesus Christ!' Max said. 'That's enough for ten movies.'

'Plus Max Webber in the lead, of course,' Jack said.

'Excuse us,' Max said. 'We need to talk.' He got Harry off the sofa and took him for a walk along the corridor. 'What the fuck is going on?' he said. 'My hearing starts in under an hour. I don't need to listen to this guy's ravings.'

'I know, I know,' Harry put an arm around Max's shoulder. 'Forget *Logjam*. Here's the thing. Warners has a big problem. The Committee is minded to subpoena two, maybe three Warners stars. Big names in big movies that Warners wants to release soon. Imagine the damage the Committee could do to the box office. It could crucify the studio. This is the deal. Today, after you've agreed to appear as a friendly witness — '

'*What?*' Max shook off Harry's arm. 'You go to hell.'

'Hear me out. Trust me, it's for your benefit. We sell this idea to HUAC, you come off the blacklist *and* you get a three-picture contract with Warners. Showbiz is politics and vice versa. The Committee's in a mood to plea-bargain. They're losing momentum, the public's bored with all these same-again hearings.'

'That's a damn shame.'

'Sure. And your opportunity to make a break for freedom. Right about now, somebody's informing the Committee that Warners plans a major movie with Oscar potential as part of the great American struggle against Communism.'

'It's been done already. Anti-Red movies. Korean war shit.'

'This is different. *Logjam* will be *dedicated* to HUAC. I mean, up there on the screen, at the start, big and bold. And the lead will go to an ex-GI who was brave enough to stand up and declare that yes, he was wrong and yes, the Committee is right, and yes, he is ready to play his part as a true American patriot in the great crusade against godless Communism. When HUAC hears that, Warners will be off the hook, and so will you.'

Max got a drink from a water cooler.

'Nobody remembers me, Harry. No studio is going to risk a bundle on an unknown lead.'

Harry shrugged. 'Don't even think of that. Think of a three-movie contract. Think of working again.'

They went back to the room. Jack Delmonico was on the phone. 'Doris Day?' he said, and laughed. 'She's wonderful, but not for this . . . Ben, they've just come back, I'll put him on.' He held out the phone. 'Ben McHenry.'

'Warners vice-pres,' Harry said softly. 'Watch your language.'

Max took the phone. 'Hullo,' he said.

'Good morning. No, I guess it's afternoon where you are. My brain takes a while to get in gear.' McHenry's voice was rich and smooth, calm and unhurried. 'I met Elia Kazan last night. You know Elia?'

'Not personally. By reputation. Great director.'

'Then you know he was subpoenaed last year, and he publicly volunteered to do anything that HUAC thought necessary or valuable to help their cause.'

'He named names. Actors, mainly.'

'I asked him why he did it,' McHenry said. 'He told me that if the Committee were to bar him from the only work he knew, the only job that mattered, then he was dead. He's not alone. Edward Dmytryk made great movies.'

'*Farewell My Lovely*,' Max said. '*Crossfire. The Caine Mutiny.*'

'You know your stuff, Max.'

'It's my profession. *Was* my profession.'

'Dmytryk got blacklisted, went to jail, had time to think, to ask himself: what am I accomplishing? What am I *wasting*? My whole life? He came out, helped the Committee, he's using his God-given talents again.'

'You want me to testify as a friendly witness, Mr McHenry.'

'And my real name isn't Ben McHenry, any more than your real name is Max Webber. I'm Lev Goncharov. My parents came from the Ukraine. They taught me: first you survive; after that, maybe you can have options. Options are a luxury. Your parents came from Poland and you're Josef Zaluski. My guess is they told you the same. There are two kinds of people in our world: the survivors, and the rest. Which means there's really only one kind.' Short pause. 'Don't waste your life, Max. You won't get another.' Click. Buzz. Max hung up.

Harry was back on the sofa. Jack was back at the window.

'I can always take the Fifth,' Max said.

'A lot of people think that,' Harry said. He checked his watch. 'We've got twenty minutes before you need to leave. Let me tell you something, Max. The Fifth Amendment is a tricky little thing. Everyone knows it protects the citizen against incriminating himself. But there are pitfalls.'

'Stumbling blocks,' Jack said.

'I prefer pitfalls,' Max said. 'Cut to the chase, will you.'

'Suppose, for instance, the Committee asks you if you ever knew General Patton,' Harry said.

'We met.'

'He decorated you, didn't he? In Italy. So you'd have to say

91

yes, because in no way can a knowledge of Patton be damaging to you. Quite the reverse. So the Fifth can't apply. Next they ask if you know . . . say . . . Ring Lardner, or Joseph Losey, or Carl Foreman, or even Larry Adler, the harmonica king? Do you know them?'

'Some. They're all blacklisted. If I say I know them, that incriminates me in the eyes of the Committee.'

'So you plead the Fifth.'

'Damn right I do.'

'How does that sound?' Jack asked, without turning. 'Yes I know Patten, and I plead the Fifth on four alleged Communists.'

'Sounds like you fingered them,' Harry said. 'And in the process you didn't do yourself a whole lot of good, either.'

Max was silent while he thought it over.

'Shit,' he said. 'They've got me by the balls, haven't they?'

'One thing I've learned in life,' Harry said. 'When they've got you by the balls, always move in their direction. It reduces the pain.'

The HUAC hearing was being held in the Old House Office Building. They went in Jack's limo. 'If I have to name names,' Max said, 'I'm going to lose some old friends.'

'And make some new ones,' Harry said.

'Look at it this way,' Jack said. 'The sooner we root out the last Red, the sooner we can all get back to living a normal life.'

A cluster of news photographers and TV cameramen was waiting. 'You go ahead,' Jack said. 'Don't smile, don't frown. Hold your head up and look patriotic.'

'And when you testify, no jokes, no speeches. Keep it snappy,' Harry said. 'If we're lucky we'll make the early editions.'

Max got out. Flash bulbs popped. He went up the steps.

'Jokes and speeches?' Jack said.

'Actors,' Harry said. 'Always trying to pad their part.'

2

Luis made martinis. The penthouse had a small terrace. They leaned on the rail and drank and talked and threw peanuts at the passing pigeons. Julie was thinking that this was better than waiting on tables at Mooney's. At the back of her mind was the thought that living with Luis without going to bed with Luis was like holding a martini without drinking it. Further back was her memory of the two phoney uniforms who had been poking around in the 84th Street apartment. Spooks? Or genuine burglars? Must have been really dumb burglars to expect to find anything there. Some burglars *were* dumb. Those guys had looked very professional.

Luis was thinking how delightful it would be to coax her into bed and how painful it would be if she disagreed and slugged him in the face. Better not risk it. At the back of his mind was the safe deposit box. Emptying rapidly. That wouldn't do.

They went inside and watched the evening news.

A lot of people came and went on the screen but none of them was Max. 'Maybe the hearings got fouled up,' she said. 'Maybe Max got rescheduled.' The station did sport. It did Wall Street. Then it did Max.

'Finally,' the man said. 'The House Un-American Activities Committee met today and questioned actor Max Webber, whose movie career came to a halt in 1950 when screenwriter Martin Berkeley informed the Committee that Webber was one of the 152 known Communist sympathizers in showbusiness. Well, Webber today denied all such sympathies, claimed any contacts he might have made were accidental, and promptly named ten of his old pinko pals, including film director Billy Jago. Oh, and Warners has just announced that Webber will star as the good guy in a major motion picture about Communist infiltration of the US, the movie to be dedicated to . . . guess who . . . the House Un-American Activities Committee. Some days it's hard to tell where Washington ends and Hollywood begins. Now for the weather. Got a nice cool breeze for us, Larry?'

Julie killed the set.

'The schmuck,' she said. 'The prize prick. He finked on us. What an asshole.' Her voice was harsh. 'All that shit about telling the Committee to go fuck themselves! What a . . . what a . . .' She couldn't think of a bad enough word and it was making her so furious that Luis took the highball glass from her hand before she threw it. That was a five-dollar glass.

'Okay, so Max is a schmuck and a pig and he's betrayed all his finer principles,' Luis said. 'But what actual harm has he done anyone?'

'He sold Billy down the river.'

'Billy was already so far down the river, he was lost at sea. Besides, he has no TV. He'll never know.'

'Jesus Christ! Whose side are you on?'

'Posterity. I'm for the winners. The rest is noise. Thunder and blunder.' He was impatient with her rage. So Max fluffed his lines; who cared? They were crappy lines to start with.

But any second now, he or she would say the unforgivable and, bang! all today's enjoyment would go out the window. They were saved by the bell. Bonnie Scott phoned. Julie answered and they swapped profanities. Luis finished both martinis and went out, ate a hamburger, saw a movie at the Biograph. *Casablanca*. The audience knew every line. When he got home she was in bed.

★

They understood each other well enough to stay apart for a while. She took the train to Westchester, met some old friends, came home late. He explored New York in his Studebaker. He stopped often at diners or coffee shops: the great American invention, he thought. Iced tea, iced Coke, chilled milk. Then out in the baking heat again. He got lost, often. Didn't matter. Had money, wouldn't run out of gas. Got home late.

She was fresh out of the shower. Her hair was still wet; it coiled like a mass of little black snakes. She was wearing old jeans and one of his new shirts, loose. He approached cautiously, kissed the side of her neck, and sniffed. 'Peachy,' he said.

94

She opened his shirt and licked the hollow above a collarbone. 'Salty,' she said.

So that was all right.

They had dinner at a small French restaurant where they could eat in a quiet courtyard: onion soup, chicken grilled with tarragon, a bottle of chilled rosé. 'I used to bring clients here,' Julie said. 'That was before I got caught in the flood.'

'Everyone else knows your scandalous past.' He poured more wine. 'So tell me.'

She was tired of not telling him. She told.

She had worked for Newport, Bowie, Scutt, Mayo, an ad agency. She was what they called 'copy-contact'. Most agencies used account executives to present the stuff; NBSM believed in letting the client meet the creative people, especially when she had good legs.

Julie was at lunch with her client, plus a couple of suits from NBSM and – unusually – the art director who worked on that account. Eugene Sulakov, born in St Petersburg a few years before it became Leningrad, father killed fighting the Austrians, mother escaped to America. Eugene was medically 4F: he wore glasses as thick as ashtrays, and spent the Second World War in Kansas, designing camouflage for the army. That was about all anyone at NBSM knew of him. If you smiled, he smiled. Eugene let others talk. He ate.

The client was Brandon LeBeq, ad manager for Snowy Mountain Coffee, the stuff which kick-started half of America into a better day. LeBeq had been an intelligence officer all through the Pacific war. Then, men's lives depended on his judgement. Now he sold coffee.

Somebody mentioned Korea. 'Looks like that mess is finally over,' LeBeq said. 'Three bloody years. I suppose it was worth it.'

'Sure it was,' one of the suits said. 'Communists had to be shown that aggression doesn't pay.'

'They keep pushing, don't they?' the other suit said. 'The Berlin blockade, then Korea. Couple of months ago, some MIGs took a pot at an American weather plane near Alaska! I mean, where next?'

'They've got China,' LeBeq said. 'You'd think that would satisfy any dictatorship.'

'The Chinese have got China,' Julie said. 'Just to keep the record straight.'

'We should never have let Stalin get his hands on Eastern Europe,' the first suit said. 'Big mistake. I mean, did we win the war just so Russia could have an empire? I think not.'

Eugene stood up so fast his glasses jerked sideways. '*Russia* beat the Nazis,' he said. 'Not America. Start to finish, two-thirds of Hitler's army was fighting on the Russian front. Two-thirds!' He was so excited, he was spitting slightly. 'Twenty million dead in the USSR!'

'Cool it, Eugene.' Julie tugged his sleeve. 'Nobody's arguing.' He sat down.

'Sure, the Russians fought a hell of a war,' LeBeq said. 'Cost them plenty. So for the life of me I can't understand why they want another. Damn it, they've turned Eastern Europe into a barracks for the Red Army. I've *seen* their Iron Curtain and —'

'First World War!' Eugene announced. 'Germany attacks Russia! Also . . .' He counted them on his fingers. 'Hungary attacks Russia, and Austria, Bulgaria, Poles, Czechs, Turks, all attack. Nobody here remembers Turkey invaded Russia. But *Russians* remember.'

'Save the history for another time, Eugene,' the second suit said.

'History? This is my childhood! German army *invaded* Russia, took Odessa, took Kiev! Like someone invaded the East Coast and we lost Pittsburgh.'

'That's not such a bad deal,' Julie said, and got a laugh from the others. She was trying to flag down a waiter, get the check.

'Forget Pittsburgh.' Eugene was unstoppable. 'But remember the West sent its armies into Russia in 1919. British army, French, American, Japanese, Czech. We don't teach that in our schools.'

'The fog of war,' LeBeq murmured.

'But Russians remember, and twenty years later Germany invaded them again! So I ask you, Mr LeBeq. It is 1945. You are Stalin. Three times in thirty years your country has been invaded from the west. Twice your country has sacrificed millions of citizens. So what does military intelligence tell you to do?'

LeBeq flicked some crumbs from a sleeve. 'Very interesting,' he said.

Julie gave the waiter a pile of bills. 'No change,' she told him. They began to stand, but Eugene wasn't finished. 'You'd make damn sure it wouldn't happen again, wouldn't you. Make a buffer zone between you and the goddamn bloody krauts, right? Build an iron curtain and keep the bastards out.' His shoulders were hunched.

'Thank you, Julie,' LeBeq said. He had a good smile, and he knew when to use it. 'You know more good restaurants in New York than *Gourmet* Magazine.'

'We're too many for a taxi,' the second suit announced. 'Eugene and I will walk back. We need the exercise.'

The art director was sacked that afternoon. 'It was a straight choice,' Julie's boss told her. 'Either we lost Eugene or we lost Snowy Mountain Coffee.'

'LeBeq thinks we're soft on Communism, is that it? Eugene's been putting too much red in the Snowy Mountain artwork?'

'Wise up, kid. LeBeq can't take the risk, and neither can we.'

'Sure. And if we all hold our breath, Russia will disappear. It worked with China.'

Julie went around the agency and tried to organize a petition. Dead loss. Eugene had gone. Signatures wouldn't change that, but they might get other people fired. She told her story to the reporters who covered the ad industry. Some wrote it up. NBSM fired her. The publicity was small but lethal. No other agency would hire her. 'I told you already,' she said to Luis. 'Blacklist is just a word. You can't look it up in the public library. But everybody knows, so it adds up to the same thing.'

They were strolling towards the Studebaker, hand-in-hand, which stimulated the supply of blood to Luis's brain, and he said: 'There's nothing to stop me getting a job with an ad agency. You could stay at home and create the advertising.'

She squeezed his hand until it hurt. 'That's the worst idea you've had so far.'

'Oh. Well, I'll just have to go back to being a contract killer for . . . um . . . thingummy.'

'Stevie. She wasn't going to pay you in money.'

'That's true.' They stopped, and looked at each other. The bruise under his eye was a deep purple. She remembered the fight, and laughed. He said, 'This is a very serious matter, you know.' It exhausted their conversation, so they kissed. 'That simplifies things,' he said. They kissed again. 'And now?'

'Oh . . .' she said. 'You know.'

He tapped her head. 'Brain like a runaway dynamo,' he said. 'Whatever that is.'

3

Next morning they taxied down to Schrafft's on Fifth Avenue so they could have breakfast and watch the commuters hurrying through the heat to get to their offices because the Long Island Railroad had broken down again, poor slobs. Luis had a small steak and eggs with home fries. He was feeling thin. Julie had about a pint of orange juice and stole bits of his steak. She was feeling sleepy.

'That's twice you've robbed me of my virginity,' she said. 'Mind you, it was in pretty crappy condition to start with.'

'I've been thinking about our future,' he said, 'and I want to make it clear that I can't support you in the manner to which you're accustomed.'

'Christ, I hope not. Poverty stinks.'

'That was my joke. You stole my joke.'

'This is New York, buster. Nobody waits.'

'I'm waiting for an answer to my idea. I get a job with an ad agency. You write the ads.' He signalled for more coffee.

'You wouldn't last a week, Luis. The ad game's a serious business.'

'So was the Double-Cross System. We told people what

98

they wanted to hear. Some of it was almost true. Like advertising.'

Julie propped her chin on her fists and studied his face. Good looks meant zero, she knew plenty of handsome men who were pure Jello and some uglies who were heroes. Luis wasn't a hero. He thought he was indestructible when he was just highly resilient. How would she feel about him if he crawled out of a car wreck with only half a face? Everything was luck. Enjoy it while you have it.

'What have we got to lose?' he asked.

They went back to the penthouse. She scanned the columns in the *Times* and the *Trib* that reported comings and goings in the ad industry; made a few phone calls; and told Luis she'd fixed him up with an interview at an agency called Dent & Bellamy Inc. 'I've got a pal there, a secretary willing to help as long as the job's not for me. You meet Joe Steel at noon tomorrow. The agency's just won a pharmaceuticals account, Drexon. They need copywriters.'

'Easy.' Luis wrote in the air with his finger. '*Attention rheumatism sufferers! New magic drug ZX40 cures all aches and pains!* See? Piece of cake.'

'Horseshit. You can't say "magic" and you can't say "cures". Most you can say is the stuff relieves pain. Nothing cures anything permanently.'

'Except death.'

'Which can't be patented. Read this. Memorize it.'

She had created a career for him. It began with Young & Rubicam in San Francisco, moved to Ted Bates in Chicago, then McCann-Erickson Ltd in London, followed by six months with Rotblat Advertising in New York, and ending up with Benton & Bowles in LA.

'I move around a lot,' he said.

'Good copywriters do. Joe Steel won't check you out. Too late in the day to phone London, too early to phone LA. He can't ask Rotblat because Phil Rotblat blew his brains out when the agency went bust. Here's some proofs you can show him. I was with Benton & Bowles for a while, out West. Worked on some pharmaceutical campaigns.'

Luis flicked through the proofs. 'Why are all these people smiling?' he asked. 'They're suffering dreadful afflictions. What is there to smile at?'

'You have a lot to learn about the ad game,' she said.

Dent & Bellamy had offices on Madison in the high Forties, above a bank which Luis felt reasonably sure he had robbed by proxy. Joe Steel had a corner office on the fifth floor. His body was so bulky that he looked as if he were wearing two suits. His heavily muscled face had been battered by teenage acne and never fully recovered. But he was pleasant and courteous. He read the CV at a glance and seemed to like the proofs. 'Ever had piles?' he asked. Luis said no. 'Me neither. But two out of five Americans get them. Drexon manufactures this stuff.' He gave Luis a tube labelled 4DT. 'People won't go into a drugstore and ask for haemorrhoid cream. Embarrassing. But they'll say 4DT. All the product information you need is in this leaflet, and here's some ads from Drexon's competition. Give me five or six full-page ads for 4DT. Headlines, scribbles for pix, forget the body copy.'

'When d'you need them?'

'Yesterday. Let's say in half an hour.'

His secretary gave Luis a block of paper, a chair and a nice smile.

In twenty minutes he was ready. Steel was impressed.

'My guess,' Luis said, 'is that a major difficulty with advertising this type of product is that newspaper publishers won't let us illustrate what we're talking about.'

Steel blinked. 'It's a pain in the ass. Everyone knows where their ass is. Don't they?'

'Everyone knows where their brain is, but the makers of headache remedies show pictures of heads.'

'Uh-huh. So what?' Steel sat at his desk like a giant bump on a small log.

'So we can't illustrate the product at work, and we can't even ask the reader: *Do you suffer from this unspeakable ailment*? Which is why the best that our major competitor can do is tell his story beneath one large word which he hopes will attract attention. That word is: *Because*.' Luis showed the proof.

'Move it along. I've got to catch a train in five hours.' Steel was beginning to slump.

'My idea trumps that campaign. It also conveys to the sufferer the great benefit of applying 4DT *without using an illustration*.' Luis held up a sheet of paper.

Steel had slumped another six inches. He stared without expression. The headline read: *Insofaras*.

'Should be two words.' His voice was as flat as his desk. 'Insofar as. Two words.' He looked up at Luis without moving his head. 'This is a joke?'

'Wordplay, perhaps.'

'No, this is a joke. My ass is on fire, I'm desperate for help, and Drexon's 4DT wants to tell me a joke. What else you got?'

Luis showed him another rough. The headline said *Piledriver*.

'More funny business.' Steel glanced at the CV again. 'You ever taken a loyalty test?'

'You mean I have to demonstrate my American patriotism before I'm allowed near the nation's piles?'

'Damn right you do.'

'If you don't like *Insofaras*, how about *Uppermost*? Slightly less brutal.'

'You spent too long in London,' Steel said. 'This ain't Socialized Medicine. We take our health seriously. We don't joke about health.'

'I was in England when they were planning their National Health Service,' Luis said. 'I'd have voted for Socialized Medicine.'

'You're a Lefty. A Comm-Symp. Get out. I wouldn't hire you if the Red Army was marching down Park Avenue.'

'*Were* marching. Subjunctive.' Luis got out fast. Steel was heaving himself up from his chair, and it wasn't to shake hands.

★

He bought a stupendous sandwich: liver pâté, cream cheese, smoked salmon, lettuce heavy with mayo, the combination

101

thick enough to strain his jaws. 'Excellent choice,' the counterman told him. 'Enjoy it with pride.'

He nibbled his way into it, sitting on the steps of the public library at 42nd Street, quietly sweating through his undershirt. The penthouse would be cool but he wasn't ready to tell her he'd failed.

He felt better with food inside him. Failure wasn't an absolute. It was like poverty, it was relative. Nearby, a yellow cab and a city bus intercepted the same point in space. There was a bright bang that turned heads. A fender got ripped off. A shouting-match broke out. Luis felt even better. 'What happened?' a woman asked. 'Difference of opinion,' Luis said. 'I didn't want the lousy job anyway.' She wasn't listening. 'People ain't safe nowhere,' she said. 'Cops don't care. You see a cop? It's worse'n Russia, this city.'

'There's a cop.' Luis pointed. 'In fact, there's two.' She glared at him, said: 'Smartass. Fuckin' smartass.' New York women were dangerously unpredictable. He moved away, heading up Fifth for no especial reason.

Scribner's Bookshop looked a good place to escape the heat and the traffic and the madwomen. He was browsing the shelves when he came upon a section marked *Intelligence/Espionage*, and was surprised to find that most of the books were about the spy, not as hero, but as traitor. The words 'betrayal' and 'treachery' often appeared in titles. Atom scientists, diplomats, politicians, businessmen, soldiers, spy-catchers, everyone down to clerks and copy-typists had sold out. 'Heaven help us,' Luis murmured. 'Is nobody to be trusted?' The answer rang in his brain like a great bell.

4

Kim Philby was eating toast and marmalade and doing *The Times* crossword more easily than was proper. The telephone rang; he ignored it. Another wrong number, probably. Every summer the trees grew, the branches scraped the phone lines, result: more wrong numbers, for which some poor bugger had to pay the GPO, when the sodding GPO should send a man round to prune the damn trees. Aileen came into the kitchen. 'It's for you,' she said. 'Harding. British Consulate. New York.' She had a tumbler of whisky.

'Isn't it a bit early for that?' he asked.

'Yes. I like to start early, in case there's none left, later.'

The phone was on the hall table. 'My dear chap,' Philby said.

'Good morning, sir. It's about that new book you were interested in reading. I've had a phone call from the author. He says he's made changes.'

'I see. Did he elaborate?'

'Heroes have become villains, and villains have let the side down. His very words.' Short pause, while the transatlantic cable softly hissed and buzzed. 'He quoted Alfred Hitchcock: the better the villain, the better the story.'

'Did he, by Jove?' Philby found a chair.

'He says he has to pay the typist a thousand dollars. I told him to contact me tomorrow.'

'Many thanks, Mr Harding. I'll get back to you.'

Philby phoned Peter Cottington-Beaufort. An hour later they met in a pub car park on the edge of Sevenoaks. Kim got into Peter's car, an old Armstrong-Siddeley. It smelled like a warm afternoon in the House of Lords.

'I knew he'd come back,' Peter said. 'They always do.'

'And now his heroes are villains. Could mean anything.'

'Don't fool yourself, Kim. He's threatening exposure.'

'But he has no proof,' Kim said. 'I know precisely where in MI6 Cabrillo worked. He was nowhere near my show. He's bluffing, Peter.'

'Not the point.' Peter turned his head and sniffed the tiny, creamy rose in his buttonhole. 'Point is, Cabrillo's dangerous, even if he invents everything. He might invent something about *you* that's more convincing than the real thing.'

'He's good at that.'

'Go to New York, tonight – 7 p.m. flight, Pan Am. The ticket will be at Heathrow. Hullo America, goodbye Cabrillo.'

'All right.' Kim stared through the windscreen at a pair of

sparrows, dog-fighting around the car park. Such energy, from such small and unimportant creatures. 'He might be more accessible if I had a thousand dollars to give him.'

'Yes. And you'll need money to live on. All will be arranged.'

They shook hands. Kim got out of the Armstrong-Siddeley and into his own grubby Fiat. The sparrows were still hard at it. 'She's not worth it,' he told them.

5

A black man with a salt-and-pepper crewcut, wearing a white singlet, slacks and tennis shoes, was dribbling oil on to Julie's naked body when Luis came in. She was lying face-down on a bath towel on the kitchen table. 'Hullo, uncle,' she said. Luis came to a stop and breathed so deeply that his ribcage creaked. He thought she looked as sleek and as slim as a dolphin. Did dolphins have neat bottoms with little dimples? Probably not. He cleared his throat. 'I see you've met my daughter,' he said. The man smiled. 'This is Carl,' Julie said lazily. 'Ask nicely and he'll massage you too.'

'Um . . . Not today, thank you.'

'You're scared. You think the blackness might rub off his hands. Ain't that true, Carl?'

'Hush yo' mouth!' he said. 'Whatever that means.'

Luis took a shower, changed his clothes, counted his money. Carl had gone. Julie was wearing a white cotton robe, printed with soft yellow lemons. 'That's new,' he said.

'Yup. I opened a credit account at Lord & Taylor. We're rich, and you're working at Dent & Bellamy, so we can afford it.' She kissed him on the ear. She ran her fingers through his damp hair. She rubbed a leg against the inside of his thigh. 'Wealth is such an aphrodisiac,' she whispered.

'Dent & Bellamy,' he said. 'They didn't cut the mustard. I turned them down.'

'No you didn't. Joe Steel kicked your sweet ass into Madison Avenue.'

'The man is a buffoon.'

'My pal the secretary phoned me. When you left, Joe had to send out for ice packs. His blood pressure went off the dial. What happened?'

Luis told her. 'I still think "Insofaras" is a brilliant headline, but I've thought of something even better. How about "Notwithstanding?"'

'Forget it, Luis.'

'I'm tempted to manufacture the stuff myself, just so I can advertise it. Has the name "Piledriver" been patented?'

'Forget it! You're crazy, but I'm not. I didn't get this cotton thing at Lord & Taylor, it was on sale at Klein's. Just relax.'

'Money is no problem,' he said, and dismissed it like an idle servant. 'Anyway, someone's offered me a 1,000-dollar advance on my memoirs.'

'Am I in them? Show me.'

'They have yet to be written,' he said. 'So I had better start.'

★

When he got into his stride, when something pleased his imagination, Luis could write non-stop. After five or six thousand words he was wet with sweat and starving hungry. Julie knew a good Chinese restaurant. He showered in three minutes and got into one of his classy new summerweight suits, and they walked to the Studebaker. Stephanie, whom everyone called Stevie, was lying on the back seat, reading *True Detective*. She wore a sky-blue boxer's singlet, very loose, and plaid shorts, very short. 'Hey!' she said. 'Whyn't you come see me again? You promised.'

'I promised nothing. Anyway, how did you know — '

'Oh, I seen you drivin' around in this cute boat. Look, pal, I need you more'n ever. Vince is drivin' me bats.'

'Julie, this is Stevie. Stevie, Julie.' They got into the car. 'Vince is your problem. My problem is I've got to eat before I lose consciousness.' He pulled out from the kerb.

'Men,' Stevie said. She sat up and leaned forward. 'They don't understand a woman's needs. You noticed that, honey? Take me. Married three times, an' still a virgin. Can you believe that?'

'I think I read it in Walter Winchell,' Julie said.

'Five hundred bucks,' Stevie told Luis. 'Take you ten minutes, for Chrissake. Fifteen, tops. In and out.'

'So *you* do it,' Luis said. Dazzling rays of sunset carved Manhattan into blocks and sanitized the streets.

'Ain't work for a lady.' She looked at Julie. 'Bet you never get the spiders out the bath. Bet you make *him* do it.'

'Sure I do, but not with a handgun.'

Stevie wasn't listening. She said, 'I mean, it's just one bang, and bingo. Hey, is that a natural curl? You'd look terrific with bangs.'

'Stevie: go and see a priest, get some help,' Luis said. Lights changed to red and he stopped. Stevie reached forward and dropped a brown paper bag into his lap. He gasped; the bag was heavy. 'My priest said I was doin' Vince a favour,' she said. 'The sonabitch has it comin' to him, those his actual words.' She vaulted nimbly out of the car and trotted to the sidewalk.

First out of the bag was a roadmap of Connecticut. A red arrow pointed to a cross, labelled SWAMP. Next out was a piece of cardboard, showing a hand-drawn map of part of Greenwich Village. An arrow and a cross marked the address in West 10th Street of Vinnie-the-creep Biaggi. Stevie had also written it in full, together with his phone number. 'Make sure he's in,' she had added. 'He goes out a lot.' Third and last out was a Colt revolver. It had a barrel as long as a Cuban cigar. Luis opened the chamber. Fully loaded. A man in the car on his left said, 'Betcha can't hit the Chrysler Building.' The lights changed. Julie took the gun from him and hid it under his seat. 'A cop sees that, you'll eat dinner in jail.' Luis was busy driving. 'This town is full of kooks,' Julie said, 'and she's leading the parade.' Luis nodded. 'Awfully pretty, though,' he said.

TRAITORS
ABOUND

1

Kim Philby checked into the Harvard Club. His membership of the Oxford & Cambridge Club gave him reciprocal rights there, and at 44th and Fifth it was about as central as you could wish. He had a soak in a hot tub to ease the stiffness of a night in an airliner, shaved, took a stroll around the block, and met Harding in the lobby. They had breakfast in the calm, wide-open spaces of the club dining-room.

'You know I can't claim to be acting in any official capacity,' Philby said.

'Good gracious, sir, half our work here is not done in any official capacity. Besides, if what I hear is true, you'll soon be back in harness.'

'Time will tell, John. We must win back the trust of the Americans. No more shock-horror spy revelations.' Philby was prodding a poached egg as if the yolk held secrets. 'A pity you haven't got an address.'

'He'll be back,' Harding said. 'He needs money.'

'Not a problem. But he must bring his manuscript. No manuscript, no money. D'you think the appalling J. Edgar Hoover knows I've arrived?'

'Certainly.'

'Strange man.' Philby looked at the fork he was holding; it had a fine tremor. 'As powerful as Beria, they say.'

'Beria's been arrested, sir.'

'So I believe. Betrayed by his own secret police. A very Russian

107

ending. But we shouldn't patronize them, should we? Three hundred years ago, we were chopping the heads off ministers of the Crown when they outlived their usefulness. Tidy solution. As someone remarked: "Stone dead hath no fellow".'

'That was certainly Beria's philosophy,' Harding said. 'So he has no cause for complaint.'

2

All evening, Luis had worked hard on his memoirs. He kept up the momentum next morning and finished by lunchtime. Seventy pages: about twenty-five thousand words. The more astonishing revelations needed to be fleshed out, but he could do that later.

'I hope you put plenty of conspiracies in it,' Julie said. 'Americans are obsessed by conspiracies. If they can't find one, that's clear proof of a cover-up.'

'My story is one long conspiracy from beginning to end,' he said happily. 'It abounds with traitors.' He clicked his fingers. 'I'll call it *Traitors Abound*. Excellent! Thank you.'

He ate a sandwich. He phoned Vinnie Biaggi, thinking to warn him, he wasn't sure how; and got a busy signal. At least the man existed. He phoned Harding and made an appointment for four o'clock; felt suddenly weary and was asleep within minutes.

Julie looked in the mirror and saw a wreck. She went out to get her hair done. Not by Stevie.

3

Max sometimes wondered whether or not he had courage. True courage. In Italy the army had given him a medal for bravery, and the citation commented on his total disregard for his own safety. He often thought about that ferocious little fire-fight and what a horrible mistake it had been.

It had happened in the mountains, in the rain. His unit turned a corner and collided with a German unit coming the other way. One of them must have been lost, maybe both, it didn't matter. No time to think about escape, anyway escape was impossible because automatic fire was hacking and scything and grenades were flying, and both sides knew that the only way to live was to kill, wipe out the enemy fast before he wiped you out. So Max Webber took the most insane risks to kill German soldiers, risks that were not real risks since he had no choice and they were not insane because all sanity had vanished. Where was the bravery in killing to survive?

He was lucky. The bullets missed him. In less than three minutes all the enemy were dead, and so were most of Max's unit; but in the crude arithmetic of war that was victory.

He was awarded a medal, and felt ashamed about getting decorated for saving his own life. Now, sitting in the club car of the Super Chief, skimming across the Midwest of America, he remembered that day and he dismissed the memory and drowned it in whisky and water.

He could have flown to Los Angeles. Warners was paying. But he'd never crossed the country by train and, besides, it gave him time to think.

His agent, Harry Pinckney, was sitting opposite, reading the Chicago papers.

Farms and fields and small towns went streaming past. People waved. They looked small and dispensable. The real world was here, inside this rich, fast, sleek piece of machinery. Max felt he was riding in the future and looking at the past. 'You say the Committee wants more names,' he said.

Harry lowered his paper. 'You know any more names?'

'Write these down. Herb Kizsco. Bonnie Scott. Julie Conroy. All in New York.' Harry wrote them in the margin of the sports page. 'Well, that's a start,' he said.

'There's a guy called Luis Cabrillo,' Max said. 'Alien. Radical. Probably subversive. What the hell . . . Definitely subversive.'

'Attaboy,' Harry said.

'Oh dear,' Kim Philby said to Luis. 'I was afraid this might happen.' They had just come out of the Consulate and he was blinking in the blaze of afternoon sunlight. 'How tiresome. Excuse me a moment.'

He crossed the road and greeted Special Agent Fisk as an old friend. 'My dear chap! Have you been waiting long? You should have come inside, out of the sun! Too late now . . .' Philby was backing away, speaking as he went. 'Look, we're off for a spot of tea at the Harvard Club, you won't get in, you're not a member, jolly hard cheese . . . And besides, scarcely anyone gets murdered in the Harvard Club. My regards to the Director.' He rejoined Luis. 'The FBI,' he said. 'So concerned about my safety. Quite unnecessary. I keep telling them.'

They walked on. 'Had you met him before?' Luis asked.

'No. But the haircut, and the stench of duty hanging over him like a cloud of gnats: quite unmistakable. I met a lot of FBI types when I was with MI6.'

'This one's following us.'

'Yes, they follow everyone. Ernest Hemingway told me they've been following him ever since the Spanish Civil War. You were in that, weren't you?'

'Up to my neck.'

'You've read *For Whom the Bell Tolls*?'

'Nobody should write a novel about a war unless he has been killed in it.'

Kim enjoyed that.

Luis had locked the original of his typescript in his safe deposit box. Now he had a carbon copy in a briefcase. As they walked into the blessed gloom and cool of the club, Kim said, 'They don't like people doing business in here. Let me take your creation to my room. I'll speedread it while you have some tea. Charge it to me. See you in half an hour.'

He appeared after only twenty-five minutes and approached Luis with a wide smile. 'Permit me to shake the hand that wrote *Traitors Abound*,' he said. His grasp was firm. Luis's adrenaline flow kicked in and his blood pressure jumped ten digits. He trusted Philby's judgement beyond that of any man. 'Let us migrate to greater comfort,' Kim said.

They moved to a room of overstuffed armchairs. Kim chose a quiet corner, far from other members.

'It needs more work,' Luis said. 'The ending . . .'

'The ending is superb. The opening is a masterpiece. The middle is a magnificent romp. Don't touch a word of it. Not a comma.'

'I see.' What Luis saw was a lengthening line of zeros. He'd asked Harding for a thousand bucks. Make that ten thousand. Fifty thousand. 'Glad you found it so . . . um . . . readable.'

'Oh, it's a page-turner.'

Luis began to feel uncomfortable. Philby should be offended, or at least hurt; but the man was jovial. He had the chubby smile of a schoolteacher whose student has won a scholarship. 'Some people might find the revelations rather shocking,' Luis suggested. Kim nodded. Luis said: 'That's why I thought the British government would place a certain value on seeing the book *not* published. Of course, that value would have to match the royalties I would forfeit. Otherwise – '

'Dear boy, no publisher in his right mind will touch your book.'

Luis stared, but Kim was looking at an elephant head mounted high on the wall.

'You said it's a masterpiece. A page-turner.'

'I did. It also happens to be the most libellous document I've ever read. *Malicious* libel: the worst kind.'

'How can the truth be libel? I've identified thirty-seven agents of the British Secret Service who were active Communists. I've described their Soviet contacts. Listed their code-names, the secrets they betrayed. The whole kit and caboodle.'

'They'll sue you and your publisher,' Kim said comfortably. 'They'll sue your socks off. You'll both leave the courtroom stark bollock naked.'

'Freddy de Silva won't sue. He was part of your outfit, wasn't he? His car went over a cliff in 1944. I know, because I gave half-a-crown towards a wreath. A much-loved husband and brother, it said. Missed by all.'

111

'Missed by some. When Freddy's car ran off the road, he wasn't in it. The de Silva we buried was a different chap, same name. Minor civil servant in the Ministry of Agriculture. Appendectomy, peritonitis, dead in a week. But the KGB wrote off old Freddy, and that was very helpful to us at the time.' One of Kim's shoes had come loose. He let it swing from his toes. 'Freddy's married to a lawyer in Colorado. He won't like being called Communist. Legal fireworks will ensue.'

Luis had slumped in his chair, looking bored and feeling bruised. 'Fireworks make good publicity,' he said. 'I'll take my chances in court.'

'You'll never get that far. You'll never find a publisher.'

'Yes I will. I'll drop Garcia and every other actual named person. That still leaves two dozen Red agents in the British Secret Service. I gave them phoney names. *They* can't sue me.'

'One of them being Gus Brandon.'

'Yes.'

'Funny how certain names stick in your mind. I used to play golf with Gus. You didn't *invent* him, you *remembered* him. Gus was MI6, and I can guarantee that he'll sue. He's a Tory MP now.'

'I'll change *all* the names.'

Kim yawned; he hadn't slept well. 'Forget it, Luis. There's a grapevine in publishing, top-level, official-unofficial. Already, word has gone around: stay away from Cabrillo, he's a mad dog, he'll bite you in the arse.'

They walked to the lobby. Kim gave him back the typescript.

'There's one name in here that you didn't mention,' Luis said. 'And after I gave you top billing, too.'

Kim beamed. 'That was your private joke, wasn't it? Very flattering, but . . . I honestly don't think I'd make a very good KGB colonel. Just a humble bumf-shuffler on the lower slopes of MI6, if truth be known.' They shook hands. 'Mind the traffic,' he said. 'Everything's on the wrong side here.'

112

5

A man wearing flip-flops, Bermuda shorts three sizes too large held up with string, and a sweatshirt bearing a portrait of Albert Einstein, shuffled alongside Luis as he waited for the lights to change. 'Spare a quarter, buddy?' he said.

Luis looked. The sweatshirt was ragged where the sleeves had been torn off, and what remained was seriously creased and stained. 'You're not doing Einstein any favours,' he said. 'He looks old and tired and he's got ketchup in his moustache.'

The man squinted down. 'That's blood. Got in a fight.'

'It's red. Blood turns black.'

The man rubbed the stain and licked his finger. 'Damn, it *is* ketchup.' He sounded worried. 'I ain't got no money for no damn ketchup.'

'Triple negative. That's real firepower.'

The lights changed, and they walked. 'All I need's a quarter,' the man said. 'You won't miss a quarter.'

'What's it for?'

'Get me downtown . . .' He lost a flip-flop, rescued it, had to hustle to catch up. 'Gotta get me to NYU, see, or I miss my class an' they'll flunk me, them bastards — '

'Class in what?'

He took a chance. 'English,' he said. What the hell.

Luis stopped. He was outside the garage where he had parked the Studebaker. 'English?' he said. 'Okay. Listen. This has been a bad day. Things have not gone well. Tell me a joke. Tell me the funniest joke you know.'

'Jeez.' He scratched his face, and scabby flakes fell off. 'I ain't heard a good joke in a long time.' He saw Luis begin to turn away, and desperation jogged his memory. 'Hey! Here's one about General Grant. Seems Grant was takin' a parade once, on his horse, sittin' his horse, an' the horse lifted a hind foot, an' it put the hoof in one of Grant's stirrups, so Grant says, he says, "If you're gettin' on, I'm gettin' off."'

Luis didn't laugh but he smiled happily. 'Excellent!' he said. He gave the man a ten-dollar bill and went into the

113

garage. Ten dollars was wildly generous, cock-eyed, crazy. So what? Philby had tripped him and stamped on his balls. It was time to fight back. He gave the Studebaker ticket to Mickey Rooney's kid brother. 'You old enough to drive?' he asked.

'Nobody drives better'n me. You sooner have nobody? He's on his break.' The kid didn't wait for an answer. He'd heard them all before.

Outside, Special Agent Fisk was talking to the bum, asking him who he'd just met. 'That guy?' the bum said. 'He's my professor at NYU.' Ten bucks had changed the day. Changed a man's life. 'What's it to you?'

'He teaches at NYU?'

'Whadya think? He washes the floors?' That was funny. That was very funny.

'He got a name?'

'You got a buck?' Fisk gave him a dollar. 'Shorty Rogers,' the bum said. 'Professor Shorty Rogers.'

'What did he give you just now?'

The bum looked at Fisk and saw a suit and a hat. All his life, a suit and a hat meant trouble. Plus Fisk had mean eyes. He looked like he was born with a sour apple up his ass. 'You're fulla shit,' the bum said.

Fisk hesitated. No crime had been committed. If he tried to search for evidence, there might be violence. But he hated to lose a possible witness. Then a cream-and-brown convertible came out of the garage and nosed through the crowd on the sidewalk. Fisk saw Cabrillo driving, saw him find a gap in the traffic, drift away. Fisk forgot the bum and looked for a taxi. This was the curse of surveillance in Manhattan: you couldn't use a car, too many one-way streets, a subject on foot could lose you without even trying. Taxis hustled past, none empty. Defeat made his shoulders slump like a milk bottle. A taxi halted beside him, the door swung open, nobody got out. 'Hop in, old chap,' an English accent said. Fisk hopped. He saw a stocky, youngish man with a fighter pilot's moustache. 'If you're not Fisk, I've blundered,' the man said.

'I'm Fisk. I'm following — '

'Of course you are. And so am I. Frobisher, old chap. The

114

Studebaker's up ahead, waiting for the lights to change. Don't worry, I shan't lose it.'

★

Luis felt better now that he was driving somewhere, anywhere, it didn't matter as long as he was in command.

The hour in the Harvard Club had flattened him. Philby had destroyed *Traitors Abound*, casually, without raising his voice. Luis had sweated blood creating the code-names, making character sketches for so many traitors, developing KGB operations in Europe and America, keeping the whole shebang balanced and full of pace and surprise. Massive betrayal on that scale was exhausting. It hadn't bothered Philby. He'd side-stepped it. No publisher, no book. Simple. Made Luis looked childish and foolish.

Now he was on the rebound. He gunned the motor and hit the horn, heading west, into the sun, that's what they always did in the movies. He saw a hole in the traffic and swung the wheel but a battered Chevy jumped faster and stole it. Luis stamped on the brakes. The tyres gripped like glue. The car lunged. Ironmongery shot forward from under his seat.

By the time he found a space to park, he'd remembered what it was. A Colt revolver, fully loaded. Beside it, a road-map of Connecticut and a piece of cardboard bearing directions to West 10th Street. Stevie's stuff. Hidden under the seat while they ate in Chinatown. Forgotten.

Luis sat, fingering the gun. Marriage was no joke. Suppose he married Julie and she gave some stranger $500 to kill him. No. Not socially acceptable. People married for better or worse, not for a bullet in the head.

The least he could do was warn Vinnie Biaggi. Show him the evidence. Give him a break.

He drove south on Seventh Avenue. A taxi followed.

115

6

Four men sitting at a table, playing cards, was not what Luis expected to see. West 10th was a friendly street of small cinemas and coffee shops and stores selling fake Indian moccasins. Parking was impossible. Luis drove around, found a garage, dumped the Studebaker, and walked back to Vinnie Biaggi's address. There was no doorway on the street; instead, a wide iron gate opened on to a courtyard. This was lined with four houses. Warm brick walls, dove-grey shutters, big pots of geraniums. Vinnie's house was on the right. A large china bullfrog propped the door wide open.

Now that looked wrong. Luis had been trained in survival techniques by the Madrid *Abwehr*. When something feels odd, they said, don't hesitate, keep moving, get out. And here was a man at risk of being shot who leaves his front door open. Beat it. *Ausgang! Schnell, schnell!*

On the other hand, who won the war? Not the *Abwehr*. Luis was here on a mission. If he turned around now and walked away, how would he explain that to Julie? He stepped into the house.

Somebody was big on photography. Pictures covered the walls: people, animals, mountains, ships. A cat sleeping on the carpet woke up, saw nothing to get excited about, yawned, closed its eyes. Luis smelled coffee. His nose led him to a back room. Four middle-aged men were playing canasta. He knew canasta when he saw it. In Caracas he'd been king of canasta.

'Be with you in a moment,' a hefty, balding man said. All the players had removed their coats. Their sleeves had French cuffs with small, tasteful cuff-links. Buttondown collars. Club ties. They were serious about their canasta. 'Permit me a moment to complete this act of demolition.' Two moments was all it took. 'Many thanks,' he murmured. 'I'm so brilliant I frighten myself.' He left the table and steered Luis back into the hallway. 'You have my full attention, sir.'

'Would you be Mr Vincent Biaggi?' Luis asked.

'That's what the *New York Times* says.' He saw that Luis didn't understand. 'For my sins, I am music critic of the *Times*.'

'Ah.' Luis was thoroughly wrong-footed. 'Oh.'

'I assumed you were here on matters musical.'

'Um . . . no. Perhaps it's your son I should be talking to.'

'Alas, I have not been blessed with progeny.' He smiled affably. 'A blessing for the unborn, my friends would suggest.' He gestured at the card game. 'But they too are music critics, and so their judgement is deeply suspect.' His eyes twinkled.

Luis relaxed. 'Someone's played a joke on me, Mr Biaggi. God knows why. I came here to warn you that a woman tried to bribe me to murder you. She gave me a gun. Said you're her third husband. Her name is Stephanie.'

'Third husband . . .' His eyes bulged a little at the wonder of it all. He was gently leading Luis towards the front door. 'I would gladly die for, say, Maria Callas, but the prospect of marriage . . .' He gave a tiny shudder. That was when a little old lady carrying a bag of groceries appeared at the doorway.

'Mr Biaggi, there's a Fed in the street an' he's lookin' this way,' she said. 'I know you hate them lousy bastards, so I thought . . . Hey.' She leaned forward, and squinted. 'You ain't Biaggi.'

'Dear Lady, you have been standing in the sun too long. And without a hat too.' He advanced, waving his arms to shoo her away. 'Remember, I warned you about such reckless exposure.'

'You ain't Biaggi.' She tried to look past him.

'Go and lie down before you have another of your nasty turns.' He gently revolved her and sent her on her way. 'A sweet creature,' he told Luis, 'who lives in a world of her own. Well, the canasta calls. So kind of you to take the trouble.'

'Think nothing of it.' They were smiling and shaking hands. 'By the way,' Luis said, and he knew that it was asking for trouble but he was tired of losing, it was time he won something. 'That's a good photograph of Stephanie Biaggi on the wall behind you.'

The handshake tightened. The music critic of the *New York Times* sighed softly and did not turn to look at the picture. 'Nobody likes a smart-ass,' he said, sadly, and with his other hand he gripped Luis by the throat and hoisted him

117

until he was on tiptoe. 'You have talked yourself into the grave . . .' The thumb and fingers were squeezing arteries, and the words began to sound faint, distant, cracked, weary. 'The saddest part is that there is no profit in this solution for anyone . . .' Somewhere, it might have been in Iowa, a car engine roared and died and a door slammed. 'Hey, uncle!' someone called. Luis's sight was blurring, everything was turning grey. He heard the newcomer say, 'Lay off the guy, uncle. He's kosher.' The words were frail. 'What's he doin' here, anyway?' The *Times* music critic released Luis, who didn't even feel his legs begin to fold. Sammy Fantoni grabbed an arm and lowered him until he sat on the carpet. The rest of the canasta school were crowding into the hallway, carrying handguns and shotguns. 'You know this bum?' one asked.

'Sure,' Sammy said. 'He's Luis Cabrillo, visiting from Caracas.'

'Well, he brought the Feds with him,' the uncle said. 'Old Mrs Prodnose from next door saw them in the street.'

Vision returned slowly to Luis. Through a haze of wandering sparks he saw a thicket of legs. He tried to stand, collapsed to his hands and knees, and was carried upstairs to a bedroom that overlooked the street. They sat him on the bed, and moved to the window. They quickly spotted Fisk. 'Feds are getting younger every year,' the uncle grumbled. 'They have no style. See that suit? Those shoulders are a crime.'

'Who's he with?' Sammy asked. 'Can't be a Fed. Hoover don't allow face-hair.'

'Undercover agent, maybe.' Someone objected. A guy seen yacking to a Fed on 10th Street couldn't be working undercover. An argument began. Luis felt left out. He got up to see for himself. 'The moustache is Frobisher,' he said, croaking a little. 'British Intelligence. The other man is FBI. He followed me.' By now everyone was looking at him. 'I had tea in the Harvard Club,' he explained. 'I shook him off.'

'Then he shook himself back on,' the uncle said.

'You got the Feds *and* the spooks chasin' you, both,' Sammy said. 'Waddya do, screw Mamie Eisenhower?'

'Hey, hey!' the uncle said. 'Where are your manners? This

gentleman is a guest in our country.' Sammy mumbled an apology. Someone said the Fed and his pal were crossing the street. Everyone moved to a different window. They saw Fisk enter the courtyard and look at the red Pontiac convertible. 'Sammy,' the uncle said, 'take our visitor and leave.'

Sammy hurried Luis downstairs, through the kitchen, into a storeroom. A Maytag washing machine was bolted to the floor. Sammy pulled on it, and the machine hinged towards him. A piece of the floor came up with it. The hole it exposed was lit. Luis went down a slanting ladder. Sammy followed, reached up and pulled the Maytag upright, using only one hand. There was a soft clunk as the piece of floor locked into place. 'Hydraulics,' he said. 'Same as the undercarriage of a B-52.'

They were in a large concrete cellar. An air-conditioner throbbed softly.

'I never flew in a B-52,' Sammy added. 'Infantry, me. In Germany.' He was switching on more lights. 'Went to fight for freedom against the Commie hordes.'

'Goodness.' Luis's throat felt like pounded steak. 'Who won?'

'Goddam Reds never came at us. Too bad. I won medals for sharpshootin', could of dropped them Ivans easy as pickin' cherries.'

Luis was looking about him. 'Mr Biaggi keeps his larder well stocked.'

'This here is a nucular shelter,' Sammy told him.

It was about the size of a small tennis court. Boxes of tinned food were piled around the sides. There were crates of Pepsi and stacks of toilet paper. Luis saw a folding bed, deckchairs, a table-tennis table, cinema projector, camping stove, a laundry basket containing a variety of automatic weapons, and much more. 'Nucular,' he said.

'Yeah. In case the Reds start anything. The city got nucular shelters all over.'

Luis's head hurt. He sat on the nearest object, a chemical toilet. 'Your friend upstairs,' he said. 'He's not a music critic, is he?'

'That's my uncle. He was the smart kid in the family. Went to Princeton, played tight end, nearly killed a guy in the army game. You were lucky I came along. He tears phone books in half. I'm not talkin' Residential, I'm talkin' Yellow Pages. Another coupla minutes, your head would have been a bowling ball.'

Luis looked away, grunted with shock, shut his eyes, and when he opened them he could still see the toes of a pair of tan loafers poking up. The rest of their owner was hidden behind a year's supply of Ritz crackers. He pointed. 'Please tell me that's not Vinnie Biaggi,' he said.

'Hell, no,' Sammy said. 'Come see.' Reluctantly, Luis got off the toilet and followed him. *This must be the worst part,* he thought. *After this, today must get better.* And when he looked behind the cases of crackers, it wasn't so bad. The man lay on his back with his mouth open, just an average guy of about forty with a shirtful of congealed blood. Completely relaxed, eyes almost shut, he might have been taking a nap. 'That ain't Vinnie,' Sammy said, 'That's Sonny Deakin, a much-loved soldier in the Profaci family, greatly missed by all, only they don't know it yet. Vinnie Biaggi's over here.' He pushed a filing cabinet aside, and now this was the worst part. Most of the clothing was missing, and a knife had been used on large areas of the exposed body. It was a chubby body, and it had been hacked about clumsily, like a pig-roast at a drunken barbecue. Bullet holes were evident, too. Luis walked away and was sick into the chemical toilet.

Sammy opened a case of toilet rolls and gave him a few yards of tissue to mop his face with.

'See, the trouble with Sonny Deakin, he never knew where to stop,' he said. 'It wasn't enough he plugged Vinnie, he had to leave a message too. And we caught him doin' it and terminated his employment.'

'I came here to warn Vinnie.'

'Don't feel bad,' Sammy said. 'We all warned Vinnie, but he was the type guy can't be warned. He kept on doin' it.'

'Doing what?'

'Oh, whackin' the wrong fella.' Sammy was starting to

sound depressed. 'See, Vinnie had this goofy wandering eye. He kept hittin' innocent bystanders, and the Profaci family got blamed. It was vanity, he wouldn't wear eye-glasses, they spoiled his looks. But he wouldn't stop whackin', it was embarrassing, everyone was laughin' at him. Not the Profacis, they weren't laughin'. And his wife, she's got Profaci cousins, they were pissed off. So she left him.'

'Would she be Stephanie Biaggi?'

'Yeah. Stevie. Cute broad.'

'She told me she was a virgin. Blamed Vinnie.'

Sammy thought about it. 'Jeez, I dunno. The guy was a lousy shot, but missin' a target like that . . . I never heard of it before. Still, Stevie should know. You ready to go home?'

He opened a massive steel door. Luis got a whiff of air that smelt of stale electricity. 'I gotta stay. I got body-bags in the Pontiac,' Sammy said. 'Genuine government issue. They come in all sizes.' He led Luis down a narrow passage, unlocked a steel-mesh door, and they were at the gloomy end of a Subway platform. 'Take the IRT uptown,' he said. 'You want the west side, change to the BMT at 14th Street. Put a token in the turnstile on your way out. You got one?' Luis shook his head. Sammy gave him a token. 'We gotta finance the Subway system,' he said, 'or one day it ain't gonna be there when we need it.'

★

The music critic of the *New York Times* was impressed when Fisk identified himself. 'A G-man!' he said. 'What a thrill. How may I help?'

Fisk asked permission to search the house, and was given a guided tour. Frobisher went along too. They ended up where they began, in the card room, where the other three men were playing gin rummy. 'Not for money, I assure you,' the host said genially. 'I'm sorry to have to hurry you, but I must review a Bartok recital at Carnegie.'

They all shook hands. He showed them out. 'Aren't you going to take your car?' he called. They stopped. 'Oh dear. I

121

assumed the Pontiac must be yours,' he said. 'None of us here can drive. Well, cheerio once more. Mind the traffic. It's quite *ruthless* around here.'

Fisk and Frobisher stood in the shade in 10th Street and wondered what to do next. 'Sammy drove that Pontiac into that courtyard,' Fisk said. 'He's a crook. We saw Cabrillo go in there. Now that's a hell of a coincidence unless Cabrillo's in the same line of business.'

'I honestly can't see Cabrillo robbing banks,' Frobisher said. 'He was one of our chaps during the war.'

'If he's such a regular guy, why chase him?'

'He's bloody elusive,' Frobisher said. 'Let's face it, he went in there and he didn't come out, and he's not there now. That's what we call bloody elusive in British Intelligence. What do you call it?'

'I'm going to stick around,' Fisk said. Frobisher was beginning to irritate him.

'Wasting your time, old boy. Both those blighters left by the back door. By now they're having a beer in the Men's Bar at the Biltmore, and that's where I'm heading. Goodbye.'

Fisk stuck around and nothing happened. He worried about Cabrillo's car, parked in a garage. If he went looking for it, he might miss out on developments here. Maybe the car was hot, maybe Cabrillo had dumped it. On the other hand . . .

The problem was resolved, abruptly, as – for the second time in a day – the cream-and-brown Studebaker drove past and Fisk was running, searching for a taxi. Again.

★

Luis was lost, but it didn't matter.

He'd got out of the Subway station fast. Its grime and gloom depressed him; he wanted the open air and freedom. He found the garage more or less by accident, and when they brought his car and took his money he realized he didn't know whether he was pointing east or west, uptown or downtown. So he just drove, followed the cars in front, tried to relax and enjoy being in control of his life once more. He was so relaxed that he didn't even recognize 10th Street when he went along it.

Fisk found a taxi. Well, something had to go right eventually.

Luis went with the flow of traffic, crossed Broadway, which didn't look exciting. Crossed Fourth Avenue, also nothing special. Part of his mind was still down in the cellar, discovering bodies. A truck pulled out in front, so he followed it, across Third Avenue. Up ahead the lights changed to red and he stopped. Now at last he began to get his situation straight. He was heading east. That was no good. East went nowhere except into the frightful urban desert where Max had lived. To get back to Central Park West he must first drive north. The lights changed. The truck moved on. Luis turned left, north, uptown, into Second Avenue.

Fisk's driver saw the Studebaker turn and he laughed. 'Ain't goin' *there*,' he said. 'You ain't got nuff money to pay me to go *there*.' Horns blared behind them. He crossed Second.

Luis stopped, halfway up the block. He faced a tidal wave of traffic. Second Avenue was one-way, downtown. Five lines of traffic came at him, all meeting green lights in a relentless surge. He spun the wheel, pulled hard over, stopped, shut his eyes, let everything roar past, blasting him for his idiocy. Then he made a screaming U-turn and fled, soaked in sweat.

Fisk saw none of this. He had given up the chase. The cab took him back to the FBI Building. Its driver was still amused. 'One guy against the world,' he said. 'I think I saw the movie.'

★

Fisk found a message: his boss wanted to see him. He walked down the corridor, wondering how best to summarize recent events. Prendergast pointed to a chair. 'I lost him,' Fisk said.

'Well then, it's just as well I found him.' Prendergast was so calm he must be happy. 'As the movies say, the Bureau never sleeps, and a round-the-clock search has located the suspect's place of residence. So we're off and running.'

'I got the number plates of his convertible,' Fisk said.

123

'It is not a crime to drive a Studebaker,' Prendergast said. 'It should be, but it isn't.'

'And he's in cahoots with Sammy Fantoni.'

'Cahoots is not a crime either, except to the English language. Now listen. There's more to this Cabrillo than bank robbery, on which we have no hard evidence anyway. He's linked with Philby, and our file on Philby is thick as a brick. He knows where the bodies are buried. I'm talking about Un-American Activities. This could turn out to be big. This could knock Senator McCarthy on his ass. So we play this fish carefully.'

'I knew it,' Fisk said. 'I knew it as soon as I saw those boots.'

7

Senior staff at the British Consulate could join the Williams Club. It was far smaller than the Harvard Club but the fees were a lot more affordable. Also it had squash courts. Harding and Frobisher got changed, went into a court and began smacking a couple of balls about. Philby, in stockinged feet, stood between them and got ready to dodge. American squash balls were as hard as little apples, and they flew like hornets.

Harding liked to hold especially sensitive meetings in this squash court because it was almost impossible to bug the place. Noise echoed off four hard walls and cancelled the voices. Yet the three men could hear each other. This was high-grade low-budget technology, and when the discussion ended you could have a damn good game of squash.

'He's in a penthouse on Central Park West,' Harding said. 'HUAC got some new addresses out of Max Webber, and the FBI had the list in no time.'

'HUAC leaks like a sieve,' Frobisher said. He volleyed hard, three times.

'Hoover hates the Committee, of course,' Harding said. He slammed a fierce backhand. 'Hoover wants to catch all the

Reds himself.' Another backhand. 'Anyway, as soon as his New York office got the details, they started cross-checking.'

'Basic legwork,' Frobisher said. He hit some forehand drives.

'Bend your knees, for God's sake,' Harding told him. 'Watch the ball.'

'And are they going to arrest him?' Philby asked.

'Doubtful,' Harding said. 'The FBI is short of hard evidence against him. And Mrs Conroy has already been blacklisted. They don't give a damn about her.' *Whack-bang* went the backhand.

'How does this affect us?'

'Options, sir,' Frobisher said. 'If Cabrillo is a really serious threat, we can use expunction.' *Whack-bang*. 'Or we can leave him to the FBI. They've always been keen to nail him for bank robbery, and now that he's mixed up with the Mob, they're keener than ever.'

'Expunction has clear advantages,' Philby said. 'It closes the file.'

'Depends how it's handled, sir.' Harding caught the ball and checked it for cracks. 'Cabrillo can easily be expunged, but what happens to the remains?'

'Suppose Cabrillo vanishes,' Frobisher said. 'Mrs Conroy raises merry hell. The FBI intensifies its search. Heaven alone knows what embarrassing material they dig up.'

'And if a body *is* found,' Harding said, 'the FBI's bound to come looking for you, sir. They know you met him today. That's not going to help your reputation, is it?'

'So expunction is out,' Philby said. 'For the time being, anyway. A pity. Such a useful word. Where did you find it?' he asked Frobisher.

'In the *New York Times* crossword, sir.'

'Golly. I wish I had your brains . . . Well, at least we know where he lives. That's something.'

Philby left. They played their squash and Frobisher won, 3–1. He was stocky, but he was fast.

8

Julie was on the phone when Luis came in. He kissed her on the back of the neck and she tasted salty, so he licked his lips and realized that the salt was his, a deposit he had leaked at Second Avenue and Tenth when he saw five lanes of traffic charging at him head-on, lined up like cavalry, lights flashing, horns blaring, raising a surge of sweat that had soaked his scalp and dribbled into his eyes. Even now, his undershirt was drenched.

He stripped and stood under the shower. The spray pounded his skin and stripped it of sweat, but the memory remained. Five lanes of angry traffic could not easily be washed away.

He was sitting on the laundry basket, cooling off, when Julie came in with two large gin-and-tonics. He reached for one. She stopped. 'What happened to your neck?' she said.

'Oh. That.' He didn't have the strength to get into a long explanation. 'Accident. Head got caught in the elevator. The doors sort of banged . . .' The drink was only six inches from his grasp.

'Bloody liar.' She turned away, and ice chinked. 'I've seen bruising like that before. Someone tried to strangle you.'

'My fault. He was music critic of the *New York Times*. I upset him. He strangles people who upset him.' She didn't believe that either, and he had to tell her everything. His voice croaked occasionally. She relented and gave him his drink. It cooled and calmed his voice-box. He decided to finish the story fast. 'Traffic was bad on the way home. Still, I made it.'

She wasn't interested in traffic. 'You went to Philby and he spiked your memoirs,' she said. 'So you went to Vinnie Biaggi and he wasn't here, but you couldn't leave it at that, and you annoyed a gorilla from Jersey. All the time, you've got a Fed and a moustache from MI6 tailing you. Then Sammy Fantoni shows you out through the Mob's fresh-meat department. Here comes the bad part. You hit the rush hour. Well, some days nothin' goes right.'

Luis used his toes to try to pick up his undershirt. 'Look at all that sweat,' he said. 'What a waste.'

'Survival mechanism, Luis. Fight or flight. Didn't you do any biology at school?' She went off to make more drinks.

'The Jesuits prohibited biology,' he called. 'We did Advanced Guilt instead.'

She came back, looking thoughtful. She said, 'Technically, in the eyes of the law, you're a witness to murder, aren't you?'

He didn't want to talk about it. He sucked an ice cube instead. She recognized that mood: he had regressed to the age of twelve. He made his legs pigeon-toed and knock-kneed. 'Let's hope they dump the stiffs in the Jersey swamps,' she said. 'Then maybe they'll forget you exist.' He stuck out his lower lip and squinted downwards, trying to see the lip. 'I told you this city's dangerous,' she said. His mouth hurt, so he relaxed it.

'Haven't you got an opinion?' she said.

'Yes. One. I'm naked and you're beautiful.'

She tipped her head to one side and looked him over. Why did he have to act so dumb? Though sometimes he was right. This was one. He was naked, and she wasn't the ugliest broad on the block. Sometimes he was smarter than the entire Nobel Prize Academy on skates. 'If you put it like that,' she said. 'Why the hell not?'

9

Kim Philby was on the slide. He was forty-one, which meant fewer years ahead than behind. He knew it shouldn't matter. Seize the day, for tomorrow is never more than a promise. Or a threat. Now he sat in his room at the Harvard Club and thought of a man who had said to him, 'Fuck the facts. How old would you *think* you were, if you didn't know your actual age?' That man was dead. Dead at forty-five. Keeled over on the ninth green at Wentworth. What could you say? Time ran out.

Bloody time. Bloody age. Bloody golf.

Bloody Cabrillo.

He looked at his watch. Another thirty minutes gone,

wasted, lost. He got his hat and went downstairs and walked the half-dozen blocks to the Consulate and met Harding as he was leaving. That was lucky.

'I've been thinking some more about our problem,' he said. 'The simple fact is Cabrillo knows too much. He was up to his neck in the Double-Cross System throughout the war. It's still top secret, for the very good reason that all those double agents we used might come to a sticky end if their controllers in German Intelligence learned the awful truth. Ex-controllers, I should say.'

'Those types never retire,' Harding said. 'They just brood. But Cabrillo was a double agent, wasn't he? Won't that make him keep his mouth shut?'

'You've met him. What do you think?'

'He's a loose cannon. Normal rules don't apply.'

'Exactly. We've agreed that expunction is out, because of J. Edgar bloody Hoover. But what about semi-expunction?'

'A warning shot across the bows?'

'Perhaps *into* the bows?'

'It wouldn't backfire? Make him dig his heels in? You know him better than I do, sir.'

'He's never experienced physical pain. A bullet in the leg will come as a nasty shock. He won't risk another.'

'And there's his partner. She has legs, too.'

'Double the discouragement?' Philby tried to picture the scene. 'No,' he said. 'One bullet in the leg is just another statistic here. Two bullets in two legs is a news story. We don't want that.'

They went up to Harding's office. He flicked through a file and gave Philby a card. The name on it was Spence Mallaby. His business was Pest Control. Philby cocked an eye.

'A sense of humour does no harm,' Harding said.

STUPID IS DANGEROUS

1

They were talking about dinner, and what kind of food they felt like, when the phone rang. Julie took it. The call was brief.

'We're eating Italian,' she said. 'That was Sammy. His uncle in Hoboken invites us to dinner.'

Luis felt his neck. 'He'll kill me again.'

She shook her head. 'Doubt it. These people are hot on manners. Nobody's allowed to read the sports pages at funerals.'

'Yes, but Hoboken . . . I was snubbed by a bum at Hoboken. Why do we have to go?'

'One, the Mafia always eats well. Two, if we don't go, he'll send for us. Put your pants on, Luis. I'm hungry.'

The sky was heavy with cloud, trudging north like a beaten army. Somewhere south, Maryland maybe, the fag-end of a tropical storm was pushing air ahead of it, making a breeze that shook the tops of the trees in Central Park. Below the trees, two dogs, one big, one not, stood and barked at each other. They barked as if they were getting paid by the bark and it was steady money. They were still barking when Luis and Julie drove away.

They took the West Side Highway to Holland Tunnel. Luis was wondering why the FBI had followed him to 10th Street. And why Frobisher? Maybe they were following him now. In the movies, the guy driving the car said *I think we're being tailed*, and the other guy looked back and by God, they always were. Luis looked in the rear-view mirror and saw about a hundred cars.

Julie was not wondering why the FBI had followed Luis – the FBI followed all her friends, had done for years, it was a badge of friendship. But Frobisher was different. Philby was different. Was Luis tap-dancing back into their world of smoke and mirrors? Nobody could think seriously in a convertible. She rested her head and watched the sky and the gulls and the tops of buildings drift past.

Sammy's blood-red Pontiac was waiting in Hoboken. He led them out of town, many miles, deep into wooded country-side, and turned on to a blacktop driveway that wound between fields. There were a lot of white fences and sleek horses, the kind who dropped their dung regularly, confident that some lackey with a shovel would be around later to clean up the paddock.

The cars turned a corner and stopped in front of a big, handsome house, all faded red brick and mullioned windows. The drive went on, to a stableblock and a scattering of barns. Two boxer dogs came out to meet the visitors. They did not bark. This was not Central Park.

Sammy's uncle followed, introduced himself as Jerome Fantoni, and they all shook hands and went inside, to a room that was twenty feet high and forty feet long. The chintz sofas were king-size. There were coffee tables big enough for dwarves to play table tennis. Ancient Navajo blankets hung on the walls. Huge vases were full of flowers, mainly roses.

An elderly man in a white jacket and black pants brought the drinks they wanted and then got discreetly lost.

'Let's put business out of the way, so that we can enjoy our dinner,' Jerome said. He wore tennis slacks, a dark green blazer, a creamy open-neck shirt with the collar turned up. His voice had the deep charm of an ambassador to a small but well-heeled nation. 'Mr Cabrillo: I'm sure you appreciate the need for utmost security in a sensitive business like mine. It was a matter of security that brought you to 10th Street, wasn't it?'

'Well, now.' Luis almost smiled. He twitched his nose. Julie knew the sign: Luis was in a hole and scrabbling to get out. 'This is not a simple matter,' he said. 'There are – how shall I put it? – wheels within wheels.' He frowned, trying to give his waffle some weight.

'I have a proposal,' Jerome said. 'I'll tell you what I know, and if I'm right, you tell me what you know.'

'Excuse me.' Julie got up. 'I'll just go and smell the roses.'

'My house is your house,' Jerome said. He turned to Luis. 'You work for British Intelligence, don't you? That's why you went to 10th Street. Vincent Biaggi was aware that something un-American was taking place. You were, too. Furthermore, you weren't trying to shake off the two men watching the house. They were part of your team.'

'It's an international conspiracy to subvert the Free World,' Luis said soberly. 'It calls for a vigorous, coordinated response from intelligence agencies throughout the West.' He took a deep breath. Nearly out of the hole.

'So who's the rotten apple in my barrel?' Jerome asked.

'I was hoping that Vincent Biaggi would tell us that. Somebody got there first.'

Sammy saw his chance to contribute. 'Sonny Deakin aced Vinnie.'

'Yeah, but why?' Julie asked, from a distant corner. 'And who aced Sonny? Before he could talk to Luis?'

'It's all right,' Luis told Jerome. 'She knows everything.'

'Mrs Conroy is a very smart lady,' Sammy added.

'Here is the sequence of events,' Jerome said. 'Three of my associates went to 10th Street to play canasta with Vincent. A regular arrangement. They caught Mr Deakin red-handed. He resisted them and paid the price. They informed me. I arrived and assumed command. Sammy left to make arrangements, we had time to kill, so I made the fourth at canasta. You know the rest.'

'So who shot Sonny Deakin?' Julie asked. She was back on a sofa again.

'Tony Positano,' Sammy said. 'He came to play canasta and — '

'Hey!' Julie pointed a finger at Luis. 'You thinkin' what I'm thinkin'? Sonny Deakin could be Wallpaper. Or maybe Garlic.'

'Good Lord.' Luis widened his eyes. Wallpaper and Garlic had been code-names in the Double-Cross System. 'Then Mr Biaggi might be Seagull. Could Mr Positano be Nutmeg?'

'It all fits,' she said. 'Code-names,' she told Jerome. 'Red networks always use code-names.'

'It all sounds rather comic-opera,' Jerome said.

'We take it seriously,' Luis said. He was into his stride now. 'We broke the code for their New York network and got all the code-names. Yours is Pinetree. Mrs Stephanie Biaggi is Bluebird.' Sammy laughed, but he was alone and he quickly stopped. 'Our information was that Seagull was being black-mailed by Wallpaper into joining the Communist Party.'

'Code-named "Hotdog",' Julie said.

'Where does Mr Positano fit in?' Jerome asked.

Luis shrugged. 'Difficult to say. We were hoping Wallpaper could tell us, but unfortunately . . .'

'Nutmeg shot Wallpaper,' Julie said.

'If he *is* Nutmeg,' Luis added.

'This ain't right.' Sammy sounded upset. 'Sonny knocked off Vinnie on account of Vinnie couldn't shoot straight.'

'That's what they want us to think,' Luis told him.

'So you can't name names,' Jerome said.

'Only code-names,' Luis said, 'and they may be phoney. The investigation is ongoing.'

That ended the business discussion.

2

The apartment block didn't have twenty-four-hour doorman service. After eight p.m. the tenants used their keys to get into the building. It was a nice old building and the front door had a nice old lock and Spence Mallaby had a set of picks that opened it in seven seconds flat.

He took a pride in blending with his surroundings. For

Central Park West on a summer evening he wore a pair of old but well-polished cordovans, wool trousers in a quiet brown check, a faded russet shirt and a grey windcheater. He was pushing fifty, medium height, absent-minded expression. Right now there were ten thousand guys between the Park and the Hudson who looked just like him: out for a stroll in the cool of the evening.

Nobody in the lobby. He took the elevator to the penthouse. Tapped on the door. He was sorry to bother you, but he had the apartment down below and there was water dripping from the ceiling. Nobody answered. Tapped again. Nothing. This time the lock was modern and expensive and his picks took twelve seconds.

Ever since he gave up smoking he enjoyed a cup of coffee at this time. The penthouse had coffee: Colombian, his favourite. He brewed a pot and turned out the lights and took a mug – black, no sugar – on to the terrace and waited for the young couple to return.

3

They went in to dinner.

It was not Italian; it was English: mushroom soup, crown roast of lamb with mint jelly, strawberry fool, a small Stilton. Jerome carved the lamb. 'I believe in the right of the individual to better himself,' he said. 'The Bolsheviks want to share the misery equally. That's not the American way.'

'How would you define the American way?' Luis asked.

'Let me give you an example.' Jerome tasted the claret and nodded. The elderly servant poured. 'Major construction projects. The lifeblood of the economy. Years ago, each union was demanding bigger kickbacks than the next union. Chaos. New York was getting a very bad name construction-wise. For the sake of the city, we had to step in. Today, in return for a small, fixed percentage of the budget, we guarantee that every union will perform as promised, and harmony reigns. Harmony expands opportunity. That's freedom to build. I'm a libertarian, always have been.'

'And take fish,' Sammy said. 'That Fulton Street Fish Market was a disgrace until we knocked a few heads together. Now you can eat the best sea bass in the country. Clams, too.'

'Any plans for expansion?' Julie asked. She sounded like NBC talking to General Motors.

'The banks are letting the city down,' Jerome said. 'They open late and shut early and treat customers like cattle. The place that really cries out for reform, however, is City Hall.'

'You ever tried to renew your driver's licence?' Sammy asked her. 'Better take sandwiches. Take a sleeping bag. Take three days off, for Pete's sake. It's worse'n the Kremlin down there.'

'You've got a point,' Julie said.

'I'm concerned about extortion by the City's building inspectors,' Jerome said. 'In Manhattan, for the simple restoration of the gas supply to an apartment, I'm told they demand thirty dollars.'

'Forty, I paid,' Julie said.

'If we put our guys in City Hall we could get it down to fifteen,' Sammy said.

'It's a matter of resisting the arbitrary restraint of trade,' Jerome said.

For coffee, they returned to the room with the sofas and the roses. Rain had begun to patter on the windows.

'This is all very civilized,' Luis said. 'Would it be indelicate of me to recall our first meeting, when you seized me warmly by the throat?'

Jerome sighed, not entirely with regret. 'Sometimes we act, not as we wish, but as we must. This afternoon my associates expected strong words and prompt action from me. You see, I'm obliged to play a dual role: sometimes Hamlet, sometimes Henry V.'

'Sometimes Ivan the Terrible,' Luis suggested.

'Well, you pushed your luck,' Julie told him.

'You want I should get the Yellow Pages?' Sammy asked helpfully. They wanted. He came back with a directory three inches thick. 'This is merely a party trick,' Jerome said. He flexed his fingers and slowly ripped the book in half.

'Crikey,' Luis said. 'Did you learn that at Princeton?'

For the first time, Jerome smiled. 'I majored in music. I still play the piano for three hours every day.' He looked at his hands. 'Bach deserves all the credit.'

When it was time to leave, thunder was grumbling around the horizon and rain was punishing the driveway.

'Your little convertible will drown in this,' Jerome said. 'Sammy, fetch one of the Buick sedans.'

They waited in the hall. The boxers, eternally good-mannered, came to see them off.

'You needn't answer this,' Luis said, 'but exactly how did you know I worked for British Intelligence?'

'I didn't know. I took a chance, and guessed.' The Buick swished up to the front door, and they all shook hands. 'It's almost flattering to be a victim of Red infiltration, isn't it?' Jerome said. 'They target the vital organs – the State Department, the Atom Bomb, the Army, Hollywood, and now my operation. Almost flattering.'

★

The storm had sucked up a large part of the Caribbean and it still had a lot left to dump on New Jersey. Luis was glad to be driving the Buick. It felt big and safe and rich. The interior smelled of the hides of rare animals, lightly smoked over a fire of ten-dollar bills. Luis felt pleased with himself, and grateful for Jerome's generosity. 'The man may be a thug but he's a prince,' he said. He turned the wipers to maximum. They flung the rain back into the night.

'I was right about good food,' Julie said. 'Everything else, I'm not so sure.'

'We bamboozled him. Eldorado strikes again. Bullshit baffles brains.'

'You reckon? All that stuff about saving the construction industry? And straightening out City Hall? Who was bullshitting who?'

'Wasn't it all true?'

'Yeah, sure, City Hall stinks. And nobody lays a brick in New York without the Mob skims a percentage off the budget. It's a racket, everyone knows that. It's *his* racket, and there he was, giving us this civics lesson.'

'Well . . . maybe he was relaxing. Maybe he has a wry sense of humour.'

She grunted. 'Mafia jokes usually turn out to be as funny as a boil on the backside. And I'll tell you another bad joke. You just missed the turning for Montclair.'

'I don't want to go to Montclair. I want Richfield, then Rutherford — '

'Luis, whatever you want, you're on Interstate 80 heading west. Keep it up, and you'll hit Pittsburgh, Pennsylvania. Okay?'

'That's no damn good. I want Route 46, south. Where's 46? You've got the map.'

They argued about it. He had to drive a long way before he found an exit that let him get off Interstate 80 westbound and on to Interstate 80 eastbound. 'Don't do anything clever,' she said. 'Just stay on this and we'll hit the George Washington Bridge into Manhattan.'

'I don't want the bloody bridge. I want the bloody tunnel. It's not raining in the bloody tunnel.' They began arguing again.

4

Jerome Fantoni smoked a long cigar and played backgammon with Sammy. They always played for a dollar a point. Money was the only thing that made his nephew shut up and concentrate on the game; and Jerome liked backgammon because it let him think clearly about other matters.

He won twenty dollars and they stopped.

'Flattery,' he said. 'I find it depressing how much flattery most people can take. Look how Cabrillo leaped at my suggestion that he was a British Intelligence agent.'

136

'The guy's a phoney?'

'Sammy, a real intelligence agent would have a cover story ready to hand, a legit reason for being in America, a job, whatever. Instead, Cabrillo tried to bullshit me with that flim-flam about code-names. That was not smart.'

'That was stupid,' Sammy agreed.

Jerome studied the stub of his cigar. 'Stupid is dangerous. Cabrillo blunders into something which is not his business and then believes that his bullshit will erase his blunder. Instead he has doubled it.'

'That was *real* stupid.'

'You know where he lives? Yes, of course you do. Take his Studebaker, go there now and delete him from the records. Not the girl, unless you have to. Lose the Studebaker, I don't want to be associated with it. Bring back the Buick. Dump the body in Connecticut.'

'Long Island's nearer.'

'No. Connecticut went Republican. I don't like Connecticut.' Jerome walked with Sammy to the door. 'I should have known better when I saw them arrive. What sort of clown drives a Studebaker?' All around, thunder was still grunting and growling. 'Drive carefully, Sammy. The roads are full of homicidal maniacs.'

5

Spence Mallaby thought that Manhattan was at its best in the rain. Everything wet looked clean. That was one of the first things he'd learned in the military: when an inspection takes place, if it's wet, it's clean. Later, his career in the military became more hazardous; now he was grateful to be alive. The world looked good, especially at night, when he was on the penthouse terrace, enjoying the rain, watching headlights that had lost their glare and tail-lights that were deeply and softly reflected by the soaking pavement. It was the only time when traffic was a pleasure to see.

He waited a long time, over two hours, but that was nothing; there had been occasions in the military when he had waited motionless, all day and night, until small animals came up and sniffed him and decided he was dead. Now he watched the traffic and thought about the quadriceps extensor muscle, the biggest muscle in the leg. From the pelvis to the knee there was nothing but muscle and perhaps fat and only one bone, the femur. The thigh made a large, clean target, unlike the lower leg, which was guarded by much bone; or the abdomen, packed with gastro-intestinal plumbing. He had studied these things.

A cream-and-brown Studebaker convertible appeared and parked down below. A man got out and entered the building. No woman. Well, Mallaby was glad of that. Simplified the job. He left the terrace and opened the penthouse door. There was a light outside but the penthouse was dark. After a minute or so the whine of the elevator ceased and he heard its door slide open. Soon, Sammy appeared, silhouetted, and Spence Mallaby shot him in the left thigh. The sound was softer than a popped balloon. Sammy made more noise falling on his rump.

'There's a message,' Mallaby said. 'Go back to Venezuela.'

'Jesus Christ,' Sammy wheezed. 'What the shit you do that for? That goddam hurt.' He felt his leg, and groaned. 'I never been to fuckin' Venezuela, pal.'

'Uh-huh. I have to leave now.'

'You do that an' you're a dead man. I got blood pourin' out of me. I'm Sammy Fantoni, you asshole. Get me to a doctor, fast. Otherwise my family's gonna blow your fuckin' brains out. Christ Almighty, look what you did!'

Mallaby turned the lights on. He recognized Sammy, and he saw blood spreading rapidly outwards from his thigh. 'Maybe I clipped an artery,' he said. 'Your femoral runs through there.' He took out a knife and slit Sammy's pants.

Blood was throbbing over the leg. 'Where did I hit you?' Sammy's fingers groped for the hole. 'Press hard on that,' Mallaby said. He went away and came back with a kitchen spoon and a handful of neckties. 'You like the blue or the green?' he asked.

'I feel like shit,' Sammy said.

'Nobody's wearing shit this year.' Already a necktie was around the thigh, and knotted. Mallaby made a pad from a handkerchief, slid it under the knot, and tightened the tourniquet with the kitchen spoon. Blood still pulsed through Sammy's fingers. Mallaby shifted the tourniquet, forcing his thumbs into the inside of the thigh, hunting for the spot where the artery could be jammed against the bone. He found it, moved the tourniquet, used another tie to lash the spoon in place. The flow stopped.

'You got your knee in my balls,' Sammy said weakly.

Mallaby dragged him into the apartment, searched him, found a short-barrelled automatic in his hip pocket. 'You here on business?' he asked. Sammy nodded. 'Well, business is closed for the day. Remember when you said you felt like shit?' Sammy nodded again. 'You've gone downhill fast since then,' Mallaby said. He shoved the gun back in the pocket.

His training in the military took over. First priority: get the casualty treated. Problem: moving Sammy out of the building. Solution: create a diversion. He called the Fire Department. Then he made a heap of newspapers, magazines and books on a table near the balcony, put a match to it and waited until it was burning hard. He picked up Sammy by the armpits and carried him to the elevator, put him inside, leaned him against a corner. Two floors down, the elevator stopped and a young couple got on. 'Just a fainting fit,' Mallaby told them. 'It happens.' He smiled, so they smiled too. Smile and the world smiles with you. Hitler had a nice smile.

There was a couch in the lobby. He and Sammy sat there for a short while, until he heard the fire siren whooping joyously. He slid his right arm under Sammy's coat and got a good grip around his ribcage and half-carried him out of the building. Everyone was looking at the firemen, or pointing up. There were cops, but they were busy keeping the traffic moving. And the rain helped. Mallaby got Sammy into the

Studebaker, found the keys in his pocket, drove away. Stage one completed.

★

Luis was drifting along, searching for a parking slot, when Julie saw the flames. 'That's us!' she said. 'The penthouse is on fire!' He swung the Buick into a space reserved for buses and they watched a fire truck blare a hole through the traffic. 'How extraordinary,' he said. 'And look, all the lights are on. We didn't leave the lights on.'

She had nothing to say about that. The whole experience was bizarre: sitting in comfort, watching her home burning through curtains of rain, while Nat King Cole sang *Stardust* on the car radio. It was totally cock-eyed.

'And I think that's my Studebaker.' He pointed to the opposite side of the street. She nearly said it was impossible, the car was in Jersey. But what were the odds against a different cream-and-brown Studebaker convertible being parked on this block? It wasn't a car you saw every day. Or every week. As they looked, it drove away. 'Fantoni keeps the Studebaker, which turns up here just as our apartment burns. This is not a healthy place,' he said. 'We are not wanted.' He pulled out and joined the traffic. She felt sad; she had begun to like the penthouse. There were books of hers, and records, up there . . . Now what?

'I timed that nicely, didn't I?' Luis said. 'Spot-on.'

'You didn't time anything, you schmuck. It was luck.'

'Ten minutes earlier, you'd have got your eyebrows singed.'

'Pure luck! Jesus Christ, Luis, you got *lost* three times, just getting here.'

'I was one hundred per cent right about the tunnel. It's definitely faster than the bridge, isn't it? If we'd taken the bridge, we'd never have seen the Studebaker.'

'And if I hadn't turned you round, we'd be in Ohio, you moron.'

'Perfect timing,' he said. 'It's an instinct we Spanish have.'

140

'My American instinct tells me we have nowhere to sleep. Think you can find a hotel?'

'I'll find you six hotels, sweetheart, all different colours. Which d'you like?' Luis was feeling buoyant. He was glad to be out of the penthouse. Too many people knew about it.

★

The dealer had sold the Studebaker cheap because he knew it was a lemon. The previous owner had spent zero on servicing, and now, at the worst possible time and place, in the rain, halfway between the apartment building and the hospital, the car died of neglect.

Spence Mallaby was driving one-handed, using the other to hold Sammy upright. He was heading uptown on Broadway, aiming for Warners Presbyterian Medical Centre, talking to Sammy, asking how he felt and was there any blood running down his leg, and getting mumbled answers, and not seeing the red light glowing on the dash. Up ahead, someone changed lanes without looking, a truck-trailer slammed on its brakes, the trailer fishtailed, a bus swerved and sideswiped a couple of cars and in a few seconds, uptown Broadway was jammed. Heavy rain, heavy traffic, it happens.

The Studebaker wasn't hit, but the road was blocked. Mallaby couldn't go forward, couldn't go back. The red light still glowed. Clogged oil filter. The engine was being starved of lubricant, the pistons were hotter than hell. Soon, the Studebaker died. By then, Sammy wasn't even mumbling. Mallaby had a flashlight. He meant to check on the tourniquet but the flashlight showed a spreading pool of blood at Sammy's feet. His heart had been young and strong and it had pumped him dry. Well, deep potholes, poor suspension, thumps and shakes, what else can you expect? No tourniquet lasts for ever. This one must have slipped.

Mallaby wiped his prints off everything he might have touched, got out and ran through the pelting rain to the nearest Subway station.

Win some, lose some.

CATCH THE WIND
OR YOU CRASH

1

The day after the fire, they left New York as soon as Luis could get to the bank and empty his safe-deposit box. He had about fifteen hundred dollars. The *Times*, the *Trib* and the *News* ran short reports on the finding of Sammy Fantoni's bloodless body in an abandoned Studebaker. No mention of a double slaying on 10th Street, but the *Trib* carried an interview with Stevie Biaggi. Asked when she last saw her husband Vincent, she said their different careers kept them apart. Clearly the *Trib* had been tipped off.

'No tunnels, no bridges,' Luis decided. 'I don't like toll gates. Too easy for the FBI to watch.'

'The FBI doesn't know we've got the Buick.'

'Jerome Fantoni could have reported it stolen.'

'Why would he do that?'

'Why would somebody kill his nephew?'

Silence, while Luis studied a road map.

'I don't know,' Julie said. 'Sammy wasn't smart but he wasn't a total schmuck. He deserved better.' She still couldn't believe he was dead.

'We take Broadway to Route 9,' Luis announced. 'Same way we went to lunch at Tarrytown, remember? But we keep going, alongside the Hudson, north, past Ossining, Croton, Peekskill . . .' The map ran out. 'Until we find a bridge over the river without a toll. Then we'll think again.'

They drove 150 miles to Albany, ate lunch, bought suitcases, pyjamas, toilet kit, changes of clothing and more maps.

North led to Canada. They turned south-west into the mountains and cow pastures of New York State. Julie drove. 'Now that we're not in Manhattan,' she said, 'where the hell are we going?'

Luis was studying a map of the East Coast states. 'It seems to me that all roads lead to Washington, DC.'

'That's so decent people can get away from it.'

'I smell power. Greed. Vanity. Lust. All that man needs to make life a thing of simple joy and staggering wealth.'

'Uh-huh.' She tried to think of a better place to go. Philly? Baltimore? Pittsburgh? She had an aunt in Roanoke, Virginia. Not necessarily still alive, though. She gave up. 'I guess DC is as good as anywhere,' she said.

By mid-afternoon they were in Pennsylvania, following back roads. The land looked prosperous; the folk were friendly: often they raised a hand in greeting. 'Hey, this is nice,' she said. 'This is tranquil. Let's stay here for a week or two. My nervous system needs a break. DC can wait, can't it?'

Luis agreed. 'Smell the flowers. Walk in the woods,' he said. 'As a matter of fact I could use some peace and quiet. There's a screenplay I've been thinking about. Brilliant idea. Just needs to be put on paper.'

They found a small hotel: nothing more than a large inn but it was comfortable. Luis borrowed a typewriter from the owner and spent the days writing his screenplay. He never discussed it, and Julie never read it. In the evenings they walked, often arm in arm, while the sunset turned the air to a golden haze and fireflies provided free entertainment. Julie thought: *This is too good to last*, and of course she was right. After a week they packed up and drove to Washington, DC. She checked into a motel and took him to the airport. 'Well, I hope it stinks,' she said. 'Hollywood loves crap.' They kissed. Luis flew to Los Angeles, a reckless extravagance but justified by his raging talent; rented a black car; bought a dark suit and a snap-brim hat; and headed for Warners.

★

The guard on the gate at Warner Brothers was not easily surprised. When a man gets to salute Gregory Peck arriving in the morning and June Allyson leaving in the afternoon, he regards the world differently. But he was surprised to see a modest black Ford hardtop drive up and stop. Black was not fashionable in Los Angeles. Must be a tourist got lost, looking for directions. The driver got out. Didn't dress like a tourist. Dark blue suit, black shoes, grey tie, snap-brim felt hat, aviator glasses.

'Howdy,' the guard said.

'Special Agent Cabrillo, FBI,' Luis said, and flashed a silver badge with a gilt star, the gift of the Chief of Police of Caracas after Luis had donated generously to his re-election fund. 'I am here, on the authority of Senator Joseph McCarthy's Senate Sub-Committee, to speak with an actor by the name of Max Webber.' He showed a long, brown envelope. 'And you, sir, have a statutory duty under federal law to assist me. Where is Webber?'

This sort of thing had never happened before. 'Well, now just hold on there,' the guard said. 'You need a pass, I can't just — '

Luis showed another envelope. 'This, sir, is a subpoena for you to appear before Senator McCarthy and answer why you obstructed the work of his Sub-Committee, if you so obstruct.'

'Shit . . . Third building on the left. Park at the back. Anywhere except the slot marked Kirk Douglas.'

Luis thanked him, quietly and soberly, and drove in. *Jesus Christ Almighty,* the guard thought. *I could have lost this job right there, in ten seconds.* It scared him so much that he gave Richard Widmark a really crisp salute as he drove out.

Max Webber liked Los Angeles. He liked getting paid, wearing new clothes, living in a roach-free house with a front door not made of sheet steel and four locks plus two bolts. He liked the sunshine, the palm trees and the endless, easy parking. Above all he liked being a working actor again. The angry hostility of New York, the looming shadow of HUAC – all that was behind him. Three thousand miles and three time zones behind. Max was sitting in the sun, reading his script, marking his lines, when Luis came and sat beside him.

'Jeez . . . you look like a morticians' convention,' Max said.

'That's a nice healthy tan, Max. It suits you.'

'Yeah. I bet you say that to all the stiffs.' Reluctantly, Max closed the script. He had named Cabrillo as a Red subversive. Now the bastard had come three thousand miles to see him. 'Why do I have this dull, sickening sense of dread?'

'Relax, my boy.' Luis had a briefcase, and he patted it. 'I have here what all Hollywood has been waiting for.'

'It better be the world's best pastrami on rye with pickle,' Max said. 'Or you're dead in the water.'

★

The screenplay was called *Double Trouble*. Max refused to read it. 'Give me an outline,' he said. He was afraid to take his eyes off Cabrillo. The guy might have an ice-pick up his sleeve.

'Comedy-thriller set in Nazi Germany,' Luis said. Max winced. 'Hitler has a double, a guy who appears instead of him, decides to save Germany by killing the Nazi leaders, starting with Himmler. But when he tries to kill Himmler's double, he discovers that she's a woman. They fall in love and agree to kill Goering, but — '

'Don't tell me. I'm three reels ahead already.'

'They have an idea — '

'Enough!' Max said. 'Wait here.' He took the screenplay, went inside, and came back without it. 'Lunch?'

They ate in the commissary. With people all around, Max felt less afraid.

'Tell me,' Luis said. 'Why did you change sides?'

'Americans are restless people. We thrive on change. Once it was ragtime and railroads, then the Charleston and wing-walking, and after that, Prohibition and the yo-yo. Now it's television and blacklisting. You can't tell people what they

146

want. It's like flying a glider, you've got to catch the wind or you crash. No point in fighting the wind, that gets you nowhere. America knows best, Luis.' Max felt safe.

'No regrets, then?'

'This is Hollywood, chum. Like I said, we give the people what they want.'

'What they want is names. It amazes me. Lots and lots of names.'

'Sure. They had mine and they seemed to enjoy it.' A little bitterness was spilling out. Max was no longer acting.

'And this is reputedly the land of the free.'

'Yup. Everybody's free to be screwed by McCarthy. That's equality. The Jews have been fucked. The Indians have been fucked. The niggers have been fucked. That only leaves the goddamn Christians unfucked. Well, now they're getting their share. Makes a man proud, don't it?'

Luis could smell a fight in the air. He nodded, although he didn't know what he was agreeing to. He looked around the commissary. 'Hey!' he said. 'Isn't that Piper Laurie over there? Wearing green?'

'That's not green,' Max growled. Which brought the conversation to an end.

They were leaving when a stubby man with a silvery crewcut came in. 'This the guy?' he asked. Max nodded. The crewcut handed Luis his screenplay. 'Let's get out of here,' he said. They went into the sunshine. 'You should know better,' the crewcut said to Luis. 'We can't take your stuff. You're on the list.'

'Welcome to the club,' Max said. 'Now you're fucked too.'

Luis was so startled that he smiled. The crewcut continued to look disgusted. 'How is that possible?' Luis asked. 'This is the first screenplay I've written.'

'You pissed off the New York publishers, Mac,' the crewcut said. 'They liaise with us. We don't want Un-American writers any more than they do. Beat it.'

Luis had nothing to say. They wouldn't have listened anyway. He left.

'And you,' the crewcut told Max. 'Keep your pinko pals out of here.'

Max shrugged. 'I didn't ask him to come,' he said.

'Since when was that an excuse?'

Luis sat in his car and counted his money. Not enough. He had bought a one-way plane ticket, banking on a Warners deal to take care of the return. He could still fly home but it would knock another big hole in his savings. Then he'd have to tell Julie that he'd bombed in Hollywood. Three failures in a row: Madison Avenue, the British Consulate and Hollywood. Poor show.

Glenn Ford strolled by, in cowboy gear. Luis sneered at him: a grown man who made a living out of waving a gun that fired blanks while a crew of thirty people took moving pictures of him sneaking around a gulch, whatever that was. 'At least I haven't sunk that low,' Luis said aloud, and immediately felt better.

The car was too hot. He drove to the gate, and beckoned the guard. 'Banks,' he said. 'Where are all the banks in this town?'

2

San Francisco. That's where the banks were.

The guard, anxious to please, told Luis the big bank headquarters were in Downtown Los Angeles, around Bunker Hill. Or, if he just wanted a lot of banks, Wilshire Boulevard had a fine selection. Luis took Sunset Boulevard to Downtown LA and didn't like it: too much space, not compact like Madison Avenue. And nobody walked, everyone drove. Hopeless. He found his way to Wilshire Boulevard and kept driving. Wilshire was sixteen miles long. It had more banks than he needed but they were all remote from each other. Not helpful. LA sprawled. It was everywhere and so it was nowhere.

He parked, and looked at the road map of California. San Francisco was on a narrow peninsula; it seemed a lot like Manhattan. And he was already on the Pacific Coast highway, so that clinched it. Four hundred and one miles, the map said. Good. Gave him time to think.

The FBI would certainly have warned all its offices about a new style of bank robbery, involving messengers. They would be alert. Maybe his method needed refining. He drove, and examined various refinements.

The Pacific gleamed an emerald blue to his left. Mountains reared dramatically to his right. The tyres of the Ford drummed softly. Two girls in a sports car waved as they passed, and he waved back, easily, almost lazily, just as Cary Grant would have done. In fact he was better than Cary Grant. This was better than Warners. Hollywood was dreams on a screen. This was *happening*, and he was making it happen.

Refinements came and went. He stopped for gas at Ventura. Coffee at Santa Barbara. A steak at Santa Maria. Checked into a hotel at San Luis Obispo. He was standing in the shower, trying to get his mind into fine focus, when he remembered the motto of the Double-Cross System. 'Tell them what they want to hear,' he said aloud. 'And keep it simple.' It had helped win the Second World War. It should be good enough to knock over a few banks.

★

San Francisco was a nice city. The air was fresh, the views were dramatic, the people were pleasant, and in less than an hour he found seven banks, all within easy walking distance of a messenger agency and an office building with small suites to rent by the week. He took one. It was too late in the day for crime, but he spent a pleasant couple of hours in the office with scissors and paste, cutting up headlines and making threatening demand notes. 'Dynamite' was not in the news. Pity. He assembled 'TNT' from different typefaces, added an exclamation point, then removed it. 'Moderation and restraint,' he said. But when he found a string of dollar signs in a department-store ad, he created GIVE ME YOUR $$$$$$$$. Neat but not gaudy, he thought.

149

Next day, at about one-thirty, he was finishing off a cream cheese and anchovies on rye when the first messenger came limping along the corridor. Luis was sitting in the office swivel chair, wearing the snap-brim hat, the aviator glasses, the dark blue suit. He signed the man's worksheet. 'Leave it on the desk,' he said. He tipped him a dollar. Two more messengers made deliveries, took their dollar and left. Then the fourth man came in, followed by a plain-clothes cop. He had cop's eyes: a little weary, rarely blinking, and able to take in the whole room at a glance. He was fifty plus. He'd bought the jacket when he was forty plus and he would never button it again. He had jowls like a bulldog, and they seemed to weigh down his shoulders.

'That blows it,' Luis said. His voice was as flat as last night's beer. 'He won't come here now.'

'Who the hell are you?'

Luis's arms were folded. He unfolded them, displayed the badge in his left palm, refolded them. 'Special Agent Carlos, FBI. You?'

'Lieutenant Dwyer, robbery.'

'They know you're here, lieutenant.' Luis made a tiny nod towards the window. 'They follow the messengers. If all the messengers arrive, and they reckon they're safe, they complete the operation. But they saw you bring this man.' He signed the worksheet and gave the tip. 'Let him go. You know where to find him.'

'Sure-Thing Messengers,' the man said.

'Beat it,' Dwyer told him. He sounded disgusted. 'You knew this was coming down? Why didn't the Bureau tell us?'

Luis looked at the ceiling and stroked the front of his neck. 'You've had experience, lieutenant.' He spoke quietly: one pro to another. 'Police departments don't always co-operate when they see a chance for kudos, do they? Too bad. The gang hit seven banks, didn't they?'

Now Dwyer was thoroughly disgusted. 'You knew so much, why didn't you nail them?'

'How many banks get hit in California every week? In the US? These men hide in the general run of crime. We've been

150

on this case for a year now. They hit seven banks in Pittsburgh, seven in Chicago, same in Detroit, St Louis, Denver, Dallas and Omaha. Seven is their favourite number.'

Dwyer had not moved from the doorway. He looked from Luis to the bulky brown envelopes on the desk, and back to Luis. 'This is the strangest bank heist I ever come across.' He disapproved of strange robberies; that was clear from his voice. 'Too cute. Way too cute.'

Luis stayed motionless. He counted to twenty, thinking: he's old enough to be a grandfather and still only a lieutenant. No genius, but good at waiting. Guys like him can wait for hours. 'We live in cute times,' Luis said. He glanced at his watch. 'I'm permitted to tell you something. Not everything. The dollars from these bank hits go to finance left-wing extremists and agitators.'

'Reds?' Now Dwyer's expression changed. 'Commies?'

'The FBI is acting in strict liaison with Senator McCarthy.'

'Uh-huh. Well, you handle the politics and I'll take care of the money.'

'You'll get a subpoena to appear before McCarthy if you touch those envelopes. They're evidence. An FBI forensic unit will examine them.'

Dwyer and Luis exchanged stares. The detective couldn't read Luis's expression. Luis was pretty sure he knew what Dwyer was thinking. He was thinking that he was two years off retirement. Did he really want to risk his pension by getting accused of prejudicing a McCarthy Senate Committee investigation? A guy could get fired just for being subpoenaed. The hell with it. Let the banks wait for their dough. 'I'd better report in,' he said, and moved towards the phone.

'Don't touch it. Prints.'

'Shoot. Nearly forgot.'

'Take these.' Luis gave him head-and-shoulder photographs of three men, two serious, one grinning. He had found them in a Sausalito junk shop that morning. 'Names are no help. They change their names as often as their socks.' Even now, Dwyer didn't want to go. 'Every minute you stay here,' Luis pointed out, 'is an extra minute they use to get away.'

'I guess you're going to stick around.'

'This is my post,' Luis said. 'I have no other.'

Dwyer left. Luis packed the four envelopes into his suit-case. Two more messengers arrived. 'Are we late?' one asked. 'Bumped into young Jimmy here, his birthday, had a beer to celebrate. Seventy today, I mean what the hell.'

Luis signed for the envelopes and gave them ten bucks each. 'Have one on me,' he said.

'Okay if we have two?' Jimmy said. Very funny joke. They laughed all the way down the corridor. Luis let them take the elevator. He took the stairs to the basement. The central heating furnace was roaring softly, like a sleeping giant. A door opened on to the car park. San Francisco was a trusting city. Nobody had stolen a central-heating furnace in living memory.

He drove unhurriedly to Salt Lake City, 751 miles, most of it uninhabited for obvious reasons. It took a day and a half. He went by plane to Denver and then got a first-class flight to Washington DC, another reckless extravagance now totally justified by his undeniable and staggering talent, and met Julie at the motel. 'You're far too beautiful for a dump like this,' he declared.

'Does that mean we're rich again?'

'Moderately.' Six banks had provided $10,712.00. Presumably the messenger from the seventh bank had run off with its money, the scoundrel. 'Nothing to excess,' he said.

Lieutenant Dwyer had a bad day. When he reported in, he got roasted by his captain for leaving the banks' money. Then a detective recognized one of the photographs the FBI agent had provided. 'He played short stop for the Brooklyn Dod-gers in the 1930s,' the detective said. The captain phoned the FBI and the FBI said they had no Special Agent Carlos. The nearest police car went howling to the office building. Empty. The bankers were indignant. San Francisco FBI were ex-tremely pissed off. The cops had steam coming out of both ears. Dwyer got sudden chest pains and had to be sent home. 'I don't see how I could of handled it any different,' he told his wife.

'That bastard Hoover's to blame,' she said bitterly. 'You cops take all the risk and he takes all the credit.'

'It's a bitch.' Dwyer lay on a couch. The pains were coming back.

Soon a report clattered out of the teleprinter in the Bureau's New York office. Prendergast was amused. He could afford to be; he wasn't the one with egg dribbling down his chops. 'I said this guy was a smart-ass, didn't I? It wasn't enough that he conned the banks, he had to con the San Francisco PD. He enjoys his crime. I like criminals who like risks. Now for the bad news.'

'Is there bad news?' Fisk asked. 'He hasn't hurt anyone. The banks have been warned.'

'To do what, exactly? How can they distinguish between the messengers our smart-ass sends and the hundred other desperate men who hold up banks every week?'

Fisk thought about it. 'We could expose him,' he said. 'Use the newspapers . . .' Prendergast looked sideways at him. 'Copycat crimes,' Fisk said.

'This could be a different smart-ass, impersonating Cabrillo. Assuming it *was* Cabrillo in New York. Whoever the criminal, he's a showman. Good. Soon he'll trip over his own feet and fall off the stage.'

'And meanwhile, we don't think Cabrillo killed Sammy Fantoni.'

'Why would he? No motive. He's too smart to be a gorilla. Fantoni was a dumb hit-man. My reading is that his uncle sent him to whack somebody, Sammy loaded his gun in the car, accidentally shot himself in the leg. Gangsters are not immune from error, Fisk. Don't make something of nothing.'

Fisk thought: *But he was in Cabrillo's car. Nobody heard a shot. And what about the fire?* He knew what Prendergast would say: Life is messy. Disorder is normal. Purity is suspect. Let it lie. So Fisk said, 'Jerome Fantoni is very dissatisfied. Says he wants justice.'

'Then he should pay his taxes,' Prendergast said. That was that.

★

Harding and Philby met in the Metropolitan Museum of Art, which was unlikely to be bugged by the FBI. Philby read the case summary that Harding had brought; then they strolled through the galleries.

'On the debit side, sir, the Bureau doesn't have a clue where he is, or what to do next, or even if he is the real Cabrillo.'

'Oh, he's the genuine article.'

'On the credit side, our pest control man has fumigated the premises. Pity he winged the wrong bird. Understandable mistake. Made Cabrillo jump, didn't it? All the way to California.'

'Yes.' Philby stopped. They were looking at a huge canvas depicting a blood-smeared warrior, holding a sword and naked except for a helmet, doing battle with an angry lion. 'The director of MI6 in discussions with HM Treasury,' he murmured. They walked on. 'The publishers' blacklisting is helpful, but it won't silence Cabrillo for ever.'

'He doesn't need funds, sir. Not since San Francisco.'

'I was thinking of his Spanish temperament. Have you heard the old saying: "Scratch a Spaniard and start a fire"?'

'No, sir.'

'I'm not surprised. Cabrillo invented it, which doesn't mean it's not true. I say, just look at this.' It was a painting of Leda and the swan. 'Here we see the FBI and the CIA earnestly seeking ways to fuck each other. Hence the baffled expression on the swan.'

'Isn't the swan supposed to be a Greek god?'

'Zeus. He took the form of a swan to improve his chances of sexual intercourse with Leda.'

'He should have asked my advice first, sir,' Harding said. 'It would have avoided a lot of fuss and feathers and frustration.'

3

While Luis was in California, Julie checked out the real estate scene in Washington. This didn't take long. Washington wasn't the murder capital of America, but the US army trained its surgeons for Korea by sending them to Washington hospitals, a good place to learn how to treat gunshot wounds, especially on a hot Friday night. Usually, the wounded were black. Two-thirds of the citizens were black. Segregation simplified the real estate business. 'Unless you're very brave and very poor,' an agent told Julie, 'it's got to be Georgetown. Trust me.'

He found her a small house in Potomac Street, a turning off M Street. It was another short sub-let: the owner was a State Department official who'd gone to Paris to replace a colleague who had shopped often but paid seldom.

Luis didn't like the sound of it. 'M Street?' he said. 'Presumably between L Street and N Street? That displays a pathetic lack of imagination. What happens after Z Street?'

'It's all swamp up there,' she said. 'Nothing but bears and Indians. Grab your hat.'

He didn't like the look of the real-estate agent either. Gregg DeWolf was a younger, slimmer version of Burt Lancaster. He wore a cool tan-coloured suit. The crease in his pants was as sharp as the prow of the *Ile de France*. He was three inches taller and half an octave lower than Luis. He was pleased to meet Luis and very pleased to see Julie again.

Potomac Street was delightful and the house was perfect: two-storey Georgian, painted cobalt blue with black shutters. Luis parked the Buick next to a fire plug. DeWolf advised against this. Luis ignored him. He paid three months' rent in advance, in cash, counted the notes into DeWolf's hand, waved away the offer of a receipt. 'I taught unarmed combat to Commandos all through the war,' he said. 'There are six ways to break a man's arm without using weapons and I invented three of them.'

DeWolf knew when to look impressed, and he looked impressed now.

'Everyone needs a hobby,' Julie said. 'Me, I play tennis.'

★

The house on Potomac Street was fully furnished. Life was easy. Julie explored Georgetown and bought clothes to replace the stuff abandoned in the penthouse. After too long serving beer and burgers at Mooney's, this was an unreal, fairy-tale existence. Luis seemed to be rich and she was willing to wallow in luxury. She knew Luis: it wouldn't last.

He got a ticket for parking next to the fire plug. He began to read it and found it long-winded and heavy-handed and he gave up. He used the car again, and came back and parked next to the fire plug again. Soon the car had another ticket. He stuffed it where he'd stuffed the first, in the glove compartment. The Buick had a deep glove compartment. Its designers had thought of everything.

A DEMOLITION
JOB

1

The radio warned that it was going to rain. 'The sun is shining,' Luis said. Julie was curled up on a sofa, happy, with a bunch of new novels from the owner's bookshelves. 'Take an umbrella,' she said. 'This is federal territory. They got federal rain here.'

He didn't take an umbrella. He took a bus, the first time he had been on a bus since London in 1945. A small boy in the seat in front turned and stared. His narrow features had a middle-aged look. He was chewing bubble gum. A bubble swelled and burst, sounding like a slap on a wet thigh. He sucked in the tattered debris. 'Gimme a quarter,' the boy said softly, 'or I'll tell the driver you took out your pecker.'

Luis leaned forward. 'You're a smart kid,' he whispered. 'You know any Commies?' He flashed his Caracas police badge. 'The Bureau pays a dollar a Red.'

The boy still stared but he stopped chewing. Saliva dribbled from a corner of his mouth. He suddenly turned away and slumped. Luis relaxed. The bus went past the White House. It looked much bigger in the movies. Then the boy was back, bubble gum garaged in his cheek. 'I got a Red for you,' he said, quietly but urgently. 'Math teacher at my school. Bastard's a Commie. That's worth more'n a dollar, ain't it?'

Luis patted his shoulder. 'The FBI already identified your teacher. But keep your eyes open, son. The enemy is everywhere.' He gave the boy a quarter. 'Get off at the next stop. We can't be seen together.'

Luis rode the bus to the Mall, feeling slightly ashamed for having bamboozled the kid so easily. Espionage was such a potent drug. He walked to the Washington Monument. Against a grey sky it looked massive but not majestic. He strolled around it twice. Now what? A tourist wearing a porkpie hat with a plastic hat-protector sidled up to him. 'Some piece a stone, huh?' he said. 'Five hunderd an' fifty-five feet. Hell of a thing.'

'That was last year,' Luis said. 'What they don't tell you is it sinks an inch a month.'

'Thatafack?' He took a pace back and revalued the monument. 'So . . . not five fifty-five, you reckon?'

'Five fifty-four. They lost twelve inches since last year.'

'Yeah, but . . .' He had a guidebook. 'They finished building in 1884. If it kept sinkin' like you said, that's damn near seventy feet it sunk. Ain't possible.'

'You're no fool,' Luis said. 'Once a year, the government sends up a construction crew to add an extra twelve inches to the top. They work by night. It's one of the best-kept secrets in Washington.'

'How come you know so much, then?'

'I'm the crew boss,' Luis said simply. 'We climb tonight.'

They stood for a long minute, looking at the phenomenon that was the Washington Monument, until the man said, 'Nice talkin' with you, sir. Now I got to go see where they make the money.'

Luis gave him a hundred yards' start and followed him. An occasional breeze hunted in the grass, chased bits of litter, gave up, came back from a different angle. It was soon obvious where he was heading: a hulking lump of a building, as boring as a brick. Yet there was a line of people waiting to get in. Everyone wants to see money being made, and the Bureau of Engraving and Printing made dollars day and night, all year round. Billions of dollars.

The tour fascinated Luis. He looked down at presses creating sheets of thirty-two bills as easily as making wrapping paper. Men scanned each sheet for defects. That was all they did. Came to work, scanned half a million bucks, put their hats on, went home. A different press added serial numbers. A cutter chopped the sheets into bills. The bills got lumped into chunks, four thousand to a chunk. The chunks went to the banks. End of story, except the story never ended. What pleased Luis was the aura of craftsmanship. American dollars were made with care. With pride. With respect.

He was strolling across the Mall, thinking about those chunks of money, each as clean as a brick, when it began to rain. He sprinted to the Capitol building, and just made it before God pulled the plug and soaked the tourists.

Luis was lost in five minutes and bored in ten. Too many marble columns, too many bronze statues, and miles of bloody corridors that led to staircases that went God knew where. Architecture didn't thrill Luis. What this Capitol building needed was someplace to nurse a martini and talk to a friendly barman until it stopped raining, instead of which he got a cop with brass buttons for eyes who said, 'You look kinda lost, mister.'

'Ah, constable. Just the chap I need.' Luis smiled with his eyes and adopted his best Cary Grant accent. The *Abwehr* had coached him in how to deal with nosey policemen. Relax. Stand tall, speak calmly, request advice. If possible, associate yourself with authority. 'Got here early for my appointment. Seem to have lost my way, rather.'

'Who's your appointment with, sir?'

'McCarthy. Senator McCarthy.' As soon as he heard himself, Luis knew that McCarthy was the real reason he was in the Capitol. In fact, McCarthy was the magnet that had drawn him to Washington.

'Senate's not in session. Probably in his office. That's in the Senate Office Buildings, across the street, on Constitution Avenue.'

'Outside?' Luis looked at the rain-streaked windows. 'One would arrive quite drenched.'

'Take the Subway,' the cop said. 'In the basement.'

'What a thoughtful arrangement.'

159

'We like it.'

The Subway train was made of small, open-top cars. The seats were generously upholstered and they faced each other. Luis sat in an empty car and thought about money, lunch, Julie and sex, all in the space of ten seconds. Sex made him hungry. An omelette would be nice. Three men got into the car. Suits, hats, briefcases.

'Hi,' one of them said. 'You're not an accountant, by any chance?' Luis shook his head. 'Too bad,' the man said. 'Our client has mislaid a million dollars.'

'Can it, Charlie,' an older man said, mildly.

'Maybe he just mislaid the decimal point,' the third man said.

'Forgive my colleagues, sir,' the older man said. 'Zeroes excite them. Are you a visitor to this fair swamp?'

'Oh, no,' Luis said. The fellow mistook him for a tourist. 'I have an appointment with Senator McCarthy.' That silenced them.

The train moved and carried them through a tunnel and stopped. They got out. Charlie said, 'You're going to see Joe McCarthy, right?' Luis nodded. 'Met him before?' Charlie asked. Luis said no. 'Well, get ready for a ride on the tiger,' Charlie said. 'And I hope you brought plenty of red meat, preferably poisoned.' Anger had deadened his voice. He hurried after the others.

My goodness, Luis thought. *Such a welter of images*. But he was thoughtful as he made his way upstairs. His mind offered up faint echoes of an ancient adventure, when poverty had sent him strolling into the German embassy in Madrid, offering to spy on the British. But that just took nerve. Senator McCarthy was an American politician, and therefore much more formidable an opponent than an *Abwehr* brigadier. Tackling McCarthy would demand nerve and fast footwork and high intelligence and a truckload of bullshit.

2

He found the right building, the right floor, the right corridor, the right office, but nobody answered his tap on the door; so he opened it.

A secretary blinked to acknowledge his presence. Her eyes were the only way she had to communicate. She was typing. Her mouth gripped a ballpen. Her shoulder squeezed a telephone. 'Uh-huh,' she told the phone, and typed. 'Uh-huh.'

'The senator . . .' Luis began. She nodded, and her eyes swivelled towards an open door. 'Uh-huh.' The typing never stopped.

Luis went into the next room, which was bigger and better furnished. Nobody was there. Another door was, if not open, not entirely shut. He kept going, into a room that was even more spacious. A king-size desk was covered with books, files, documents. A man was writing fast on a yellow legal pad, filling line after line, no pause, no hesitation. Left hand spread across forehead, shielding the eyes. Shirt sleeves rolled up.

He filled a page, flicked it over, began the next. Luis lost patience. 'Well, goodbye, senator,' he said. 'Finish that letter to your mother.' The writing stopped. 'Red spies in the US can wait.'

The man sat back. He was surprisingly young, certainly under thirty; but Luis reminded himself that McCarthy was the *junior* senator from Wisconsin. The man spoke. He had a scratchy, high-pitched voice. 'One: I am not the Senator. Two: you are a horse's ass. Three: get your horse's ass out of my office.'

'Yes, I suppose I could do that.' Luis looked around for a comfortable chair and settled into it. 'After all, what do I owe you, a man with no manners and the speech-patterns of a baseball manager? Why should I care if you reject information crucial to the security of the United States? If you decide to blow your career when it's scarcely begun, who am I to stop you?'

'Damn good question. Who the hell are you?'

161

Luis studied him. He had a narrow face and small features except for his teeth, which were big and very white. His eyes seemed to hold a permanent glare. He was four weeks late for a haircut. 'I'm the man who is here to see the senator,' Luis said gently. His heart was pumping hard, a not unpleasant sensation. It was like the excitement of watching horses rounding the last bend in a good race.

'I'm legal counsel for the senator's Sub-Committee. I can have you tossed out of here in ten minutes flat. Now tell me what you want.'

'Well, now,' Luis said, 'that depends entirely on what you've got.'

'I've got a keen desire to bust your chops. I'm sick of finks like you, wasting time, on the take, full of crap.' That was when a green light, mounted high on the wall, began blinking. Counsel was on his feet, grabbing a fresh legal pad. 'You're not staying here, mister,' he said.

'Senator McCarthy wants you. Good. We'll go together.'

They had a short staring-out contest. Counsel was shorter and thinner than Luis, and dressed like an undergraduate: tweed jacket, grey pants, white tennis socks, loafers. His tie hung loose. 'We can't go in with you looking like that,' Luis said. He rapidly fixed the tie, smoothed the collar, buttoned the coat. Counsel was shocked. No man had ever touched him so intimately. 'Get off me, you punk,' he growled.

'During the war, I taught unarmed combat to British Commandos.' Luis took a pencil from the desk. 'There are seven ways to break a man's arm without using weapons.' He snapped the pencil. 'And I invented four of them.' He tucked the bits into counsel's breast pocket. 'Punks like me won the war for kids like you.'

Counsel loosened his tie as they went out. Luis's soft touch disgusted him. He would have relished a healthy knock-down fist-fight, but this wasn't the time or the place for a brawl. Later, perhaps.

★

They arrived in the middle of a demolition job.

Two men were in the room: both middle-aged, heavy-set, dark-suited; but Luis immediately identified Senator McCarthy. He was pacing up and down, and using a rich, deep senatorial voice to denounce a man for betraying this country's sacred heritage of liberty and justice for the sake of cheap and sensational headlines.

'Who's the other guy?' Luis murmured.

'Jim Patterson,' counsel said grudgingly. 'Canadian reporter.'

'God knows we live in a bleak and bloody world, sir,' the senator boomed. 'But you and your grubby henchmen, with your greed for cheap applause, daily make it bleaker and yet more bloody.'

'Uh-huh.' Patterson was sitting on a couch, searching for something in an overloaded briefcase. Luis noticed that he had not shaved well that day.

'Your sweeping condemnation of responsible citizens is the language of the gutter. Your own words betray you.'

'Uh-huh.' He abandoned the briefcase and searched his pockets. 'I know I got it here somewhere . . .'

'Despite your rabid lies, one voice will always survive. The truth remains the truth. I take comfort from that.'

'Uh-huh.' The pockets failed him. 'I'll find it. Look, take a drink, for Christ's sake. Bobby, where's that piece from the Milwaukee paper?' Counsel hurried forward.

'Let there be no misunderstanding, sir. I despise and reject you and your policies.'

'Sure, sure. Now for God's sake have a drink, take the weight off . . . Ah, thanks, kid.' Counsel had found the piece from the Milwaukee paper, lying on a desk. 'Get a copy of that for Mr Peterson, will you?'

'Patterson,' the other man said.

'Yeah, sure, Patterson, hell of a writer, I read your stuff all the time, now will you for the love of Christ take a drink? I hate to drink alone.'

'If you insist,' Patterson said wearily. 'Bourbon and ginger. But it won't alter my — '

163

'Sure, sure. You write what you like. I got the great people of America behind me and we're fightin' the Red Menace in every crack and corner it dares to show itself. Read what Milwaukee says there. The good voters of Wisconsin want me to run for president. Would that kind of thing happen in Russia? How's your drink?'

'More ginger,' Patterson said.

'Okay, good, now we're comfortable,' McCarthy said. 'Fire away.'

Luis sat in a corner and got used to the switch. The well-dressed guy who'd delivered the blast was not the senator; he was the reporter. The guy in the baggy suit who needed a drink and a new razor was Senator McCarthy.

Patterson did the interview. Luis thought McCarthy won without breaking sweat. 'Americans don't mess with Russian politics,' he told Patterson, 'so what brings Communists to this country except to cause trouble?' Patterson had no answer to that. The session ended. McCarthy gave him a souvenir jug of Wisconsin maple syrup, a signed copy of his book *McCarthyism, The Fight for America,* and a warm handshake. 'Any time,' he said. 'Ain't just sayin' that. My door is never closed to the gentlemen of the Press.' Patterson left, looking flat. 'How about that,' McCarthy said. 'Two yards of piss and a Princeton Ph.D., and he never laid a glove on me. Do I know you?'

'I sincerely hope not,' Luis said crisply. 'I spend considerable time and money on preserving my anonymity.'

'Claims he had an appointment,' counsel said. 'He lied. He's here on false pretences.'

'Oh, don't be such a sore loser, for Chrissake. Half of Washington is here on false pretences.' McCarthy boosted his drink and groped for a handful of ice cubes. 'This guy says he's a spook, I believe him, the other half of Washington are all spooks, why not him? Got a code-name, Mr Spook? Something we can put in my appointments diary, keep our little friend here happy?'

Luis searched his memory. 'Arabel,' he said. 'Call me Arabel.' It had been the *Abwehr's* code-name for him during the second half of the war. To the British he was Eldorado; to the Germans, Arabel. Eldorado might still mean something to intelligence veterans in Washington but the *Abwehr* was long since dismantled and demolished. And Arabel was a name that Luis could easily remember.

'Sounds like a floozy to me.' McCarthy would never be handsome. Too bulky. Between receding black hair and dark jowls was a job-lot of features: heavy eyes, bulbous nose, slanting mouth. But he had an easy grin. 'Not that I got anything against floozies. Well, that ain't true. I got my tumescent genital organ against 'em, every chance I got. Only kidding, Mr Arabel. I say things like that to give our little friend here a vicarious and illicit thrill, on account of his family never lets him have any fun. Take a drink, Mr Arabel, and tell me somethin'. You here to buy or to sell?'

'Buy?' Luis was surprised and a little amused. 'What should I buy?'

'Oh . . . well . . . folks sometimes value my goodwill. My good works. My good nature.' Now McCarthy was amused.

'Senator, this man told me he had crucial information,' counsel said. Not amused. We were not put on Earth to enjoy ourselves.

'I'm here to sell,' Luis said. 'You investigate and expose Communists. I can supply you with Reds. Top quality. All fresh.'

McCarthy strolled across the room and straightened a framed photograph of himself shaking hands with Eisenhower in uniform. Ike's grin looked like it had been set in stone. 'Mr Arabel . . . I've been doing this job for a few years now. Reckon I know as much as any man. How come I missed what you say you found?'

'Maybe we're talking about two different kinds of Communists, senator. There's the kind that goes about like a snail, leaving a trail behind it. And there's the other kind that leaves no trail. Really dangerous Communists don't address meetings, or publish newsletters, or carry membership cards, or get elected to party positions.' He felt the kick of spontaneous creation and knew it was time to take a break before he

165

pushed it too far. He walked to the drinks cabinet and poured a glass of tonic water. He plopped a lump of ice into it. He dried his fingers on a bar towel monogrammed with the senator's initials. The tonic fizzed against his palate. Everything in the room seemed heightened, the colours, the shapes, even the silence. Especially the silence.

'Well, you got a point, Mr Arabel,' McCarthy said. 'Question is, how d'you catch these snails? The no-trail kind.'

'Do you care how I do it, senator?'

McCarthy laughed. 'No, sir. I don't give a damn. Hey . . . I'm late for lunch. Politics is all food, you know. Steaks are going to kill me. Good to meet you, Mr Arabel.' They shook hands. 'Stop by again, we'll compare slime. Bobby knows how to find me.'

'Bobby?'

McCarthy aimed his glass at counsel. 'Bobby Kennedy. Didn't you guys meet?'

'Not formally.'

McCarthy took his drink with him as he went out. 'Don't you mess with Bobby Kennedy,' he said. 'Medical Science ain't got no antidote to Bobby's venom.'

They listened to his footsteps fade.

'And it's *Bob*, not Bobby,' Kennedy said, in a cracked monotone. 'I wish people would get it right, for God's sake.'

3

The Central Intelligence Agency did not exist. That's why the food there had to be so good. It wasn't like the FBI, where you could set your watch by J. Edgar Hoover and his sidekick Clyde Tolson stepping out to lunch at Harvey's restaurant. The CIA fed its workers on the premises, and fed them well. It says a lot for Mrs Bailey's dedication to duty that she damn near worked through her lunch break.

Mrs Bailey was an audio typist. She listened to spools of tape and made transcripts of what she heard: not absolutely everything, not chit-chat about the weather or sexual long-ings or borrowing ten bucks; just serious business. The trouble with audio was people wandered, coughed, mumbled, chewed gum, interrupted. Mrs Bailey was patient, persistent. She replayed the tape. Even so, some words troubled her, so she added a query in red ink in the margin.

She did this with *Arabel*, if it really was Arabel. Sometimes it sounded like Annabel. Mrs Bailey had only ever come across *Arabel* as a girl's name and this was a man talking. She couldn't find it in any of her dictionaries: English, French, Italian, Spanish, German. She was now very hungry. In the margin she wrote *Arabel or Annabel?* and went to lunch.

The CIA operative who read her transcript was not impressed by big talk in McCarthy's office. 'Same old stuff,' he said. Then he noticed the red-ink query. It intrigued him. Why would a male use a female code-name? There was a reason for everything, and he wanted to know it. He sent a memo to all departments of the agency, asking if the names rang a bell.

Wagner had been a brigadier in the *Abwehr*, German military intelligence. When The Second World War ended, he was in a prisoner-of-war camp. At first it was scoured by Allied investigators, picking out individuals to stand trial for war crimes. Wagner was not one. Soon the Soviet Union was building its Iron Curtain, a buffer zone from the Baltic to the Black Sea. That was a lucky break for Wagner and many like him. Some of their *Abwehr* colleagues, unlucky enough to be captured by the Russians, found themselves back at work in East Germany. Wagner's wartime operations involved send-ing spies into Britain and receiving their reports: exactly what American intelligence now wished to do in East Germany. It made sense to counter one set of *Abwehr* officers with another. The US cherrypicked the best, including Wagner. When the CIA was set up in 1947, Wagner was one of several ex-*Abwehr* men on the strength.

He was still there in 1953, looking at a memo that was all about a name.

'Arabel,' he said aloud. Agent at the heart of the *Abwehr*

triumph of the war. Could there be two Arabels? Coincidence? No, he knew this must be the same man. But here, in Washington, dickering with Senator McCarthy? Bizarre. Wagner was quite excited. He must find out more.

ALL SORTS OF
FREAKS AND WEIRDOS

1

Every day the garbage scow went down New York's East River and far out to sea, where one of the crew pulled a lever, the hull opened like bomb doors and another several hundred tons of metropolitan crap got dumped into the Atlantic.

On the way back, midway between the Statue of Liberty and Brooklyn Navy Yard, a deckhand saw an unusually large piece of garbage drifting with the current. The skipper ordered that a striped buoy be dropped near to it, and he got the Harbour Police on the radio. 'It's a floater,' he reported. Let the cops get their hands dirty.

Ten minutes later, a police launch found it. The cops slid boathooks under the ropes and hauled it over the stern and on to a tarpaulin. Nobody got his hands dirty, which was just as well because Sonny Deakin was coated with oil and sewage. At one time there had been a concrete block around his feet, but the salty Atlantic had quickly found so many weaknesses where it could penetrate and degrade that it had nibbled the block down to nearly nothing, and the bloat in the body brought him to the surface.

Too much sand in the cement, perhaps. Or maybe not enough patience to let it harden.

Sloppy.

2

The bullet that clipped Sammy's femoral lay in the sodden carpet of the penthouse until the police found it. They already knew he hadn't been shot when he was in the Studebaker: no slug, no hole in the seat, and the angle of entry of the leg wound was wrong. Plus he'd been in the penthouse. They found the same carpet fibres plastered all over the bloody seat of his pants. Also, blood splashes in the elevator and the lobby matched Sammy's type. He was a Fantoni, so the NYPD was happy to let the FBI have the case as part of its investigation of organised crime. But shooting a guy in the leg, torching somebody else's apartment, driving the guy up Broadway in the rain until he's dead and the vehicle quit because nobody ever took the trouble to change the oil filter: that wasn't organized crime. That was dishevelled crime.

The coroner kept Sammy while the FBI went poking around, listening for leaks from the other New York families and hearing nothing but disbelief and disdain at the decline of professional standards, no wonder you couldn't find a good plumber nowadays. So the coroner released the body. Jerome Fantoni organized the funeral. It took place in Jersey, at the church of St Nicholas of Tolentino, a spacious venue, it needed to be, with three hundred and twenty mourners. An orchestra of fifteen and a choir of thirty performed a Monteverdi Requiem, after which everyone retired to the residence of Jerome Fantoni to restore their fluid balance.

This was announced, briefly, in the *New York Times*. The notice added that a private interment would take place next day at Yonkers cemetery. Prendergast and Fisk attended.

They stood under a majestic chestnut, out of the sun, and watched a small group of people walk down a winding driveway through parkland that would cost a hundred dollars an inch in Manhattan. The hearse followed, crunching the gravel as softly as a burglar. The mausoleum had been built in the Yonkers house-style: a square room and a gable roof, all made of simple white stone. FANTONI was carved above the entrance in foot-high capitals. In this leafy setting, the place looked more like a pretentious Wendy house than a tomb. 'Even when they die, the rich live better,' Prendergast said. 'It's a lousy shame.'

A man who was either the funeral director or the *maître d'* at the Waldorf-Astoria walked over to them and said this was a private occasion and would they please move on.

'We're family,' Prendergast said. 'I'm Uncle Sam, and so is he.'

The man liked that. His left eyebrow climbed one millimetre. In the circumstances it was as good as a standing ovation. He turned and went back.

Folding chairs had been arranged in a half-circle. The party sat and listened to a violinist and a cellist play Bach. Even the birds shut up, out of respect. Then the casket got carried inside. Finally there was more Bach, much livelier. The chairs were packed away. Limos drifted down the drive, collected the party, drifted away. Now only Jerome Fantoni was left. He lit a pipe and ambled across the grass to the giant chestnut.

'The purists will never forgive me for tampering with a sonata for unaccompanied violin,' he said, 'but the cello adds such gravitas. The arrangement is my own.'

'I wouldn't change a note,' Prendergast said. 'I'm a tenor sax man myself, and Fisk here favours the harmonica.'

'Yes? Very brave of him. Have you any news?'

'Well, a pattern is emerging, sir,' Fisk said. 'Sightings at Hoboken docks, then at East 84th Street, West 10th Street, your own residence in New Jersey, plus the arson attack on the penthouse on Central Park West. We have your nephew at all those places when Luis Cabrillo was there too.'

'And, of course, we have him ultimately in Cabrillo's Studebaker,' Prendergast added.

'Cabrillo had been my dinner guest. Sammy's idea. There was a girl, too, I fancy Sammy was more interested in her. Nothing memorable happened. I have a lot of dinner guests.'

'This one disappeared,' Fisk said. 'The girl also. Could be they had a lot to disappear from. Cabrillo has known Communist Associates. They're both blacklisted.'

171

'So he's a Red. That's no reason to kill my nephew. What is Cabrillo's motive, for God's sake?'

'Sammy wanted his girl. We found a .38 in Sammy's coat pocket. Maybe Cabrillo fired first.' There was a silence while they all thought about that.

'We found another .38 in the Studebaker,' Prendergast said. 'Under the seat. With written directions about how to find Vinnie Biaggi.'

'Cabrillo.' Fantoni tapped out his pipe on his heel. 'It's all Cabrillo, isn't it?' he said. They walked towards the drive. A squirrel saw its chance and ran to the shreds of tobacco lying in the grass, sniffed, hesitated, backed off. It might be a trap. You got all sorts of freaks and weirdos in this cemetery.

'Three dead, and two on the run,' Fisk said. 'A pattern is definitely emerging, sir.'

'You know where to find us if they turn up for dinner,' Prendergast said. They left him staring at the mausoleum as if someone had told him it had a spelling mistake but he was damned if he could see it.

They turned a bend in the drive, walking slowly because of the heat.

'I feel uncomfortable about using the Mob to find Cabrillo,' Fisk said.

'I don't,' Prendergast said. 'Their budget's bigger than ours.'

He was right about that. Fantoni had one potential clue as to Cabrillo's whereabouts: the black Buick Cabrillo had driven away in. Had vanished in. Fantoni's organization had associates and affiliates all up and down the East Coast. Quite quickly they knew the licence-plate number. It was a start.

3

Time passed. This was out of the control of the CIA, the FBI, the NYPD, or even the Mafia.

Jerome Fantoni was surprised how much he missed Sammy. In his industry, people came and went; and Sammy hadn't been the sharpest knife in the box, but he *had* been loyal and attentive, and in his uncle's scale of values that rated high. There was too much dishonesty in the industry. You hijacked a truckload of booze and then people stole. They got paid for hijacking yet still they stole, a case of Scotch here and there, it all added up. Sammy never stole. He did as he was told and whacked the guys who stole. Now Jerome had lost that portion of loyalty and honesty, and he didn't know why, and this upset him. Jerome wanted balance, equity, closure. He wanted Cabrillo. He had his people out looking for him.

Kim Philby missed Cabrillo in a very different way. He knew – because the Consulate knew what the FBI knew – that Luis had probably gone to San Francisco, presumably after being scared out of Central Park West. Maybe the fright would persuade him to stop making a nuisance of himself; but Philby remembered the Cabrillo of the Double-Cross days: tireless, restless, never satisfied. 'I think he'll be back,' Philby told Harding. 'I'll hang about for a while.'

4

Frank Magee was a cop in Washington, hardworking, honest, reliable. In fifteen years working the toughest part of town, the harbour area, Magee racked up commendations and scars equally. Then, in six months, a burglar with a knife slashed his face and a drunk with a baseball bat broke his arm. The bone healed but most days the arm ached. The Department transferred him to Georgetown, where the crime of choice was adultery. Burglary was left to the possums. Nobody's peach trees were safe. It was a scandal.

Magee was walking down Potomac Street when he saw the Buick parked beside the fire plug, and he said, 'You bastard.' He'd already written five tickets for this car, same offence, same place. He could see the goddamn tickets now, poked in

173

the glove compartment. Son of a bitch. A fire crew would waste valuable seconds, dragging a hose around this heap. He checked the licence plates again. Not even diplomatic! Registered in New goddamn Jersey! He wrote another ticket, slapped it behind the wipers, went and found a phone and told his sergeant.

It was a quiet day. The sergeant didn't like Buicks. His first wife had wanted a Buick, bitched about their Chevy, wasn't going to be happy until they got a fat stinkin' Buick, so in the end he took out a lousy bank loan and bought a Buick and guess what? She still wasn't happy. The sergeant told the captain that Magee was papering a Buick with tickets in Georgetown.

The captain didn't like Georgetown. Everyone there made three times the money he'd ever make and their neurotic wives phoned the police department if the garbage men dropped half an eggshell in the driveway. He talked to an assistant DA and they agreed that this was blatant and persistent contempt of law, aggravated by the fact that the car belonged to a shithead who lived in New Jersey. The assistant DA had gone through Marine Corps boot camp in New Jersey. He drew up a warrant for the arrest of the owner of the Buick and began the process of extradition for trial in DC. It probably wouldn't work, but at least it would pay back New Jersey for shaving his head.

★

Jerome Fantoni had friends in DC, and these friends had friends in the DA's office. One hand shook another. Where was the harm in that? It was only a goddamn parking offence. Before the warrant and the extradition order had been completed, Jerome knew the details.

He could have contracted the job to a local affiliate. But this thing was about Sammy. This was family. He chose one of Sammy's cousins, Chick Scatola. Scatola listened when you spoke, did what you said, and dressed like he worked for IBM, so nobody should look twice at him in Georgetown.

174

'Luis Cabrillo,' Jerome said. 'Your age, height, build. Probably lives on or near Potomac Street. Took my black Buick. Here's the licence number, spare keys. Find the car, you'll find Cabrillo. He knocked off Sammy and he's a Communist sympathizer. Erase him. Lose the man, lose the car, call me when.'

'Cabrillo was never there, sir,' Chick said. 'Nobody will miss him, except the Reds, and who gives a shit about them?'

★

Chick Scatola had the face of IBM but it concealed the soul of MGM. He was a passionate man. He cried at hockey games. He took sex very, very seriously, and as a result he got very little of it, but his prospects had changed since Vinnie Biaggi was made into veal. For years Chick Scatola had lusted after Stevie; but he was too decent, too stupid, too honourable, too scared to make his move: Mount Rushmore on the outside, Mount Etna in the inside. Now she was free and when he offered his deepest sympathies she French-kissed him even deeper and said she was still a virgin after three marriages, what was wrong with men, caught their whanger in their zipper, or what? From then on, their friendship blossomed. He was into her life. Now all he had to do was get into her pants.

He telephoned her at the hairdressing salon, asked did she feel like a trip to Washington, couple of days, see the sights, eat a bucket of clams maybe. 'Why the hell not?' she said. He picked her up in his Chrysler half an hour later. When they hit the Jersey Turnpike the sun was so bright she put on her Ray-Bans. He thought she looked like Audrey Hepburn. And she could share the driving. It was 220 miles to DC. He wanted to arrive fresh. Scatola was not all pure lust. Inside MGM there lurked a piece of IBM.

A MICK FROM
THE STICKS

1

Luis spent a lot of time in the Library of Congress. Intelligence reports must be convincing, especially when they were faked. He researched the Red threat to America. There was much to read.

He took a break, went outside to stretch his legs. A young woman of elfin beauty approached him. 'I saw you in the library,' she said. Big grey eyes and a tiny, whispery voice. 'You were reading that wonderful book by Senator McCarthy.'

'Yes.'

'That man is this nation's moral compass.'

'I'll remember to tell him that.'

'You actually know him? What a privilege! He fights fire with fire, and let the chips fall where they may. He smoked out the Communists in our midst. It had to be done.'

'You're nobody's fool, are you?'

'Well, somebody betrayed America.' Her eyes were huge with patriotism, her voice fine as gauze. 'Somebody stole our atom bomb secrets and gave them to the goddamn Russians, and that was after we went over there and beat that bastard Hitler, and then this sonofabitch Stalin takes all eastern Europe from us, and now we had to save Korea from the Chinese, and today no country, not even America, is safe from the evil tentacles sent to suck our blood by the Communist fucking juggernaut.' There was a little foam at the right-hand corner of her mouth.

When Luis got home, he repeated the conversation to Julie. He mentioned the foam. 'She felt very strongly,' he said.

'Well, I was blacklisted,' Julie said. 'I feel fucking strongly too.'

'I forgot to tell her that.'

'No, you didn't. You chickened out.'

'My mind was on higher things. Money,' he said, before she could ask.

'Bullshit.'

'The two are often confused.'

2

The rain drifted north and left Washington to stew in the kind of humidity that grows fungi in clothes closets and sweaty headlines in newspapers.

A bunch of reporters were hanging about in the shade of the Capitol building, hoping that some news would fall out of the sky like birdshit, when they saw Senator McCarthy heading for the Senate Office Building and they closed in on him. Later they pooled their shorthand notes and agreed on a common record of question and answer.

Q: How you feeling, Joe?

A: Fine. You ought to ask how America feels about President Eisenhower's promise to clean out all the security risks he inherited from the treasonous Truman administration.

Q: The White House say they're working on it. What's the rush?

A: I'll tell you what's the rush: regaining national honour, that's the rush. Our government is still riddled with Communists, fellow-travellers, Truman-type Democrats guilty of blood-stained blunders and when the Soviet agents scream so loudly about McCarthyism, they betray themselves as obviously as they've betrayed their country. You got all that?

Q: Got it. What about the senators who criticize your methods? Accuse you of improper conduct?

178

A: You mean Ralph Flanders.

Q: That's one.

A: The guy's a medical miracle. Only man in the world who has lived so long with neither brains nor guts.

Q: So this flak doesn't bother you, Joe?'

A: Not a bit. But the Commies like it. See the *Daily Worker* yesterday? 'Throw The Bum Out', it said. That's me. Their hatred knows no bounds. And if the Commies hate you . . . Work it out for yourself.

Q: You must be doing something right, is that it?

A: You said it.

Q: Got a story for us, Joe?

A: Soon. I got names, big names. Can't say more. Not yet. Got to protect my source.

Q: Give us a quote, at least. Something.

A: Sure. Want to know what makes me see red? Streaks of yellow in high places.

3

This time the secretary recognized Luis. 'The senator will see you straight away, Mr Arabel,' she said. She opened the inner door and was about to lead the way when she glanced at a black woman sitting in a corner. About forty years old, plain dress, plain face, you saw thousands like her every day in DC, clearing tables, mopping corridors, walking somebody else's dogs. 'I guess he forgot you're here, honey,' the secretary said. 'Let's see if we can smuggle you in too.' The woman stood up and flicked a look at Luis, just enough to check him out: see he was not old, not poor, not sick and not black. Lucky man.

In the senator's office, men were laughing. Except Bobby Kennedy, who stood apart, silent, hands in pockets, looking like he'd found a dollar and lost ten. The noise came from two young men who were bragging to McCarthy. 'We hit the deck running,' one said.

'Dust hasn't settled yet,' the other said.

'You want evidence of subversion, senator? We found a truckload over there.'

'That's terrific,' McCarthy said. 'I mean, that's appalling.' He led the laughter. He saw Luis and waved him forward. He did not see the black woman and she retreated to a corner. 'Mr Arabel! Come in, have a drink . . . Meet these gung-ho foreign investigators. David Schine, consultant, Roy Cohn, the Sub-Committee's chief counsel, this is Mr Arabel, he trained Commandos, so Bobby says. Be good to him or he'll break your arm in five ways.'

'Seven,' Luis said. 'Bourbon and water, please.' They all shook hands. At first glance, Cohn might have been McCarthy's son: same black hair combed straight back, same thick brows over heavy-lidded eyes. But the nose was short and blunt, where McCarthy's was a snowplough; and plenty of girls would have settled for Roy Cohn's shapely mouth and lips. By contrast, Schine had well-groomed blond hair and a chubby, forgettable face. He looked like the sidekick.

'We've been fumigating the State Department's activities in Europe,' Cohn told Luis.

'Libraries and stuff,' Schine said.

'You wouldn't believe the sheer quantity of subversive Red literature we threw out,' Cohn said.

McCarthy gave Luis his drink. 'I'm gonna kick State's butt until I shake out the traitors responsible,' he said.

'We really hustled those guys,' Schine said. 'The goddamn librarians were clearing their shelves before we arrived. Biggest purge since they invented California Syrup of Figs.'

'The newspapers said you purged Dashiell Hammett's detective stories,' Luis said.

'Hammett's a Red,' Cohn said. 'Refused to testify. Contempt of Congress. Went to jail.'

'He's a fine writer.'

'And he was a Party member, for Christ's sake!' Schine said. 'True Americans don't need Red propaganda disguised as detective stories.'

'Interesting. So who should a true American read?'

'Mickey Spillane,' Schine said confidently. 'He's got a great private eye. Mike Hammer. Enjoys killing Commies and he isn't ashamed of it.'

'We don't kill Commies,' McCarthy said. 'We simply make sure they don't louse up America. Simple problem, simple solution.' He noticed the black woman, patiently waiting. 'What you here for, sweetheart? Delivery? Pick-up?'

'Senator,' she said, speaking softly because it never did any good to raise your voice to a white person, 'I've come to ask you to get me my job back again. Please.'

McCarthy was munching peanuts. 'You mean, your boss done sacked you? He's a Red, huh? Got evidence?'

'No, sir. Your Sub-Committee, it got me sacked. You told the Army, you said I was a code clerk, sir.'

'Yeah, I remember,' Cohn said. 'Pentagon employee. You're Mrs Sarah Stone.'

'I worked in the kitchens, sir,' she told him. 'Prepared vegetables and such. Never was a code clerk.'

'But, you had Communist links,' Cohn said. 'We connected you with a staff writer on the *Daily Worker*.'

'Deputy editor,' Schine said. He clicked his fingers. 'Ted Randolph. Right?'

'Sir, I never knew him,' she said. 'Man I knew was a different Ted Randolph, coloured gentleman, drives a truck, married my cousin. I told the Army, but . . .'

McCarthy tossed ice-cubes into his glass and made them swirl.

'I got three children, senator. Their daddy's dead. I can't get no job, nowhere, not since . . .'

Luis could smell boredom in the air. Everything had been going nicely until this black woman made a damn nuisance of herself. Shee-it.

'Bobby, take care of it, would you?' McCarthy said.

Kennedy ushered her out. The door thumped shut.

'Anybody's drink need freshenin'?' McCarthy asked. 'Mine does.'

Schine moved fast to fill the silence. 'Senator, we think you could score big on this book-purge idea. Here's a lady on the Indiana State Textbook Commission discovered that Communist teachers have orders to push the Robin Hood story hard, because he robbed the rich and gave to the poor.' Schine held up a newspaper clipping. 'She says, quote *It's just a smearing of law and order* unquote.'

McCarthy half-closed his eyes. 'Can we ban Robin Hood?' he wondered.

Cohn said, 'We need fresh meat, senator. All those showbiz radicals, Paul Robeson, Larry Adler, suchlike, they've been done to death. That horse won't run.'

They sat and drank and watched him prop his head on his fist and try to make a pencil stand on end. The fifth time it fell over, he quit and straightened up. His knuckles had left a white mark on his face. 'The American Legion's gonna turn up here in half an hour,' he said. 'You boys go and write some crackerbarrel ad libs for me.' Cohn and Schine went out.

McCarthy put his feet on his desk and rested his glass on his stomach. Luis, sitting on a sofa, put his feet on a coffee table. For a while the only sound was the sigh of air-conditioning.

'Politics is work, Mr Arabel,' McCarthy said. 'Folk don't realize how much work. Some soda jerk in Broken Arrow, Wyoming, watches TV, sees a guy in a Brooks Brothers suit, nice tie, white Stetson, makin' a speech full of bullshit that ends *Thank you, my friends, God bless America!* And everyone cheers, and the soda jerk thinks *Jeez, I could do that, easy.* Wrong. Ain't easy.'

'The art is to make it *appear* easy.'

McCarthy thought about that, and moved on. 'I get hate mail. That really burns me. Get plenty of love mail too, but some people out there want me dead. Say I'm just a tool of Wall Street, mouthpiece for millionaires. Say I'm in this anti-Communist crusade for what I can get out of it . . . Jeez, if I wanted money I'd never have left the law. I was the youngest circuit judge ever elected in Wisconsin, did you know that? Fastest, too. I granted divorces on the courthouse steps, two people decide their marriage is bust, why horse around? They know best. You married?'

'Thinking about it.'

182

'I dated Bobby's sister Pat for a while. Not to be. Kennedy kids all fart in perfect pitch. I'm just a Mick from the sticks. Didn't keep me from becoming godfather to Bobby's first-born. That's why I love America, this great democracy, it took me all the way from a tarpaper shack in backwoods Wisconsin to the chairmanship of one of the most powerful Senate sub-committees.'

'The giddy heights,' Luis said. 'Where eagles soar.'

McCarthy wasn't listening. 'See, I'm not an innovator,' he said. 'Not a pioneer. Definitely not a radical, God spare the mark. I'm a simple man, and I simply give America what it wants. What it needs. What it's thankful for.'

He took a swig of drink. Luis realized he was a test-audience for a speech the senator was rehearsing. Hence the little gestures.

'I didn't introduce loyalty boards. The Truman gang did that. They panicked when they knew Americans ceased to trust their government. I didn't smoke out the atom-bomb traitors. Staunch patriots in the House Un-American Activities Committee, led by now Vice-President Richard Nixon, did that good work. But Americans everywhere could still smell rotten apples in the barrel. They asked me to enhance the crusade against security risks. I've done much. There's still much to do.'

'Enhance,' Luis said. 'Enhance. I like it.'

'Yeah, well.' McCarthy yawned. 'Sorry. Had a late night.'

'Your crusade needs enhancing, senator, because from what I read you've made enemies in Washington, important people who are not security risks.'

Now the rehearsal was over. 'There's a few delicate flowers,' McCarthy said. 'Supersensitive sonsofbitches. You've got to enjoy the rough-and-tumble of politics, swap punches and share a drink later, no hard feelings. Soldiers are the worst cry-babies. Marshall won't even say hullo to me.'

'Marshall.' Luis recalled the name from his Double-Cross days, misinforming the *Abwehr* about Allied plans. 'Not the legendary General of the Army George Marshall?'

McCarthy shrugged modestly. 'I upset him.'

'Quite an achievement.'

183

'Well . . . let me see . . . This is from memory, now . . . I said he was involved in a conspiracy so immense and an infamy so black as to dwarf any previous such venture in the history of man.'

'And he took offence?'

'Two years ago. Won't speak to me, won't shake my hand. He's either very, very touchy or . . .' McCarthy hoisted his brows '. . . I scored a hit. Take your choice, I don't give a shit, what matters is *now*. You brought me some of those non-slime snails you were talkin' about, Mr Arabel?'

Luis took a sheet of paper from an inside pocket, unfolded it, and wasted a moment checking its contents.

'Henry Tappan,' he said. 'Lansford Hastings. Stephen Meek. All in the State Department. In the Treasury: Osborne Cross. At the Pentagon: Byron McKinstry and Lucius Fairchild. Bureau of Indian Affairs: Helen Carpenter. Central Intelligence Agency: Marcus Whitman. That's enough for now.'

McCarthy swung his feet off the desk. He opened a drawer and took out a directory, wet a finger, raced through the pages. 'Pentagon's got no Byron McKinstry and no Lucius Fairchild.' The book got slung into the drawer. The drawer got kicked shut. 'You're jerkin' me off, Mr Arabel.'

Now Luis took his feet off the coffee table, but instead of sitting up, he stretched out on the sofa, hands linked behind his head. 'You didn't really expect to find them listed under their real names, senator,' he said. 'You're too smart for that.'

'Real names. You're saying you've got the real names of . . . what?'

'Of cuckoos. Communist agents who have been inserted into government departments where they operate under new identities. In KGB jargon, cuckoos. After the heartless habit of the bird — '

'Yeah, I know about cuckoos. Toss the eggs out the nest and lay their own.' McCarthy rubbed the stubble on his chin. 'Kind of crude, isn't it?'

Luis turned his head and stared. 'I didn't select the code-name, senator. Blame the KGB. Their jargon has always been

184

slapdash.' The pulse in his neck was hammering. Last bend before the home straight.

'The hell with cuckoos. Question is, what can I do with these names?'

'Surely not. The first question concerns remuneration. No money, no more names. And I can get plenty.'

'Yeah? Where from?'

'From an expert cuckoo-wrangler,' Luis said. 'And believe me, cuckoo-wranglers don't come cheap.'

McCarthy found that so funny, he spilled his drink. He walked over to the sofa and Luis had to raise his knees smartly or McCarthy would have sat on him. 'Maybe *you're* a cuckoo, Mr Arabel. Maybe the Kremlin sent you. Why should I believe you?'

Grudgingly, Luis got ready to play his ace. It wasn't much of an ace, the card was old and bent and dog-eared, but it was all he had. 'This is utterly confidential,' he said. 'Men's lives are at stake here.'

'Sure. Speed it up, I've got the Spanish ambassador at three.'

'Certainly. My whole career has been in counter-intelligence. I'm a spycatcher. Throughout the war, I was at the heart of Allied planning. Now I'm a freelance consultant. I'm not short of contacts. We spooks stick together. Friendships forged in battle. General Eisenhower described our operations during D-Day as masterstrokes that bamboozled the German armed forces.'

'Hot shit. How did you do that?'

'Rather like fly-fishing. You see, the trick—'

'Fuck flies.' McCarthy got up and found a putter and practised strokes with an imaginary ball. 'Who can vouch for all this bullshit?' His grip was wrong; he changed it.

'If you want confirmation, call the British Consulate in New York, ask for Harding or . . .' Luis hesitated, then burned another bridge. '. . . or Philby.'

'Fuck golf.' McCarthy tossed the putter into a waste basket. He opened a desk drawer and took out money. 'Here's five hundred,' he said. 'Now you're a consultant. Give me those names.' He took the list. 'I must be crazy,' he said. 'These goddamn cuckoos are using different names now. How can I trace . . .'

'Don't even try,' Luis said. 'Let the State Department do it. And the Treasury. And the Pentagon. You've uncovered the treachery. Now it's their job to smoke out the scoundrels.'

McCarthy thought about it while he turned the list into a paper aeroplane and sent it floating across the room. 'Come back soon,' he said.

On his way out, Luis saw Bobby Kennedy at his desk, head down, writing hard.

'Mrs Sarah Stone seemed an honest lady,' Luis said. 'Has the Pentagon given her job back?'

Kennedy stopped writing but he didn't look up. 'I advised her to write a letter.'

'Can she write?' Luis asked. Kennedy didn't move, didn't speak. 'May I say what a pleasure it has been to meet you,' Luis said, and offered his outstretched hand. Kennedy got to his feet. It was not a handshake. He gave nothing to it. He allowed only the tips of his fingers to be touched, and he withdrew them immediately. It was like shaking hands with a dowager's glove.

Luis went out into the hot, dank midday air, feeling thankful on two counts: he had five hundred bucks, and he wasn't cursed with whatever it was that afflicted Bobby Kennedy. He drove home and parked by the fire plug, where there was always a space. That made three counts.

4

Wagner took a seat in the coffee shop on the fourth level, south side, inner segment of the CIA building and re-read the transcript. Before he could finish it he turned it face-down. He knew the bloody thing by heart. An iced doughnut on a plate looked up at him. Why had he bought the wretched thing? His stomach was in knots. Hot knots. What the Americans called heartburn, damned idiots, it was nowhere near the heart, it was acid in the guts, *magenverstimmung*, that was the word. Thank God, here came Manfred Sturmer. 'Bad news,' Wagner said. 'Terrible, shocking news.'

'You broke your recording of *Tannhäuser*?' Manfred said. 'No? Then it can't be so bad.' He had brought a glass of tea and a thick slice of chocolate cake with whipped cream.

'Read this.'

They were an unlikely pair. The Second World War had brought them together in Spain, which was neutral and therefore convenient for sending spies to Britain. Wagner still looked like what he had been before he took command of Madrid *Abwehr*: a tough, fit brigadier of infantry who enjoyed having his staff on the carpet for the pleasure of pulling it from under their feet and seeing them bounce on their backsides. Manfred could never be mistaken for a soldier. He was chubby and a little dreamy; he seemed always to be remembering something amusing. At Madrid *Abwehr* he had been senior analyst. Everyone had liked working with Manfred Sturmer, he so obviously enjoyed eavesdropping on the enemy. Nobody had liked Wagner but he wasn't there to be liked, he was there to drive the station forward. In 1953 they were not the only German ex-officers in the CIA, but they had shared many experiences in the *Abwehr* and for that reason they valued each other's company.

'This is surreal,' Manfred said. 'Arabel dealing with Joe McCarthy? It's like finding Hitler in bed with Donald Duck.'

'We sent Arabel to spy in England,' Wagner said. 'Here he's boasting of being at the heart of Allied counter-intelligence.'

Manfred spooned down whipped cream while he studied the text. Wagner watched him and swallowed hard to dispel the taste of bile. 'Maybe it's a hoax,' Manfred said. 'McCarthy attracts a lot of *schmucks*.'

'He gave this one five hundred dollars.'

'All right, suppose this is Arabel talking to McCarthy. He never actually *says* he was a double agent, does he? And even if he was, maybe he was screwing the British.' Manfred started on the chocolate cake.

'No, no. Look at what he says about Allied deception at D-Day,' Wagner said harshly. 'Eisenhower called it a counter-intelligence masterstroke. He said it bamboozled the *Wehrmacht*.' His stomach clenched. 'How can you shovel down that American muck when I'm telling you that we spent the entire war throwing money at a traitor and a swindler for selling us a pack of lies?'

'My dear Wagner, do not agitate yourself. It's not as if this scoundrel Arabel lost the war for the Third Reich. The Russians did that.'

'Not so loud, man.'

'Oh. Sorry.'

'That sort of talk doesn't go down well in the CIA.'

'I forgot.' Manfred gave back the transcript. 'I am shocked, of course, but surprised? No. I never had total faith in Arabel. Too good to be true. Consider the facts. We sent a flock of agents to England. How many were caught? One in ten? My dear Wagner, was that credible? Convincing? And Arabel's informants were such staunch spies, so fearless, always harvesting such valuable, such secret information, never getting caught! Transmitting oh-so-long radio reports, night after night, yet constantly evading detection! Did you never think twice about our astonishing good fortune? I know I did.'

'I don't care.' This was a lie: Wagner's thunderously black expression said as much. 'Arabel betrayed the Reich. He turned us into unconscious collaborators in his damned counterfeit deceptions.'

'The deceptions were not counterfeit,' Manfred said. 'The deceptions were genuine. Let us be precise about our confusion.'

'When I think of all that wasted effort,' Wagner muttered. He made his hands into fists, and took a deep breath. 'He made puppets of us, Manfred. And if this Arabel thing leaks into the CIA, our careers will be finished. We must find a way to deny it.'

'Good diagnosis,' Manfred said. 'Wrong prognosis. If you gave the problem more thought, instead of sitting there looking like Siegfried after he has trodden in a heap of fresh and steaming dragon's dung, you would realize that Arabel will be a threat as long as he lives.' Manfred had finished the chocolate cake. He nibbled on the iced doughnut. 'Either he or we must die. It can't be me, I've just paid for a series of tennis lessons.'

'I'll kill him. I'll strangle the swine. It will give me pleasure.'

'First you must find him. Would you recognize Arabel if you saw him? He was one of forty agents whom we sent into England, and that was ten or twelve years ago. People change, Wagner. Arabel might now be bald, or bearded. Or both.'

'Maybe. Or maybe neither. I kept a picture of Arabel on the wall of my office. He can't change his thieving eyes, can he?' Wagner scowled at Manfred. 'To think I got that bastard the Iron Cross.'

'And all the time he was selling us horseshit,' Manfred Sturmer said. 'You're looking awfully gaunt, you know. Why don't you get something to eat?'

5

Julie was not at home. Luis was disappointed. He'd had a small triumph; telling her would have doubled the pleasure. He stared at himself in a mirror. A bit thin, he thought. Working too hard, maybe. Immediately he knew what to do. A Frenchwoman in Caracas had taught him how to cook real bouillabaisse. He felt armed and confident.

He went out, found a fresh-fish shop, and bought some halibut, baby cod, red mullet and whiting. Also shrimp. Elsewhere he got garlic, pimientos, leeks, canned tomatoes and olive oil. The rest, he knew, was in the kitchen.

She was getting out of Gregg DeWolf's car as he reached the house. Her tight tennis shirt and short tennis skirt gave Luis the sour taste of jealousy. He swallowed it. 'Awfully kind of you,' he said to DeWolf. 'I do hope your real estate activities haven't suffered from your absence.'

'He talks like Henry James,' she told DeWolf, 'only worse.'

'Hell of a backhand,' DeWolf said. 'I got murdered.' He looked quite happy about it as he drove away. His car was an opentop Morgan, a brisk little English sports job. Its exhaust growled like a well-fed lion.

They went inside. 'Just as well I turned up, or you'd have kissed him goodbye,' Luis said.

'I did that already, *at* the club, *on* the lips, and what the hell business is it of yours?' she asked cordially, and went away to take a bath.

★

Potomac Street drowsed in the afternoon heat. Too early for anyone to come home from work. Hired help had quit for the day. No kids in the street. This time of year, Georgetown kids were high in the hills, in summer camp. So all was calm and quiet. There was even a parking space near the corner. Chick Scatola slid the Chrysler into the slot. 'Dunno how long I'll be, gorgeous,' he said. 'You have to go someplace, the can maybe, leave a message on top of the dash.'

'Like sayin' what?'

He looked at Stevie. She was serious. A knockout, yes, but also serious and difficult to figure sometimes. 'Like sayin' *Gone to the can, back in five,*' he told her.

She hunched up, arms wrapped around her legs, and made her mouth sulky. 'Five ain't enough. First I got to find a place, a bar probly, then us ladies ain't built like a guy, you just poke it an' pee, we need time.'

'Fine,' Chick said. 'Back in ten, fifteen. Whatever. Twenty. Take as long as you need, babe.'

'This message I wrote. Someone comes by, they know. See me come back, they know where I been an' everythin'.'

'So what? Everyone goes to the can.'

'Ain't nice. Ain't ladylike.'

Jesus H. Christ, Chick thought. It had not been an easy trip. When Stevie drove, she drove too fast. Last thing he needed was to get pulled over by a highway patrol wanting to know what was his hurry. And when he saw a motel, suggested take a break, couple of hours, share a shower, make some whoopee, she just said, 'I hate that motel.' Mostly what she did was

190

chain-smoke and change the station on the car radio. Now they're in DC and he has a job to do, she's pissed because some passing stranger might know she had to take a leak. Ain't ladylike, for Chrissake. 'I never met a lady had any choice,' he said. 'I mean, we're not talkin' about some optional extra here. Ain't like you signed up for whitewall tyres.' It was a joke, he had a nice smile on, but she just hunched down deeper. *I drove two hundred an' twenty miles to argue about female bladder problems*, he thought. But look, she was a dish. Even tied in a goddamn knot, she was a dish. 'Listen, this is easy,' he said. 'Write the stupid message in code. Write "Gone fishin'." Write "Gone crazy." Write *any*thin'.'

'Mental health ain't somethin' to joke about.'

He took his briefcase and got out and shut the door and walked away. He did not look back. Women. You couldn't live with them and sometimes you still couldn't live with them, and this was one.

The steambath heat swamped him. He slowed to a saunter, strolling from one shade tree to another, moving like the natives did, nice and easy, and within half a block he saw the Buick, right where he'd been told to look, next to a fire plug. He had Jerome's spare keys. Nobody was around. He unlocked the car and got into the back. He locked the doors and stretched out on the floor behind the front seats. Not a bad fit. Comfortable enough. He had a compact-model body, five-nine, ten stone, no fat, all he ate was fruit and salad and pasta and every morning he did ten lengths of the pool at the Y, year in year out, result he had stomach muscles so clearcut you could play chequers on them. One reason he'd wanted to stop at that motel was so Stevie could admire these muscles, trace them with her fingertip. Maybe stroke his ass too. It was a perfect curve, that ass of his. Two perfect curves.

Back to work.

He took a sand-coloured dust-sheet from the briefcase, shook it loose and draped it over himself from head to foot. Didn't want any snoopy passerby to see him lying there, get curious, call a cop. Next to his hands he put a six-inch butcher knife, a spring-loaded sap, and a short-barrelled .32 Colt automatic. He would let this creep Cabrillo get behind the wheel, smack him hard twice and then chop something vital while the creep's mind was elsewhere. Chick had taken a course in first aid at the Y, he knew what parts were vital. He wouldn't need the gun. The gun was purely for self-protection. Biggest industry in DC was crime, everyone knew that. Next came politics, which also was crime, well-known fact. Damn city was riddled with Commies, robbing the taxpayer blind. Only man with guts enough to fight 'em was Joe McCarthy. Now *there* was a guy who kept swinging with both fists. That was the spirit of 'seventy-six. The spirit that made America great. Chick rested more easily, knowing that the senator was out there, fighting the good fight. He used the briefcase as a pillow. This could be a long wait. Wrong. It lasted seventeen minutes.

★

People never learn. They open the trunk to lift something out, a box maybe, and it's heavy enough to need both hands, so they drop the keys in the trunk, lift out the box and slam the trunk shut. Force of habit. Now they've locked themselves out of their car. Happens all the time.

Demand creates supply. Walt Garrison, a mechanic with a Washington garage that took a lot of calls for breakdowns, became expert at opening locked cars for people who couldn't believe how stupid they'd been. He was thirty-five and in line for promotion and a lot more pay when that job went to his boss's wife's cousin, also a mechanic but a knuckle-head who couldn't count to eleven without taking one sock off.

Walt quit.

Plenty of other garages wanted to hire him. He didn't want another boss.

Next Sunday, as he came out of church, he told the pastor he was searching for a new career but . . . And he shrugged. 'Every man has a gift,' the pastor said. 'The trick is to find your gift and make it pay.' Walt thanked him. The pastor

192

smiled: another satisfied customer. Walt strolled around town and stole a blue Mercury sedan, just for practice, and next morning a used-car dealer who wouldn't know a scruple from a cocktail olive bought it for $500. Walt had found his gift. That was four years ago.

Three rules kept him out of trouble. He never stole more than one car a week. He only stole cars he could sell immediately. And he never took longer than twelve seconds to get into a car. Longer than that, he moved on, left it.

He worked Georgetown about once a month. He liked the summer afternoons because the heat kept people indoors. There was a Labrador dog stretched out on the sidewalk of Potomac Street but all it did was open one eye as he stepped over it. He saw the black Buick, liked it, and fingered the assortment of picks in his pocket, feeling for the right ones.

Chick Scatola heard the scratchy tickle of steel and came wide awake in a hurry. This wasn't right. He held his breath and felt his pulse pounding the sides of his skull. Cabrillo had keys, this was *wrong*. Then the door opened, someone grunted as he dropped into the driver's seat, and the door clunked shut. Walt Garrison looked at what he'd got and was pleased. Recent model, low mileage, clean condition.

Chick Scatola eased the dustcover off his body. Slowly and silently he got to his knees and peered over the front seat. What he saw was Walt Garrison, also on his knees, fumbling behind the dash. 'Shit,' Chick said. That was a mistake.

Walt was so startled that he turned fast and banged his head hard on the wheel. He ended up sprawling on the floor, blood chasing down his forehead, spilling off his nose. It was only split skin but it looked like a hatchet attack. 'Who the fuck are you?' he demanded.

'Get your ass out of here. This is my car, you dumb prick.'

'Yeah? You sleep in your car?' Walt suddenly found the situation very funny. 'Let's see your licence and registration, then.' He tasted blood and now it wasn't at all funny.

Chick shook his head, a gesture of disgust but Walt didn't know that Chick had just driven from New York and didn't need an argument with this schmuck who was lying beyond his reach or he'd use the sap to bust him up good, except he couldn't do that because if he did, the creep Cabrillo wouldn't get into a car with a body in it. Double-shit. 'Just beat it, for Chrissake,' he said. 'You're out of your depth, Jack.'

The blood made the difference. Normally Walt would have tipped his hat, cut his losses and left. But he was bleeding because of this piece of piss who didn't even want the lousy Buick except to sleep in. Walt spat a stringy mix of blood and saliva. 'I need a handkerchief,' he said, and took an automatic out of his pants pocket. 'Move your ass!' he shouted and fired a shot past Chick's head. That too was a mistake. Chick dropped out of sight, grabbed his .32 and pumped rounds through the seat. Most missed. Two hit, the throat and the chest. Then Walt was fighting for his life, aiming low, guessing where Chick was, finally getting lucky with one shot to the head. The firing was all over in eight seconds and both men were dead within a minute, a total waste, the product of arrogance, poor judgement and the taste of blood.

The best place for a quiet gunfight in a street is inside a sturdy car such as a Buick, loaded with soundproofing. A couple of neighbours thought they heard a ripple of back-firing, went to the window, saw nothing. 'People should fix their mufflers,' they said.

Luis worked fast. Olive oil, chopped carrot, leek and onion went into a heavy pan with a crushed clove of garlic, and all cooked to a golden brown. Meanwhile he boned and cut the fish into chunks. Slid them into the pan, added half a can of tomatoes, some herbs, didn't have fish stock so a cup of white wine and a splash of water had to do. Simmered the lot until he felt that the fish was nearly done, threw in the shrimps and the chopped pimientos and simmered a few minutes more, seasoned it, squeezed a lemon into it, gave it a healthy drink of wine, and one minute later she came downstairs in a while sleeveless dress that made her look so virginal that his toes curled. Well, some days things ended up right.

194

'Bouillabaisse,' he said. 'Notorious aphrodisiac. Hungry?'

'Yeah. Peckish.'

He poured the bouillabaisse into a large tureen and carried it to the table. She brought bowls and spoons and bread. They sat and looked. 'You're six inches off the deck, Luis,' she said. 'You're going to burst into flame unless you tell me, so for Pete's sake speak. What's happened?'

'Oh, nothing of huge significance. I met Senator McCarthy again, and this time I conned him out of five hundred dollars.'

'I see.' She put her elbows on the table and rested her chin on her hands. 'And how did you do that, Luis?'

'The old Eldorado technique. Tell 'em what they want to hear. McCarthy wants names, so I sold him names. Easy money.'

'You're serious? You sold names to McCarthy?' When Luis nodded, she stood and picked up the tureen by its handles and dumped the bouillabaisse on his head and left the dish there, upside-down. It was swiftly, deftly done. She had excellent hand-to-eye coordination. DeWolf had found that. Luis was too shocked to move. The bouillabaisse was hot and thick and for a long moment he couldn't see. When he blinked his eyes back to some sort of sticky vision, she had gone.

He didn't move. The carpet was ruined. No point in trying to talk. He knew her too well for that. He collected a piece of halibut with his tongue and chewed it and wondered if other couples behaved like this. Something was stuck to his upper lip. Baby cod, perhaps. And he could smell a trace of garlic.

She came downstairs, dressed differently and carrying a suitcase. She scooped up the car keys.

'I may have overdone the paprika,' he said.

'Just stay away from me, you pathetic bastard.'

'A little parsley would have helped.'

The front door slammed.

A mouthful of food had slithered into his right hand. He raised it to his mouth before it could get away. The tureen was securely lodged on his head, so it must be his hat size, more or less. What a curious coincidence. His face was drying quickly. Bits of fish began dropping off it. Should he catch them, or let them fall? If he caught them he could eat them, but it would never amount to a full meal, would it? He was trying to decide, when the front door opened and she came in. 'There are two bodies in the Buick,' she said.

'Oh.' Luis licked his lips and tasted tomato. 'Well, there's a surprise.'

'Is it? Feels more like routine.' She dropped her suitcase and leaned against the doorway. 'And you look like the King of Siam.'

★

When Senator McCarthy first exposed the grim scale of Red subversive activity, back in 1950, he took a few shots at the CIA. If the agency had done its job properly, McCarthy said, it would have flushed out all these traitors. Made you wonder whether they were being protected by Leftists inside the agency. So the CIA bugged his office. Just routine.

McCarthy suspected this and asked the Justice Department to protect his privacy. The FBI sent a man to sweep the rooms. He found the CIA's bugs and taps, cleaned and dusted and tested them, and installed a feed to the FBI's department of electronic surveillance, a thousand yards away. Hoover didn't like McCarthy. Bastard was stealing his thunder.

The name Arabel meant nothing to the headquarters of the FBI. Then Arabel was linked to Harding and Philby at the British Consulate in New York, and Washington asked the New York office to find out what the hell was going on.

'You're cosy with Frobisher,' Prendergast told Fisk. 'Take him to lunch. Take his moustache too.'

They met at the Oyster Bar in Grand Central Station.

'Cabrillo,' Fisk said. 'Now a.k.a. Arabel.'

'My goodness. Has he robbed another bank?'

'He's in Washington DC, doing business with Senator Joseph McCarthy.' When Frobisher chuckled, Fisk said, 'Surprised us, too. We're hoping your chaps in British Intelligence can shed some light.'

'Nothing to do with us, old boy. Scout's honour.'

'Then why is he hiding behind his wartime code-name?'

'Beats me. Tell you what: give me his address, I'll go and ask him.'

'Shall we order?'

'You've lost him again, haven't you? You can't find him.'

'I recommend the clams,' Fisk said. Enough was enough.

★

You couldn't see the bodies unless you looked in the car. Death had pulled the pins out of the joints and gravity had done the rest. They sprawled on the floor of the Buick, each looking as if he'd shovelled fifteen tons of Number One coal and was too bushed to climb into bed.

'How do you know they're dead?' Luis asked. He had got rid of the tureen and put his head under the cold tap for a few seconds, but his eyes still felt sticky. He leaned against the car and blinked a lot.

'That one's got a hole in the head. This one isn't breathing. Still, don't take my word. Check 'em out, maybe they're playin' possum.' Julie opened the driver's door. The peppery stink of explosives surged out.

'Holy smoke!' Luis said. He elbowed the door shut.

'It ain't smoke, and it ain't holy,' she said. 'And unless you want to choke as you drive, I say let it all out.' She opened the door again. Luis had his mouth open but no words came. 'Or you could tell the cops,' she suggested. He shook his head. 'Then we're gonna have to drive this shambles out of here,' she said.

He looked at her as if she were a stranger. His eyes were wide open and blank, like a child's. 'Hey, snap out of it!' she said, and kicked his ankle. He stumbled, and bit the inside of his mouth. The pain shocked him out of his stupor. 'Look,' he said, very calmly, and pointed. 'It's the triple virgin.' He was calm because calmness was all he had left.

'Hi, you guys,' Stevie called. 'Small world, huh?' They watched her approach. There was no way they could stop her. 'I was parked by the corner,' she said, 'saw you guys

197

come out, knew you straight off, fifty yards away, I got twenty-twenty vision, my optician says I could have been a fighter pilot, or maybe if I took up skeet shooting, you know, I could win Olympic gold, just takes *hot shit in the fuckin' springtime!*'

'Did you kill these two?' Julie asked.

'Not me. Did you?'

'We never met them,' Luis said. 'Every time I meet *you*, however, it's guns and homicide and bodies left lying.'

Stevie took a closer look. 'That's my date, in the back. Chick Scatola. Him an' me came here on business. This other . . .' She shrugged.

'Your date?' Julie said. 'You don't seem too knocked out about what happened to him.'

'He kept tellin' me I drive too fast. He got on my tits.'

'Hell of an epitaph,' Luis muttered.

'I drive better'n most men. Sammy Fantoni drove like he was leadin' the Veterans' Day Parade. Sammy and Chick were cousins. Maybe that explains a lot.'

'I don't really believe I'm saying this,' Julie said, 'but we gotta get rid of these bodies. This is Potomac Street. They got *standards.*'

'Dump 'em in West Virginia,' Stevie said. 'They got lots of wilderness over there. Hell, they got wilderness in West Virginia ain't hardly never been touched yet by nobody at all.'

'A triple negative,' Luis said. 'And in all this heat.'

'You got fishy gunk on your shirt,' she told him.

'West Virginia,' Julie said.

★

Kim Philby made a transatlantic call to Peter Cottington-Beaufort and told him that the Consulate had traced Luis Cabrillo to Washington and to Senator McCarthy's office, where they discussed naming names.

'When he tried to blackmail me with his so-called memoirs, I thought he was bluffing,' Philby said. 'But maybe he really knows something. Why else would he go to McCarthy?'

198

'Yours would be a considerable scalp for the senator to wave from Capitol Hill.'

'So would yours, Peter.'

'How could Cabrillo possibly . . . No, I withdraw the question. Irrelevant. Pity you weren't able to achieve expunction when you had the chance. Still, you know where your man is, don't you? Hurry down to Washington and do it yourself this time.'

Long pause. The line crackled.

'Either you're scratching your head,' Peter said, 'or a hungry crab is chewing on the transatlantic cable.'

'I've never done an expunction. Arranged plenty, but never actually done one.'

'Remember that the bullet does the expunging. All you do is squeeze the trigger. I'm told that's hugely reassuring.' The line went dead.

★

West Virginia was easy to find. Interstate 66 came out of Washington and barrelled straight across Virginia for sixty or seventy miles until it hit the Appalachian Mountains, got discouraged and called it a day.

Luis was hungry. Lunch had been skimpy. He'd taken a quick shower, then driven the Buick with Julie sitting alongside and both corpses stiffening in the back, under a sand-coloured dust sheet. Nobody had said much. Now he signalled to Stevie, who was following in the Chrysler, and they pulled off at a roadside diner. Luis was getting out when Julie said, 'News on the hour.' She turned on the car radio and searched for a Washington station, WMAL or WTOP. 'Might have something about the Potomac Street massacre. You never know.' What she got was a live broadcast of Senator McCarthy's four p.m. press conference. She groaned. Luis brightened like a dog hearing his owner's key in the door. 'Bet you he uses my names,' he said.

A couple of hundred miles to the north, Kim Philby was in a bar at Idlewild Airport, waiting for his flight to be called.

The television set showed *Tom and Jerry* until the station suddenly cut to Senator McCarthy. 'Goose the volume a bit, would you?' Philby asked the barman. Together they watched the unlovely image, listened to the drumroll of accusations. 'Dunno if he scares the Kremlin,' the barman said, 'but he makes me want to hide in the broom closet.' He went away and came back. 'I done nothin' wrong,' he said. 'Nothin' un-American.' Philby nodded and the barman left him alone.

'. . . *and this crusade – I make no apologies for calling it that, because I speak for all decent, loyal, Christian Americans in our struggle against brutal and Godless Communism – this crusade has not made me popular in certain quarters of Washington. They call me a muck-raker. Well, ladies and gentlemen, I was born an' raised in the fine state of Wisconsin, an' my family kept hogs, an' it was my job to clean out them hog-pens, an' I speak with the voice of experience when I say you can't rake muck unless there's muck to be raked. We didn't call it muck, but I won't go into that. Spell it how you like, it's here in Washington DC, and the stain of treachery and disloyalty has leaked into all the main departments of government, and soaked so deep into the fabric of America that I believe it'll take a carload of picks an' shovels to dig it out, and a river of disinfectant to wash it clean. Why, just this morning, a young man came to me with a list of names.'* [McCarthy unfolded a piece of paper.] *'I cannot and will not reveal that young man's identity. Unlike some, I do not betray my friends, who have taken great personal risks to secure intelligence that is crucial to this nation's security from foreign foes.'*

'Damn right!' Luis said. Julie turned up the volume.

'I will say this: these names shocked me. I've taken a few licks recently from the high-falutin' bleedin'-heart liberals who don't like my style but cannot deny my facts, and I thought my skin was pretty tough, but I'm here to admit that I shuddered when I saw these names and knew the powerful positions they hold – in the State Department, the Pentagon, the Treasury, a dozen other agencies of government where card-carrying Communists or

Commie sympathizers can secretly – secretly – inflict lethal damage. These names . . .' [McCarthy flourished the paper] *'. . . represent a deadly virus which seeks to invade Americanism. I intend to reverse its course. I intend to turn this into the death warrant for all twisted, warped, Leftist traitors who have infiltrated our great country. It won't be easy. I have some experience in this area.'* [McCarthy allowed himself a knowing grin.] *'For a start, I pledge to place this list in a secure lodgement. When I leave here, I will hand it over to the senior partner of the most respected firm of lawyers in Washington, the eminent firm of Grant, Delaney, Meyer & Stubbs, for safe keeping. And I'll tell you why. There is a Presidential Order – think of that, a Presidential Order – which states that nobody, nobody, in the State Department is allowed to give any information as to the disloyalty or Communistic activities of any, I repeat any, State Department employee. It gets worse. Nobody in the State Department can say anything, not one word, about the employment of anybody there! You see what we're up against. You see what barriers are raised. You see why certain men . . .'* [McCarthy glanced at the paper and shook his head.] *'. . . why these men remain in office. But I'm not going to quit. I want you to know that as soon as Secretary of State John Foster Dulles gives us all an indication of his good faith by lifting this odious veil of secrecy, then I will be glad to give him these names, and then the Senate Sub-Committee of which I am proud to be chairman can get down to the business of investigating those alien agents who are dedicated to selling America down the river. These men are well hidden. Well disguised. I have their real names, the names they were born with. But today, acting on instructions from their foreign masters, they hide behind false identities. Masks they have worn so long that their faces have grown to fit them. They may be listening to me right now. I hope so. They know who they are. Who they think they are. But not for long. The masks will soon be off. I have dedicated my life to exposing subversives. Ain't gonna stop now.'* [McCarthy clenched the fist that held the paper.] *'Can't stop. It just ain't in me.'*

End of statement. Back to the studio for news, traffic, weather.

'Love it!' Stevie said. 'Ain't he somethin' special? McCarthy makes Errol Flynn look like he's runnin' for dogcatcher.'

'He didn't use the names I gave him,' Luis complained. 'I went to all that trouble, and he never used a single damn name!'

'He's a smooth operator,' Julie said.

'Love him.' Stevie kissed the radio. 'I'm gonna send him money.'

'He missed his chance,' Luis said. 'He dropped the bloody ball.'

'No, he didn't,' Julie said sadly. 'I detest the bastard but that was a brilliant piece of politics.'

'Brilliant bollocks. He missed — '

'Shut up and listen. Look how he handled it. He used his old familiar technique, the list of names. Done it before. This time he puts a new hat on it: secrecy. These are *secret* names. We're privileged to know of the *existence* of the secret but not the actual names. Once he reveals the names, he's played his cards, got nothing left. So he hands them to his lawyers and blames it on State Department secrecy! Now that's smart. If State can have secrets, so can Joe.'

'Yeah!' Stevie said. 'They're just bums in stripey pants.'

'Hey, wait,' Luis said. 'Where's the logic?'

'Who gives a shit? It sounds good, and everyone hates Washington.' Julie batted away some flies, probably attracted by the smell of death. 'What matters is the way he dumps all the blame on Dulles. And what's perfect is his timing. Late afternoon. He'll grab headlines in the evening papers but it'll be too late for the Administration to reply. The news'll be all McCarthy.'

'There's still tomorrow,' Luis said.

'Tomorrow's another world. Tomorrow nobody's listening. What everyone remembers is Joe McCarthy found another bunch of Reds in the government.'

'He did, too,' Stevie said.

'Let's go and eat,' Luis said.

At Idlewild, Philby had ordered another drink. He too had been impressed. The brave young man whom McCarthy would not name was probably Cabrillo. And if McCarthy could create such high-grade hokum when Cabrillo gave him ghosts to work with, imagine what uproar he would provoke if Cabrillo provided some flesh-and-blood traitors. Philby felt the skin crawl at the back of his neck.

6

They took Route 55 over the Appalachians, past Star Tannery, Wardensville, McCauley, Needmore, and Fort Run. 'Extraordinary country,' Luis said. 'The bigger the name, the smaller the town.' Julie wasn't interested. 'Keep goin',' she said. Farmland, farmland. Useless. Where were the swamps when you needed one?

At Petersburg they stopped to check out the map. South and west lay Monongahela National Forest, 100 miles of it or more. Monongahela had mountains, creeks, caverns, and rugged names like Red Lick, Elkwater, Smoke Hole.

'Real wildernessy,' Stevie said. 'You should of brought quicklime. Or acid.'

'You done this kind of thing before?' Julie asked.

'I go to the movies.'

'Where do we get quicklime?'

'Yellow Pages?'

That ended the discussion.

A month ago, Julie thought, *I was a happy victim of the witch hunt, poor but harmless, bugged by the FBI, slinging burgers and beers on Mooney's graveyard shift. Then Luis appears and I get sacked, evicted, torched, hustled off to DC and now look at me: deep in the sticks, trying to find a home for a pair of bullet-holed cadavers that I never met before, with the help of a fruitcake who believes everything Warner Brothers ever said.*

'This has turned into a very peculiar day,' she said. 'Let us for Christ's sake do what we have to do, and go get a good steak somewhere.'

They drove into the forest. In the early evening, the slanting rays of the sun made it magnificent. The road climbed between vast stands of oak and sycamore, merging with pine and cedar as they penetrated the mountains. Cliffs stood sheer, and large birds wheeled up there, and streams rushed below. It looked virgin, untouched, superbly original. It probably was.

After twenty miles of this, Luis pulled over at a scenic viewpoint and they got out. Stevie in the Chrysler pulled in behind them. It was odd to feel a chill in the air. Washington was virtually at sea-level. This place was not far off a mile high.

'Any suggestions?' Luis asked.

'My ears popped twice,' Stevie said. 'Bet they get a hell of a good TV picture here.'

'I say we find a lake,' Julie said. 'Dirt road leads down to it. Handbrake off, windows open a few inches, big splash, air bubbles, two-three minutes, out of sight. In the movies — '

'No, no. Jesus!' Stevie waved at the scenery. 'This Buick is gassed up, the motor's pumped full of oil an' shit, you can't just pollute their water! Which people drink!' Julie was silent. 'You wouldn't like it,' Stevie said, 'if West Virginia folk dumped their cars in the Central Park Reservoir.'

'Forget lakes,' Luis said. 'The oil floats to the surface and someone gets suspicious . . .' He shrugged. 'I've got a better idea. Set fire to the wretched thing and shove it over the edge. That's a five hundred foot drop. Gas tank cracks open, raging inferno, nothing left to identify.'

'Gets my vote,' Julie said.

'I'm ashamed of you guys,' Stevie said. 'Here it is, middle of summer, here we are, middle of a forest, trees down there must be dry as tinder, you want to start a forest fire? Jesus! Get smart.'

Julie flung a small rock into the abyss. 'I can see how you wore out three husbands, honey,' she said.

'I just go by what the signs say. No camp fires except in designated sections of Official Recreation Areas.'

'How big is a designated section?' Luis asked. 'Could we burn a Buick in one?'

'I threw that rock real hard,' Julie said, 'and look where it landed. Brambles and briars an' suchlike. Never reached the trees. What say we just tip these two over the edge and hope they make a hole in the bushes? Seems like nobody ever goes down there.'

''Cept the buzzards an' the coyotes,' Stevie said.

They looked at her. 'Is that an obstacle?' Luis asked.

'Hell, no. It's a solution.'

They perched the bodies, one at a time, on the parapet, gave a shove, and watched them tumble through space until they got swallowed by the undergrowth. 'Now it'll be easier to lose the car,' Julie said.

'I'll give the bloody thing away,' Luis announced.

By the time they got out of the forest and across the Appalachians and into the town of Harrisburg, dusk had fallen. They drove to a large, noisy bar-diner. Luis left the keys in the ignition and the windows open. They came out an hour later and the Buick was still there. 'It's cursed,' he said. 'There's a hex on it.'

'So just dump it,' Stevie said.

'Nobody dumps a new Buick,' Stevie said. 'The cops find it, they'll be in Potomac Street within the hour.'

'Damn.' Luis kicked a tyre. 'Damn damn damn.'

They drove on, until Luis pointed to a roadsign that said Washington Airport. 'I have an idea,' he said. 'We'll lose it in the crowd.' He took the airport turnoff. Stevie followed.

He drove into the long-stay parking lot and tossed the keys to an attendant. 'Your lucky day,' he said. 'My company just transferred me to Tokyo for ten years. Shan't need the Buick. She's all yours.'

'Kind of low on gas, ain't she?' the attendant said. But by then Luis and Julie were striding towards Stevie's Chrysler.

Nobody had much to say until they crossed the bridge into Washington.

'Anyway, I never wore out three husbands,' Stevie said. 'Luis here shot Vinnie. He shot him with that pistol I gave.'

'You've got to get that idea out of your mind,' he said.

'Never think I don't appreciate what you done, 'cus I do. You got my appreciation, Luis, any day. Or night.'

'Forget it!' he shouted. 'You got the wrong guy! I never saw Vinnie. Not alive anyway. Never used the lousy pistol. Not me, lady. Look elsewhere.'

'Yeah, yeah,' Stevie muttered. 'They all say that.'

She parked the car, not by the fire plug. They went into the house. Julie took her to the guest bedroom.

He was brushing his teeth when Julie said, 'Where did you get the names, Luis? No bullshit. I just need to know.'

He rinsed his mouth, went away and came back with a book called *Oregon or Bust: How The Pioneers Crossed America*. 'I lifted the names of men who went west by wagon train. Good, solid, convincing American names.'

'Phoney. Not real people.'

He nodded. 'Senator McCarthy isn't obsessed with the truth.'

As they lay in bed, he said, 'If Chick Scatola was Sammy Fantoni's cousin, it's a fair bet he got sent here by Jerome Fantoni.'

'Yes. You just worked that out?'

'Do you think Jerome wants his car back?'

'Sure. That's why his gorilla was carrying a sap, a butcher's knife and a loaded automatic. Stevie told me he was here to do a job, that's all she knows, but go ahead and ask her yourself, she might open up to you since you gave Vinnie the Creep a hole in the head.'

Luis went to the guest bedroom. He was soon back.

'She sleeps in the buff,' he said. 'A lesser man would have faltered but as you know I have the pluck and courage of a British grenadier.' He got into bed. 'Chick Scatola's line of work was population control. He whacked people. It's too risky to live here now.'

'Damn,' she said. 'Just as I figured out how the stove works.'

FAKE
EARTHQUAKE WARNINGS

1

Wagner had been writing his memoirs for five years. The stack of manuscript stood a foot high.

1953 was too soon to seek publication. Timing was everything in life, and when the moment came, Wagner would be ready. Ready to demonstrate that the Third Reich had not been defeated in 1945. The *Wehrmacht* had run out of war materials – bullets, tanks, fuel, men – but the *Abwehr* had triumphed in the intelligence war. A victory that nobody could deny.

And Wagner had been fortunate enough to be in the vanguard of this stunning success. Right to the very end, the *Abwehr's* network of agents in England had sent a stream, a river, a flood of secret information. They had given the German High Command a precious insight into what the enemy was doing and planning to do. And Wagner's best agent, by a mile, was Arabel.

Wagner's memoirs were rich with gems from Arabel's reports. In fact he had enough material to make two books. 'I might as well burn it,' he told Manfred Sturmer.

'Shred it, burn it, dance on the ashes,' Manfred said.

'I'll tell you what's worst. Little episodes keep coming back to me. Do you remember when Arabel complained we were making him work too hard? And we parachuted another agent into England to help him?'

'Arabel told us he met the man. Said they made a good team.'

'The truth is, our man must have been caught the minute his boots touched the ground.'

'Nasty shock,' Manfred said. 'Probably got shot. Even nastier.'

'I'm going to shoot that treacherous bastard as soon as I find him.'

'Of course you are.' They were silent for a moment, and then Manfred laughed. Wagner frowned. 'You must admit,' Manfred said, 'Arabel brightened up our dull lives.' Wagner turned away. His *magenverstimmung* was biting again.

2

Kim Philby had checked into Hampton Hotel, near Union Station. Very near. Sometimes his room vibrated as a train pulled out. The bathrooms were shared, the furniture was gothic, the elevator clanked like a Sherman tank. Not important. It was only half a mile from Capitol Hill. He didn't know how long he'd be in DC and he hated having to keep tapping Peter Cottington-Beaufort for more money. The rouble was down everywhere.

He sat on his hammocky bed and thumbed through the Yellow Pages. Washington had enough gunshops to beat off the Red Army. He picked out Tab's Guns because it looked small and simple, and the address was in the Waterfront area. Guide books had two words to say about the Waterfront: *Stay away*. The area was a generous contributor to Washington's murder rate, most of which was by gunshot.

Philby walked there. Everyone he saw was black, or at least brown. He avoided all eye-contact, but he knew he was being stared at, sometimes shouted at. Soon he felt that this trip was a very bad idea. On the other hand, he was unlikely to have been followed here by the FBI. The further he walked, the more he felt that the Waterfront represented the failure of capitalism. Not that it promised the triumph of Communism, either. If anybody rules here, Philby thought, it was Smith & Wesson. So he was in the right place.

Tab's Guns was in a side street that had weeds growing in the potholes. Tab was small and thin, and his face was as creased as old brown wrapping paper. Khaki work pants. No shirt. Wire wool for chest hair.

'I want to buy a rifle,' Philby said.

'Uh-huh.' Tab made the bar stool rock back and forth. 'What you plannin' on shootin'?'

'A young buck.'

'Got your huntin' permit?'

'Certainly.'

'No, you ain't.' Tab slid off the stool. 'This is closed season for deer. Right now the mama deer are havin' their little baby deer.'

'Well, later on then.'

'Man needs a heart of stone to shoot Bambi.'

They looked at weapons. In the end, Philby bought a high-powered deer rifle with a cracked stock, no sling, and a scratch on the telescopic lens, plus half a box of ammunition, for fifty dollars. Tab watched him handle it, and said sadly, 'Only way you'll kill that buck is he dies laughin'.' He showed Philby how to break down the rifle into three parts. He put them in an old canvas bag stencilled *Property of A1 Fruit Farms*. 'I got a coupla bazookas out back,' he said. 'You whack Bambi any day you like. Whack that shit Disney too.'

Philby walked back to the Hampton Hotel. In his room, he assembled the rifle and aimed at his flyblown reflection in the mirror. He made an unconvincing figure, but the bullets were real enough. One squeeze of his finger could change everything. For years, he had been the highest-ranked Soviet agent in the British Secret Service, and even now he was only retired, not sacked, never exposed. He still had good pals, well placed in the Service, who felt that he had been badly treated and who would welcome him back. But not if this bugger Cabrillo sold him to that sod McCarthy and put him on the American Red Peril hit list.

One squeeze.

He put the gun in the bag and hid the bag under the bed and went out in search of his target.

209

3

Luis woke up full of ideas and eager to get to work on McCarthy's Red Scare campaign, but Stevie was a problem. She came down to breakfast wearing one of his shirts, mainly unbuttoned, and nothing else. 'Is he good in the sack?' she asked. 'Some guys are all talk an' no dick, know what I mean?'

'You got a real knack for picking losers,' Julie said.

'Us, we'd make a real good threesome.' Stevie drank orange juice. 'Him bein' such a stud, stands to reason — '

'Forget it. We don't even make a good twosome.'

'Ain't the point. See, I owe him one, from that Vinnie thing he did.'

Luis chewed bacon. 'He was stone dead when I got there, you stupid woman.'

'It's the thought that counts. Ma always said — '

'Listen! We're leaving here. Moving out today. Where you go is up to you. Just depart. You understand the word *go*? Here, I'll write it on your hand, so you won't forget. Go!'

'See his eyes flash?' Stevie said to Julie. 'That's the stud in him comin' out. This boy is *hot*.'

The doorbell rang. Luis came back with Gregg DeWolf. Julie poured him some coffee. 'Sorry if this louses up your paperwork.'

'Real estate is all about comings and goings.'

'The house is fine. It's a business decision,' Luis said. 'Put it down to adverse trading conditions.'

'The Mafia are chasing us,' Julie said.

'Us wops always get the blame,' Stevie complained. 'It's un-American. You got any more eggs?'

'Stay away from this woman,' Luis told Gregg. 'She killed three husbands, a boyfriend and a passing stranger, the last two right out there on the street, yesterday afternoon.'

'I'm sure your motives were of the best,' Gregg said.

'Sure,' Julie said. 'Her boyfriend came here to pull the plug on Luis and me.'

'A not unfamiliar situation,' Gregg said. 'Many of my clients prematurely vacate their lease.'

'Chick did that,' Stevie said. 'That was his line of work. You stepped out of line, he prematurely vacated your lease.' They were surprised and impressed. 'Ain't stupid,' she said. 'People don't give us wops credit. Who invented spaghetti? Not the Pilgrim fuckin' Fathers.'

Luis wanted to go to work. Julie and Gregg discussed where else to live. Gregg suggested an apartment near Dupont Circle: big Victorian building, off the tourist track yet handy for Foggy Bottom, Old Downtown, Capitol Hill. And such good bookshops!

'Ma said a house without books is like a meal without wine,' Stevie told them. 'She wrote books. Not paperbacks. Real books.' Nobody was about to argue.

★

Luis worked hard in the Library of Congress, ate lunch, and took the Capitol Subway to the Senate office building on Constitution Avenue. He was so excited that he stopped at a men's room, locked himself in a cubicle and forced his lungs to breathe slowly. And after all that, Senator McCarthy was out.

His secretary made a brief call. 'Mr Cohn will see you,' she said.

Cohn and Schine were in a conference room. Luis stopped at the doorway and watched. A curious ceremony was taking place. A long table was loaded with cardboard boxes. Cohn was sitting on the padded seat of a library ladder, looking down at Schine, who took a book from a box and held it up for inspection. He said, 'Mrs Eleanor Roosevelt's book on — '

'Who cares?' Cohn said. 'She's a goddamn menace.' He gave a thumbs-down.

Schine tossed it into a bin, and took another from the box. 'Biography of Larry Parks,' he announced.

'Hostile witness,' Cohn said. Thumbs-down. Into the bin. Cohn noticed Cabrillo. 'Hi! Joe's not here. Still drinking his lunch. You brought us some goodies?'

'And then some.' Luis held up a fat envelope.

'David, go get Bobby. I need him to take notes.'

Schine left. Luis moved forward. 'What are you doing?'

'Fumigating. Some jockstrap university got the jitters about its library. Asked us to weed out the pinko authors.'

'Larry Parks made *The Jolson Story*. It's a masterpiece.'

'He had Red friends, he taints the cinema industry, he won't work in it again. Want to help? Pick a book.'

Luis pulled out a handful. Cohn gave a rapid thumbs-down to George Orwell's *Animal Farm*, some Dorothy Parker short stories, and John Steinbeck's *Grapes of Wrath*. Then he rejected the Revised Standard Version of the Bible.

'Now I know you're joking,' Luis said.

'I don't believe so. Ninety-five clergymen took part in preparing that book. Thirty have identifiable links with Communism, such as they sponsored the World Peace Movement or they signed the charter of the Civil Rights Congress, both of them notorious Communist Front organizations. By definition, that means the other sixty-five clergy willingly affiliated themselves to Red Fronts. Their book has no place in a patriotic American university.' Schine and Kennedy came in. 'Got your little notebook, Bobby?' Cohn said. 'I want this on the record.'

'Mr Arabel should report to the senator.' Kennedy's voice was flat as sandpaper, and as harsh.

'It's my call,' Cohn said. 'I'm senior counsel.'

'Satisfy my curiosity,' Luis said to him. 'How old are you?'

'Twenty-five.'

'Eighteen months younger than me,' Kennedy said.

'It's what you do with the years that counts,' Cohn said, crisp as cross-examination. 'I graduated from Warners Law School at age nineteen, was admitted to the New York bar and got sworn in as assistant US attorney the day I reached twenty-one. Where were you when you were twenty-one, Bobby? Playing touch football with your sisters?' But Kennedy wouldn't answer. 'How about you, Mr Arabel?' Cohn asked.

Luis thought. At twenty-one he'd been in Spain, snooping on both sides in the civil war, behaving so recklessly that he deserved to have died a dozen times. 'Top secret,' he said. 'I could tell you, but then I'd have to kill you.' Cohn and Schine enjoyed that; Kennedy scowled. 'Want to see what I've brought?' Luis said. 'Not typed up. No time. Had to translate and return the originals in rather a hurry.'

That got their full attention. 'Translate?' Schine said. 'What language?'

'Mind your manners, David,' Cohn said. 'Go ahead, Mr Arabel.'

'First . . .' Luis selected a page. 'Headed: Report to controller code-name Hammer from agent code-name Sparrow. Begins: First phase testing new US army tactical radio at research facility, General Electric, Schenectady, New York State, now complete. Performance figures exceed actuality by 27 per cent in range, 35 per cent in clarity, 61 per cent in anti-static capacity.' He produced another page. 'Next: report by code-name Arrow to — '

'Hold it, hold it.' Cohn came down the library ladder. 'Who the hell is Sparrow and why should we care?'

'Senior technician at GE Labs. Tests their new radio for the US army. Secretly alters the results, persuades the Pentagon the equipment performs far better than it actually does. So, millions of dollars wasted, and American soldiers fail to communicate.'

'Sabotage,' Schine said.

'Well spotted,' Kennedy muttered.

'Kinda technical,' Cohn said. 'Percentages . . . Next?'

'Code-name Artichoke to code-name Rattle. Message begins: Have infected Idaho crops with Oregon potato blight. Outcome sporadic. Need funds. Message ends, although there's a page of figures plotting blight density against ambient temperature throughout June.'

'Outcome sporadic?' Cohn said. 'What does that mean?'

Luis clicked his tongue. 'Translation is a problem. In the original language, one word can have different shades of meaning. It could mean "sporadic" or "emphatic" or "explicit".'

'Son of a bitch,' Schine said.

'There's also a poetic meaning of "ecstatic", but we can ignore that.'

Kennedy put a line through what he'd written. 'So which is it?'

'For you, perhaps "dyspeptic",' Luis said.

Cohn laughed. 'He gotcha,' he said, and patted Kennedy on the shoulder. Kennedy recoiled. 'Keep going.' Cohn said.

'Code-name Blanket to code-name Engine. Re Operation Badmouth. Strategy is to smear eminent scientists by alleging Leftist background, thus exclude from university employ. Long-term effect must be . . .' Luis looked up. 'He said "must" but then he used the subjunctive. Russian grammar is tricky. Damn.'

'I knew it was Russian,' Schine said brightly.

'List of names,' Luis said. 'Long list.'

'Skip it,' Cohn said. 'Next?'

Luis flicked through the pages. 'Plan to introduce bogus data to the US Treasury's records in order to distort its economic forecast . . . Communist propaganda infiltrated into the high school syllabus in Ohio . . . Deliberately falsified analysis of the San Andreas Fault, aimed at demoralizing California with fake earthquake warnings . . . And there's more.'

Ten minutes later he finished reading.

'Very impressive,' Cohn said. 'But . . .' He shrugged.

'We have to protect Joe,' Schine said. 'We gotta make sure.'

'Where's your goddamn *proof*?' Kennedy demanded. 'Where's your *authentication*? Where's your *corroborating evidence*?'

'Where's your money?' Luis said crisply. 'I'm risking my neck. What are you doing? Making a reading list for some jockstrap university? I need five hundred dollars now. I have people to pay off. Or the senator will never see these reports. Or the next lot.'

For a long moment Luis thought he had pressed too hard. Cohn gazed at him with his hooded, lawyer's eyes. Kennedy doodled and sneered at the doodles. Schine picked up *For Whom the Bell Tolls* and tossed it into the reject bin.

'Five hundred,' Cohn said. 'For that, we expect the Holy Grail.' Luis said nothing. It was a time for letting the other man talk. 'Come with me,' Cohn said.

Luis left the building five hundred bucks to the good.

An hour later, Senator McCarthy returned from lunch. Alcohol flushed his face and slowed his speech but it didn't seem to dull his brain. He read the copies of Arabel's reports, skimming some, studying others. 'What d'you think?' he asked.

'If they're kosher,' Cohn said, 'he's got a terrific source.'

'Bobby? Your opinion?'

'I don't like him, he's on the take, but . . .' Kennedy shrugged. 'Some of these reports are so damn *boring*. Only a bureaucrat writes like that. It's turgid, it's tedious . . .' He pressed his lips hard together.

'So it's true?' McCarthy suggested. Nobody was ready to agree out loud. Or disagree. 'He's either a goldfield or a minefield. And that, men, is what makes politics so interesting.'

4

He liked the new apartment. It occupied the fourth floor. Big rooms, ceiling fans, French windows on to a large balcony, the traffic on Connecticut just a faint throb, far below. The wallpaper had wide stripes in the colours of the ribbon of the Hungarian Order of Virtue, Third Class, and the air smelled of lemon soap. He heard singing from the bathroom. 'She's still here,' he said to Julie.

'Yeah. You throw her out, Luis. If you can. She's got a brain like a pin-ball machine on a flying trapeze. I told her it was dangerous here, she could get hurt, look at Chick Scatola. She said plenty places are more dangerous. I said – '

'What places?'

'New Orleans. Dallas. She reads the FBI Crime Index in bed. Then she said she could teach me how to save a marriage, she'd had three, all disasters.'

'We're not married.'

'We're as good as married, Luis. We've lived in three apartments, a house and a motel, all in the space of a month. Look what I've done for you. I dumped your fruit-boots, I read your crappy memoirs, I helped you toss a couple of bodies into a canyon. If you were any sort of husband you'd drown her in the bath before she murders Cole Porter entirely. Why are we running from the Mafia? Jesus, I need a drink.'

'We're running because they're chasing.' Luis poured bourbon into glasses, added ginger ale. 'Why they're chasing, I don't know. We never harmed them. I had a small problem with the FBI. Does the FBI hire Mafia hitmen?'

'I never heard of it. Cheers.' They drank. 'Let's face it, Luis. We just don't know what happened in that Buick. Maybe somebody else shot both those guys.'

'It's pretty certain Uncle Jerome sent Chick Scatola. If we kick the Triple Virgin out, what are the odds she'll go straight to Jerome and tomorrow another of his gorillas will ride into town, looking for us.'

Julie sighed. 'Let her stay, then. Better to have her inside the tent pissing out than outside the tent pissing in. Did you have a good day at the office?'

'So-so.' Luis showed her the sheaf of reports, supposedly transcribed from Russian files of subversive work by Communist agents scattered across the US. She enjoyed reading them, knowing it was all bullshit but admiring the skill with which the bullshit had been applied. It was like the old days in the Double-Cross System, telling the enemy what he wanted to hear. 'Those goddamn cunning Bolsheviks,' she said. 'I like this stuff about scaring the pants off California with phoney data on the San Andreas Fault. Los Angeles is too pleased with itself anyway. And when all this crazy sabotage is exposed as hokum, McCarthy's gonna look foolish. We win either way.'

'Yes. Perhaps.' Luis took his drink for a slow walk around the room. 'There's a problem. The senator's staff want cast-iron evidence that the transcripts are from genuine Soviet files. I need a smoking gun. My subversive agents are all ghosts. I need just one All-American hero who has genuinely betrayed his country to the Commies . . .'

'That ain't easy.'

'Who sez?' Stevie had come out of the bathroom and was drying her hair. 'Would Jerome Fantoni be any good? He was a card-carrying Communist at Princeton, back in the twenties. I got his card at home. Ma gave it me as a keepsake. She was membership secretary of the Princeton Communist Party. They were married, see. To each other.'

Julie said, 'That makes you . . .'

'I'm his daughter. We don't speak. Three husbands, no kids, he blames me.' She lifted Luis's drink and took a deep swig. 'Also he criticized my driving. You want the card?'

5

Kim Philby ignored three-quarters of the city. That was where seven out of ten lived: blacks, Hispanics, poor whites and illegal immigrants on the lam from Uncle Sam.

He looked in the other quarter: from Capitol Hill through Old Downtown to Foggy Bottom, and in the comfortable Northwest, from Georgetown to Adams Morgan. Philby walked, and walked. Then he rented a bicycle. It bruised his crotch. He was dripping with sweat long before midday, the taste of salt on his lips. His sinuses suffered from the humidity. He called at every real estate office he saw. All said the same: not their policy to reveal clients' names. He kept hoping for a streak of luck. Perhaps if he tried to call on Senator McCarthy . . . No. Rotten idea. If Cabrillo saw him, he'd go into deep hiding.

Philby read the Washington papers, dreading to see his name. In the evenings he sat on his bed and practised assembling his rifle. And counted his money. Not much left.

★

They drove Stevie to the airport, put her on a plane to New York, and came back later to pick her up. She was carrying a box file tied with a floppy mauve ribbon.

'Ma gave it me the year before she died. Said it was all she had worth remembering. "We had some times together, your father and me. We were gonna turn the world on its head." All she said.'

They drove to a bar, took a corner booth, nobody nearby, ordered beers. Emptied the box on the table.

Birth, marriage, death certificates dating back more than a century. Yellowed snapshots of self-assured men sporting too much hair and tired women wearing too many clothes, and bored children staring, mouths open. Autographed dance cards. A cancelled cheque for two hundred dollars from a publisher. Written on the back: *First advance! For first book!* A bronzed baby-boot. A champagne cork with a foreign coin embedded in it. A chain of coloured paper-clips. A police whistle. A George Gershwin songbook for piano. Some book reviews, stapled together. And a strong buff envelope containing a dozen American Communist Party membership cards from the 1930s, a pocket-size cash book listing names and dues paid, and a pile of glossy 8-by-10 photographs of young men and women in groups, camping, swimming, playing tennis. Names were written on the back. Stevie pointed out her parents. Young, slim, unworried.

'I guess they were in love in them days,' she said. 'Didn't last. See, he was never home. The Mob came first. Runnin' the rackets, it takes up a lot of time.'

'These other people,' Julie said. 'Were they all at Princeton?'

'Hell, no. Mostly with the Mob. Younger sons. Ma said Jerome thought he'd recruited them, you know, fighters for the cause. Bullshit. It was a joke to them. Joined the Party for the party! Good booze, get laid. It was the Depression, lots of people were Reds. Jerome's crowd were kind of silk-stocking Bolsheviks.'

Luis was studying the names. 'Any of these guys still active?'

'Let's see.' She spread the photographs. 'Him. And him. Fitz Delaney and Bender Costello.'

'Just two? What happened to the rest?'

'Oh,' she said. 'You know.'

218

ONE BALL, AT LEAST

1

The elderly man in a white jacket and black pants served iced coffee, and got lost. The boxer dogs waited until everyone was seated before they stretched out, one on each side of the great brick fireplace, mirror-images of each other. Manners were not dead in New Jersey.

'If you had made an arrest I would have known,' Jerome Fantoni said. 'So Sammy's murderer remains at large.'

'Yes and no,' Prendergast said.

Fisk handed Jerome a head-and-shoulders photograph of a man. 'Spence Mallaby,' he said. 'Had a pest-control business in Queens. Astoria Boulevard at 94th Street.'

Jerome put on half-moon glasses, took the picture to a window, gave it a ten-seconds appraisal, came back. 'A total stranger. I know nobody called Mallaby.'

'Too late to start with this one,' Prendergast said. 'Heart attack. Dead before he hit the sidewalk.'

'Couple of cops went to his apartment to break the sad news,' Fisk said. 'No family. But they did find a small armoury.'

'Ah,' Jerome said.

'We made the usual tests,' Prendergast said. 'One handgun fired the bullet that killed your nephew.'

Jerome had guessed what was coming. 'God help us,' he said. 'Pest control. What would drive a man like that to shoot Sammy?'

They drove away. 'He's beginning to look old,' Prendergast

219

said. 'My guess is he had his nephew snuffed. Little Sammy went moonlighting, ran a little racket of his own, screwed up. Rustled the wrong herd. These people are all the same: get greedy, get reckless, get dead.'

'He still bled to death in Cabrillo's Studebaker when it was stalled on Broadway,' Fisk said. 'Nothing explains that.'

'You're obsessed with neatness. You crave precision. I keep telling you, crime is messy because criminals always bungle. Find a neat and tidy answer and I guarantee you haven't solved the crime.'

Forget answers, Fisk thought. *We're still working on questions.*

2

In the morning Luis spent a lot of time thinking and then got down to writing.

Julie took Gregg DeWolf's advice and went to Hecht's, the classiest department store in town. She bought a bitter-chocolate outfit with matching shoes, just what a working girl would wear if she owned the company.

Stevie went to the zoo.

In the afternoon, Julie and Luis went to see McCarthy, by appointment. Also present were Cohn, Schine and Kennedy. Luis ignored them. He introduced Julie to McCarthy. 'Miss Conroy,' he said. 'My agent. She's smarter than I am, a terrifying thought.'

'And a stunning addition to this dreary gang.' McCarthy took her hand in both of his.

'My client does the stunning, senator,' she said. 'I just take ten per cent of the concussion.'

He liked that. 'First time I've done business with an intelligence agent's agent,' he said.

'May I have my hand back? Or should I invoice you first?'

'Ideally, I'd like to take an option on it.' He kissed it, and released it, all done with a kind of aw-shucks backwoods charm.

The kidding was over. Down to business.

'Yesterday I brought copies of certain transcripts,' Luis said.

'I read 'em.' McCarthy was still admiring Julie. 'Eye-openers.'

'And your associates asked for supporting evidence.'

'I'm in the public's eye, Mr Arabel. Everything I do has to be squeaky-clean.'

'We're not selling dishwashers here, senator,' Julie said. 'You can't expect *Good Housekeeping*'s Seal of Approval.'

McCarthy tugged gently on his left ear-lobe. He appeared to be thinking. Maybe he *was* thinking. 'So what can we expect?'

'Hard evidence of Communist penetration of a billion-dollar American industry,' Luis said. He paused to enjoy the silence, huge as an empty stadium. 'Undeniable proof that card-carrying Party members operate at the highest level of organized crime. You've got Reds running the Mafia, senator. The Mob in New York is a puppet of the Kremlin.' Now everyone was talking.

McCarthy pounded the desk until they shut up. 'I need names, Mr Arabel. Give me a name.'

'Jerome Fantoni.'

'Oh, brother!' Kennedy said, leaking excitement for once. 'The Fantoni family is up there with Gambino and Costello and Trafficante and the rest. If you've got Fantoni you've got the Mafia by the balls.'

McCarthy looked at Cohn. 'One ball, at least,' Cohn said.

'I need to see Fantoni's Party membership card,' McCarthy said to Luis.

'Negotiable,' Julie said.

Luis handed McCarthy a file. 'Carbon copies of subversive reports, transcripts of Soviet policy discussions, analysis of economic disruption in the New York area . . . My Russian is a little rusty and the translations were hastily carried out, so the language is sometimes stilted, but the gist is clear.'

McCarthy flicked through the pages. 'How about you and Miss Conroy go enjoy a coffee and a Danish and come back in half an hour?'

★

221

Pages were passed from hand to hand. Speed-reading took place. Minutes passed.

'Enough!' McCarthy said. 'Somebody for Christ's sake stick his neck out. I got Jap TV coming here to interview me in an hour.'

'I think it's sensational,' Cohn said. 'You'll get three-inch headlines from here to Honolulu. And there's incredible mileage to be got from it! That's assuming the Party cards are genuine.'

'I'd feel happier if we knew more about this Arabel,' Kennedy said.

'You wouldn't know happiness if it came up and blew smoke in your face, Bobby,' McCarthy said. 'What's botherin' you, boy?'

'The entire way he operates. He shimmies in here, no introduction, no credentials — '

'Secret agents don't carry credentials, dummy,' Schine said. 'Except fakes. You want fakes?'

'Soviet embassy's sprung a leak,' Cohn said confidently. 'That's what it smells like to me.'

'So why didn't the leak go straight to the FBI?' Kennedy demanded.

McCarthy dismissed the question with a flap of the hand. 'Arabel would never have got this far unless he'd convinced his source that the set-up was safe and solid and secure. If you guys poke around and make his source nervous, Arabel's gonna cease making deliveries. Lay off him.'

'Just thought of something,' Schine said. 'Maybe one of them's an *agent provocateur*.' They all looked at him, waiting. 'Maybe not,' he said.

'Go suck a rock, David,' Cohn said.

'Third delivery inside a week.' Kennedy tapped some pages into a pile. 'Suggests the source may be plural. Two people, even three.'

'HUAC would kill for this stuff,' McCarthy said. 'J. Edgar Hoover will cry himself to sleep, and the Russian ambassador will say it's lies, lies, capitalist lies.'

'Well, Arabel sure as hell didn't make it all up,' Cohn said.

'Just to translate it, he'd have to work twenty-four hours a day.'

'And then some,' Schine said, with a big smile. He liked having the last word. It irritated Roy, and it really pissed off Bobby, but then Bobby was always pissed off.

★

Luis and Julie wanted fresh air, not coffee. They strolled around to the Capitol building and sat on the steps and watched the gulls patrolling the Mall, snooping on picnickers, swooping on tidbits. After a week of dank, overcooked weather, the air tasted like a suddenly opened fridge. 'You know these clowns,' Julie said. 'What's on their minds?'

'They're bound to be twitchy about naming Jerome Fantoni. I bet McCarthy has never exposed a big-time gangster before. Fantoni will deny everything. He might sue. It wouldn't surprise me if McCarthy chickens out. Naming the Mafia isn't like taking a shot at the Indiana State Text-book Commission.'

They sat and thought about all that.

'Time's up,' she said. 'Come on. He can't kick us out until we've crawled in.'

They got it wrong. If McCarthy could bad-mouth five-star General Marshall and get away with it, he wasn't afraid of naming Jerome Fantoni and others like him. He was relaxed and affable. His staff had gone; now it was just the senator and Arabel and Miss Conroy sitting around a coffee table. Booze, mixers, peanuts, pretzels, ice, napkins, all there, help yourself.

'I assume you have the Party membership cards,' McCarthy said. 'Okay. Now let's think about the press conference. On live TV. How to handle that.'

'Your speech writes itself,' Luis said. 'Exposed, the Red Tsar of Crime. For decades, Stalin's men in the New York Mafia have conspired to sell America down the river. Jerome Fantoni, the double traitor. First he betrays justice, then he betrays patriotism. When the Mob takes orders from the Kremlin, what hope is there for decency and honour in the USA?'

223

'Hold it there.' McCarthy was scribbling fast. 'Okay . . . Listen . . . People are going to wonder how this conspiracy works. Fantoni's business is corruption. How can the Commies subvert corruption?'

'Let's not get bogged down in detail,' Luis said. 'Let's just remember the strategy of Red infiltration. They target the vital organs: the State Department, the Atom Bomb, the Army, Hollywood, and now we discover their tentacles inside the Mafia, probably the biggest business operation in America.'

'Vital organs,' McCarthy said. 'Good point.'

'It's no wonder the FBI can't capture Communist agents,' Luis said. 'They've never got a grip on the Mafia, who are one and the same thing.'

'Dandy.' McCarthy made a note. 'But if I was Fantoni, I'd be saying something like, "Look, I'm a successful businessman, why should I be a Commie? What's in it for me?" Answer that one.'

'It's not for us to answer,' Luis said. 'History does that. What was in it for diplomats? Atom bomb scientists? Pentagon officials? They all turned traitor. Why not leading Mobsters?'

'Enough,' Julie said. 'Before my client says another word, senator, you and I need to agree contractual terms, with particular regard to financial remuneration.'

'Sure. Toss a figure in the air.'

'Thirty thousand dollars' retainer.'

'Hey!' McCarthy collapsed as if shot, clutching his heart. 'I don't have that.'

'You can get it. Ask one of your millionaire campaign supporters. When this story breaks, you'll be the hottest ticket in the Republican Party. You'll make ten grand a night on the rubber-chicken circuit. Plus radio, books, magazine interviews. I can see a whole TV drama series coming out of it. Roll the credits: Joseph R. McCarthy was played by himself.'

'Twenty-five grand retainer. Only after I get the originals of all these documents.'

'Twenty-five, and a thousand a month. Plus bonus payments to be agreed for special discoveries by my client.'

They bickered professionally for five minutes, but the deal was done. 'I'll draw up the papers,' she said. 'Obviously my client retains all literary rights, stage and motion-picture rights, radio serial rights, newspaper and magazine one-shot and serial rights, Book Club rights, translation rights and strip-cartoon rights, both US and worldwide.'

'Lady, I got a cute birthmark on my right butt,' McCarthy said. 'You can have the rights on that too.' They shook on it.

3

'I want to be clear about one thing,' Julie said. 'Just what exactly are we trying to do?'

'Make money, sweetie.' Luis was still slightly manic. They had opened a bank account on the strength of McCarthy's twenty-five grand, and they were walking back to the apartment. Success made all the colours brighter. He could see that she enjoyed being his agent; she had known literary and theatrical agents in New York, knew their tone, style, language. Her pleasure doubled his feeling of fizz.

'We're boosting Joe bloody McCarthy too,' she said. 'Is that part of the plot?'

'He's a windbag! We keep pumping him up, one day he'll explode.'

'No more names, Luis.' She grabbed his arm and made him stop. 'No more blacklisting. You start sticking pins in the phone book, just to sell names to that miserable monomaniac Fascist fart, and I'll kill you.'

'Me? Why me? Kill *him*. He started it.'

'I don't care about him. I do care about you.'

Happiness flooded his being. He embraced her and they kissed, long and hard. A passing convertible played *La Cucuracha* on its horn. They waved, and walked on. *Jolly good*, Luis thought. *But I've still got to feed the senator a steady diet of red meat, and if not names, then what?*

4

Kim Philby sat in his room, newspapers littering the floor, and told himself that he had been in tighter corners than this, often when he was just one slip from disaster. Burgess and Maclean had been huge risks. Maclean had soaked his tattered nerves in so much alcohol that when he bragged of being a Soviet spy, his friends put it down to booze. Burgess had flaunted pictures of the pretty boys he'd seduced, and generally buggered everyone about until a Foreign Office report said he was "dirty, drunk and idle". Kim shuddered at the memory. Hard questioning would have cracked either of them, and then Kim would really have been in the hot seat. Someone would surely have remembered the Volkov affair. Kim had nearly come a cropper over Volkov. When the head of Soviet Intelligence in Istanbul tries to defect, and says he knows the names of Soviet agents inside the British government, one name is bound to be Philby's. Kim had flown to Istanbul, alone, and on his own authority had rejected Volkov as unreliable. Kim returned to London, Volkov to Moscow, strapped to a KGB stretcher. Touch-and-go, that. Compared with hairy episodes like that, the threat from Cabrillo was a flea-bite. But a man could die from a flea-bite.

Cabrillo was still in Washington: he was convinced of that. He was sick and tired of the search; literally sick and tired: his sinuses were inflamed, possibly infected, and the bicycling gave his calves the most painful cramps. And now Jack Anderson, a political columnist for a Washington paper, was telling his readers to expect another bombshell from Senator Joe McCarthy. Shocking revelations. Commie treachery. Big names.

Kim assembled the rifle and practised by aiming out the window at the guy who ran the corner newsstand. One clear shot. That was all he asked.

5

The Second World War had been a piece of cake. All it took to baffle the *Abwehr* was a bucket of warm sympathy, laced with a generous splash of convincing technical data. Warm sympathy was not Joe McCarthy's diet. He needed hot blood.

Luis prowled around the Library of Congress, brooding over his problem: how to find evidence of the damage that Communist treachery was doing to America, when America was conspicuously wealthy, and getting more so by the minute. Chrysler had power steering. Hotels had vibrating mattresses. RCA was introducing colour TV. Remington Rand had built a revolutionary computer as big as a locker room. *Playboy* magazine made men glad to be alive. Ike was in the White House. A six-pack of Bud cost a buck and a quarter. Who's complaining?

The library's card index system was just standing there, doing nothing, like him, so he went over and poked around in it. Nothing under *crooks* or *gangsters*. He tried *Organized Crime* and struck gold. In 1951 Senator Kefauver chaired hearings of the Senate Crime Investigating Committee. The cream of the underworld took the stand. Big TV audience.

Luis spent the rest of the day picking the plums out of the Kefauver reports, and then writing intelligence summaries about Mob leaders who were secret Communist party members or sympathizers, doing the Kremlin's dirty work by siphoning the life-blood from the American economy.

He went home and showed it all to Julie.

'They're crooks,' he told her. 'They steal from the poor, they bankrupt small merchants with protection rackets, they corrupt judges and cops and politicians. You can't object to their names being named, can you? They're scum. We're doing a public service.'

'They're not Party members,' she said.

'Oh . . . steady on. Some of them *might* be.'

'But you can't prove — '

'Who in hell cares? They'll deny it, and nobody'll believe them, because they're *crooks*, for Christ's sake! They always lie.' Luis was so pleased with himself that he performed a slow foxtrot across the room to the balcony. Slow, so that he wouldn't spill his gin and tonic.

Julie, cool in a running singlet and beach shorts, stretched out on a divan and browsed through his stuff. After a while she said, 'All this flim-flam about labour racketeering in Illinois is damn dull. Of course, I know it's meant to be dull.'

'Look at my graphs of economic inactivity.' He waved to a girl on a balcony across the street. 'Look at my box summaries of wage-dollars stolen during the last ten years. I sweated blood on those.'

'Sure you did. Still damn dull. This thing you did about businesses in southern California going bust when they can't pay for protection: that's not bad. Everyone knows someone's brother-in-law who got screwed that way.'

'Larry "Boom-Boom" Garcia,' Luis said. 'He's to blame. Dreadful man. The pride of the KGB.'

'The Cleveland story's okay, too. City taxes are high because so much gets skimmed off by the Mafia. Nobody likes taxes.'

'Everyone pays for the Mafia,' he said happily. 'I reckon the Kremlin takes twenty per cent. Moe Dalitz runs Cleveland.'

'That's all crap,' Stevie said.

She had come out of the bath, hair still dripping wet. Already the towel wrapped around her was losing its grip. On its left a nipple showed. On its right there was more leg than towel, and the parting was growing wider by the second. 'Wear a robe, can't you?' Julie said.

'I heard you say that stuff about Garcia in LA and Dalitz in Cleveland. It's all crap. You ain't foolin' nobody, believe me.'

Luis came in from the balcony. 'It may be crap to you, but it's bread and butter to me,' he said.

'It ain't the done thing to say "Mafia" in Cleveland.' Stevie fixed herself a drink. 'And John Scalisi has the Cleveland territory, not Moe Dalitz. John would show you the door if you said Mafia. It would cause offence. Like if I called you Benny instead of Luis. You wouldn't like being called Benny.'

'I might.' Luis was fascinated by the glimpse of nipple.

'No, you wouldn't,' Julie told him, 'and don't get horny. I want to eat soon.'

228

'In Cleveland, it's always "the Combination",' Stevie said. 'That's because of the Greeks an' Swedes an' Irish they let in.'

'An Equal-Opportunity Employer,' Julie said. 'God bless America.'

'What's wrong with my report on the notorious West Coast mobster, Larry "Boom-Boom" Garcia?' Luis asked. 'The guy's an enormous thug.'

'He's *stoopid*.' Stevie hitched up her towel, hid one nipple, exposed the other. 'Garcia couldn't organize a walk in the woods. The guy running the protection racket out of LA is Frankie DeSimone. That man is an artist, he loves his work. In San Francisco, Jimmy Lanza. You speak of Garcia in the same breath, you make yourself look foolish.' She took a swig of gin and nearly lost the towel again. 'Who you got for top banana in Chicago?'

'The Fischetti brothers,' Julie said.

'You're pathetic.'

'Paul Ricca?' Luis suggested.

'All gun, no brain. Sam Giancana runs the Mid-West. If you want to put the fix in, Murray Humphreys knows the price of every Chicago politician down to the last nickel.'

Luis said, 'So the Mafia actually — '

'Not the goddamn Mafia! In Chicago it's called "The Outfit". Maybe "The Syndicate". Jeez, you guys see too many movies.'

'Who runs Buffalo?' Julie asked.

'Stefano Magaddino. His organization's called "The Office".'

'New Orleans?'

'Carlos Marcello. The Syndicate. He's got Louisiana and half Texas, too.'

'How come you know so much?'

'How come you know so little? I'm a Fantoni. I was brought up to take a pride in my heritage.' She strode away with such dignity that the towel fell off. She let it lie.

'Triple Virgin,' Julie said. 'And she's built like Miss America with new Ultra-Glide Hydromatic Suspension.'

Luis was staring into space. 'Nobody says Mafia in the Mafia,' he said softly. 'Isn't that wonderful?'

'I'll tell you what's even more wonderful.' She stood up. 'Dinner can wait. Can you decode that message?'

'I may need help.' He got to his feet. 'Meanwhile, can I interest you in a roll in the hay?'

'Is Garibaldi a cookie?'

It was dusk when they wandered out of the bedroom, showered, dressed, and took Stevie to dinner, oyster-stuffed fish fillets, all you can eat for $5. She ate her fill, but she was not happy. 'They say there's somebody for everyone. Why is it I keep finding somebody who's nobody?' she said.

'A good-looking woman makes a man nervous,' Julie said. 'He takes one look, he knows he's not in the same league, his poor little prong goes AWOL.'

'Yeah, but not in the dark with the lights out.' Nevertheless, Stevie was slightly encouraged.

'I would be a huge disappointment to you,' Luis said. 'Just a moth in the flames of your beauty.'

'I'll wear a paper bag over my head,' she said.

'You are a truly desperate woman,' Julie said.

They went back to the apartment and worked through the pile of Soviet-Mafia intelligence reports. Stevie corrected the names, added convincing details. 'Joe Zerilli runs the Syndicate in Detroit,' she said. 'Very thorough. There's seven men on the Detroit Police Review Board and Joe's got five. This here, where you mention Tommy Lucchese in New York? He should get credit for double-boxing. It's his way of disposin' of stiffs when a lot of guys been whacked. Two bodies in one box, the top one bein' the genuine customer. Who's gonna go pokin' about in a coffin? People got more respect.'

They finished at two in the morning.

'One thing puzzles me,' Julie said. 'Your father went to Princeton. Where did you go? Hell's Kitchen?'

'He sent me to Bryn Mawr. I got my letter in lacrosse. Bust three heads wide open when we played Sarah Lawrence. But I quit. They was too polite. I like to be around people who speak their minds.'

'No shit,' Julie said.

'There you go,' Stevie said.

230

HOW CAN YOU
FIGHT DEATH?

1

Ella Wheeler Wilcox, Edna St Vincent Millay, Henry Wadsworth Longfellow. All born to be poets. With names like that, what else could they do? Some people live up to their names. Some people live down to them. Wiley Foxx, for instance, had to be a small-time crook. What is it, an act of premature vengeance against an unwanted child? The Stones have a daughter they christen Cherry. The Carts have a son and they reject Elmer and Duke and Floyd because, hey, Orson, that's a nice name. Orson Cart. It's not enough the kid gets their tattered, battered genes; they have to make him a cartoon character. A lot of people thought Wiley was Foxx's nickname. No such luck.

Wiley was twenty-two when Luis gave him the Buick. So far his life had been a bad joke. Kicked out of high school for attempted arson (the matches were damp), medically unfit for the army, barely literate, he was too stupid to know he was stupid. It made him just a digit in the stats that require a certain number of schmucks to counterbalance the clever people. You can't reward genius without penalizing the putz.

Wiley got a temporary job as attendant in Long-Stay Parking at Washington International Airport while the regular guy recovered from sciatica. The job was easy, plenty of dead time between flights when Wiley could steal. People left cars unlocked, windows a half-inch open, spare keys on a magnet stuck inside a wing. Pickings were slim: a pack of

231

Lifesavers, a thermos flask, a Zippo lighter. On a good day, a travel rug. Not enough to feed Wiley's greed. When travellers collected their cars and paid the parking fee, Wiley short-changed them, if he felt brave.

One day he short-changed an off-duty Washington cop, back from a wedding in Bermuda. Big mistake.

The cop let the bills lie on his open palm. 'I gave you a twenty,' he said.

Wiley gave him more money and apologized with a grin that sent out waves of dishonesty as loud as if he'd fouled his pants, which he almost had.

The cop put his thumb on the bills to stop them blowing away but he still did not close his fist. He thought: *This piece of piss needs to suffer. Needs to bleed.* He nodded at the attendant's hut. 'That where you guys hang out?' Wiley grunted, yeah. The cop said, 'Mind if I go in, take a look around?' Now Wiley wet himself, a hot rush down his left thigh. In the hut was stuff he stole. Hidden, but . . . 'Locked,' he said. 'Ain't got the key. Other guy, he got the key. But he ain't here . . .' His bladder pumped itself empty. 'That's how come it's locked.' Wiley wanted to cry.

'Too bad.' The cop looked at the sky. 'Rain on the way. You're gonna get wet.' He drove on. When he glanced at the rear-view mirror, the attendant was sitting on the ground. You ask a guy, can I look around your hut, he doesn't know you're a cop, he says go to hell. This sad specimen, he panics.

Washington airport is in Virginia. The cop phoned the local law. Fifteen minutes later, two State troopers in a handsome tan-and-bitter-chocolate patrol car swung into Long-Stay Parking, and Wiley discovered a fluid ounce he thought he'd spent. He was going to jail. He wouldn't last ten minutes in jail.

They were friendly, just wanted to check out security arrangements. 'We talk inside this hut of yours?' one said. Fat splashes of rain were blackening the ground. The cop had been right. Wiley's nerve was as limp as old lettuce, he couldn't con these big, smart troopers with his shit about keys. He opened the door and let them in. That was when he

232

got lucky. A car horn blared. 'Customer,' he said. 'Be right back.'

The rain became serious while he was taking the money, giving the ticket, leaning on the counterweight to raise the barrier arm. He left it upright. He ran to the Buick, his crappy old sneakers skidding on the wet tarmac, got in, rammed the key into the dash. More luck. The motor fired. He set the wipers to max and slipped the brakes and rushed such power to the wheels that his head bounced. What a punk.

If he had driven quietly and modestly out of Long-Stay, he might have got away. It was a parking lot; naturally cars came and went. But he slammed his foot to the floor, created a rage of noise, left a wake of blue smoke from burning rubber, fishtailed through the exit. He was Wiley Foxx. The troopers chased him.

He saw the flashing lights and heard the coyote wail behind him. Traffic was thin. They'd catch him. Any cop drove better than Wiley, he knew that. His right leg was shuddering, he had to grip his knee to keep his foot hard on the gas, but that took one hand off the wheel, and the wheel was wet, slippery, he needed both hands. Fuckin' rain. Now the lights behind were brighter, the wail was louder, he had to get off this road, and he knew there was a chance soon on the right, an escape, a sharp exit into a side road, narrow, just a lane. Wiley knew if he waited and then fired the Buick hard right, the troopers would scream past him and he'd be gone, man, gone! He'd seen it done on TV, in *Dragnet*. The turn-off hurtled towards him. He hit the brakes and spun the wheel. What he wanted was a long sideways skid, as seen in *Dragnet*. What he got was a full-circle spin, and then some, which slammed the Buick broadside at a pine tree, 126 years old, five foot diameter, in perfect health. Car and driver embraced the base like a candy wrapper. In an instant, the average intelligence of the population nudged upwards by an infinitesimal amount.

The Buick was identified; so was Wiley Foxx. The information travelled via the DA's office in Washington to Jerome Fantoni. It deepened his depression. All his life, he had regarded serious crime as the solution to his problems; now he was bedevilled by trivial crime, almost *facetious* crime. A pest control operator killed one person close to him. Now an airport parking attendant was tied to the loss of another. Probably killed him. What made it worse, these nobodies, these nebbishes, they went and killed themselves before he could get to grips with them. How can you fight death?

★

'Wiley Foxx,' Prendergast said. 'A pitiful jerk who gets a headache making change at Long-Stay Parking. What did I tell you?'

'You said crime is messy,' Fisk said.

'And Foxx has Jerome Fantoni's Buick. Which disappeared when Cabrillo, if it was Cabrillo, dropped out of sight when Sammy ran out of blood on Broadway. What else did I tell you?'

'Criminals always bungle.'

'Because they're bums. This Foxx was a bum. That's why this whole thing has never made sense. Bums have no brains. Wise up, Fisk. You keep looking for a pattern of behaviour. Tell me this: if you ever find a pattern, what will it be?'

'An accident. A mistake. An aberration. Because crime is messy.'

'You're learning at last,' Prendergast said.

2

The TV crews cursed McCarthy for holding his Press conference halfway up the steps of the Capitol Building at four p.m., the hottest, stickiest part of the day. To get a good shot of the senator meant building a temporary camera tower of scaffolding. The networks and the local stations competed for space with foreign TV crews. Riggers, sound engineers and cameramen sweated and swore, but the reporters relished the setting. It was pure McCarthy. Look at that bank of microphones: studded with idents from all over. Look at the background: noble, soaring pillars pointing to the stately Dome. Look at the crowd: a great mob of tourists, ready for a free show, something to boast about when they got back to Elk Lick, Dakota. Best of all, the newsmen were guaranteed hot headlines, because McCarthy always delivered. In spades. For that, any true newsman would sweat blood.

The crowd applauded McCarthy when he walked out of the Capitol. A team of six men took positions behind him. He began to speak at four p.m. on the button. Another reason why television loved him.

'The price of freedom,' the Senator said. 'Think of that for a moment. The price of freedom. What is it? How much are we willing to pay?' That was to give the sound engineers a chance to balance their levels. Now for business. 'The price of freedom is eternal vigilance – well, you knew that. But vigilance is just a down payment, when there are people hellbent on taking away our freedom who are prepared to spend blood! That's no figure of speech. When I say blood, I mean the very essence of life itself which we know the Communist dictators squander with ruthless indifference. Stalin . . .' McCarthy spoke very slowly, delivering the words as if they were playing-cards. 'Stalin . . . murdered . . . several . . . hundred . . . thousand . . . colleagues.' Back to normal speed. 'Not enemies. Colleagues, comrades, taken away, shot, never heard of again. Why? Who knows? Before that, Stalin had already murdered his Kulaks, his farmers, by the million. Some say eight million, some say ten million, maybe more. Why? Who knows? Red leaders don't have to explain their massacres. Don't have to explain anything! But one thing needs no explanation because it cries out so loudly that even the deaf, blind but unfortunately not mute liberal-loving Comm-Symps in this country cannot ignore this simple question. If that is how Stalin treated his own people, his countrymen, patriots who saved his skin against Hitler, then how do you think the Reds would treat us, the American people, if we let them dominate this fair land? Impossible, you

235

say? Think back. Remember Japan. I served in the Pacific. I saw the blood our boys shed. The price of freedom. So it's with a heavy heart that I find it my inescapable duty to report that the Communist infiltration of the United States has created a more insidious, a more deadly Fifth Column on American soil than ever before in our history . . .'

Wagner was at home, holding a book, not reading. He was thinking of his future. Manfred had been right: Arabel was a threat as long as he lived, a threat to Wagner's career, which meant his life. He was an ex-brigadier of a defeated army and an ex-head of a disgraced *Abwehr* station. He knew how very lucky he had been to get into the CIA. If the Arabel scandal came out, he was a three-time loser. Finished. It was maddening to know that Arabel was not far away, in killing range so to speak, if only he could find him.

Wagner let the book drop. He switched on the television. Senator McCarthy was blaming everything on the Communists. Wagner watched, hating himself for wasting his time. But what else could he do with it?

A row of serious-looking, sober-suited men stood behind McCarthy, one step up. One of them smiled and nodded, endorsing the Senator's claim. Not Secret Service, then. Wagner blinked. He moved closer to the set, kneeled and stared. Arabel? Arabel, yes, beyond any doubt. The director cut to a wide shot. The Capitol steps.

Wagner grabbed his car keys and ran.

'Folks write to me,' McCarthy said. 'All kinds of folks. That's good, I want to hear what the good people of America think, even including what they think about *me*. I'm told that's not the way it is with every US senator . . .' Laughter could be heard. McCarthy looked puzzled. 'Oh, you noticed it too . . . Huh . . . Well, some folks ask, they

236

say, "See here, senator, if you know so much about Communist dirty tricks, why don't you arrest the scoundrels?" Answer is: I wish I could. But I don't have the power. I have the honour to chair the Senate Sub-Committee on Investigations. Yes, *investigations*. We turn over rocks and some pretty slimy things crawl out, but we can't arrest them. Not our job. What I can do is *alert* the American people to the kinds of sabotage that Red agents trained in subversion would like to see succeed. Let me give you an example of how they might possibly seek chinks in our armour. For instance, I've learned that a new military radio which is being tested for the Pentagon has been reported as having an unbelievably good performance. I'm no expert. All I know is, if it's unbelievable, I don't believe it, and I wouldn't want American soldiers to depend on it in battle. Wouldn't do any harm if the Pentagon double-checked the loyalty of that team doing the testing, would it? And I was shocked to learn how vulnerable to sabotage the state of Idaho is. Soviet scientists have been experimenting, developing a new type of potato blight. Maybe it's still in Russia, maybe it ain't. Now, as you know, a lot of your tax dollars go into the Department of Agriculture. I just hope Agriculture's on the ball. I hope nobody's draggin' his feet, for whatever reason. I think you know what I mean. And if you want to know just how smart the Reds can be, imagine how much damage it would do to the economy of our richest state, California, if the folk out there got demoralized by repeated earthquake warnings that were faked. How? By falsifying the data obtained from studying the San Andreas Fault! Experts tell me that, with the wrong man in the right place, it could easily be done. If I were Governor of California . . . I need say no more. It's kinda worrying, ain't it? I'm just one man, but if my intelligence system can pick up these kinds of risks, I sure hope our law officers and the head honchos in this Administration are keepin' their ears to the ground. I say this because I have – and I have it here – hard evidence, clear evidence, physical evidence, of a total failure, a devastating and a shameful

237

failure at every level of your government, to detect the hand of the Kremlin at work in one of the places where you might least expect to find it . . .'

★

The Shamrock Bar was closed between four and five but Tommy the barman knew Kim Philby well enough by now to let him bring his bicycle in so it wouldn't get stolen and watch the TV while he rested in the cool, sawdust-scented gloom.

'It's himself, at it again,' Tommy said. 'God knows what part of Ireland his people are from, but he has the gift of the gab.'

Almost at once, Kim saw Luis Cabrillo, above and behind McCarthy's right shoulder, and couldn't believe his luck. He squinted and blinked. Yes, definitely. Outside the Capitol. 'Forgot something,' he said. Grabbed his bike. Ran out.

The English, Tommy thought. *Running, in this heat. Never stop to think. That's how they lost India. One day they'll lose Ulster too, God willing.*

★

'You all know how Red subversion works,' McCarthy said. 'It's an evil formula, polished and perfected by evil men. It's how they seized power in Russia, in China, in a dozen nations that once were free and now are slave. Communism targets the vital organs of a nation! It infects them with its evil virus, a poison that spreads and grows unseen until it is no longer the parasite, it becomes the host, the master! What are the vital organs of America but those centres of power and influence where I have exposed treachery, callous and persistent treachery, year after year: the State Department, the Atom Bomb, the Universities, the Army, Hollywood. Yet there is one other centre of power. Some say – and it gives me no pleasure, but the truth must not be denied – some say it is the biggest business operation in America. I speak of the Mafia, organized crime, which has been infiltrated and con-

238

trolled and manipulated by the Kremlin. And when the Mob takes orders from Moscow, what hope is there for decency and honour in the USA?'

Stunned, shocked silence.

'I want you to look at this. It is a Communist Party membership card.' McCarthy opened it, held it where the cameras could zoom in. Fifty flash bulbs popped. 'The man whose face you see is Jerome Fantoni, head of one of the biggest New York crime families. For decades, Fantoni and his henchmen have conspired with Stalin to sell America down the river. Henchmen like Mafia leaders Fitz Delaney and Bender Costello, whose Party Cards I also show. These crooks are double traitors. First they betray justice, then they betray patriotism. They will deny it. Of course they will deny it! But here is hard evidence that the tentacles of the KGB are deep in the Mafia, and that must mean they are deep in America . . .'

Uproar. Reporters swarmed around McCarthy. Questions, questions, questions. Thirty minutes later he was still talking, naming names – Stefano Magaddino in Buffalo, Carlos Marcello in New Orleans, John Scalisi in Cleveland, Frankie DeSimone in LA – and hinting at rackets that were linked to the Kremlin, extortion, protection, tax-skimming, judge-bribing, union-corrupting. Luis Cabrillo was at his shoulder, quietly pleased with the sound of words that he had suggested.

Wagner was in the crowd. So was Philby. When the party was over, Luis walked away and got a taxi home. Wagner followed in another taxi. Philby, pedalling so hard that he got chest pains, followed by bike. It was rush-hour; traffic was sluggish. They both reached Connecticut Avenue in time to see Luis leave the cab and enter the apartment building. For a brief moment, Philby thought of abandoning the bike and chasing after him, to get his apartment number. But Philby was dripping sweat, he was gasping for breath, and stars were wandering across his eyeballs. He quit while he was winning. He went back to the hotel.

Wagner took the taxi back to his car, and drove home. He had a shower, sat on the bed, and thought the problem through, as a good infantry commander should.

★

'No.' Prendergast clicked his fingers and Fisk killed the TV. 'No, no, no. That doesn't hang right. It's cock-eyed.'

'The senator sounded very confident,' Fisk said.

'Think, man. Where's your training? The Mob doesn't do politics. It would be like baseball on ice. Fundamentally wrong.'

'We saw Fantoni's Party card.'

'And you saw the shit-eating grin on Cabrillo's face. I tell you, something is seriously wrong here. Why would the Kremlin infiltrate the Mafia?'

'Money,' Fisk said. 'Power. Influence.'

'But they kill each other!' Prendergast shouted. 'The Profacis shoot the Bonannos, the Gambinos shoot the Costellos! Where in God's name is the Party discipline? You can't hear the *Internationale* for the sound of gunfire!'

'Messy,' Fisk murmured.

3

The colonists licked the British; wrote a Constitution and elected a president; and made their capital in a place where the air is soggy as a hot dish-rag for three months of summer. The British sent a peace-keeping mission in 1814 and, as a gesture of goodwill, burned most of Washington. The colonists came right back and rebuilt it, which displayed that gung-ho can-do pioneer spirit, but it couldn't change the climate. Even after the sun goes down, Washington in summer still cooks at a steady simmer.

Luis wore a pair of basketball shorts, and he swaggered about, bare-chested, with a gin-and-tonic in a pint tankard,

240

while they all watched highlights of McCarthy's Press conference, switching channels from ABC to CBS to NBC and any other station they could find.

'Is that true, about the San Andreas Fault?' Stevie asked. She was wearing a man's shirt, loosely buttoned.

'It doesn't have to be true,' Luis said. 'As long as it's not proven untrue.'

'Yeah, but . . . I seen pictures. I mean, San Andreas Fault exists. It's this big long crack, keeps gettin' wider.'

'On the subject,' Julie said, 'keep your legs together, sweetheart, or go put some panties on.'

'Too damn hot . . . You got a fine brown frame, Luis.'

'Look!' he said, pointing. 'There I am again. Damn, I look good in profile.'

'McCarthy, he ain't married, am I right?' Stevie asked.

'He's a lush,' Julie said. 'Don't ever marry a lush.'

'That's me again,' Luis said. 'Not such a good shot.'

'I bet Jerome's looking at these same pictures right now,' Julie said. 'You being on TV was not a smart idea.'

'Jerome's going to be looking at a subpoena tomorrow.'

'How much sex do you guys have in a week?' Stevie asked. 'Average week?'

'Go take a shower,' Julie said.

'God, it's hot,' Luis said. He strolled on to the balcony. It would be dusk in an hour. There was a bucket of shrimps in the fridge and much white wine. 'We should eat out here,' he said.

4

Kim Philby went to the Shamrock, had two Irish whiskeys with beer chasers and made himself eat a hamburger. It would do no good if his hands were shaking from hunger as well as nerves. Also, eating killed some time.

He was not nervous about killing Cabrillo. He was nervous about missing him with the first shot, maybe just winging him, having to reload and fire again. By then Cabrillo might be running, or crawling, trying to hide. A poor target. Two or three shots must attract attention. It would get awfully messy.

In the old days, Moscow would have found a technician to handle this sort of problem. Philby was too valuable to risk, then. No longer. Now Moscow expected him to clear up his own mess.

He went back to his room and looked at his bed. An hour's sleep would settle his nerves. No. He knew that if he fell asleep, the night would be lost. He washed his face, scrubbed it dry, combed his hair, and stared at the reflection. It blinked back at him. *Don't think*, he ordered. *Do it now. Go.*

He went downstairs and fetched his bike. Bullets were in his pockets. Rifle was in the old canvas bag. He hung it on the handlebars. Nobody was likely to stop a middle-aged white man who was riding a bike with an old *A1 Fruit Farms* bag hanging on it.

The block where Cabrillo lived was all apartment buildings. Philby stopped near the front door where he had seen Cabrillo enter, and immediately he knew he couldn't go inside. Even supposing he was lucky enough to find Cabrillo, Philby knew he couldn't shoot him at close range and walk away. Or, worse still, run away. Not possible.

Small things tumbled out of the darkness and rattled softly on the sidewalk. They crunched under his foot. He picked one up. Peanut shell.

More followed. There was laughter high above.

He crossed the avenue and got a better look at Cabrillo's building. Each apartment had a balcony. Lights were burning in most apartments. Anyone on a balcony was silhouetted at worst, illuminated at best. Philby began to feel a strange emotion. It was hope.

★

Wagner waited until the dusk was a deep purple, and he drove into Washington. He parked on Connecticut Avenue and wrapped the rifle in his jacket. He was an infantryman; it

242

took him only a few seconds to appraise the terrain and decide that the best way to kill Arabel was from the roof of an apartment building on the opposite side of the avenue: good view, clear shot, no witnesses.

It was surprisingly easy to get on to the roof. He just kept climbing the stairs and went through the last door. The roof was a public space, with a couple of kids playing ping-pong, and an old guy watering his pot plants. Not a problem. If anyone got in his way, Wagner would shoot them too.

5

Had Wagner not been so eager, he would have chosen the next apartment building. It was one floor higher but it had an elevator. Philby took the elevator and found stairs leading to an open door. The roof was flat and empty except for a man practising the tenor sax. He was at the back of the building, and he didn't seem to notice Philby. He was working on *Bess, You Is My Woman Now* and having trouble with some of the octave jumps.

Philby took the telescopic lens from the bag and used it to study the apartments across the avenue. Most were lit. Many of the balconies had people on them. It took him about twenty minutes to find Cabrillo. By then the tenor sax had moved on to *Summertime, An' the Livin' Is Easy*. Fewer octave jumps, but some tricky sustained notes in the lower register. Philby assembled the rifle.

★

Stevie did the cooking. 'My second husband said he loved Shrimp Jambalaya,' she said. 'Reckoned it put poke in his pecker. That was the night he jumped off the Brooklyn Bridge.'

'No disrespect,' Julie said, 'but your sexual track record depresses the hell out of me.'

'In the morgue, I had to identify him, the corpse had an erection you could hang your hat on. The bum was mockin' me from the grave.'

'I'm going to watch TV,' Julie said.

'I'm not sayin' they wear hats in the morgue,' Stevie told Luis. 'Don't get me wrong.'

'Never,' he said. 'Call me when the shrimps are ready.'

He took plates and cutlery and glasses to the balcony and put them on a wrought-iron table that lived out there. He added garlic bread and he took the salad out of the fridge. The wine was uncorked. The night looked like black velvet. Smelled of burned barbecue, but looked like black velvet. He went inside and found Julie lying on a couch, looking at the ceiling. 'Where is this roller-coaster going to end?' she said. It wasn't a real question and he didn't give an answer. 'I worry about the McCarthy–Fantoni stuff,' she said. 'It's too rich.'

'Relax. It can't fail. Piece of cake.'

'Yeah. That's what General Custer said.'

Silence. End of discussion.

'Come and get it,' Stevie called. They strolled to the balcony.

★

Wagner was unsure until Arabel lit the candles. They dipped and flickered in the occasional breath of wind, but candlelight made all the difference. Then the difficulty was Arabel: he was too restless, he wouldn't sit. He strolled about, poured wine for the others, performed the odd dance-step, waved to neighbouring balconies. Wagner settled down and waited. The click of ping-pong went on behind him. The old guy with the potted plants had disappeared. Wagner felt very comfortable with a rifle. A rifle was a simple solution to the most complex problem. His mind was weary but, as long as it held that one, single, simple thought, he knew that, sooner or later, all would be well. *Alles in ordnung.*

★

The telescopic lens made Luis big. Philby's hands made the image shake. The cross-hairs wavered and wandered. He was holding the rifle too tightly and pressing the butt into his shoulder too hard. He told himself to relax. Gripping the rifle as if that alone would stop Cabrillo escaping was no damn good and it made his hands sweat. He laid the rifle on the parapet and dried his hands with his handkerchief. Without the telescopic lens, his vision was blurred, his eyes felt sticky. Probably more sweat. It was trickling down his forehead, dropping off his ears. The night wasn't *that* hot. So this sweat had to be the product of stress. Yet his mouth was dry. He couldn't swallow. What a bugger. You'd think the body would make a greater effort to help when a chap needed help the most.

The tenor sax had moved on to *It Ain't Necessarily So*. The tune was straightforward enough but too often the fellow ran out of breath in mid-phrase. Must be inhaling at the wrong time. Someone should tell him.

Philby wiped his eyes. He rested his elbows on the parapet and tried to imagine the rifle was fragile, delicate, not to be bruised. The telescopic lens made Luis leap into view, bare-chested, happy, waving a drink in one hand and a stick of celery in the other. Philby had stopped breathing and was allowing his forefinger to touch the trigger, when a hand raised the barrel. 'Not a good idea, Kim,' a man said. His voice was deep and rich. A good trial attorney's voice. 'We can do better.' Now the rifle was completely off target. Philby released it.

'Whoever you are,' he said, 'you cut this very fine, didn't you?'

'Well, I wasn't sure whether your target was Mr Cabrillo or the assassin on the next roof.'

Philby looked where the man was pointing. 'Nobody I know,' he said.

'Nor me.' He raised Philby's rifle and shot Wagner through the head. Wagner tumbled sideways as if someone had hooked his feet. His finger jerked the trigger and he fired at the sky. The tenor sax was reaching for a high F sharp; he heard nothing. The table-tennis kids were battling furiously through a long rally; they dimly heard shots but they were so excited they ignored them. Luis, Julie and Stevie heard noise, but they also heard echoes bouncing off apartment buildings, and they weren't sure which way to look. Cities are full of inexplicable bangs, a lot of them much louder than rifle fire. Nobody screamed. They quickly forgot about it.

'And who are you?' Philby asked.

'Mikhail. Otherwise known as Michael.' He was chunky, fortyish, clean-shaven, well dressed in a dark blue lightweight suit and knitted white tie. Already he had taken the rifle apart and stowed it in the bag. 'We can leave now. Even in Washington, I don't think more than two people will try to shoot Mr Cabrillo tonight, do you?'

'I don't know what I think. I need a large drink.'

'Easily arranged. We'll go to the Embassy.'

'I thought we might. May I ask your title there?'

'Cultural attaché.'

'Of course.' They made their way down to the elevator. 'I wonder who on earth he was,' Philby said.

A BARRAGE
OF BOMBSHELLS

1

Gregg DeWolf knew his stuff. By noon he'd found a small but smart suite on the fifth floor of a new office building on 8th Street and Pennsylvania Avenue, until recently occupied by a music publisher, now bankrupt. Luis got the rest of the lease, including furniture and fittings, for a song. Well, a sing-song. By mid-afternoon, a signwriter had painted *Metal Exchange Inc.* on the door. 'The metal is money, right?' Julie said. 'Exchanged for what?'

'My genius,' Luis said.

'I had a boyfriend was a genius, once,' Stevie said. They waited. 'With hair,' she said. 'Erik had magic hands with hair. With my body, I never found out. Dad would've killed him if he touched me.'

'Because he was a hairdresser?' Luis asked, surprised.

'No.' Stevie's eyelids were heavy with regret. 'Because he was Norwegian.'

'Life with you is one long soap,' Julie said.

'Go back and marry him,' Luis suggested.

'He quit the salon. Went to Brooklyn and joined the Bonanno gang. They didn't know Norway from Rockaway.'

'So where is he now?' Luis said.

'Oh . . .' She sighed. 'You know.'

'Jeez, that's depressing,' Julie said. 'Look, here's five bucks. Go to Alaska, men outnumber women ten to one up there, find a lumberjack who's hung like a horse, keep the change.

I'm going back to the apartment to read a history of bubonic plague for laughs.' She left.

'She's mad at me,' Stevie said.

'We're all mad at you. Every man you touch turns to mashed potato. It's unhealthy. It's un-American.'

She wasn't listening. 'I wouldn't have married those jerks if I'd known they were such creeps,' she said.

Soon the man from the telephone company came and hooked up Metal Exchange Inc. Luis's first call was to McCarthy's secretary, to give her the address and phone number. Then he put his feet on the desk and began planning what McCarthy might like to buy next. He could hear Stevie practising on a typewriter. She wasn't going to Alaska. She'd made herself the company receptionist.

★

The man took off his hat, but even so he ducked instinctively as he came through the door. He wore a lightweight rust-red blazer and tan slacks, with a soft shirt in a green check and a bottle-green bow tie. He was built like a heavyweight and dressed like a golf professional. Behind him came Senator McCarthy, built like an ex-middleweight and dressed like a crow. But McCarthy had the gun.

All this Luis took in as he swung his feet off the desk. Stevie had gone; it was early evening; the building was quiet. The gun was a military pistol. McCarthy's forefinger was hooked through a ring set in the base of the butt. So nobody was about to get shot; not without three seconds' warning, anyway.

'Colonel, meet Mr Arabel, my Chief Co-ordinator of Intelligence,' McCarthy said. 'Or Coordintel, as the jargon has it. Mr Arabel, Colonel Washington.'

'How d'you do, colonel,' Luis said.

'The privilege is entirely mine, sir.' Washington's grip made Luis's knuckles slide like ball-bearings.

'The colonel has motored here from South Carolina especially to give me this fine pistol, his personal handgun, plus what he calls clandestine information.'

'How interesting,' Luis said. 'Some Clandinfo, as the jargon has it.'

'I heard the senator's speech,' Washington boomed, 'regarding the threat of Communist agents in government departments where they operate under new identities.'

'Operation Cuckoo,' McCarthy said.

'I know the names of twelve traitors,' Washington said. 'Both their real names, that is the names they were born with, and the new identities invented for them by the KGB.'

'And you say they're all in the Pentagon, colonel.' McCarthy slumped on a couch so heavily that he hurt the springs. 'A massive example of Soviet infiltration at the heart of the military.'

'What we call Sovinfil,' Luis said. He was working hard to keep up with them. 'This is crucial intelligence, colonel.'

'Well, sir, there are times when a man must run with the ball or lose the game, and I reckon this is one of them. Now, to look at you, I'd guess you were a quarterback, sir.'

'Damn right he was,' McCarthy said. 'Prince of the Pigskin, they called him.'

'Modesty forbids,' Luis murmured.

'Last time I was in Washington was for FDR's second inauguration. Extremely cold, that day. Gentlemen, I have a train to catch. I say: no mercy. Shoot the traitors in the head. In the head, sir.'

'Depend on us, colonel.' McCarthy got up, with an effort.

'Operation Goodnight Vienna, we call it,' Luis said. The colonel stared so hard that Luis's eyes went out of focus. 'Huh,' the colonel said. They all shook hands. He left.

'No jokes,' McCarthy said. 'Guys like him got no sense of humour.'

'It's an operetta. *Goodnight Vienna*. Very popular. Very apt.'

'Fuck operetta. Jesus, I'm bushed.' He stretched out on the couch. 'What a day. What a night *and* a day. You and your goddamn Mafia Reds are killin' me. All last night, TV interviews, radio, the Press, they never stopped, when the East Coast went to bed the Midwest was askin' for more and the West Coast was just hittin' its stride. I got a couple hours sleep at four in the a.m. and then the breakfast shows started up, and after that . . .' He yawned, hugely. 'I must have done a hundred interviews. Even the *Ladies' Home Journal* wanted a slice of me.' His eyes had bags like inkwells. His body lay where it had fallen. His voice was husky but still strong.

'So the Mafia thing worked,' Luis said.

'Oh, it worked, Jack. Worked too damn well. Look: I don't enjoy formality, Mr Arabel. I'm Joe. Who are you?'

'Luis.' He got his feet back on the desk. 'How could it work too well?'

'Listen. Politics is news, and news is politics, and we run around like convicts shackled to each other. I have to keep runnin' because every ten minutes I get a new partner chained to me. News is a colossal business in America, Luis. You got three-year-old kids out there watchin' TV, for Christ's sake. All those networks, all those newspaper chains, all those smart-ass magazines like *Time* and *Newsweek* and *Dog's Life* and *Muckshifting Monthly*, and ten thousand others, they all eat news, it's what keeps 'em alive, but they're a *monster*, Luis. A goddamn monster. And I'm chained to it. The more you give, the more it wants. Exhausting.'

'Plenty of senators stay out of the news, Joe. They survive.'

That made him chuckle.

'They hide in the Party, Luis. Do what they're told, vote as they're told, crap in their pants if the Whip says so. I'm not smooth enough for that living death. I was the runt of the litter, Luis. Nine kids in my family, dirt-poor Irish, and the ugliest and the dumbest was me. So how did I get to be a United States senator at the age of thirty-eight? Not by bein' a nice guy. I climbed that greasy ladder fast by stampin' on my opponents' fingers. Kickin' 'em in the teeth. Bootin' 'em in the balls. Picked up a deal of scar tissue on the way. I'm a survivor, see. Kick a man when he's down, that's the best time to do it, so he won't get up an' bother you again . . . Where was I?'

'Clawing your way into Congress.'

'Gettin' in was one thing. Gettin' *on* was another. The

Republican Party had no time for me until I exposed the new and deadly threat to our national security.'

'Communism wasn't new, Joe.'

'Not Communism, pal. The Democrats. We'd had a Democrat in the White House since 1932. Thirteen years of FDR, then seven years of Truman. The Republicans were in black despair. And all the while, the Democrats were covering up their Commie pals who were selling America short. Well, I exposed those twenty years of treachery, Luis. My anti-Communist crusade blew the lid off the Dems, gave the Republicans the lever they needed to get Eisenhower into the White House, and saved America from betrayal, disgrace and spurious infamy.'

'If it's spurious it can't be infamy, Joe.'

'Whatever. I saved the Party, and look, I'm still on the outside, ploughin' my lonely furrow. Half the Republicans on the Hill owe their seats to me. I get no thanks. No job in the Administration – that'll never happen. Ike never mentions my name. What keeps me alive? It's the news, Luis. As long as I can make the news, I've got a place in politics. But it's been three long years, pal, an' I'm beginnin' to feel kinda ground down. It's a monster, Luis. It always wants more.'

The senator stood up, which took an effort. He got his feet on the floor, leaned forward until his belly was above his knees, pushed off with his hands, straightened before he toppled. His face was cherry-red patched with white. 'Fuckin' doctors,' he said. 'Fuckin' useless.' He moved to the door.

'Wait,' Luis said. 'What about Colonel Washington?'

McCarthy was too weary to turn around. 'He's a loony. I get fifty loonies a week. Some write, some phone, some visit. I reckoned you ought to see one.'

'So his lists of names are . . . gibberish, then?'

'Hell, no. All those guys played in the Yale–Harvard football game in 1924. The colonel took his real names from the Harvard team. His fake identities, they played for Yale. He gave me the match programme as proof. Gave me the gun, too.'

'Truly loony.'

251

'Yeah. He played right tackle for Harvard in 'twenty-five. No helmets in them days. I guess he took too many bangs on the head.' McCarthy opened the door. 'Remember what I said, Luis. We gotta feed the monster.' He walked along the corridor, his feet at ten-to-two. A man who drank as much as he did learned to keep a steady balance.

2

The CIA looked after its own, especially when dead. Wagner, it said, had recently shown signs of depression and mental instability. That was enough for the Washington PD to lose interest. The coroner fast-tracked Wagner, had the autopsy report by noon, learned nothing from it, briefly considered suicide, settled for accidental death. Wagner had dropped his rifle, safety was off, impact caused fatal shot. Why was he on the roof? Irrelevant. Cremation authorized. Funeral tomorrow.

3

Washington is a good place to get out-of-town newspapers. Julie had bought a dozen and she was sitting cross-legged in the middle of the apartment, pages scattered all around. She didn't look up.

'The senator dropped by,' Luis said. 'Had a chat.'

She nodded. Went on reading.

He made himself a drink, bourbon and ginger, lots of ice, and wandered back. McCarthy looked up from every front page, stern but just, alongside four-column reports, continued inside. More pix, usually of men hiding their faces with their hats. Features. Editorials. Cartoons.

'Joe's out on his feet,' he said. 'Interview, interviews. Most of last night and all day today. He can scarcely walk.'

She didn't even nod.

'He wants to keep up the momentum,' Luis said. 'Keep the Press salivating. Lead the crusade to save America, et cetera.'

'How about you?' she said. 'What are you crusading to save?'

'Me?' This was getting heavy. 'Oh, you know me, sweetheart. I'm just along for the ride. Can I get you a drink?'

'You're only in this for the money.'

'Well, that too. The money goes with the ride. How do we know we've screwed the senator unless he pays up? Anyway, you were the one who hit him for twenty-five grand.'

'Yeah.' She was staring at the papers. 'I never thought he'd pay.'

'He got us cheap. Those headlines are pure gold to a politician.'

'He's a thug. All his rant about saving America is selfish, sadistic crap. He's not defending freedom. He's creating tyranny.'

'Well, at least it won't be a Communist tyranny.' Luis had said it before he realized what a blunder it was. Too late now.

'You promised you would make McCarthy look stupid. Now look.' She stirred the newspapers with her foot.

'No, I said if we *inflated* him, he'd burst. That's the plan. And since there's money to be made — '

'Billy Jago's dead.' She still didn't look up, still sat round-shouldered, head down. He was silent. 'Billy Jago's dead,' she said in exactly the same, flat voice. 'Billy's dead.' Then she was weeping, sobbing, her shoulders shaking. Luis was startled. Should he kneel, try to comfort her? Before he could decide, she stood up and walked to their bedroom and shut the door. He could hear the sobs. He took a long swig of bourbon and ginger.

She came out five minutes later, completely calm. She had changed her clothes and packed an overnight bag. Again. Twice in two weeks. 'Don't tell me you're sorry about Billy,' she said. 'You don't give a shit about Billy. And I don't give a shit about you. If I stay here I'll probably kill you.' She left.

He made himself another drink and replayed in his mind all

253

that had been said. He mentally rewrote parts of his dialogue. The changes were unconvincing. He gave up.

Stevie came out of her bedroom, yawning and combing her hair. 'Reckoned you'd be hungry,' she said. 'I made a whole mess of Shrimp Jambalaya.'

'Bloody hell. We had that last night.'

'You said you liked it. Certainly ate enough.' Luis grunted and turned away. 'Huh,' she said. 'No pleasin' some folk. Where's Julie?'

'Oh, you know,' he said.

He fished out the *New York Times* and found the obituary. Suicide. Shotgun. The body had been lying in the bungalow for at least a week before it was discovered. Easy to imagine the scene. Difficult to forget it.

That was why she'd bought the papers. Not for McCarthy. For Billy Jago.

4

'Checklist,' Prendergast said. 'What you got?'

'First is Philby,' Fisk said. 'Not in the British Consulate or the Harvard Club. Gone where?'

'Do we care? The Brits have retired him. What harm can he do? Next.'

'Man called Wagner, ex-Nazi, now CIA, shot dead. Only reason I included him is it happened opposite Cabrillo's apartment.'

Prendergast took a stroll around the room, tossing a coin from hand to hand, while he analysed the incident. 'First of all, CIA is stiff with ex-Nazis. Secondly, Washington is the place to go if you want to get shot. Thirdly, I don't give a damn. Next.'

'This Colonel Washington that McCarthy brought to Cabrillo.'

'Loony.'

'He gave the senator a gun.'

'First positive thing you've said. With luck, they'll all shoot each other.'

'You're thinking of the Profacis and the Gambinos,' Fisk said. 'Different spelling altogether.'

★

'History is an implacable debt-collector,' the minister said. 'Long after the peace treaties are signed, war still claims its casualties. We may never know what battles of the mind our dear departed friend and colleague was fighting at the end, but none can doubt that he fought them with a dogged determination. And now, in the sure and certain knowledge that his soul has found eternal peace, we release his body to its everlasting rest.' He pressed a button. The conveyor belt trundled Wagner into the furnace. The minister had more to say, but Manfred Sturmer wasn't listening. He was thinking that his friend Wagner, a brigadier of infantry, was the last man in the world to shoot himself with his own rifle. The CIA had the best firearms experts in the world. They had dropped Wagner's rifle a hundred times, with the safety off, and it hadn't fired. Nobody could examine the bullet that killed Wagner: it had gone through his head and vanished. But Manfred was certain that it came from another gun.

He had accumulated a month's leave. If he left now, today, he could be in Frankfurt tomorrow. He knew Frankfurt well, he would be safe there. Yes.

5

Gregg DeWolf suggested the Duncan Hotel. Clean and quiet, he said. Guests hardly ever got drunk and shot out the light bulbs.

Julie was finishing breakfast when Bobby Kennedy came in and sat at her table. 'The senator wants a brainstorming session this morning,' he said. His voice was like a crack in a piece of slate.

'Uh-huh.' She drank some coffee. 'How did you know I was here?'

'You and Mr Arabel are valuable to the senator's team.'

'You mean someone's snooping on the apartment.' Kennedy almost shrugged. 'What makes this brainstorming so urgent?' she asked.

'Not here,' he said. 'I'll tell you in the car.'

'Sinister,' she said. 'Irresistible.'

★

Kennedy drove a 1948 Chevy. It chugged like a locomotive leaving Union Station. The seats sagged. The gear stick shuddered. 'Your old man gave you a million bucks when you were twenty-one,' she said. 'I read about it in *Pravda*.'

'It's a car, it gets me there.'

'I should care. What's the panic about?'

'The senator's getting some flak over this Red Mafia stunt. He'll explain.'

'Why me? I'm the agent, not the principal.'

'The senator trusts your judgement.'

'Sure. And he fancies my ass, which isn't for rent or sale. My judgement he can have for a hundred bucks a day.' No response. The Chevy's motor rumbled as if it were running on cobblestones. A tired smell of charred rubber seeped into the car. 'Get yourself some decent wheels,' she said. 'If you wanna fight the world, you gotta fight the traffic first.'

'Everyone interferes,' he said. 'Government interferes, Communists interfere, lobbies interfere, unions interfere, special interests interfere, *you* interfere. This nation's getting interfered to death. The liberals are worse than the Communists. The Reds are fighting for Marx, the liberals are fighting to control the American soul, they want to do us all a heap of good, and when they've got their way, we won't remember how to *live* as free, strong, independent people. Free to succeed, free to fail. You liberals are destroying the freedom to fail. If we can dump the liberals same time as we dump the Communists, America stands a chance.'

'Not my America.'

'Then stand aside,' he said. 'One freedom we guarantee is the freedom to get out of our way.'

6

The flak was financial.

McCarthy was in his office with Roy Cohn and Luis when Kennedy and Julie arrived. She made brief eye-contact with Luis, just to get it over with. They sat on opposite sides. McCarthy looked sober, well shaved and statesmanlike.

'Campaign contributions,' he said. 'The Mafia is threatening to pull the plug. They don't take kindly to my recent exposures and allegations. I reckon around half the men elected to Congress will be hurt if the threat becomes reality. At State and city level, of course, Mafia purchasing power reaches a lot deeper. So the risk is: a lot of budgets are gonna feel a lot of pain. Some folk started screamin' already.' He held up a bunch of memos. 'This morning's calls. Up to when I told my secretary I'd gone to Mass.'

Luis said, 'Is it legal for the Mafia to — '

'Of course not,' Cohn said, impatiently. 'Transactions take place indirectly, covertly. It just takes blinds or cut-outs to conceal the origin.'

'So the Institute for Moral Welfare gives the mayor a hundred thousand bucks,' McCarthy said. 'So he appreciates it.'

'Expose the racket,' Luis suggested. 'Get the Mob money out of politics.'

McCarthy let his shoulders sag. 'You aimin' to cut my political throat?'

'The racket works,' Cohn said. 'People like it. The thing ain't bust, and we ain't gonna fix it. Can we move on? Focus on what matters?'

'You're awful quiet, Miss Conroy,' McCarthy said.

'Just thinking, senator. What's the worst can happen? Is this going to be a big news story? *Politicians Rush to Defend Mafia Kickbacks*? I don't think so. You won't lose votes. Might lose friends. Do you care? Everyone on the Hill hates you already.'

'What a dear sweet lovin' creature you are,' he murmured.

'The Mafia won't pull the plug,' Luis announced.

'Go on, astonish us,' Cohn said.

'They won't because it won't benefit them. It's just an emotional gesture, isn't it? A tiny tantrum. It won't stop the senator's campaign, and it won't help the Mafia get what it wants, because . . .' He shrugged.

'Because nothing oils the wheels of government like a greasy dollar,' Julie said.

'Ride out the storm?' McCarthy said. 'That what you're saying?' The phone rang. 'This better not be bad news.' He plucked the receiver as if it were hot. 'Doing nothing won't get us out of this hole,' Cohn said quietly. 'We need a counter-attack, a bombshell, something to grab everyone's attention so they forget about this Mafia shit.'

'My client has several proposals in hand,' Julie said confidently.

Luis twitched. 'Under development,' he said. He cleared his throat.

'A barrage of bombshells,' she said.

'Fully authenticated?' Cohn said. 'No bullshit?'

Luis nodded. He was trying to think of something to say, when McCarthy put down the phone. 'They got tremors in California,' he said. 'All those damn swimming pools are goin' splish-splosh, and some folks are blamin' *me*, because I went on the radio with that San Andreas story. Everythin' was fine and dandy until McCarthy interfered. *Now* look. That's what they're sayin'.'

'They're all crazy in California,' Cohn said.

'I sent them an earthquake, just to further my political career. People will say that.'

'Tremors,' Cohn said. 'They get tremors all the time. Mr Arabel's got something ten times bigger.'

'I need a drink,' McCarthy said.

Kim Philby moved out of the Hampton Hotel and into the Soviet Embassy. As he unpacked his bag and lay on the bed, he realized how dog-tired he was. Hiding while he hunted had drained his strength. Uncertainty, isolation, worry about money had nagged as heartlessly as hungry children. Life was hard outside the solid, reassuring framework of MI6. He was remembering the comfort he had taken from being part of the department even while he betrayed its secrets, when he fell asleep.

Mikhail woke him. It was afternoon. They drank tea in the garden.

'Cottington-Beaufort should never have sent you here,' Mikhail said. 'He's been in England too long, he's started to *think* like an Englishman. Trouble in the colonies? Send a gunboat. That's you, Kim.'

'I couldn't hit a bass drum in a phone box, Mikhail.'

'Just as well. Your man Cabrillo is too valuable to lose. We need him here.'

'A fortnight ago he was vermin, to be shot on sight. Now he's a protected species.'

'Let me explain. First of all, he's forgotten about you, Kim. Abandoned his foolish memoirs, moved on, found a new career with Senator McCarthy. That's the second point in his favour. McCarthy is doing more damage to the morale of the American people than Pearl Harbor, the Crash of 'twenty-nine, and the death of Valentino, all combined.'

'A very large claim,' Philby said.

'Think how much money he saves us. McCarthy has persuaded America that there is a Russian spy on every block, a saboteur in every factory, a traitor at every level of government. He's worth fifty infantry divisions to us. Every time he opens his mouth he inflicts further damage on American pride and trust and self-confidence. McCarthy has done what years of Soviet propaganda failed to do: he has made America afraid of its own shadow.'

'Jolly good show.'

'And just when McCarthy was beginning to sound a little tired, lacking the old bite, along comes Cabrillo with a bag full of bright ideas.'

'He always had plenty of those.'

'Divide and conquer. McCarthy is dividing America into little, nervous, suspicious, demoralized pieces, Kim. He mustn't be allowed to stop. Cabrillo's help is crucial.'

Philby felt lost. This wasn't hard-nosed espionage. He got up and wandered about the garden. Noisy bees were plunging head-first into the yellow flowers of a big bush. 'Look at this,' he said. 'Such a mad rush. And when all is done, they don't even get the honey. Some interloper comes in and steals their glory. Makes a chap wonder if it's worth the effort.'

'Stay here for a while,' Mikhail said. 'Read the transcripts. I don't always get the sense of American slang.'

'Who *was* that on the next roof?'

'CIA. Not quite right in the head, it seems.'

'Not after you'd finished with him,' Philby said.

8

After the crisis meeting, Julie and Luis went to Metal Exchange Inc. Stevie was there, practising her typing. She had bought roses to go on the reception desk, a coffee-maker, magazines for clients to look at. 'You got any work for me?' she said. 'I'm gettin' bored.'

'Write your memoirs,' Julie said.

Stevie shook her head. 'Story of my life is gonna be called "He Died with His Pants on",' she said.

They left her typing the title to see how it looked, and went into the conference room. 'I thought perhaps you'd left town,' Luis said.

'It crossed my mind. Then Bobby told me your pal Joe was in deep trouble, and I had to see the show. Congratulations, kid. Your Commie Mafia exposé was dynamite. I hope it blows his tiny brains out.'

'Tiny brains.' There was a fake fireplace at the end of the room, and he stood on a chair so as to perch on the wooden mantelpiece. It was narrow and uncomfortable, but it gave him height. He felt in need of superiority. 'You're the expert there. Why did you tell Joe I have several proposals in hand? That's lunacy.'

'No, it's policy. You said we were going to keep inflating him until he exploded.'

'He'll never explode. The more I give, the more he wants.'

'And the more he pays.'

'I haven't got any damn proposals. I'm burned out.' He flexed his buttocks. 'I'm running on empty.'

'Horseshit. I'm your agent, I say when you're empty. Get your ass in gear, Luis. Feed the senator some five-star crap.'

One end of the mantelpiece gave way. Luis crashed. He knocked over a set of fire irons. Bits of plaster fell on him. He lay on his back and watched a small cloud of dust drift away. 'You're fired,' he said. 'Take your crass irresponsibility and go.'

'Not until I get my ten per cent,' Julie said. He flung the poker at her. Not even close. 'No back-lift,' she said. 'Poor follow-through.'

TIME THE COSSACKS
RODE TO THE RESCUE

1

Cohn and Schine came up with some good new ideas, so they said. Ways to get the senator back in the headlines. He hated them. 'The good shit isn't new,' he told them, 'and the new shit isn't good. We got to regain the initiative, goddamn it. Draw blood, Commie blood. Keep leaning on Arabel. He's gotta deliver. Twenty-five grand, for Christ's sake.'

Cohn telephoned Luis.

'I've got some hot projects in the pipeline,' Luis said.

'Pipeline.' Cohn sucked his teeth. 'How long is this pipeline?'

'My source can't be hurried. He's in a very delicate position. It's not like inserting a coin and getting a bottle of Coke.'

'And how hot is hot?'

'Red hot,' Luis said. 'In both senses.'

'We're not talking picayune politics here. We're in a war to save America.'

'In a must-win situation,' Luis said, 'there can be no room for complacency.' Cohn couldn't argue with that.

★

Stevie was alone at Metal Exchange. She sat at her desk and wondered what James Stewart was doing that very moment. Making a movie in California, probably. Riding a horse. Tipping his hat to a lady. Not boozing, not jumping off a bridge, not putting bullets into passers-by, and not the kind of man that she would ever, *ever* get a chance to meet. Growing up in northern New Jersey put her out of reach of James Stewart permanently.

The fact hit her like a jolt of static. She was trapped in her family. No matter where she went, she would never be happy, because she was the daughter of a wop mobster and, if James Stewart ever saw her, he would be the DA and she would be lying dead, cut down by wild crossfire in a raid on a spaghetti joint. What a bummer.

Without knowing what she wanted to say, she phoned her father in New Jersey. The elderly manservant knew her voice. Her father was in conference with his attorney. Would she like to leave a message?

'Tell him . . . Oh, Jeez, I dunno . . . tell him I'm in DC an' I'm workin' for Luis Cabrillo, government work. Tell him Chick Scatola had a really bad accident. Say I'm sorry McCarthy's leanin' on him but he criticized me plenty times, now he knows how it feels. You want the number here?' She rattled it off and hung up. She knew he wouldn't call her back. Never did.

Everything was done politely. A man in a polite suit knocked on the door and politely asked to see Mr Jerome Fantoni. He was politely frisked and escorted to Mr Fantoni whom he politely served with a subpoena to appear before the Permanent Sub-Committee on Investigations of the Senate Government Operations Committee, in Washington DC, two days hence.

'Plead the Fifth,' his attorney advised. 'Stonewall. Bore 'em to death.'

'No. The less I say, the worse I look. I won't duck and dodge like some frightened film star. This grubby senator has blackened my character. I'll stand up and fight like a man.'

'And you'll fall like a log. They've got your Party membership card, haven't they? '

'It wasn't illegal then. How can they —'

'Forget it, Jerome. Plead the Fifth. And take a dozen handkerchiefs. Those TV lights are damn hot, and sweat has a way of making a man look awfully guilty.'

★

Kim Philby read transcripts of the meeting in McCarthy's office, reduced them to a summary, gave it to Mikhail.

'I don't like this,' Mikhail said. 'McCarthy's morale is weakening. And your Mr Cabrillo is dragging his feet. At this rate, fear will lose its grip on America. I'm appalled.'

'Can't your people do something helpful?'

'Such as what?'

'A small war, maybe. Invade a corner of Turkey, or a bit of India. Just for a little while.'

'No, no, Kim. Foreign affairs don't interest Americans. One Korea is enough. Reds under their beds, that's what they want, and so do we.'

★

'If I was Cabrillo, I'd get out of town,' Fisk said.

'If I *were* Cabrillo. The supposition takes the subjunctive. Why is it a supposition?' Prendergast began throwing paper-clips at Fisk, one at a time.

'Um . . . because . . . well, it assumes that Fantoni still thinks Cabrillo is guilty of —'

'Wrong. It assumes that Cabrillo *knows* he is guilty. If innocent, why flee?'

'I bet Fantoni whacks him.' Fisk began catching the paper-clips. 'These things go in threes. Sammy, Chick, now Cabrillo.'

'Neatness. You are obsessed with neatness.' Prendergast slung the box at him, and paper-clips sprayed everywhere. 'That's reality! Chaos! Crime is like that, random and unpredictable, otherwise we would see it coming and prevent it!'

'Of course, Cabrillo might whack him first,' Fisk said.

2

Julie and Luis slept in separate beds again. He woke at six, utterly lost in time and space, not knowing dawn from dusk, bewildered by the room and the sounds. His brain had to hunt down this town, which grudgingly explained the apartment, and then a barren yesterday swam into memory, so this must be a new day.

Exhausting.

He dozed for an hour. Got up, and was on the balcony drinking coffee, wondering more or less simultaneously if he was cut out for marriage and why McCarthy had never accused the New York Jewish community of being Communist, they were powerful enough, and how birds knew all about flying without having to practise – when did you ever see a bird crash – when the phone rang.

Bobby Kennedy. Meet the senator in half an hour at the Confederate Memorial in Arlington National Cemetery. Luis asked why. 'Because nobody dares bug Arlington,' Kennedy barked, high-pitched and half a tone flat. Wasted in politics. Should have been a high school football coach.

Luis took a taxi.

McCarthy was sitting on a bench under a tree, with Cohn and Kennedy. His elbows were on his knees, his fingers were linked. When Luis approached, he raised his eyes. No other part of him moved.

'Fantoni will plead the Fifth,' he said. 'The man will sit there with his thumb up his ass and his brain in neutral and he'll plead the Fifth to the end of time.'

'Won't that make him look guilty?' Luis asked.

'Worse. It'll make him look boring,' Cohn said. 'Pleading the Fifth is not news.'

'We'll be lucky to make page five,' McCarthy said. 'TV ratings will stink. I'll be down there with the soaps.'

Luis said, 'Fantoni has turned himself into a dummy. Our problem is how to make the dummy talk.' They looked at him with no hope in their eyes. 'Give me a minute,' he said.

He turned away and walked slowly around the Confederate Memorial; slowly because it was a small monument and he had only the beginnings of an idea. Halfway around the memorial, his mental superchargers kicked in. He saw the solution, bright and clear. He began to stride.

'Here's the scenario,' he told them. 'Fantoni's on the stand. I play the senator. Mr Cohn is Fantoni.'

McCarthy flapped a hand: proceed.

'Mr Fantoni: is a member of a political organization committed to the violent overthrow of the US government fit to be a citizen?'

'I decline to answer on the grounds — '

'Yeah, we know,' McCarthy said.

'In your line of business, Mr Fantoni, how many card-carrying Communists do you know? Apart from yourself.'

'I plead the Fifth Amendment,' Cohn said.

'I have here the Party cards of you and two of your colleagues in New York. Are there more than three?'

'I plead the Fifth.'

'More than five? More than twenty?'

'Plead the Fifth.'

'More than fifty? More than one hundred active Communists known to you?'

'Plead the Fifth.'

'More than five hundred? A thousand? If you knew over *one thousand* Communists, knew them *professionally*, Mr Fantoni, as part of your business, wouldn't you remember five? Fifty? Several hundred?'

'Plead the Fifth.'

'Okay, Mr Fantoni, you're afraid your answers might incriminate you, we all understand that. Let me ask you about your leader, your hero, Josef Stalin. In your professional opinion – and you are an expert in this field – were Stalin's massacres of millions of innocent Russians a criminal act?'

'Plead the Fifth.'

'Oh? Meaning you're not sure? Let me help you out. All

your Red friends in New York, are they bigger crooks and killers than Stalin?'

'The Fifth.'

'There's a split in the New York Communists, isn't there? That's why Trotskyites recently killed your nephew Sammy Fantoni and his cousin Chick Scatola?'

'They did?' Cohn was startled.

'Blood relatives, Mr Fantoni! Your family! Murdered by Moscow! And you call yourself an American?'

'Fifth,' Cohn muttered.

'Enough, Mr Arabel.' McCarthy stood and stretched. 'I catch your drift.'

'It might be enough to get the bastard deported,' Cohn said.

'I need a drink,' McCarthy said. 'That's helpful, Mr Arabel. Keep at it. I need more. And fast.'

3

Flying in an aeroplane is not natural. Strong adult men who can tear a phone book in half are afraid of flying. Take-off terrifies them. Once airborne, they dare not look out. Landing is one long sentence of death. And the arrival lounge comes, not as a relief, but as a sense of betrayal. All that terror, for nothing. It left Jerome Fantoni feeling angrier than ever.

He despised fear. That was why he flew to Washington, because otherwise fear would have nagged him into taking the train; but now look: fear won anyway. And it would be waiting for him when he flew back to New York. Well, he wouldn't put up with it. He'd take a gun and blow its gloomy head off.

A man was waiting for him at Washington Airport.

'It's an office block,' the man said. '8th Street and Pennsylvania Avenue.'

★

'Pull over here,' Jerome said. 'I'll be twenty minutes.'

It was a suburban church, St Brendan's, not an Italian saint, not by a thousand miles. The bricks had leaked salt, which made the walls look like a cheap liquor store. Any New York building contractor did that to the diocese would get rebuked with a baseball bat. But a church was a church. Jerome went in.

Everything was light oak. The stained glass had cost fifty dollars including tax. Incense was losing a fight with pine disinfectant. He had been in cocktail lounges where the atmosphere was more devout. Still, a confessional was a confessional. He entered the box.

Several minutes passed. He hadn't slept well, he was tired. The grill banged open and startled him. They made the routine statements. An Irish priest. Not young. Not charming. Well, he wasn't here to be charmed.

He wasted a few seconds, wondering how to begin. 'I'm in a predicament, Father,' he said.

'Is that your car out front?' the priest barked. 'The 'fifty-two Lincoln?'

'Um . . . probably. Yes.'

'It's illegally parked. Can't you read? The sign's as clear as day.'

'I'm sorry.'

'So you say. And when some poor devil has a heart attack during Mass and the ambulance can't get in because a selfish eedjit has parked like you have, what good is sorry?'

'Of course you're right. Has that happened?'

'Two weeks since. Come on, I have the sick to visit. What's your problem?'

'It's a matter of faith, Father. I think I may have lost mine.'

Silence. Then a sigh, perhaps a groan. More silence. Then: 'Like an umbrella, d'ye mean?'

'I'm sorry, Father?'

'Where didya last have it? Have ye looked there?'

'Perhaps you misheard me, Father. I said — '

'I know what you said. You've lost your faith. Hell's teeth, I lose my faith a dozen times a week. Preachin' the Glory a

God in this moral bog of a country, it sucks the marrow from a man's soul, so it does.'

Jerome tried again. 'My problem is homicide, Father. Close relatives have died.'

'The police handle that.'

'Yes. But the suspects have died too.'

'Isn't it enough? You're lucky the police got that far. Have you no idea of the clear-up rate in homicide? It's pathetic.'

Jerome had come seeking compassion, and he felt he was getting blame. 'All those meaningless deaths, Father. They make life seem pointless.'

'Most life is pointless. I have gallstones. What is the point of gallstones? Do they enjoy the pain they give me? They do not.'

'Have them out, Father.'

'I did. They returned. Sonsabitches.'

Jerome made his confession and was told to read his Bible and pray. He said that he had prayed a lot but nobody was listening. 'Try again,' the priest said. 'You never know, you might get lucky. Now move your damn car.'

Jerome came out of church feeling angry with God. He was fifty-five, he had invested time and money in God, and now God was jerking him around, telling him nothing mattered because life was meaningless, and so was death. Well, that was unacceptable. God made the rules but then he made them meaningless. Okay, that was His privilege. Now Jerome Fantoni was going to break a couple. He was going to kill Luis Cabrillo. That was one death that he, personally, would not find meaningless. And Cabrillo would have all eternity to wonder where he went wrong.

He got into the Lincoln and they drove to 8th and Pennsylvania. The man called Metal Exchange on the car phone. 'He's not back yet,' he told Jerome. 'Soon, they reckon.'

4

'All this booze.' Mikhail said. 'That's not going to do his depression any good. His crusade needs a kick-start.'

'Scandal?' Kim suggested.

'Bigger. We want Americans to wonder why their God has abandoned capitalism when they're paying an arm and a leg in taxes.'

'Maybe Cabrillo will come up trumps.'

Mikhail shook his head. 'Cabrillo is tap-dancing on one leg. He's about to fall on his face. It's time the Cossacks rode to the rescue.'

'I suppose this means he's bugged.'

'We like to call it protective surveillance. It's for his own good.'

★

Julie and Stevie were at Metal Exchange when Luis came in. 'Fantoni will plead the Fifth,' he said. 'The Senator is not a happy man.'

'That's too bad,' Julie said. 'Any chance he'll die of despair before sundown?'

'I knew a girl at Bryn Mawr, her father died of a broken heart,' Stevie said.

'Misery kind of follows you around, don't it, honey?' Julie told Stevie.

'Whatcha mean, misery? He was pissed off, that's all. His wife left him, and then he took two slugs in the chest from her boyfriend. Bust his heart wide open.'

Luis briefly forgot McCarthy. 'Why?' he asked.

'It was in Texas,' Stevie explained. 'You want some coffee?'

Luis waved no. He was eager to show off his creativity. 'I found a way around the Fifth Amendment,' he told them. He was re-enacting his dialogue with Cohn, when Jerome Fantoni walked in, his right hand in his jacket pocket, holding a revolver with a silencer as big as a beer bottle. 'Nobody move,' he said.

'Hi, Dad.' Stevie waved.

'She moved,' Luis said.

'Everyone shut up! You, you're a homicidal sonofabitch, you took out Sammy and Chick and for that I'm going to blow you away.' He was trying to ease the gun out of his pocket. It seemed to be trapped.

'Quite ludicrous,' Luis said.

'Then die laughing.' Jerome tugged harder. The gun was jammed, perhaps hooked on a tear in the lining.

'Is this a stick-up or a fuck-up?' Stevie asked. Her question sounded funnier when she heard it. She laughed. Jerome glared. He got both hands on the pocket, twisting the gun, making the problem worse. 'Take your time, Dad. Nobody's goin' anywhere. Just remember, if you kill Luis, you kill the father of your unborn grandchild too.'

'You did *what*?' Jerome demanded. He still gripped the gun but he stopped wrestling with it.

'So I married the guy,' she said. 'So what? I can marry who I like. Whom. Whatever.'

'Unforgivable. Beyond belief.'

'The marriage has been consummated,' Julie said.

'Fourth time lucky,' Stevie said. 'Worth the wait.'

Luis had caught up. 'They say it could be twins. Two boys.'

Stevie moved to her father and took his arm. 'Be happy, Dad. It's what you want. Give me a kiss, at least.' Stiffly, grudgingly, he bent to kiss her forehead. Her foot hooked his leg and her fist shoved his chest, hard. His legs went one way and his torso the other. His left shoulder hit the floor first and a splash of white-hot agony washed through him. A roar like surf rose in his ears. The last thing he saw was people diving for cover. He never heard the string of stunted detonations when his fingers tightened, blew holes in his pocket and massacred Stevie's desk. Then silence.

Julie raised her head. 'That was slick,' she said.

'Bryn Mawr. Lacrosse. You learn how to protect yourself. I knew Dad has a bum shoulder. He mashed it in the Princeton–Yale football game. Never recovered.' The gun had freed itself. She kicked it from his hand. The air smelt like the Fourth of July.

★

They rolled him on to his back. His nose was bleeding. His upper lip was split and also bleeding. It was hard to know which flow was which. He was breathing well enough to blow small red bubbles. By the time they fetched a doctor his eyes were open. 'Shoulder,' he said.

'Uh-huh. Keep still.' The doctor did his stuff. 'Dislocated it,' he said. 'What happened?'

'Beats me. Act of God.'

The doctor had noticed the bullet-holed desk, the lingering cordite aroma. He said nothing. He cleaned up the face and put the arm in a sling. He telephoned the hospital. 'Thirty dollars,' he said. 'The ambulance will be extra.' Luis paid him. He left.

There was a difficult silence. Julie drank coffee. Stevie picked wood splinters out of her typewriter. Jerome sat on a couch and sucked his fat lip.

'How are those lovely boxer dogs of yours?' Luis asked.

'You planning on killing them too?'

'You are a truly miserable ingrate,' Stevie told him. Luis was impressed. 'Yesterday's crossword,' she said. 'An ingrate is a father who never calls you back even when you leave your number.'

'I was busy,' Jerome muttered. 'I got subpoenaed.'

'You phoned your father?' Luis said. 'You gave him this number?'

'Nothin' doin' here. I got bored.'

'Oh, sister,' Julie sighed. The mood was sombre.

'These people didn't rub out Chick. I was there,' Stevie told Jerome. 'I saw it all. Chick met some guy, they didn't agree.'

'So where is Chick?' Jerome demanded.

'West Virginia,' Julie said.

Nothing to add.

The ambulance arrived. Stevie sat in the back with her father.

'What's the matter with you?' she said. 'You waste a fortune on violin lessons so I can appreciate Mozart, who in my opinion cannot hold a candle to the Andrews Sisters, and then you bust in and embarrass my friends. What you did with that gun was not a class act, it was crude, and I want to make it clear that I am not married and I am not pregnant.'

'Some lucky man,' he muttered.

'Yeah, sure, go on, be negative. Nobody likes an ingrate. Wait an' see if you got any friends in the Senate, 'cus Joe McCarthy's gonna be gunnin' for you tomorrow. He is truly mean, and you, buster, are red meat in his sights.'

Jerome's shoulder felt as if it had been shot. That would teach him for taking liberties with the Almighty.

PURGATORY SHOULD BE
A PIECE OF CAKE

1

Luis poked pencils into the bullet holes in the desk. Red pencils, green, blue, brown. 'Look,' he said 'Modern art.'

'You're babbling, Luis.'

'I'm entitled to babble. That's twice the music critic of the *New York Times* has tried to kill me.'

'He's not the music critic.'

'And I wouldn't read the *Times* if he were,' Luis said. He had run out of babble. The sense of shock that lingered after Jerome left was slowly fading.

'He's gonna make quite a picture when he takes the stand,' she said. 'One arm in a sling, a lip like a banana.'

'He'll be a basket case when Joe's finished with him.'

Julie was flicking through a copy of *Harper's Bazaar*. How could anyone spend that much on lingerie? 'You're sure he'll plead the Fifth.'

'Of course.' But he knew that tone of voice. 'What else can he do?'

She turned a page and saw a black silk bikini that was sexier than skin. 'What would be the worst thing that could happen to McCarthy tomorrow?' She asked.

'Brain tumour?' She shook her head. 'Give up,' he said.

'Go where the money is, Luis. See if you can get Fantoni out of his hole. After all, you put him there. Okay, I've done all the hard work, what I need now is a coffee milkshake.'

She went out. Luis picked up her magazine and let it fall

275

open. On page after page, half-clad women, stunningly lovely, looked insolently into his eyes. Soon a cautious optimism invaded his loins. Perhaps she had forgiven him for Billy Jago's death. Not that it had been his fault. He dropped the magazine. Time to do what he was good at: cheating.

★

It was all on two sheets of paper. Julie listened while Luis acted it out. To add a bit of drama he sat in a roller chair and scooted himself about the room while he spoke. Sometimes, for variety, he made the chair spin.

'Well, it's good and simple,' she said. 'That's a start. There's one big weakness.'

'No authentication. No documents. Nothing to wave.' The chair slowly revolved to a halt. 'Bullshit won't do the job.'

'Not in a Senate hearing.'

They looked at each other, soberly, hoping they'd over-looked something. Nothing offered itself. 'Today I boosted McCarthy,' he said. 'I almost married and impregnated the eternal virgin. I damn near got shot to pieces by the Mafia. I invented the light bulb. All before lunch. Let's go eat.'

They went to a Mexican place whose name contained one vowel and seventeen consonants, mainly x, p and q. They ate chilli with grated cheese and tiny crackers and drank Dos Equos beer. They went back to the office. A man they had never seen before was waiting. 'You got a customer,' Stevie said.

'We haven't got a business,' Luis said.

'Metal Exchange is just a name,' Julie told the visitor. 'I won it playing poker.'

'But you need something, Miss Conroy,' Mikhail said. 'You need authentication and documents. Something to wave.' Nobody in the room moved, nobody breathed. Even the traffic noise seemed to stop. 'You need help to get Mr Fantoni out of his hole, and bullshit won't do it, Mr Cabrillo.'

276

The traffic moved again. 'How did you . . .' Luis began.
'Oh,' Mikhail said, 'you know.'

★

They moved into the conference room, where the chairs were
more comfortable. He said his name was Michael; no surname.
'The only authentication I cannot provide is my own,' he said.

'Let's get this straight,' Luis said. 'We've prepared a new
scenario for Fantoni's hearing that says — '

'I know what it says.'

'Oh. Yes. Of course. Sorry. Well, it needs a dossier to
support it, by tomorrow morning . . .'

'I've done this before, Mr Cabrillo.'

'Okay,' Julie said. 'Suppose you tell us.'

Mikhail told them. They made suggestions, added this,
discarded that. After forty minutes he looked at his watch. 'If
I go now, you can have it by ten tonight,' he said.

They walked with him to the elevator. 'You know, this is
very strange,' Luis said. 'The senator believes my stuff comes
from a secret informant. But that's all balls.'

'Yes. I know.'

'And now you turn up.'

'Just in time.'

'But you haven't asked for money,' Julie said.

'Not that we have any money,' Luis said.

'You have $29,280, as of this morning,' Mikhail said.
'Relax. My services are free.' The doors opened. They all
shook hands. '*Dosvedanya*,' he said. 'Whatever that means.'

★

Jerome Fantoni had a suite in the Hotel Washington. Julie
met him in the rooftop bar. The hospital had put his shoulder
back and given him a stylish black sling, but there was little
they could do for his swollen lip. He was drinking milk: the
doctors had advised no booze for a couple of days. She asked
for a champagne cocktail.

277

'I read your script,' he said. 'I see no problems.'

'Good. We kept everything simple.'

'Too simple. I've added colour, emphasized the chiaroscuro. Or, to use a metaphor from the concert hall, I've written my own cadenzas.'

'Bully for you. You realize the hearing's liable to get kind of intense.'

'Miss Conroy, I played Macbeth for the Princeton Dramatic Society. My performance was described by the *Herald-Tribune's* critic as "majestic, manly, momentous". You have the dossier?'

'You have ten thousand dollars?'

She gave him a fat file. He gave her a briefcase. For a moment their eyes met. He said, 'It would be crass of each of us to ask the other how this was done so speedily.'

'You bet.'

After that, there was nothing left to do but enjoy the view. Jerome sipped his milk. He pointed to the floodlit White House. 'The Tomb of the Well-Known Warrior,' he said. 'I feel sorry for Eisenhower.'

'Why?'

'People tried to kill FDR, and Truman, so chances are that someone is planning to kill Ike. We are a violent nation.'

'Yeah. That reminds me: d'you want your gun back?'

He shook his head. She finished her drink. Said goodnight. Got a taxi. Hugged the briefcase. Ten per cent of this should buy a black silk bikini and leave some change.

★

'How much?' Luis asked. They were in bed.

'Ten grand.'

'Good God.' He watched the shifting pattern of moonlight reflected on the ceiling as the curtains blew with the breeze. 'Did you have to haggle?'

'No. Ten grand is the right price, Luis. Us agents know this sort of thing.'

He turned on to his side, so that his body matched hers, his knees behind her knees, his chest against her back, and he slipped an arm around her waist. 'You're brilliant,' he murmured into her hair, 'and you smell wonderfully of lemons.' She made pleasantly agreeable sounds. 'You could have tried for fifteen,' he said.

'You're a turd, Luis,' she said softly. 'A turd with talent, but still a turd. Now go to sleep. Big day tomorrow.'

2

This was theatre. The hearing had precious little to do with law. The chairman and his fellow senators sat in a row and looked down on the witness. Around him and behind, the room was packed with reporters, cameramen, public, lawyers, cops. The gallery was full. Cohn and Kennedy lurked near McCarthy. As chairman, he had the gavel and everyone expected him to hammer damn hard. The crowd wanted high drama. They hadn't come for a civics lecture, they'd come for blood.

Jerome Fantoni took the oath. He looked good: hair thick, silvering at the temples and well disciplined; a dark grey suit of conservative cut, buttoned over the sling but the left sleeve hung empty, obvious to everyone; a discreet tie of dark red and navy blue stripes; white shirt with the cuffs just showing.

The chairman gavelled until he got silence, and began, 'Now, Mr Fantoni, you live and work in the New York area, am I right?'

'That is where I live and vote. Work sometimes takes me elsewhere.' His swollen lip gave him a slight lisp.

'Uh-huh. This work elsewhere, does it bring you in contact with *Communists*?' McCarthy made the word ring out.

'Let's cut out the preliminary fencing and sparring, senator. I know you enjoy it but it's a waste of everybody's time.' Fantoni's voice was calm and confident and quiet. The shuffling and whispering in the room ceased. 'You want to hear how many Communists I've ever known, don't you?'

'Well, this makes a change,' McCarthy said, smiling, and the crowd chuckled. 'Put it like that, Mr Fantoni, then yes I do. Exactly how — '

'Three hundred and seventeen. That's by personal contact. I know *of* others whom I have not met. Perhaps five hundred.'

That popped the silence. All over the room, people were saying: *Five hundred! You hear that?* McCarthy got his gavel going. Cohn leaned forward and said something. McCarthy nodded. His eyes had the gleam of a cardsharp who knows he's won and wants the other player to keep bidding.

'Three hundred and seventeen Communists you personally know. Is that in the United States, Mr Fantoni?'

'I never said that. I never said Communists I *know*, I said Communists I've *ever known*. Some are dead. You should pay more attention, senator. Do you want the whole story?' Still calm and quiet.

'Just remember your place, Mr Fantoni. We ask the questions here.' As McCarthy shuffled some papers, Fantoni said, loud enough for the microphone to catch, 'Then why doesn't he get on and ask them?' A few in the crowd applauded.

More gavel. 'I want the facts, Mr Fantoni. Communists you've known, dead or alive, in this country, total three one seven. That right?'

'It may not be right, senator, but it's correct.'

Ripple of laughter.

Kennedy said in McCarthy's ear: 'He can't plead the Fifth now. He's hung himself, senator.'

McCarthy's hand had covered his mike. 'Craziest damn suicide I ever saw.'

'Nail him down, boss,' Cohn said.

When in doubt, McCarthy gavelled. He beat until dust rose. 'Mr Fantoni, give us the facts. Tell us how many of the three-one-seven communists you've known are involved in organized crime?'

'Some were politicians. Is that organized crime?' Big laugh. Fantoni's face never changed. 'Best Marxists I ever met were in City Hall. Best rackets, too.' The crowd agreed.

'Mr Chairman, if I may,' another senator said. McCarthy

280

nodded. 'Why did you join the Communist Party, Mr Fantoni?'

'Because the FBI asked me to.'

A blizzard of flash bulbs. The witness kept his head still. One eyebrow was raised, wrinkling his brow. Otherwise, no change.

'That's the most unheard-of thing I ever heard of,' McCarthy said.

'Tell us more,' the other senator said.

'Your chairman told me to remember my place, sir.'

'Very well, Mr Fantoni. *Why* did the FBI ask you?'

'It was J. Edgar Hoover's idea, so perhaps you should put the question to him. However, I'll do my best. Hoover invited me to form a Communist club at Princeton so that he could keep track of leftist sympathizers. You must remember that, in some intellectual circles, Communism was, in the twenties, fashionable if not respectable. Rather like gin during Prohibition. Excuse me.' He took a sip of water.

'Brilliant,' Julie said quietly. She and Luis were in the gallery. 'Now he's running the show.'

'The FBI financed the Princeton Communist Club,' the witness said. 'All done covertly, of course. No incriminating records kept by us. Without Hoover's money, Communism would never have survived at Princeton. Our treasurer was hopeless. He is now the professor of mathematics at the University of Texas, I believe . . . But Hoover got more than he expected. The Soviet Consulate in New York recruited me when I graduated. They trained me to be a longterm underground secret Communist agent – a sleeper who could infiltrate American society and be ready when the KGB had work for me. It wasn't the KGB then, of course. It was the NKVD. I told Hoover, and Hoover told me to do exactly what they wanted.'

McCarthy said, 'So you were a secret agent for the Kremlin.'

'And for the FBI. I was a double agent.'

'But you signed for the Kremlin first. How many Americans have you betrayed?'

'Mairzy doats and dozey doats,' the witness said, 'and little lamsey tivey.'

'That's an insolent answer.'

'It was a dumb question. If I didn't act like a dedicated Red when I met the Communists, I was no use to the FBI. But my ultimate loyalty was to the USA.'

'And when we ask J. Edgar Hoover — '

'He'll deny it. Standard operating procedure. Last thing Hoover said to me was that if I ever lost my cover, the Bureau would deny any knowledge of me. That's how all intelligence agencies work. I'm surprised at your naïveté, senator. Did you really expect me to come here with a double agent's badge?'

'No proof, then.'

'Not from the FBI. Plenty from the Soviet side.' Fantoni opened a document case. 'These reports are all from the archives of various Soviet embassies. They cover my knowledge of various illegal or un-American activities.' He held up a fistful of papers. 'Why has the FBI never arrested me? Because they knew about everything in advance. I told them. Copies of all these documents are in the FBI files.'

Another senator claimed the microphone. 'Mr Fantoni, would you have us believe you *stole* all those Soviet documents?'

'Yes, sir. I did.'

'But why?'

'Because I knew the day would come when I would face the difficult task of proving my patriotism.'

McCarthy gavelled. 'This hearing will go into closed session!' he announced. 'Marshals, clear the room!'

3

The Carolina shrimps were undoubtedly tasty, but after all that Jambalaya they felt shrimped out. The red snapper was sure to be good; or there were crab cakes. Or grilled salmon. Hard-shell steamed crabs. Lobster. Old Henry's Tavern was the best seafood restaurant in Foggy Bottom. Said so on the menu.

They ordered. Mikhail did the wine: Bordeaux Blanc.

'What d'you think's happening now?' Julie asked.

'They'll have to get a translator for the dossier,' Mikhail said. 'And stenographers. We have plenty of time.'

'I bet they get in experts to test the paper and the ink and stuff,' Luis said. Julie patted his hand. 'Of course it's all genuine,' he said. 'I keep forgetting.' For a moment he was flustered. 'Did you ever meet Stalin?' he asked.

'Give the poor guy a break,' Julie told him.

'Forgive me,' Luis said. 'Shocking bad taste. I'm quite mortified.'

Mikhail tasted the wine, and nodded. When the waiter had gone away, he said, 'I know the collapse of western capitalism is inevitable, but personally I hope it doesn't happen until after lunch. In fact I'm prepared to wait indefinitely.'

'I know you,' Julie said. 'There was something familiar but I've just placed it. We met a couple of times in New York, years ago, at Bonnie Scott's place. You're Gib Rail. The author. He's Gibbon Connor Rail,' she told Luis. 'Wait a minute. Weren't you kind of bald?'

'A triumph of Soviet technology.' Mikhail smoothed his hair.

'A novelist,' Luis said. 'I wish I had time to write a novel.'

'You got expelled,' Julie said. 'Didn't you?'

'All a misunderstanding.'

'I met Graham Greene once,' Luis said. 'He was in MI6.'

'I don't remember that,' Julie said.

Luis snapped a breadstick. 'He said he admired my style enormously. I appear in some of his recent novels. Lightly disguised.'

'And I'm Queen Marie of Rumania,' she said.

4

The Sub-Committee came back from lunch to find that the translations had been sorted into groups. Five groups. Five senators. A happy coincidence. Each man settled down to read his pages. Apart from the occasional muttered curse or grunt of surprise, the room was quiet.

'Hot as pigshit,' McCarthy sighed, 'as we say in Wisconsin when a virgin comes to town, which is rarely. Who wants to start? What did you draw, Henry?'

'I got labour unions,' Henry said. 'Seems our witness was a go-between for the Communist Party and various unsavoury gangsters during the twenties and thirties. See here: they wanted Machine-Gun Kelly. Couldn't get him. Too expensive.'

A senator called Sherry said, 'The Reds were fighting for the unions, right?'

'Usually. The CP helped the West Coast Longshoremen's union but when the Party tried to take over the garment industry it had a shoot-out with the needleworkers' union in New York. Then again, Communists were involved in the Memorial Day Massacre in South Chicago, 1937. Remember that? Steel union marched on Republic Steel, police shot ten workers. Party was disappointed. Not enough blood.'

'Let's move on,' McCarthy said. 'Sherry?'

'I got Race Riots, Joe, and by God the Reds found themselves one hell of a happy hunting ground.' This amused the others. 'Here's one of the best. Detroit, 'forty-three. The blacks are pissed off because the army's segregated and United Auto Workers is all white. Our witness claims he dreamed up the Double-V slogan for the blacks.'

'Victory at home and abroad,' Henry said. 'I was in Detroit that year. Double-V was everywhere.'

'Sure,' Sherry said. 'And UAW let the blacks into the union and every white man in Detroit saw his job, his neighborhood and his cute blonde daughter in danger. One hell of a riot. Thirty-four dead.'

'You're up, Chester,' McCarthy said.

'Okay. Sabotage. I found three plums in my pie. First up, there's the liner *Normandie*, burns until it capsizes at a pier on the Hudson, maybe an accident, maybe a local Red did it, our witness thinks the guy's bragging. Second, the invasion of Mexico in 1936. Seems — '

'I never heard of that,' McCarthy said.

'It never happened. Father Coughlin, the radio priest, remember him? Tried to get General Butler, ex-commandant US Marine Corps, to overthrow the Mexican government, for reasons too crass to contemplate. Our witness claims he put the priest up to it.'

'Coughlin was a rabid Fascist,' Henry said.

'So what? The Reds will get into bed with anyone who suits their purpose. Lastly, the bungled assassination of FDR in 1933, when a jerk called Zangara shot the Mayor of Chicago instead.'

'Don't see how that helped the Party,' Chester said.

'Rumour was, Zangara was paid to shoot the Mayor of Detroit. Detroit was very anti-Communist in those days.' Chester held up a page. 'It's all here.'

'Amazing,' McCarthy said. 'Who's next?'

'Economic Riots,' Byron said. 'You probably know this stuff already. Chicago Eviction Riot of 1931. Depression, no jobs, no money, families evicted by the thousand. CP organized a fight back, so they say. Likewise in Arkansas, 1935. Tenant farmers got kicked off their land. Quite a war down there.'

'Take your word for it,' McCarthy said. 'All I've got is some crap about Commie propaganda. Let's move on.'

They sent for the witness.

'Three hundred and seventeen known Communists, I believe you said,' the chairman told him. 'What are their names?'

'Twenty-four are dead,' Fantoni said. 'You can have those.'

'We want the living.'

'No. You and your subpoena have blown my cover. You've needlessly destroyed my value to the FBI. But I'm not the only double agent who is active inside the Communist Party. Other patriotic Americans are still at work. Imprison me if you wish. I shall not reveal their names.'

Byron had a question. 'Mr Fantoni . . . Why are you a crook?'

'Can you think of a better front, sir?'

'But doesn't that make it difficult for you to contact the FBI?'

'They contact me, sir, which surprises nobody.'

285

'I see. What happened to your shoulder? And your mouth?'

For the first time, Jerome almost smiled. 'I tripped over the cat,' he said. Byron recognized a coded message when he heard one. 'I'm through here,' he said. Sometimes you just had to trust the other guy.

★

On behalf of the Sub-Committee, Roy Cohn made a very brief statement to the Press. 'The hearing's over, gentlemen,' he said. 'No questions. Good afternoon.'

★

By then McCarthy was in his office, trying to catch up on his drinking.

'Sonofabitch could of pleaded the Fifth,' he grumbled. 'Would of saved a lot of trouble. Now I'm up to my neck in counter fuckin' intelligence. Whyn't the stupid bastard plead the Fifth?'

Nobody knew. Schine came in with some afternoon newspapers. 'Three hundred and seventeen known and active Communists.' He pointed to a headline. 'Congratulations, senator.'

'I've been screwed by a New Jersey mobster,' McCarthy growled. 'I feel soiled. How can you trust a man who sleeps with the enemy?'

'That's Princeton for you.' Cohn shook his head. 'No moral fibre.'

5

Luis and Julie walked across the Mall and looked at the Potomac. 'Maybe it's time to cut and run,' he said.

'Your decision. Personally, I was hoping to see McCarthy crash and burn. And I like making him pay. God knows he made me pay plenty.'

Luis sat on the grass and hooked his hands around his knees. A wandering dragonfly hovered, watching him watch it. The difference was the dragonfly saw a man, whereas Luis saw nothing but deceit, subterfuge and fraud. 'One last shot,' he said.

As they drove home, he said: 'What's in this for Michael?'

'You heard him. The collapse of Western capitalism.'

'That's absurd. He obviously enjoys living here.'

'Well, work can be fun too. This is America. A man has to do what a man has to do. Randolph Scott said it.'

'Bollocks. Anyhow, we can't afford to pay him more than five hundred dollars.'

'Forget it Luis. You never did understand money.'

Mikhail was in the apartment, waiting for them. He and Stevie were drinking chilled beer in frosted goblets while they watched TV coverage of the hearing.

'Joe ain't happy,' Stevie said. 'Got a face like a bad clam.'

'Let's go on the roof,' Mikhail said. 'Lousy acoustics up there.'

Luis got beers from the fridge, and they went upstairs. A girl in a leotard was practising dance steps in one corner. In the other an old man was squeezing gentle melodies out of an accordion.

'McCarthy's a very bad loser,' Luis said.

'One day we give him Russian documents,' Julie said, 'and next day Fantoni gives him Russian documents. He's gonna wonder, did they all come out of the same hat?'

'Fantoni told him the FBI has copies,' Luis said. 'Does it?'

'Some,' Mikhail said. 'Not all.'

'McCarthy demands J. Edgar Hoover checks the FBI files,' she said. 'Then what?' She didn't wait. 'I know what. Hoover hates the bum, hates helping him. *But* if he *does* check, then he'll know *some* stuff is phoney. What next?'

'Hoover tells McCarthy he's been conned,' Luis said. 'He'd get a big kick out of that.'

'But not for a week, maybe two,' Mikhail said. 'Millions of files in the FBI. Still time to do new business with the senator.'

'Talking of business,' Luis said. 'One thing we might as well get settled now —'

'How much do you plan to pay us?' Julie asked.

'One thousand dollars a week,' Mikhail said.

'Done.' They shook hands.

'Well,' Luis said. 'That's reasonable, I suppose.'

★

Later that evening, Stevie announced she was going to live in Paris. 'Frenchmen got *panache*,' she said. 'You see any *panache* in DC?' They asked when she wanted to go. 'Now,' she said. They drove her to the airport. Last seen, she was talking to an Air France flight engineer. Looked like love at first sight.

6

Fantoni and Fisk flew back to Idlewild. A summer storm boiled above Philadelphia and the seat-belt sign was never off. Fisk observed that his man's right foot twitched like a metronome; and when the plane landed, touched down, Fantoni kept his right hand clamped on his thigh so hard that the fingernails lost their colour. The engines stopped. Fisk undid his man's seat-belt. 'After that,' Fantoni said, 'purgatory should be a piece of cake.'

A car was waiting for Fantoni. Fisk took a cab to 44th Street and checked in with Prendergast.

'Officially, nobody's saying anything,' Prendergast told him. 'But everybody's got an opinion. What's yours?'

'Fantoni put on one hell of a show. And if his documents aren't kosher, why hasn't McCarthy said so? Either way, we can forget the senator. Mr Hoover has the facts. All the Bureau need do is look in the files.'

Prendergast didn't like the sound of that. He screwed his face up. 'The files,' he said. 'The files . . . FBI HQ in DC has million of files. Plain files. Confidential files, available only to assistant directors. And then there's the "Do Not File" files.

288

They contain all the items that are so sensitive they must not be filed. Only the Director has access to the "Do Not File" files. Maybe that's where Mr Hoover keeps the Fantoni papers. If they exist.'

'He hasn't denied it,' Fisk said, 'so maybe it's true.'

'He can't deny it,' Prendergast said. 'Any denial would only confirm Fantoni's claim that the FBI will deny everything.'

Fisk threw up his hands, walked away, leaned against a wall. 'Maybe he really was a double agent. We know he contacted Cabrillo before the hearing, and Cabrillo was a double agent once. He could be Fantoni's minder.'

'Sure. And the butler shot Sammy in the library. What happened to Fantoni's arm?'

'Shoulder. Old football injury. Princeton.'

'Dumb game,' Prendergast said. 'He should have stuck to tossing the beanbag.'

7

They were having breakfast in a coffee shop when Luis said, 'You know, we've developed a really beautiful relationship here.'

'I'm not going to marry you.'

'I didn't mean you and me. I meant us and Michael . . . And I didn't ask you to marry me.'

'So we've got total agreement on that, then.'

He watched her eat toast. 'Not necessarily.'

'Then why don't you ask me?' She seemed quite serious.

'You've just given me the answer.'

'I might have been lying. You lie all the time.'

True, he thought. Also untrue. 'My poor head is spinning. Can we get back to the beautiful relationship? Everyone is getting what he wants. Metal Exchange is making money coming and going. Michael pays us at one end and McCarthy at the other. The Red perils we expose are authentic. Michael's documents say so. McCarthy's experts test them until

289

their fingers bleed, and they're all as Russian as Dostoevsky's underpants. Isn't that beautiful? Pure harmony. Like Mozart.'

'Speaking of underpants, your fly's open.'

'Today I shall focus on the Chicago Department of Sanitation. Subversion in the garbage collecting.'

'After the Mafia stuff?' She made a face. 'Anticlimax.'

He thought about it. 'Possibly.'

They went to the office, and Luis shut himself in the conference room. He came out at lunchtime, empty-handed. 'The well is dry,' he said. 'The Communists have already infiltrated government, church, education, atomic energy, the unions, the Mafia, Hollywood, the Idaho potato crop and the San Andreas Fault. I can't find anything they've missed.'

'Roy Cohn phoned,' she said. 'The Senator is hot for those major projects we have in the pipeline.'

'Food. I can't create without lunch.'

'Mozart was the same.'

★

'Give him time, Mikhail,' Kim said. 'I know this man. He's at his best when under pressure.'

'His well is dry. What sort of feeble excuse is that?'

They were strolling in the garden. Kim had not left the embassy since the night of Wagner's death, and he was starting to feel restless. 'Artists exaggerate,' he said. 'They're not to be taken literally.'

'Momentum is everything with McCarthy. He's like a shark in the water. Stops moving and he's dead. Needs impetus. Otherwise people forget.' Mikhail snatched at a passing butterfly and missed. Some days nothing went right.

★

At two fifty-three p.m. Luis had a brilliant idea. Sport. The US missed out on a gold medal at the last Olympics when the best man in the pole vault wasn't even selected because he had been subverted by his girlfriend, a Commie agent. She subverted him between the sheets, twice a day and all night long. Yes! Michael would find a photograph of her. Stunning. Naked. Shameless.

No. This wasn't an Olympics year, so who cares? Most American men would sooner be subverted silly by the lovely Olga than go home with a medal. No. Forget sport. Lousy idea.

By four p.m. Luis's backside was numb and his eyes weary from looking at nothing. He quit. The well really was dry. He went into the next room.

'Cohn phoned again.' Julie said.

'Well, fuck him.'

'That won't solve his problem.'

Luis got a Dr Pepper out of the office refrigerator and flicked through the magazines Stevie had bought for their non-existent clients to read.

Brain-washing.

It was in an article in *Time*, about the Korean War. Chinese propaganda. Captured American pilots confess to germ warfare and urge the US military to leave Asia, so the Chinese claim. Followed by stuff about hypnotism and magic mushrooms. 'Hey!' he said. 'Got it! Brain-washing drugs.'

'All drugs scrub your brain. Heroin, coke, grass. So what?'

'These are new. These drugs change the face of battle. Now you can spray the enemy and make him friendly. The Chinese have started doing it in Korea! Read all about it.' He tossed her the copy of *Time*. 'No more gunfire! No more bloodshed!'

She read. 'Nothing about that here. This is about prisoners-of-war, allegedly drugged.'

'Of course they were brain-washed. The Chinese have them on film, saying terrible things about America. Why else would a red-blooded patriotic US Navy pilot say China is the future and he wants to settle there and grow rice?'

Julie scanned the article. 'I don't see that.'

'You will when I finish my report.'

'So . . . no more war. Is that it?'

'No more *violent* war. The Chinese will defeat us in the

laboratory. The US Marines will advance into a chemical fog and come out laughing and skipping and eager to embrace their Chinese foe. Not a shot will be fired.'

'Cute. Does the Pentagon know?'

'That's the whole point.' Luis was so pleased with himself that he was walking in circles. 'The Pentagon has been so slow in recognizing the threat of brain-washing that it has tested only one antidote. You'll never guess what.'

'Astonish me.'

'Anadin,' Luis said. 'Three times a day. Or as prescribed.'

★

Kim Philby took off the headphones, picked up his notes, and went along the corridor. 'The well is wet again,' he said.

The more he read, the more Mikhail liked it. 'China is a raw spot for the Americans,' he said. 'They sent flocks of missionaries for decades and how did the Chinese show their gratitude? Went Red, the whole inscrutable lot of them.'

'Clever devils. Invented gunpowder.'

'And now they've got anti-gunpowder.' Mikhail stuffed the notes into his pocket. 'No time to waste.'

THE LITTLE SOD
GUESSED RIGHT

1

Julie read the first draft, corrected the spelling, and had some questions. The senator was always the guy in the white hat, the straight-shooter, riding to save America. He always had the answer: boot out the Reds. But that wouldn't beat Chinese brain-washing, would it? Luis waved the problem away. Leave that to the Pentagon. The CIA. Meanwhile, scare every taxpayer who expects the US cavalry to come riding to his rescue. But this is America, Julie argued. Americans like guns. Love 'em. Exactly, Luis said. That was when Mikhail arrived.

'I hear you have struck gold,' he said.

'How . . .' Luis began.

'The same old way,' Julie told him.

Mikhail took a seat and read the draft. 'Very interesting,' he said, and re-read it. 'Hugely interesting. Congratulations.'

'Julie thinks it might be too scary.'

'For McCarthy? Nothing is too excessive for him. No, this is pure wind in his sails. May I keep this copy? I'd like to start work straight away.'

'Music to my ears, dear chap.' Luis was as blithe as a bluebird. He escorted Mikhail to the door, then stopped. 'One tiny fraction of a second,' he said. He strode to his desk, pulled a page out of the typewriter, separated the carbon copy and handed it to Mikhail. 'A mere afterthought,' he said. 'A footnote to a footnote. But you might as well have it.'

★

Kim had a nose for trouble; it had helped him survive for all these years. When Mikhail returned, said nothing, disappeared into the upper floor where the KGB heavyweights had their offices, Kim smelled bad news. He did the London *Times* crossword to settle his nerves. In a treacherous world, the *Times* compilers never cheated.

When Mikhail came down he had a bottle of pepper vodka and two glasses. 'I suppose it was bound to happen,' he said. 'Your Mr Arabel-Cabrillo has stumbled on the truth.' He poured the vodka. 'To Lady Luck,' he said, 'who has just abandoned us.' They drank. 'Arabel's got to go, too.'

'Words of doom and gloom.'

Mikhail took three pages from his inside pocket. 'Pages one and two describe the mythical Chinese brain-washing drug, which reduces whole armies to a state of inoffensive serenity. Read page three. He calls it a footnote.'

Kim read it in twenty seconds. 'Bloody hell,' he said.

'That's not what they said upstairs. They burnt the air to a crisp upstairs.'

'The concept is brilliant. A brain-washing drug that actually *recruits* enemy troops, reverses their loyalty, and makes them attack their comrades! Such ambition! And the Soviet military has it?'

'I wasn't sure. Nothing's impossible. That's why I took it upstairs, a long way upstairs. They nearly had multiple heart attacks.'

'The little sod guessed right.'

'Near enough.' Mikhail topped up their glasses. 'Have we got this damn drug? Does it work as described? Nobody's going to tell *me*.' He knocked back his vodka. 'But we've got scientists working on it, or something like it. He nearly guessed the code-name. He calls it Operation Boomerang. We've been calling it Project Rebound. Yet this thing is

294

extreme ultra top five-star secret. Imagine how Moscow will react if McCarthy tells the world about it.'

Kim stared. He could feel the vodka burning his gut but it didn't seem to have done him any good. 'We'll be blamed,' he said. 'You and I.'

'We'll be shot.'

'Then let's kill Cabrillo, now, fast. Before he can cause any more chaos.'

'That's what I said Upstairs. They rejected the idea, flat. No killing.'

'For God's sake, why?'

Mikhail took off his tie and loosened his collar. 'Because,' he began, 'as they say in Hollywood, this thing is bigger than both of us. To start with, Upstairs are afraid that Cabrillo and Conroy are CIA.'

'Bloody ridiculous.'

'I thought so too, at first. Now I'm not so sure. Look what they've accomplished. Penetrated McCarthy's inner circle. Made contact with the KGB.'

'That was *your* idea,' Kim said. 'Wasn't it?'

'Was it? I went fishing. They were the bait. Who caught whom?' Mikhail raised his eyebrows. Kim had no answer. He was trying to catch up with the idea that Cabrillo was back in the double-agent business, now with the CIA. Mikhail said: 'Upstairs, they believe Cabrillo and Conroy must have had CIA help, before I got involved. How else could they have fed McCarthy so much high-grade stuff? The quantity, the quality, the sheer rate of output . . . And look at their cover: they're both blacklisted. Upstairs think that is pure CIA camouflage.'

'Upstairs has gone soft at the knees, if you ask me.' Kim said. 'I don't understand this sudden twitchiness about the CIA. We've killed their agents often enough. They've killed ours. Who cares?'

'This may take a little time.' Mikhail picked up the phone and ordered food: cheese, smoked eel, pickled gherkins, anchovies, stuffed olives. Then he began to explain.

Stalin was dead. The Korean war was over. The world was

changing. Moscow and Washington had been working on an exchange of spies for many months. Now was definitely not the time to rock *that* particular boat. Furthermore, there might be a Soviet mole inside the CIA; perhaps two. Upstairs had given a hint of that possibility. It would be a fatal mistake to frighten the Agency and make it tighten its security. Moles were an endangered species at the best of times.

'But this is DC,' Kim said. 'Murder capital. Cabrillo could be shot for his loose change. It happens every day of the week.'

'And the woman too? No loose ends, remember. Do you really want to murder two consultants of the most powerful senator in America? Think of the uproar.' Mikhail waited as food was brought in and the servant left. He ate an olive. 'Upstairs appreciates all you have done in the past, Kim, but that was then and now is now. Ask yourself a simple question. Would it be more convenient for Upstairs to decide to shoot Luis Cabrillo or Kim Philby?'

Kim was chewing on some smoked eel. 'After all I've done,' he mumbled.

'And when I was Upstairs, the vote was very close,' Mikhail said. 'Now, for the love of heaven, have some more vodka and stop looking so damned miserable. I may have a solution. For a start, I don't believe that Cabrillo is a full-blown CIA agent. He may *know* an agent, perhaps someone who is moonlighting, passing him information, getting a percentage. I'm guessing. But Cabrillo doesn't strike me as CIA material. Too flippant, too self-centred, too volatile. That's what makes him vulnerable. He spins like a top. Well, let's knock him off-balance. Upstairs says expunction is out. All right: what's the next best thing?'

'Better than death?'

'How about being frightened to death? What would scare the wits out of him? Send him running as far and as fast as possible?'

'Nothing less than dynamite up his rectum,' Kim said.

'Dynamite,' Mikhail said. 'Well, that's a start. Now let's try and improve on it.'

They talked, and killed the bottle. Something had to go, and the bottle was nearest.

★

Next morning was hot and heavy. Luis hadn't slept well: the air was too humid and his brain was too active. He wanted to get back to work. He took a shower and couldn't get completely dry. 'Appalling climate,' he said.

'It's a swamp,' Julie said. 'But it's our swamp so we like it.'

Mikhail arrived at nine, carrying a briefcase. He accepted a coffee, and said, 'The situation has changed for the worse. I'll go so far as to say it is grave, extremely grave. Your lives are in danger.'

'Not bloody Jerome again?' Luis asked.

'Not Jerome. But there are hostile forces, more deadly than Jerome, ranged against the senator. Assassination now would make him a martyr, so he is safe. But his associates . . .' Mikhail spread his arms in a helpless gesture. 'Well, this is America, and Americans have their own way of eliminating difficulties. Believe me: you're in their way, so you're in their sights.'

'How d'you know this?' Julie asked.

'We're the KGB.'

'Yeah. Sure. Sorry. Forgot.'

'Nobody's threatened us,' Luis said.

'They never *threaten*,' Mikhail said. 'They *act*. The bullet you never hear is their threat – to others.'

'If it's as bad as you say, okay, we can move, find some place more secure. But frankly, I feel pretty safe here.'

'I was afraid you'd say that. Please come with me.' He went to the balcony. They followed, making baffled faces to each other. 'It was on this very spot that Luis was very nearly assassinated as you ate dinner.'

'Shrimp Jambalaya,' Luis said. 'Too much chilli.' Nobody laughed. 'Not a funny joke,' he said.

Mikhail pointed. 'You see that rooftop? A man armed with a sniper rifle was within seconds of killing you. A single shot to the head.'

297

'What stopped him?' Julie asked.

'I stopped him. I shot him before he could shoot Luis, and probably you too.'

'To quote the Senator,' Luis said, 'this is the most unheard-of thing I ever heard of.' Again, nobody laughed.

'One's own violent death is hard to imagine,' Mikhail said sadly. 'Look there, across the street.' He waved an arm, and a man appeared on the rooftop, leaned on the parapet, aimed a rifle towards them. Instantly the crack of a hammerblow struck the stonework ten feet to their left, and a bullet sang as it ricocheted and was lost. '*Jesus*!' Luis cried.

'Look down. You see? Nobody noticed,' Mikhail said. 'Silencer.'

'Damn your bloody silencer. I've been hit.' Luis was clutching his left wrist. Blood dripped.

Mikhail examined it. 'A chip from the wall. Clean cut, quite small.' He saluted the man on the roof, who disappeared. 'Run water on it. Then ice.'

They all went to the kitchen and watched Luis hold his wrist under cold water. 'Stings like a bastard,' he said. Bloodstained water swirled pinkly in the sink.

'You set that up.' Julie's voice cracked, so she tried again. 'You arranged that. The guy with the rifle was your guy.'

'I was afraid words alone would not persuade you to leave.'

Luis was outraged. 'You had me shot? For nothing?'

'To demonstrate the danger —'

'Thanks a million. I was in perfect shape until you began protecting me.'

Mikhail went into the study while Julie patched up Luis with king-size BandAids and a yard of bandage. When they joined him, he was quick to apologize.

'Forget it,' Luis said. 'Forget the whole stupid shambles. Let's get down to business.'

Mikhail sat with his hands interlocked, shoulders hunched, face wooden with worry. 'This thing is on my conscience. If it hadn't been for me, the Arabel affair would never have reached these proportions. Please, just go away for a month or two. Don't pack, don't call anyone, come with me now, I'll get you on a plane to Mexico City, Venezuela, Costa Rica, you name it. Here, take these.' He pushed passports into Luis's hands.

'We have passports.'

'I don't,' Julie said. 'Blacklisted. Remember?'

'Hell's teeth . . .' Luis stuffed them into his hip pocket. 'Listen, it's kind of you to worry. Tomorrow maybe we'll take a trip, Miami, New Orleans, God knows where. Today I'm a freelance. Slightly wounded, but still working. The motto of the freelance is: waste nothing. So, can we talk brain-washing? Chinese, Russian, Eskimo, whatever you've got.'

Mikhail emptied his briefcase and gave Luis a brief account of the documents. They were all in Russian. Half concerned Chinese development of mind-control drugs, he said, and half were about Soviet advances in the field. 'We are a long way ahead of our Chinese comrades. That is, assuming our spies in China have not had their brains washed already.'

Nobody smiled. Julie said: 'Looks like you worked through the night.'

Mikhail had reached the last page. 'Perhaps it would be wiser to omit this.' It showed a single line of printing. 'The chemical formula for a new mind-control drug, still being tested. Very powerful but highly experimental. Risky.'

Luis looked. The long line of letters was cluttered with symbols and figures. 'Hideous,' he said. 'Chuck it in. McCarthy likes flim-flam.'

He fetched his papers, added Mikhail's documents, and locked his briefcase. 'Into battle,' he said, 'or maybe not, if the drugs work.'

'My car's parked downstairs,' Mikhail said. 'The least I can do is give you a lift to the Capitol.'

'Don't worry about me,' Luis told Julie. 'Michael will have his sniper riding shotgun.'

2

Washington never had much of a morning rush hour. By now the streets were fairly empty. Mikhail's Lincoln cruised quietly. Luis made his seat recline and let his eyelids droop. Thank God for air-conditioning.

'I'm told that Molotov preferred a Buick,' Mikhail said. 'So did half the Politburo. But Stalin's car was usually a Packard, because it could be more heavily armoured. Bullet-proof. So they say. Odd to think that the Kremlin depended so much on Detroit.'

Luis grunted. After the carnage on the balcony, he felt no obligation to chat.

'This car isn't new, by any means. Third-hand, perhaps even fourth. The embassy got it cheap. Lincoln is a good, safe, democratic name, isn't it? Government of the people, for the people, that sort of thing.'

Luis nodded. Minimum effort.

'Only fault is it's a thirsty beast. Gets through a tankful in no time. In fact, I'd better get a few gallons now.'

Luis opened one eye and watched him swing into a gas station and pull up at the pumps. 'Relax,' Mikhail said. 'Shan't be a second.' The door opened, letting in a whiff of clammy air, and shut. Luis was thinking, rehearsing his opening remarks to McCarthy. *The history of the next war, senator, can be written in a single line* . . . All the Lincoln's doors opened at once. A man in a blue boiler-suit barged Luis sideways. Luis grabbed the wheel for support. Someone behind him slipped a hood over his head and gripped him by the neck. By now the Lincoln was moving and someone was tying his wrists. The hands around his neck were released. The hood hung down to his chest. He could breathe easily but see nothing. The cloth smelled of old apples. Someone put a hat on his head.

★

They drove for what might have been an hour. Luis dozed occasionally. The shock of being kidnapped had lasted only seconds; after that, nobody spoke and he was wedged comfortably between the driver and the man who had barged him. Nevertheless, the mental stress was huge and exhausting.

300

Trapped inside the hood, Luis could think only one thing: he was going to be killed. Logic told him to make the most of every minute that remained, but that idea was exhausting too. Fatigue won. He nodded off. Each time he woke, he felt worse. He thought of West Virginia, the mountains, the long drop into the gorge. Why did people scream as they fell? Screaming wouldn't save them. Maybe they only screamed in the movies. Just like in the movies, he was being taken for a ride. He dozed again.

The car stopped. He was pulled out and he lost the hat. 'Never liked it,' he said, not in his own voice. Too high, too thin, too weak. His knees were made out of wet paper towels. He clung to somebody's arm and breathed deeply. This wasn't the mountains. Not cold enough. Very unprofessional. He thought about saying so, in his borrowed, feeble voice. Too late: they were making him walk. Not far. Into a building. A door shut behind him. More walking. A chair was shoved against his legs and he sat with a thud. He heard a familiar click and much rustling of papers. They had opened his briefcase.

He counted to a hundred and then backwards to zero. Time to speak. He said, 'Tell me . . .' Someone slapped him, not gently; enough to make orange blossoms parade before his eyes. So now he knew the ground rules.

The rustling of paper went on and on. Then there was the unmistakable sound of pages being shuffled together and tapped into a block. 'Your formula,' a man said. 'Interesting, on paper. Wars are not fought on paper.' Neutral accent, neither American nor British. 'The next stage is to convert the formula to reality, and test it on your mind, which is in urgent need of control.'

'It's risky.' Luis waited. Nobody hit him. 'Might not work.'

'That will be your funeral.'

'I have to pee.' Pathetic but true.

'Nobody is stopping you.'

People walked away. A different voice said, 'Do not move. You are being observed.'

At last he had something to think about. They didn't want him, they wanted the formula. What then? The stuff was raw,

301

untried chemistry. Pumped into him, it might scramble his brains. Fry them. Braise them, poach them, broil them with sprigs of parsley. Horrible thought. In an hour or two, he might be incapable of thinking it. Or he might be thinking something more nightmarish, against his will, if he still had a will. He should have listened to Michael, should have quit, got out. Too late now. Too late to control his bladder, too. The flood of hot urine down his left thigh soaked his calf and ran into his shoe. It was shameful and then it was pleasant. If he was going to lose his mind he might as well enjoy the pleasures of infancy while he still could. Nobody seemed to object.

Evidently the door was open, if there was a door. He heard distant sounds. Vaguely chemical smells reached him. This must be a laboratory and the kidnappers must be scientists. All brains and no humanity. The last trace of hope slipped away.

★

Sometimes he dozed. He awoke, swaying dangerously, and spread his feet wide to stop himself falling. Time had lost all meaning. His left leg was dry but the underpants stuck to his skin. He was thirsty. He swallowed repeatedly. Maybe if he kept recycling his saliva it would lessen his thirst. After a while he forgot to swallow. Thinking was very tiring.

He woke up suddenly when someone grabbed his arm, pushed the sleeve up and stuck a needle in the forearm. 'Look at it this way,' a man said. 'You're either a guinea-pig or a martyr. No future either way.' The needle came out.

'Wait,' Luis said. 'I've been thinking. That formula is wrong. We put in deliberate mistakes as safeguards.'

'Such as.'

'Um . . . replace potassium dichloride with sodium pentathol. And add ethylene glycol. And use benzenes as a catalyst.' Luis was gabbling. The last chemistry test he took, he failed, and that was when he was thirteen. 'Heat everything to 500 degrees Fahrenheit.' His imagination failed. Was the man still there? Long silence. He must have gone. Perhaps they would repeat the experiment. So what? His brain would be bent like a pretzel by then. Ethylene glycol . . . Where had that come from? He murmured the words and immediately he remembered. It had been the coolant mixture in RAF piston engines. Oh well. At least he'd tried.

Then his pulse began pounding. He stopped breathing in order to listen better. His heartbeat was kicking his ribs. Blood was throbbing in his throat, his ears, his skull. Now he knew his arms were bloated, they felt inflated, his fingers were as big as bananas. All he could see was the hood, but he knew his limbs had stretched enormously and his head was so high that it made him giddy, and it was getting higher. 'This can't go on,' he said, and the growing stopped at once. 'What's the point?' he asked. He sounded angry. 'What does it prove?' That was when a hurricane of hot air knocked him over and blew off the hood.

He saw a flash like a sunburst, although some of that might have happened when his head hit the floor, it was hard to tell. There was certainly a bang like a battleship's broadside. The air was thick with dust and torn paper. He looked at the ceiling and waited for it to fall on him.

The fog thinned and he saw his hands. Tied with electric flex. No knots, the ends just twisted tightly together. He got one end between his teeth and made circles until it all came loose and he was free. He walked out of the room and along a short corridor and into another room, heading always for a bright light. It turned out to be a hole in a wall. In fact it was all hole and no wall. He walked through the hole and into a fine, refreshing rain.

★

'I was . . .' Luis turned his head and spat. Dust still coated his teeth and tongue. 'I was out for a stroll.'

'Out for a stroll,' the cop said. He looked at the sergeant. 'Guy says he was out for a stroll. In this dump.' It was a street of abandoned buildings, empty car parks, demolition sites, potholes, weeds.

'Free country,' the sergeant said. 'How you feelin', son? You look like shit.'

Luis was sitting on a broken wall in front of the holed building. 'I stopped because I heard a cry for help,' he said. That was good. That placed him *outside* the crime scene. It made him feel better. 'I feel better now,' he said.

'This cry for help,' the cop said. 'Came from inside?' Luis nodded. 'Ain't nobody inside,' the cop said. 'We just looked.'

The sergeant went to the car, talked softly on the radio, came back. 'We need a name and address,' he said. Luis told him the truth. His imagination wasn't strong enough to think of a false name and address. 'Now, the way we see it,' the sergeant said, 'we got you, an' we got an explosion, same place, same time, and that's the complete sum total of what we got.'

'A painful coincidence. An Act of God.'

The cop didn't like that. 'Let's see some ID.'

Luis searched his pockets and found a billfold and a membership card for the Caracas Golf Club. The cop was not satisfied. 'Perhaps tomorrow?' Luis suggested. Not acceptable either.

'Looks like you're coming with us,' the sergeant said, 'Acts of God being illegal in the District of Warners.' Luis was hunting through pockets he never knew he had. 'We can't get God for it, so you're next in line,' the sergeant said. Luis dug into his hip pocket. Two passports. Another Act of God.

They took the passports away and studied them in the comfort of the car, while Luis sat in the fine, warm rain.

'Diplomatic Corps,' the cop said. 'Another goddam dip. These creeps are the curse of this town.'

'Venezuelan. I thought he looked kinda Hispanic under all that dust. Well, he's got immunity, so he walks.'

They went back and gave him the passports. 'Connecticut Avenue is thataway,' the sergeant said. 'About three miles.'

They watched him go. He was limping a little and his face was raised to the rain.

'Cry for help,' the cop said. 'Total crap.'

'It's a hole in a wall, nobody's gonna steal it,' the sergeant said. 'File and forget.'

★

Mikhail was about four hundred yards away, sitting in an old Ford, watching through binoculars as Luis's figure became more and more blurred and shapeless. 'That worked out rather well,' he said.

'Enormous bang,' Kim said. 'Made me jump.'

'Mostly pyrotechnic. Only a small charge was needed to blow down the wall. I calculated that the kidnapping would scare him half out of his wits and the explosion would take care of the rest.'

Philby wiped condensation from inside the windscreen. Now Luis was just a distant blob. 'He needs to disappear, Mikhail. The man is dangerous.'

'He's an opportunist, Kim. He's in the game for money and for fun, but not for life and death. If those are the stakes he won't play.' Mikhail started the car. 'We've beaten him with his own weapons. That injection we gave him was completely harmless, yet within minutes he was twitching and flinching and squirming like a junkie. Imagination, Kim. All that stuff he invented about mind-control drugs was so convincing that he believed it. And now it's driving him out of town. If I weren't such a dour, humourless Russian I'd call it highly ironic.'

They drove down the road and passed Luis. '*Dosvidanya,*' Philby said.

3

'Leaving?' McCarthy said. 'This is a hell of a time to resign, Bobby, just when I'm up to my ass in all this Arabel intelligence.'

'I regret the inconvenience, senator, but — '

305

'Fuck the inconvenience. You hate Roy Cohn's guts. Schine makes you puke. Your problem, Bobby, is you waste your hate. Good mornin', Ralph. You're looking well.'

They were walking along a corridor in the Capitol building. The senator McCarthy greeted cut him dead: no word, no glance, no change of expression.

'Poor loser,' McCarthy said.

'I admire your work, senator, but you've got your brand all over it. I need to find my own war to fight.'

'Go fight the rich.' McCarthy sat on the marble plinth that held up a statue of a man in a toga. 'Start a war on poverty. No, I forgot, you Kennedys never had much truck with the poor, did you?' He pressed his fingers against the artery under his chin.

'I'm going after the Mafia,' Kennedy said.

McCarthy sat in silence for twenty seconds and then took his fingers from his throat. 'Gallopin' to the grave,' he said. 'What's the rush? Damn doctors keep bitchin' about booze. Shit, if I stopped drinkin', my kidneys would die of fright. The Mafia, you say. Some folks reckon those gentlemen helped your brother get elected to the Senate. You sure know how to make people hate you, son.'

'They're scum,' Kennedy said. 'They corrupt justice and brutalize American society.'

'Uh-huh. You forgot how they provide whores, drugs and bookies, that being what Joe Public wants in a country that's dumb enough to make prostitution, narcotics and gambling illegal in most States.' He stood up. 'I shall miss you, Bobby. You're like the son I never had. I refute them allegations by that red-headed cocktail waitress in Ohio, flattering though they were.' He walked away.

BOUNDLESS
DAMAGE

1

Julie took two thousand dollars in traveller's cheques and the rest in cash. That closed the account. The bank gave her some sturdy paper bags to put it all in. She drove back to the apartment and sat in the car.

After an hour she ate part of a sandwich. By mid-afternoon she was sick of sitting in the car, looking at the rain and Connecticut Avenue and not knowing what to do next. The rearview mirrors were coated with moisture and she didn't see him until he opened the passenger door and dumped himself on the seat like a sack of second-class mail.

Everything about him was wet and dirty. His clothes flopped and drooped. One side of his face was bruised and grazed. 'Had a good day at the office?' she said.

He yawned. 'Never got there. Got kidnapped.'

'Michael told me. He saw it happen, couldn't stop it.'

'Got kidnapped, got brain-washed, got blown up. Got away.' He rubbed his eyes, wiping away the rain. 'Not sure about the last bit.'

'Got away from where?'

He aimed his right index finger at nothing, then gradually relaxed it. 'Three miles, they said. It's a long story.'

His eyes closed and his whole body relaxed. Julie went back to looking at the rain and Connecticut Avenue. After a couple of minutes he woke up. 'But enough about me. What about you? Why are you sitting in the car?'

'The apartment's full of tax men, Luis. Likewise the office. We're being investigated by the Internal Revenue. Michael warned me they were on the way.'

'Jolly decent of him.'

'Yeah? I reckon he sicked them on to us.'

'Surely not. Arabel's partner? Never.'

'Arabel's dead. Crashed and burned.'

He took a deep breath and slowly released it, making a long flubbering noise with his lips. 'Tax men. That's a really dirty trick. I'm surprised they didn't arrest you.'

'I told them I was the maid. Then I went and emptied our bank account.' She showed him the paper bags.

'Crashed and burned. And this is the wreckage.' He was getting sleepy again.

'We're leaving right now,' she told him. 'This here is a Rand McNally Atlas of the US. Shut your eyes.' She put the book on his lap. 'Open it anywhere.' He fumbled with the pages. 'No peeking. Point somewhere.' He stabbed with his forefinger. 'Unbelievable,' she said. 'You have chosen the town of Truth Or Consequences in New Mexico. Let's go.' She started the car.

'Only in America,' he mumbled. Within a few blocks he was asleep and gently steaming.

★

'I was wrong,' Mikhail said. 'The temptation was irresistible, but I was wrong. I should never have tried to encourage McCarthy.'

'Don't be too hard on yourself,' Kim said. 'The man is a phenomenon, not a politician. Nobody can influence a phenomenon. It's like trying to direct a tornado.'

'Well put.' They were deep into the pepper vodka. Arabel and his agent had long since vanished. The KGB has ceased worrying about revelations concerning mind-control drugs. Wagner was dead and cremated and forgotten. Jerome Fantoni was old news. Routine had been restored. Mikhail took another slice of smoked eel. 'What I failed to realize is that the senator has no policy. We're so accustomed to sabotaging Western policies . . .'

'McCarthy is the saboteur *par excellence*,' Kim said.

'The supreme nihilist.' Mikhail enjoyed the word. 'The ultimate rabble-rouser. The prince of hatred.'

'And yet arguably the biggest democrat in Congress. He gives America what it craves.'

'Yes? What does it crave?'

'Political thuggery. A nation can get drunk on fear.'

Mikhail poured more vodka. 'Well, McCarthy doesn't need us. Never did. He can inflict boundless damage on this country without our help. You might as well go back to London, Kim.'

'Yes. This is an awful town, isn't it? My sinuses are in a permanent rage.'

★

Manfred Sturmer left the CIA. He moved to California and made a slim but steady living as a crossword puzzle compiler.

★

J. Reuben Knox, forty-seven, vice-president of a San Francisco bank, knew he'd been given the title in lieu of the stock options and a bonus he believed he deserved. He had a thyroid condition, and from all he knew of the family history, Knox men did not live long. Termites were invading his house. Treatment would be hideously expensive. Also he was keeping a woman in Berkeley who was not his wife, and he had fallen in love with a female cashier called Belinda who was a hell of a lay but not cheap.

J. Reuben Knox took a couple of days' leave and drove to Seattle. He rented an office, paid for ten messengers to go to ten banks with ten envelopes, and got arrested by the

Seattle PD while he was counting the first delivery. As the detectives drove him away, he said, 'None of it was for me. I was going to give it all away.' The detectives made no comment.

In New York, Special Agent Prendergast took the news in his stride: neither excited nor discouraged. 'Another fool takes a fall,' he said.

'Does this mean Cabrillo is right out of the picture?' Fisk asked.

'There is no picture, Fisk. No shape, no pattern, no symmetry. Crime is the fly in your wine glass. The fly gets greedy, gets reckless and gets drowned. J. Reuben Knox is that fly.'

'Uh-huh,' Fisk said.

End

AUTHOR'S NOTE

Red Rag Blues is a mixture of fact and fiction. The reader is entitled to know which is which.

Apart from the bank-robbery con, which is based on an actual crime in New York in the 1960s, the plot – Cabrillo's arrival from Venezuela, broke; his attempts to make money; his move to Washington and his double-dealing with Senator McCarthy – is invented, like most of the characters. Joe McCarthy existed, of course, and Bobby Kennedy worked for him, as did Cohn and Schine, in 1953. Kim Philby was a reality too (although he didn't visit America that year) and details of his remarkable career as a KGB agent who almost became head of MI6 are as accurate as I could make them. Philby's KGB controller, Peter Cottington-Beaufort – surely a *nom de guerre* – is fictitious. All the words spoken by these people are imagined (although, in the chapter on the Fantoni hearing, the events studied by the Sub-Committee – union disputes, race riots, sabotage – are based on fact).

The rest – from Max Webber and Billy Jago to Prendergast and Fisk, to Stevie and Scatola, and all the others – are invented characters. Two people are re-invented, so to speak. Luis Cabrillo and Julie Conroy first appeared in earlier novels of mine: *The Eldorado Network* and *Artillery of Lies*, which described Luis's career (with Julie's guidance) as a double agent in the Second World War. The Double-Cross System existed. It sold the *Abwehr* a stream of 'secret' information, largely false, all part of a hugely successful Allied deception campaign. (Wagner appears in there too.) I based Cabrillo on a real double agent, code-named Garbo, who satisfied both sides so much that he was awarded the Iron Cross by Germany and the MBE by Britain. When the war ended he vanished to South America. So there are echoes of reality in Cabrillo.

Max's U-turn with HUAC in exchange for a Warners contract is fiction. Nevertheless, Warner Brothers enjoyed a good working relationship with HUAC: in 1952 the studio made *Big Jim McClain* (John Wayne as a HUAC investigator rooting out Communist spies) and the film ends with a big credit to the Committee for its help.

As far as I know there was no Mafia family called Fantoni in the New York area. I found no record of HUAC or McCarthy's Sub-Committee accusing the Mafia of Communist infiltration although, God know, the Mobs did more damage to the fabric of American society than Larry Adler, Arthur Miller, Zero Mostel and Dashiell Hammett, who – along with many hundred of individuals – were caught up in the witch hunt for no good reason, and sometimes for no reason at all; and got harassed, sacked, jailed or exiled.

One exile who typified many was Carl Foreman, who wrote the screenplay for an outstanding Western, *High Noon*. When John Wayne gave Gary Cooper the Oscar for his role in the movie, he growled: 'Why can't I find me a scriptwriter to write me a part like that?' Too late: Carl Foreman had been blacklisted in Hollywood (he had refused to name names) and was now in England, looking for work. Soon the Duke joined the Motion Picture Alliance for the Preservation of American Ideals – one of several McCarthyite organizations – and he discovered that *High Noon* was in fact stuffed with subversive, anti-American ideas. Foreman spent the next twenty years in England, making films. He collaborated on the script of *The Bridge on the River Kwai* and got no credit. Had his name appeared on it, the film would have been refused distribution in the US. The blacklist cast a very long shadow.

Which brings me to McCarthy, a difficult man to re-create because he was so unlike his cartoon image. He joined the witch hunt late in the day. In 1950, four years after his election to Congress, his prospects were poor. He had accomplished very little, he faced re-election in two years, and the tax authorities were on his tail. He urgently needed a popular cause to boost his career. Friends offered ideas. Develop the St Lawrence Seaway? Introduce a pension for elderly Americans? Worthy, but dull. Then someone said that Americans were worried by the threat of Communist infiltration in Washington. McCarthy liked the sound of that. A month later, during a speech in Wheeling, Virginia, he held up a piece of paper: a list, he said, of 205 known members of

312

the Communist Party still working at the State Department. Or was it fifty-seven? Later, McCarthy couldn't remember. By then he'd lost the paper. No matter; and no matter that he couldn't prove his accusation. That speech was the pebble that started an avalanche of national support. He had found his cause, he had won his publicity; and by the time he was re-elected in 1952 his reckless offensive had destroyed so many jobs, reputations, even lives, that he was known as the most feared man in America.

McCarthy was not the first US senator to exploit the Red Scare for political gains. In 1949 – the year before McCarthy's Wheeling speech – Senator Lyndon B. Johnson already had his sights on the presidency. LBJ was from Texas, and he needed Texas oil money to back his ambition. The Texas oil barons hated a man called Leland Olds, who for nine years had been head of the Federal Power Commission. He was patriotic, hardworking, fair-minded and effective. LBJ used his championship of a Senate sub-committee to remove Olds. By smear and distortion, he painted Olds as a Communist and destroyed his career, a skilled hatchet-job which McCarthy must have observed. The Texas oil barons were grateful. Eventually, with their help, LBJ made it to the White House. Meanwhile, as long as McCarthyism was in full flood, LBJ never spoke out against it. (Nor did Senator John F. Kennedy.) 'You don't get in a pissin' contest with a polecat,' Johnson said privately.

McCarthy wasn't so much a politician as an operator. All he had going for him was his Red Scare. He had to keep exposing more and more security risks, attacking great institutions, because his power came from knocking over his enemies. His fall was as stunning as his rise. In 1954 he chose to fight the Army, lost, was censured by the Senate and ridiculed in the Press, and soon found himself ignored. Two years later he was dead, virtually a suicide. He drank himself to death.

Yet McCarthy was likeable; that's what is so surprising. When he wasn't damning citizens as traitors he was relaxed and friendly. He had a bluff, Irish charm. He was, at first, welcomed by the Kennedys; might even have married into the family. Bobby Kennedy worked for him loyally in the summer of 1953, a career move which Kennedy biographers have found hard to explain and even harder to justify. At that age, Bobby was a grim and unforgiving soul for whom 'liberal' was a dirty word. Later – much later – he discovered the hardships that poverty, hunger and ill health could inflict on others, and his outlook became humanitarian. But in 1953, Bobby Kennedy didn't like people. (His reluctant, fingertip handshake kept them at bay.) He liked a fight. He was impressed by McCarthy, and he respected his politics. He grieved when McCarthy died. Few politicians attended the funeral; Bobby did.

In *Red Rag Blues*, all the intelligence agencies eavesdrop on each other. This is only a slight exaggeration. By 1953, the FBI had a free hand to bug and tap. Hoover had certainly penetrated the CIA, so it is hard to believe that the CIA did not return the compliment. The FBI bugged many senators, and McCarthy must have been a prime target – he was under constant surveillance by Hoover's agents and the Bureau had a fat file on him. The CIA bugged McCarthy as a matter of course. MI6, the KGB and the CIA existed for the purpose of gathering intelligence, so it would be surprising if they didn't bug and tap everyone who interested them.

If this suggests a certain lack of secrecy in Washington, think of William Hansen, the FBI agent who spied for the Russians for twenty-two years, earning $643,000, which lay in his bank account for any investigator to see. In 1993, after a break in his spying, he contacted his handlers again. The Russians didn't trust their luck. This had to be a trap. They complained to the American authorities that an FBI agent was trying to sell them secrets. The Bureau searched, but couldn't find him, although there were many tell-tale signs that Hansen was not to be trusted. When, eventually, he was arrested, he described the FBI's security procedures in two words: 'Criminal negligence'.

Even Hansen was overshadowed by the CIA agent Aldrich Ames, Chief of Counter-Intelligence in the agency's Soviet Division, and therefore a man with a safe full of secrets. He also had a home full of debts. With no prospect of promotion to help pay his bills, he sold the secrets to the Russians. They gave him $2 million. His CIA record wasn't spotless (he'd had a bad drink problem), but no alarm bells rang when he bought two new Jaguars and a half-million-dollar house – for cash. He spied for the Russians for eight years. He was arrested in 1994. By then, despite all that Ames had done for the KGB and against the CIA, the USSR was collapsing. Ames's treachery wasn't even a footnote to history.

By contrast, anything in *Red Rag Blues* seems almost routine.